COME DRINK COFFEE WITH ME
HUSBAND HUNTING IN ISRAEL

A NOVEL
AND
GUIDEBOOK

ANNE-MARIE BRUMM

Widener and Lewis

New York, Los Angeles

Copyright © 1994

All rights reserved

This book may not be reproduced, in whole or in part, except in the case of reviews, without the permission of the publisher

Book and cover design by the author

All names are ficticious and any resemblance to living persons is coincidental.

Also by Anne-Marie Brumm

<u>Poetry</u>

Dance of life

Sea, Sand Stones and Strife: Poems of the Middle East

CHAPTER 1
WASHED UP ON SCHERIA'S SHORE

At the beginning of her stay in Israel, Debbie led a rather relaxed kind of life - or at least it appeared so from the outside. This helped her to become accustomed to the new country more easily. Jerusalem was a precious map of pleasant memories she had collected on her previous visits. One of her favorite and familiar habitats was the Givat Ram Campus of the Hebrew University. It was a sprawling campus and had a big beautiful green lawn where she liked to sit and think or just sit and watch the people go by. It was comforting to bask in the warm caressing sun and to feel the thick blanket of green grass underneath her body. Many students had the same idea and on a nice day, the grass was full of admirers.

Often she would read a book or take her poetry pad and pour colorful words onto its yellow surface. Sometimes the relaxed atmosphere was conducive to this; other times, the heat would exert a soporific effect and she did not accomplish much. The best part was that many people she knew passed by, some from folk dancing, others from her earlier visits.

One day Debbie was sitting on the grass reading a collection of contemporary Jewish short stories. Dotted over the landscape of the main lawn in front of the National Library was a galaxy of young attractive women like herself, some of them Junior Year Abroad students from a wide variety of countries and others studying for a B.A. or M.A. All were working or pretending to be thus engaged but occasionally a twinkle of the eye in the direction of the other male readers or to the spectators could be discernible and revealed an alternate purpose to their presence on the grass.

Debbie noticed what from that distance and given her near-sighted eyes, seemed to be a young man walking very slowly around the grass stopping nearby each girl as if to see what she was reading. Occasionally he would watch for awhile as though awaiting some strange miracle to occur. Sometimes he would pass a girl by without even a glance; with others he would have a brief exchange; finally he found one who apparently had been reading whatever it was he was looking for and he sat down next to her on the grass Debbie could not ascertain what his criteria of selection was. The girl he had chosen to become acquainted with was ugly and homely in comparison to some beauties he had ignored. Now that he had come closer, she could see that he was not as young as she had first thought. He was already about 35 or more, blond, average height and very thin which gave him such a youthful appearance from afar.

He had finished speaking to the girl at this point and started walking about again on the grass, once more looking carefully at the book every young girl was reading. Soon he was close to Debbie, apparently satisfied with her choice of reading material stalking his prey like an old alley cat ready to pounce on an unsuspecting innocent tweety bird.

Pounce he did within a few moments of approaching her. He was not a man to waste time, that was obvious.

"May I sit here?" he asked, motioning to the ground. What could Debbie say except "Sure"

"You are a tourist here?" he queried.

"No" she shot back quickly, then added, "I came for a long period of time to teach and to write and I want very much to stay." A fast operator, he then asked her to go for coffee and so they headed for the dining hall. They had a very lively discussion during the coffee drinking and Debbie even grew mildly interested in him.

He was 38, quite good looking in a very nordic way, and a physicist from Leningrad. He was divorced and had one son. Last year he had had a guest appointment at Columbia University and now he had returned to Israel and to Weizmann Institute where he was employed as a physicist. Although he looked very gentle and mild, Debbie sensed a very hard and tough interior. He knew what he wanted and he would get it. He had come to the Hebrew University for an appointment with a professor in the Physics department and since it was almost four, he would unfortunately have to leave her although he, of course, did so regretfully.

He quickly took her telephone number and fled.

Debbie liked talking with him but something about him had a frightening intensity and there was a kind of mechanical quality underneath the polite manner and smile. She was also puzzled that he should have an appointment so late in the afternoon. Most of the faculty left by 2 P.M. and it was rare for anyone to be available for appointments at 4. She had not actually intended to follow him but suddenly she noticed her legs carrying her in the same direction as he had gone.

He headed for the main gate - not a very likely place for an academic interview. Debbie followed at a safe distance. He left through the gates. She followed and looked out after him. As her eyes captured him, she also noticed from the periphery of her eye, a tall slim young blond girl, either English or American, with a big black brim hat and a large dangling camera waving her right hand to him and flashing him a great big smile. He nodded recognition and hurried in her direction. Debbie could not hear the exchange of talk but she could surmise from the gestures and behavior that it was the same type of flirtatious chit chat he had engaged with her and several others on the grass. The romantic mirage vanished.

It was all very clear to her now. Mikhail Galin was looking for a foreign tourist. The books he had been checking out on the grass were not for academic interest or for intellectual content but whether or not they were in English. What he was watching for was whether the reader was turning the pages from right to left (English) or left to right (Hebrew) - a world of difference for a crafty Russian refugee looking to emigrate to the U.S.A. Debbie wondered how many girls he had picked up and tried that day, all of them thinking that she was the special one he had chosen. All the time he was just stalking up as many possibilities as he could manage on one day. One was bound to work out and his life would be set on the proper course. Debbie would have to be careful!

Debbie soon forgot about Mikhail Galin because on her way

to the dining hall, she saw the star of her wildest dreams striding towards her. She was able to see him from afar because he was so tall and walked so straight and majestically. He stood out in any crowd. As he came closer, she noticed that he was beaming.

"Whew! I just finished the final exam for a really tough graduate course. I'm glad it's over. I think I did OK, fairly well, in fact."

"Oh, I'm happy for you. Come, let's go the cafeteria," Debbie proposed invitingly.

"I can't, sorry. I really have to go home." he answered hurriedly.

She also decided not to go and to accompany him instead on the bus. While waiting for the bus and then on the bus itself, they chatted amicably about many things: school, local events, folk dancing. Debbie still looked at him with a sense of awe. He had that flawless ruddy complexion that only true redheads are blessed with. He was powerfully built and had he been born in the United States, he probably would have been a star football hero.

As the bus headed into the town center where Debbie lived, she invited him to come to her room. He hesitated for a moment, then smiled that warm friendly smile of his and said "sure". They got off and walked the short distance to her apartment. She lived on the fourth floor. There was an old, small, rickety elevator but they decided to take the stairs. Debbie went first and she noticed as they turned the corners that Shimon was eyeing her behind with very much interest.

They sat and talked for two hours although it seemed like just a few minutes. Debbie played her verbal flute, her voice full of happy melodies. Again she observed that occasionally he would glance and size up her body shyly without appearing to do so. She was wearing a form fitting pink pullover and a pink flared skirt which fit snugly over the hips. Debbie was still quite shy and lacked the courage to take the initiative and "just grab him" although she certainly wanted to do so. She hoped that he would be the aggressor but he was not, so nothing ensued. What Debbie did not know was that Shimon was an extremely passive person despite his size and muscular exterior and would have welcomed Debbie's igniting the first flame. Yet she thought perhaps it was better to take it slow and to be good friends first.

There would be time for more later or so she anticipated.

Shimon left but not without asking her to come to folk dancing on Mount Scopus on Thursday night. He emphasized that it was a very good group and to be sure to bring an I.D. card with her. "They have a very strict guard and he is careful whom he allows to enter." Shimon seemed very interested in having her come to this group so she decided she would go. She certainly did not want to miss an opportunity to be with him as much as possible. She lay back in her armchair savoring even the short time Shimon had just spent with her. Her mind was slowly tempted back to the very first time she had seen him striding into her life.

It had been Saturday evening, her first in Jerusalem, and Debbie did not have any particular plans. She was restless and anxious to jump into Israeli social life as quickly as possible.

"After all, that's why I'm here, isn't it?" she coaxed herself. "Why waste time." Debbie remembered from her tourist trips that Danny Levitt, the folk dance teacher had started an international folk dance group at the Givat Ram Campus of the Hebrew university on Saturday night. She did not know how successful a group it was or if indeed it was still in existence. Yet she would take the chance and make the rather long trip, so eager was she to resume the Israeli life she had known as a tourist.

She remembered taking the number nine bus going in the direction of the Givat Ram campus. The bus wound its way through the beautiful neighborhood of Rehavia, passed Wolfson Towers, the Monastery of the Cross, the Israel Museum, the Shrine of the Book, the Knesset, the Bank of Israel and then made a stop outside the main gate of the university. This route was perhaps one of the most beautiful of all bus routes in Jerusalem because it passed so many of the main tourist attractions - all of them illuminated during the night.

Debbie "alighted" as they say in Israel and walked toward the main gate wondering if she would remember the way to Beit Sprinczak, the student center. All the gates to the university were locked at this time except one where the guard sat who carefully inspected her bag. Then she started on the twenty minute walk straight to the center of the campus. The National Library, several large science buildings, a forest, synagogue, student dormitories, then at last, Beit Sprinczak, presented themselves one by one on Debbie's journey, each assuming frightening proportions in the night. One factor she remembered very well was the truly black darkness enveloping everything along the way, especially through the forest. Here images hovered like vague ghostlike shadows which suddenly appeared and disappeared without origin, roots, or identity.

Only occasionally was there a small light, probably due to the conservation of energy. She could not help but compare it to being in a similar setting in New York and shuddered at the thought of the consequences. But it was not New York, she kept telling herself as her feet carried her swiftly on the narrow path through the forest and out to the university's white domed synagogue. She kept looking behind her if there were not someone else going her way also perhaps to the dancing. Only three young males, their faces swollen with moonlight, passed her on the way heading in the opposite direction.

As she approached Beit Sprinczak, Debbie again searched for other indications of life but despaired when she saw no one. She already anticipated that she had made the trip in vain. Little did Debbie know then that not only did she not make the journey in vain but that the quest would be a significant and tragic turning point in her life.

When she arrived at the building itself, she saw that it was lit and when she went inside to look, she found the teacher and about eight or nine people gathered around him at the stereo system. She entered and walked up to the group asking if there would be folk dancing that evening. One of the people informed her that the teacher was waiting to see if any more dancers would arrive. Danny, the teacher, remembered her from tourist days and said, "Hello, how are you? Are you here for a visit?" "More than that this time," Debbie answered proudly. He smiled, "Ah." As she discovered later, it was the week after Passover and the university was in-between semesters. Most of the regular dancers had gone home or on holiday for the vacation. Others anticipated that every one would be away and so also did not come, hence the poor attendance. Debbie thought to leave.

Just as her resolve to leave grew more firm, a very tall well built young man came in the door and also walked the long length of the hall to where the small group had congregated. He walked so erect and with so much regal confidence that it was as though he were a god that had just stepped out of an ancient Greek epic.

He had fairly long and thick reddish blond hair, a clear ruddy white skin typical of those with natural red hair and features that would have stunned even Praxiteles. Debbie could not keep her eyes off him. His profile and stance as he looked over at Danny and the stereo system reminded Debbie of the statue of Apollo in the Metropolitan Museum of Art. He was the most beautiful person she had ever seen and she became suddenly breathless. Her intention to leave had vanished completely. Debbie did not quite know what to do; she seemed to be glued to the spot, not believing her eyes. She wanted so much to touch him to see if he was really real or was his face some very fine statue of a Greek warrior?

They continued to wait and after nine o'clock more people did arrive. Danny started the music and played a few circle dances. Debbie did them mainly to show her new focus of attention that she knew how to dance. She remembered from tourist days that no one had asked her to dance assuming that she was new and therefore didn't know how to dance. It was not until she did a couple dance all by herself that people saw she knew the steps and only then did a partner join her. Debbie hoped the same would happen here.

When a couple dance was put on, she stood there trying to

appear relaxed. Then suddenly the Greek godling came forth from the primeval earth, his face shining - and smiling - at Debbie!

"Would you like to do this?" he asked. Debbie's eyes glowed, "Sure" and she moved quickly out on to the dance floor before he could change his mind.

It was truly heavenly to dance with him. He knew all the dances and he danced them well. Moreover, he seemed to want to stay with her for every dance. Debbie was overjoyed at this thinking that he really must like her and was enjoying dancing with her. She did not know at this time that it was the custom in Israel to dance with only one partner for the entire evening. Her few tourist experiences had not enlightened her about this important factor.

Debbie danced as well as she could to impress him but there were some dances which she didn't know. These were usually dances that they did not do in New York. Nevertheless, she tried hard to follow his lead and he was surprised that she could keep up as well as she did. Not realizing that Israeli and International folk dancing are as popular in New York as in Israel, he assumed she had learned them in Israel.

They danced together the entire evening and Debbie had a wonderful time. About 11:20, he said that he would have to go soon since the last bus would come through the campus then. Debbie did not know that once an hour one of the number nine buses would actually enter the campus itself and make a stop near Beit Sprinczak.

"I had planned to walk back to the main gate," Debbie told him.

"That's too far," he answered, "Besides it will take you twenty minutes, so you should also leave soon to catch the last bus at the gate at twelve," This isn't New York. Things stop here at twelve," he laughed.

"Then I'll leave too when you do and catch that bus," Debbie suddenly decided.

"Fine," he smiled. "My God," Debbie thought in wonder. "He's even handsomer when he smiles." Soon they sat together in the bus shelter waiting for the bus to appear around the corner.

He told her that he was a research economist at the Bank of Israel and that he was studying for his M.A. in Economics at the Hebrew University. He lived in the student dormitories on Mount Scopus, the campus of the Hebrew University situated at the other end of the city. She related impressions of her previous visits to Israel and how happy she was to be back.

He spoke excellent English and Debbie would have wanted to speak to him all night. She was disappointed when the bus came as scheduled.

Debbie inquired about the Wednesday folk dance group. "I would like to go to it again," Debbie announced remembering from tourist days that it had been a large and successful group.

"It's very crowded," he advised, "but maybe not now because of the holidays." The bus was nearing the town center and she would have to get off. Suddenly she realized that she did not even know his name.

"Shimon," he said, "Yours?"

"Debbie."

She quickly jumped off the bus before the door would slam shut. When Debbie walked back to her room at Mrs. Levinsky's, she felt tall as a skyscraper and so strong she thought she could do anything. Shimon had peeled away her many layers of reserve while at the same time rendering her more vulnerable. "It will be different here, I know it already," she exclaimed to herself. "I'm so glad I came." She was beside herself with joy, a feeling that had not yet come often into the life of Deborah Warshawsky.

The time between Saturday evening and Wednesday evening seemed endless. Debbie thought constantly about the tall erect Apollo that had come into her life. Finally, Wednesday arrived and she dressed with special care for the evening. She arrived early but he was already there outside the building. He was friendly and said hello although Debbie thought she noticed just a slight bit of reticence. They went in and started dancing the circle dances. Then it came time for the partner dances; "*Zugot, zugot*" was the call over the microphone. Shimon just stood still in one place not making any particular move in any direction. Debbie cleaved the crowd like a giant shark's fin and landed close to him, saying, "Care to try again?" He smiled and answered, "Sure."

Wednesday evening was all Israeli folk dancing and here Debbie was at her best. She danced as well as she could and was happy to have such a good dancer for a partner. However, during the evening, he occasionally seemed very preoccupied and deep in thought; other times his eyes wandered vacantly around the room. Debbie asked him if anything was wrong and he answered that he just had some pressing problem in his job at the bank. Debbie believed him and even kidded him about working too hard. They continued to dance and again they went home together. Gradually, she learned more about him especially his age. She had been afraid that he might be too young for her but when he mentioned that he had served in the 1973 war, she knew that he must be close to her own age. They had a very good time but still he did not ask for a date. As usual, Debbie rationalized and thought he might be short of cash. But that night she was much too tired to worry about it. She was not accustomed to doing every dance played as is the custom in Israel.

Thursday evening came and Debbie dressed with great care in a striped green and white top and a white skirt. She took along enough identification to satisfy any guard although she discovered the infamous guard to be the same man who operated the recording devices for the teacher at the YMCA when she had danced there as a tourist. She remembered him and he remembered her because she knew all the dances. There was no difficulty at all getting in.

The surprise awaiting Debbie lay within. She went in eagerly anticipating seeing Shimon and dancing with him. Instead she found him already dancing with a girl. She assumed that he would stop dancing with the girl when he saw her. Yet he continued to dance with her dance after dance. Debbie grew somewhat exasperated since she found herself sitting by the sidelines for most of the evening. It was a very small group and everyone was well coupled off for the entire session and probably beyond. Debbie couldn't understand why Shimon had asked her to come.

The girl in question was a very ugly girl in Debbie's estimation. At first glance, she looked like a light skinned Black or perhaps a mulatto with high cheekbones, a wide mouth and big lips and her dark hair tightly tied back in typical Israeli fashion. Her stance was very tough and domineering and she typically stood with both hands perched on her hips as though she were ready to shout at someone. She soon learned that her name was Dorrit. The first chance Debbie got to catch Shimon alone was when Dorrit finally stalked to the ladies room.

"Are you going to dance all night with her?" Debbie whined.

"I have to," Shimon declared discouragingly with a shrug as if it were something he did not wish to do. "She is my dancing partner for a long time, since the university," he went on to explain. "I took folk dancing as my sport requirement when I was a student and you know Shira Barkan the teacher. Well, this girl had no partner and Shira pushed me to be her partner. You know how she is! And we have danced together ever since. So I have to stay with her. I'm sorry. Can't you get a partner? The guy over there has no steady partner. Why don't you ask him."

"I came to dance with you," Debbie stated emphatically.

"I can't, really, I'm sorry. That's the way it is done here," he answered finally.

The rest of the evening was a blur. Debbie was disappointed and bewildered about the shadow that had entered her life. Who was this girl and what did she mean to Shimon were the thoughts that kept tripping in her confused mind. What was this sacred phenomenon known as a "dancing partner?"

When the dance was over, Debbie waited for him to see if he would speak to her. He did for awhile telling her again about the outdoor marathon planned for Independence Day. Then Dorrit came having changed her shoes and now busy putting on a sweatshirt. They all walked out together but most of the dancers headed in the direction of the student dormitories including Shimon and Dorrit. Soon they arched off into one of the main exits like shallow silhouettes melting together. Debbie ran for the last bus at midnight. All the way from Mount Scopus to the town center, Debbie's thoughts lingered on the strange girl that had come between her and her dream wondering if she posed any threat. Of course, Shimon had confessed that he had been forced to dance with her and he seemed not to want to very much. Debbie wanted to believe that so she did; after all, she was in love. Ah Aphrodite, is there ever any limit to what a girl in love will swallow?

Then in a more rational moment, she began to ponder the fact that perhaps they were living together or worse, married. It was not uncommon for an Israeli guy going steady with a girl or even married to "fool around" with another girl. So she decided to check on where he lived and she was relieved to find that he lived as he said with another guy. She finally convinced herself that this mysterious girl was none other than just a dancing partner he had begun to dance with some time ago and as was the custom in Israel, had continued to do so. She recalled a similar case in New York where Israeli born Miriam continued to dance with Noam, her dancing partner since age 16 even though she was dating another dancer, Joel. And besides, she argued with herself, a man as handsome, intelligent and educated as Shimon surely could get a better girl than this tough looking Carmen with the jerky movements and angry scowl. With these arguments, she bolstered her shaky faith in the god Shimon. She neglected, however, to consult the local oracle, not wanting to hear its prophetic words of doom.

Yom Atzmaut or Independence Day came with a full blast of celebrations throughout the country. It was a day of deep significance for all Israelis and they enjoyed it to the fullest. People would flock to the main streets in masses and walk about promenading. Children and people had plastic hammer shaped objects with which they would hit other people on the head as a gesture of good will and best wishes. Naturally, salesman soon stood by with a ready supply of these hammers as well as flags, horns and other merrymakers.

Debbie pushed her way through the crowds that had thronged to King George street, Jaffa Road and the Ben Yehuda mall to the number nine bus to Mount Scopus for the folk dance marathon. She thought for sure that tonight Shimon would be hers. But when she arrived and searched the rings of people dancing, the same shock greeted her. Shimon was again dancing with the same girl. He saw Debbie and waved a smiling hello but Debbie felt frozen to the ground. "What should I do," she asked herself paralyzed and helpless. She sat down on the railing and watched the mob for awhile having lost all desire to dance and celebrate. Another evening lost, she thought.

Then another young man asked her to dance. Before accepting, she glanced once more over to Shimon and saw him trying to push his partner to turn during the Israeli mazurka. Debbie had noticed already last time that this girl turned very awkwardly and jerkily. Debbie danced for awhile but her glaze always wandered back to the ring where Shimon was dancing.

The evening wore on and suddenly about 12 midnight she saw Shimon and Dorrit walking up the ramp to leave the marathon area. Debbie watched sadly thinking the night and somehow also her life to be over. She sat down on the curb dejectedly and put on her sweater for it had become quite cold or perhaps she only thought so. She did not want to stay but could not bear to go home either. She watched the dancers numbly, only the best ones being left now doing the most difficult dances. It was the best time to dance with the beginner crowd gone but her evening had ended.

She must have sat there half hypnotized, half asleep when suddenly she saw Shimon coming down the ramp again. Was she dreaming? She roused herself out of her lethargic state and saw him looking about the dancing crowd as though he were searching for someone. "Could he be looking for me?" Debbie whispered awestruck. She saw instinctually now that several girls who had no partners were beginning to eye him so she realized that she would have to move quickly before someone else would grab him. She walked towards him hesitating a little bit because she wasn't sure if it was she for whom he was straining his neck.

As she approached him and he saw her, he said eagerly, "Oh, there you are" and motioned for her to come quickly and dance. They started to dance and he said immediately, "I'm sorry about the other night but you know how it is here about keeping the same partner." Debbie replied that it was OK, only that she didn't understand why he had asked her to come.

"Well, it's a good group, plenty of room because there are not so many people and a good teacher. I thought you would get a partner," was his answer voiced in a very rational and convincing tone. He seemed to be in earnest so she accepted it wholeheartedly. She had come to life again even though it was about 12:30 A.M. and she felt happy dancing as never before. How wonderful to be dancing with someone who could dance so well and yet be so handsome and exciting at the same time? He knew all the dances and there seemed to be no end to his energy.

She felt carefree and exhiliarated dancing in the open air on the beautiful Mount Scopus campus of the Hebrew University on Independence Day, 1981 with the man she loved. One time as Shimon swung her around quickly, she laughed but out of the corner of her eye, she noticed three very dark Israeli girls standing on the curb watching her and Shimon dance in a very suspicious manner. They looked almost as if they were angry and she saw one girl whispering something to the other who then nodded in agreement. The ominous Ladies of the Night from Mozart's opera, The Magic Flute, fluttered through Debbie's mind. And yet she dismissed this disruptive observation attributing their talk to the fact that they did not have partners and so were jealous of those who did. She did not want anything or anyone to spoil this perfect moment.

Woe to the innocent unsuspecting American girl who dares to be a match for any Israeli girl! Debbie did not know that these girls were close friends of Dorrit's who couldn't wait to inform her that Shimon had returned to dance with the *Americai*. It was a crucial factor since it made Dorrit realize that she needed to take decisive action quickly before it would be too late.

Shimon and Debbie danced and danced until finally even the remaining crowd had begun to thin about 2 A.M. She was glad that she had not danced much earlier in the evening or she would not have been able to dance much now. She wondered at how strong Shimon must be to be able to dance for so many hours. Then finally the teacher announced the last dance and that there would be a *kumsitz* with an Israeli singer in the meadow beyond the Edelson dormitories.

"Do you want to go?" Shimon asked.

"Well, yes, I would but I don't know how I will get home. The later it gets, probably the more difficult it will be to get a taxi."

"Don't worry," he coaxed, "Let's go have a look." Debbie readily agreed because she did really want to see a genuine Israeli *kumsitz*. The only kind she had experienced thus far were on folk dance weekends in New York. They walked over to the field where a sizable crowd had already gathered and were sitting about a huge fire blazing in the center.

They sat down in a quiet place somewhat distant from the fire and the crowd. It was such a wonderful atmosphere. This was the happiest night of her life. She looked at Shimon adoringly and smiled, "I had such a fantastic time. I'm so glad you came back." "So am I," he whispered after they had listened to the singer wail two old Israeli songs from the days of the pioneers. Debbie felt content at having seen a real Israeli *kumsitz* but now wanted something more. Both were silent as they headed back to the dormitory area.

After what seemed to be an eternity, Shimon broke the silence and said, "You can't go home at this hour. My roommate went home for the holiday weekend so you can stay with me for the night. It's OK."

"I could call a taxi," Debbie replied weakly, convincing not even herself. "I'm sure there must be one company that operates all night."

"Come on," Shimon took her arm gently and rubbed it then put his arm around her. Debbie did not resist long and soon she found herself in Shimon's small but pleasant room.

They exchanged a few comments about the room and his roommate, then Shimon stared at her again, came close and gave her a long and deep kiss. She felt aroused and hugged his big strong body close to her. He was so tall, she remembered thinking, so accustomed had she always been to guys her own height or shorter. She felt his huge broad shoulders, his muscular arms and chest, his trim waist and hips and he likewise discovered her large soft breasts, slender waist and softly rounded hips.

"Hey, why do you keep all these nice things hidden away all the time under all this stuff?" he laughed motioning to her flary skirt, slip and panty. "You ought to show it more." He led her softly over to the bed and very gently made supreme love to her.

The weekend of the Independence Day celebration had been eventful but most weekends were quiet even lonely in Jerusalem.

The weekdays had been so full that at first Debbie welcomed a letdown now and then but after awhile, she began to anticipate the oncoming stillness on Friday afternoon with pangs of regret. It was always one of the first things even non-Jewish tourists noticed - this awesome stillness on the Sabbath. There was a general upsurge of activity on Friday morning culminating in a peak of feverish intensity about 12 to 2 P.M and then gradually lessening thereafter until the beginning of the Sabbath (depending on the time of the year) by which time things come to a virtual standstill. In Jerusalem, this meant everything! Shops were closed, people who had been hurrying home were home now, traffic ceased and in general few people were in the streets. Some could be seen coming to or from the synagogue. The quietness that suddenly descended upon a previously bustling and noisy metropolis is unparalleled anywhere. Even Jews coming to Israel for the first time find it remarkable. For no matter how observant they might have been in their own country, surrounding them was still evidences of a non-Jewish world - buses, crowds, business, noise. But here in Jerusalem, all was still as though God Himself were presiding over the Sabbath services.

With one exception - we must be honest and reveal the whole Truth and nothing but the Truth. Even in holy Jerusalem, city of three great religions, there is one tiny street, in fact, it isn't even a real street, just an alley way - very well hidden from view where the Sabbath was the furthest thing from anyone's mind. Actually, most people walk right by this pathway without seeing it, as they go down Jaffa road.

Debbie had been in Jerusalem a long time before she became aware by accident of its existence. One evening she had already passed by when she heard some music coming from this ugly unseeming opening in the wall and she dared to step a few yards inward to investigate where it was coming from. Music had always attracted Debbie and could probably lure her anywhere. Suddenly the narrow passageway opened onto a regular mall type of street. What a contrast to the somber dark stillness outside!

It was brightly lit, the noisy music was much louder now and Debbie could see a whole row of pubs on either side of the street. The head waiter (if one could call him that) of the first pub saw her immediately and motioned for her to come sit down at one of the many tables strewn around the front of the pub. Most of the pubs had outdoor tables and Debbie noticed that they were almost completely filled with merrymakers who would not let even Jerusalem prevent them from having a good time. Most were tourists, young people in their 20's, from the United States, England, Germany and Scandinavia, with probably many from the latter judging by the large number of towheads. They all seemed to be having a good time drinking beer, singing and sharing lively conversations.

In a few of the pubs, sultry sexy looking waitresses could be seen lurking at the entrances and enticing the young men going by to enter <u>this</u> pub rather than the next one. To the casual onlooker, it might have been a bohemian section or even a red light district. For Debbie, it looked like a garden of forbidden pleasures, given the holy character of what lay outside its domain. Debbie hurried out again. She was lonely but this oasis did not seem to be the place for her.

Outside, it was again like a ghost town, completely deserted. After a while Debbie learned to cope with the 24 hours of silence. She would do things she didn't have time for during the week, such as: writing letters, reading, sewing or it would be a period of introspection for herself. Yet still it was a difficult time especially for a single person when one saw all around families gathering together. It was at times like this that she would miss her parents and friends and wonder what they were doing. Past conversations played on the surface of her mind as she rewound her internal tapes.

One Friday afternoon, not long after her arrival, Debbie was feeling particularly lonely and the thought of the coming Sabbath left her depressed. She thought she would take a walk to help brighten her spirits. It was already quite late in the afternoon and the city was beginning to take on its moribund appearance. Still she kept walking losing track of the time. Little did Debbie Warshawsky know then that a girl walking alone late Friday afternoon is an easy target for men on the make.

There are some just waiting for this. For anybody walking alone at this hour especially past six is alone and perhaps consciously or unconsciously looking for some adventure.

She was walking down Straus Street when a long car pulled up along side of her. All cars in Israel are small, Fiats, Subarus, Audis, etc. so an American car of this magnitude really stood out and seemed bigger than it would have in the United States. On closer inspection, it was quite old and beaten and probably had outlived its usefulness. It was akin to an old model Cadillac frequently driven in New York by Blacks. A man about 40, dark and relatively good looking, sat behind the wheel and peered out the window.

"Can I give you a lift?" he asked smiling.

"No, thanks," Debbie said, giving him the once over out of the corner of her eye.

"Where are you going." he continued, encouraged by her attention.

"Nowhere, just taking a walk," somewhat annoyed but now looking at him completely.

"Are you a tourist? Come, I will show you Jerusalem," he smiled again enthusiastically.

"No, I can't. I have to be home soon."

The very fact that Debbie was offering him answers even though superficially negative, encouraged him. Had Debbie really wanted to avoid him, she should have walked away quickly, decisively and immediately, without even as much as glancing at him or answering his questions. Any acknowledgment indicates interest.

The conversation continued on this level for about 5 minutes and then Debbie found herself inside the old Dodge convertible. After all, she reasoned, she was not in New York or New Jersey now, but in Israel. And so, that was OK, wasn't it? What a terribly false assumption to make! Israel, like any other country has its share of criminals: thieves, murderers, rapists plus an oversupply of restless husbands looking for a quick fling before they go home to their families.

The man in the Dodge seemed nice and promised he would drive around the city. Accustomed to the traffic, she thought this would be a slow process and so she would always have the opportunity to get out should this become necessary. However, once Debbie was in the car, he proposed driving out to Ein Kerem persuading her by saying that surely there, there would be many tourist sites that she hadn't seen, since many were accessible only by car, not by bus.

One shudders to think how naive Debbie still was in her fourth month of living in Israel. She still believed at this time that an Israeli could be so interested in the tourist sites that he would want to show them to others. She did not realize the ulterior motives that lay behind each offer of "Come, I will show you."

Before long, the car was speeding out of the main portion of the city along a small country road leading to Ein Kerem. It was a winding road weaving in and out of the majestic hills surrounding Jerusalem. A breathtakingly panoramic view greeted the observer each time there was a turn in the road. Small stone houses lay snug in the hill's embrace.

For some reason, Debbie was not frightened perhaps because Avi was so good looking and such a smooth talker that he made her feel completely relaxed and unaware. This was obviously not his first experience as "tour guide." They headed deeper and deeper into the picturesque and deserted countryside.

He made a brief stop in Ein Kerem at an old church which looked like it had been abandoned for centuries.

"This is the famous Church of the Annunciation, where Mary was told she was to bear Jesus, etc. etc." he went on fulfilling his promise "to show her the sites." "Unfortunately, it is closed now, but it is very beautiful inside," he said feigning disappointment. Of course, he knew only too well that it would be closed like everything else on Friday late afternoon.

Debbie pretended to show interest just to be polite because she truly thought that he wanted to show her these things. It never ceases to amaze a more experienced Jerusalemite just how gullible tourists in Israel are. (We must still consider Debbie a tourist at this point.) They will believe almost anything. It is as if all the rational and critical faculties ceased to function once they landed at Ben Gurion Airport. Perhaps the religious and historical atmosphere of Jerusalem lends the place and its people such an air of credulity that all suspicion is suspended. An element of intoxicating magic seems to pervade the city rendering newcomers helpless victims. Were Debbie in New York now, she would be frightened to be where she was and with whom.

Then they drove on and Debbie expected to be shown another "tourist attraction." But the preface was over and the primary action would now begin. She did not notice that he had turned off the main road until suddenly they were driving through a very picturesque forest. Quiet mysterious trees were standing so close together that they shielded the road from any penetration of sunlight; indeed, there was very little light at all. It was as if it had suddenly grown dark. Debbie was surprised since she did not think that Israel had any forest of this beauty and magnitude. She had always heard of the "Plant a tree in Israel" advertisements and thus pictured the countryside of Israel to be rows and rows of stick-like saplings struggling to survive in an unkind atmosphere. But here there were lush trees, tall, thick and dark, conveying an aura of strength and power.

Suddenly he veered off this road and drove into a particularly dark and dense part of the forest and parked the car. He turned to her and said proudly, "Beautiful, isn't it?" at the same time starting to put his arm around her. Debbie was again surprised although she should not have been. She had been so enticed by the hills and forest of Jerusalem that she barely thought about him in any other way but as a friendly Israeli wanting to show a tourist around. Now as he moved closer and closer, she was forced to look at him for the first time. It was no longer an idyllic portrait.

Avi was very good looking but in a tough playboyish sort of way. His hair was a blue-black color, wavy and he wore it fairly long and in a bouffant style. He said his family had come from Morocco and he lived in Jerusalem.

At first Debbie welcomed his show of affection because she was feeling very lonely but as he became more passionate and suggested they get out and lie down on the ground, she resisted and said that she wanted to get to know and like a person first before becoming so close. Lovemaking in a beautiful forest may sound very romantic but the silence, stillness and deserted quality of the idyl frightened her and made her back off. He seemed disappointed but not angry almost as if he had expected her to refuse. They sat awhile and talked and then Debbie suggested that he take her home since it was by now quite late.

On the way home, Debbie asked him if he had ever been married thereby unleasing a torrent of anger and frustration. He began to tell her about his first marriage and his efforts to get a divorce and custody of his only son. As he spoke, his face took on a hard mean look. It seemed as if there was no fault that his wife did not have. Mainly he talked about the son and how he was plotting to take him away from her. He would have his brother watch her actions and if she went out with another man and left the child, he would have her declared an unfit mother.

"She can't be one week without a man." he declared viciously. "She knows she can't win against me. So she will have to give him up."

By this time, he had worked himself into such a state of hatred and rage that Debbie grew quite afraid of him. It was as this point that Debbie realized what a truly cruel person he was and to what lengths his viciousness would go to obtain whatever he wanted. She felt pity for the helpless wife trying to hang on to her own child and living in perpetual fear of his next unexpected move. This was certainly not someone she wanted to get involved with, no matter how good looking he was. She waited anxiously to get out of his clutches.

When they finally arrived at her door, she wanted to get away from him as quickly and politely as possible. But he asked if he could come in "just for a minute." When she hesitated, he said he was very thirsty from the trip and just wanted some juice or Cola. He was clever in appealing to Debbie's "helping" sense. She acquiesced thinking she was now indebted to him and moments later he was sitting in her room drinking an orange soda. Mrs. Levinsky had seen him enter but went to bed early so there was no problem from her.

They talked some more about marriage and divorce in general and then he once again attempted to seduce her. He was very persistent and persuasive but now Debbie was even less inclined than before. When he saw that he would not succeed in his plans, he got up and said somewhat angrily, "Well, then I'm going." He finally left and Debbie never heard from him again. When she went to bed, she once more thought of the unsuspecting wife and the enemy eyes that were watching her every move. It was like something out of a grade B movie. She began to wonder just how typical Avi had been. Were all the men in Israel so calculating and cruel? Or was she just prey to such types? Without answering the question, Debbie fell asleep.

Fortunately, Debbie learned from this experience that the best way to meet someone nice and suitable in Israel was definitely not via a car or street pickup. Usually these are very aggressive types who are highly skilled in their act because they do it all the time. Many go from girl to girl. They hang out in the five star hotels and tourist sites waiting for the innocent traveller to come along. No tourist or new immigrant could be a match for them. They know all the right things to say that will appeal to a tourist. If a girl is alone, they will assume that she is lonely and will readily welcome any offer of friendship. The timing also is important. For a girl to be walking alone late Friday afternoon is especially significant and indicates that she has no family because everyone is at home with their family at the start of the Sabbath.

Fortunately, all they usually want is a casual sexual encounter. But others want to emigrate to the United States and hope to do so by marrying an American girl. The number of psychopaths is probably small although cases have been reported of girls taking *"tramps"* (lifts) and later their bodies would be found dead somewhere alongside the road. It is usually not clear what the motivation was: terrorism, murder, theft, rape, revenge or kicks. Debbie was amazed at how common the "tramp" was in Israel and how many girls took them sometimes even just to save the bus fare. Probably most are OK but there is always that one or two that isn't. Debbie was no longer willing to take such a risk.

On another occasion, Debbie had a similar experience outside the walls of the Old City of Jerusalem. Again she was alone and just walking around when a car drove up and a very respectable looking man asked her if she "needed any help."

"You look lost," he said sympathetically. "I am from this area so perhaps I can be of some help."

Just as she was about to say "thank you, no," he asked where she was from. She answered again of course, the way most people do naturally when they are asked a question. As has been pointed out earlier, the very act of answering itself indicates or conveys interest to the person asking. Most tourists never learn that the way to get rid of someone (and sometimes this becomes necessary) is to ignore him completely and not to answer their questions, no matter how often they may repeat them. In this case, Debbie kept answering his questions, hoping he would go away.

Encouraged, he finally made a proposal, "Why don't you get in and I will show you what you want to see."

This time she did not get in. But men like this do not give up easily. When he realized that he would not succeed in getting Debbie into his car, he quickly parked the car in the nearest available space and started to walk after her.

After the veneer of "helping the tourist" was stripped off, it turned out that he also wanted sex. He was a married pharmacist who thought nothing of using Saturday as his day off not only from work but also "off" from wife and children. When Debbie stated clearly that she did not wish to become involved in such a discussion and said she wanted to go inside the city walls, he obliged (since he could not leave his car where it was) but not before giving her his "card" in case "you should get lonely and change your mind. I think we could be very good together," he added smiling.

Sometimes Debbie, as did also many Israelis, spent Saturdays in the Arab marketplace of the Old City. When the New City was closed, there was always something to do in the Old City, filled as it was with awe-struck tourists for whom the bazaar and its custom of "bargaining" was something new and exciting.

As Debbie arched her way through the crowded alleys of the market-place, young Arabs would suddenly appear as if from nowhere and be walking alongside of her. "Can I help you?" would be a typical opener, followed by "Where are you from?" then progressing to "Come drink coffee with me" or "Come to my shop. It's just down the road." (Ha, Ha, this could turn out to be anything from one to several roads. By the time the tourist gets there, she will be too confused to find her way back and so will be dependent on her "host.")

They are highly skilled in their approach since it is part of their daily business and livelihood. Many speak several languages at least to the level of initiating a conversation and transacting business. The motivation is usually just to sell a product although in some cases, there may be sexual innuendoes. Occasionally the motivation to communicate may be political - a way to make their life situation known to the Western world. One may hear very sad stories.

One time Debbie wanted to buy an olive wood vase for her mother's birthday. She looked at the vases outside one particular shop. When the shop keeper, a young Arab about 25, saw she was interested, he invited her, "Come inside, we have nicer ones." Unsuspecting, she followed him to the back of the shop. There he tried to get as close to Debbie as possible taking her arm in a sensuous way to lead her to the side. "Look over here." Then he pulled a vase out from the shelf and handed it to her again using the opportunity to touch her. When she tried to move away, he pined, "Why are you afraid?" He became so upset that Debbie actually left the shop without buying anything.

She eventually learned how to avoid such scenarios although it was not easy. Many would relent if they saw they would not be successful but some would persist. "Why don't you want to talk with me?" "Don't be afraid. Why are you afraid?" they would wine visibly insulted. When Debbie refused to be coerced into a conversation, they often went away muttering and angry. This always left Debbie upset and feeling helpless. She did not want to hurt anyone's feelings but yet she didn't want to be the victim of each guy who approached. There was also a limit to the number of conversations one had time for. In several shops, appropriate T-shirts are available which read, "I am NOT a tourist and I don't answer questions."

With Arabs, these encounters are quite different than with Israelis. Israelis usually take a "no" more easily with the attitude, "OK, if you won't, there are a thousand others who will." Israeli secular society is also relatively free sexually speaking, so males have little difficulty finding partners within their own culture.

Arab culture, on the other hand, is still very conservative and religious. Arab girls are expected to be virgins at the time of marriage, so young Arab men have less access to any kind of sexual contact. They often take rejections badly. Perhaps because the political situation has cast them into a third class minority position, feelings of having been rejected are already present. Often the social sexual domain remains the only avenue open for a young male to prove his manhood. If he is rejected there also, of course, his rejection will be more exaggerated.

Arabs also take friendship more seriously; the casual encounter is not common. Thus, if one becomes involved, it is more difficult to distance oneself later. Arab culture in general is a very complicated one for the outsider. It has an elaborate system of etiquette which can easily be violated if the person does not understand it. For example, just to raise one's voice to an Arab is insulting and enough to drive him away instantly. Concepts of honor, dignity and loyalty are strong in ways alien to the Western mind.

The tourist or new immigrant must decide for herself if she wishes to become involved. It can prove to be a very interesting and rewarding experience or it can turn out to be uncomfortable or disastrous. Each situation must be evaluated for itself depending on the person and the immediate circumstances. To have coffee in a public cafe is one thing; to go down to the deserted Kidron Valley "to see the Tomb of Absalom" or to the Jerusalem Forest is another!

CHAPTER 2
THE LAMENT FOR BION

Sometimes Debbie would forget about the time and continue to walk in and out of the narrow winding streets of the Old City. Jerusalem was a city for walking, perhaps more than any other, and no matter how long one lived there, there were always new streets and places one could stumble upon. The architecture and uniqueness of almost everything grasps one's attention so completely that it was easy to forget the time and distance one had covered.

It was at times like this when Debbie had literally spent the entire day walking and had perhaps gone folk dancing the night before that she would feel a slight tinge of pain in her left foot over the fifth metatarsal or foot bone. It was the place where she had broken this bone just two years earlier. It served as a warning to her to take it easy but it also evoked bad memories of the incident and the person who was at fault.

She had not really wanted to go folk dancing that night in New York but had allowed herself to be persuaded by Ian Rogasky, someone she had dated a few times. He didn't know how to dance very well and in one particular dance, he did not leap forward as the dance required. As a result, Debbie also could not leap forward and compensated by moving sideward, coming down hard on the side of her foot and breaking it. She knew immediately that she had done serious damage from the pain and her complete inability to step on it. She was put in a boot type cast and given crutches. For two months, she struggled about on crutches and it was six months before she could walk normally again without dragging her foot.

What pained her most was that not once did Ian Rogasky call her or come to visit although he knew what had happened. "At least he could care enough just to call and see how I am," she often argued with herself. But fact was fact. Ian Rogasky was not getting involved in or accepting any responsibility for what happened.

It was incredible, she thought that anyone could be so callous. But we know of course, that it is not only not incredible but fairly likely that a man such as this will disappear from the scene. No one wants trouble and if one can get away, why not. But Debbie's naivete and idealism would not allow her to comprehend this very simple fact. Thus, like a Proustian madeleine, the twinge of pain conjured up old feelings of anger and hatred.

On these excursions to the Old City, Debbie usually spent some time at the Western Wall. Here just the general atmosphere always gave one a good feeling. Usually she would just watch the endless stream of people come and go. It was interesting for her to observe the eager tourists approaching the wall with their hidden wishes written on little scraps of paper and putting them in the crevices in-between the stones of the Wall.

She would watch the men and little boys go to one side to pray, the women and little girls to the other. She especially envied the Orthodox woman with their long sleeve, long skirted dresses, their hair covered completely with a kerchief usually pushing a stroller with one or several other children, not much older, toddling alongside the stroller. They would go up to the Wall and pray with deep devotion.

These women had their set place in the world and knew exactly who they were and where they were going in life. Debbie often wondered if they were really as happy and serene as they appeared to be to the world. "Perhaps happiness and serenity can only be obtained at the price of freedom," Debbie pondered. "Would I be willing or even able to pay this price?" She had always been so sure of what she wanted but now she was confused and uncertain. What had happened? "Who am I, anyway?" she thought.

Deborah Warshawsky was 31, from Manhattan, New York. Actually she had been born in Flushing, Queens and went to school there, including Queens College of the City University of New York where she had majored in English. She was the first in her family to make the daring venture of seeking higher education. She arose from that social class which had been the most upward striving and pretentious about who they were and how they appeared to others - the lower middle class. Her grandparents had come to the United States from Poland and had been Hassidic Jews. Her father, as is often the case in such situations, rebelled completely against his religious upbringing and became a virtual atheist. Debbie is the blank fruit of this reaction.

Debbie had been a good hard working student; she was conscientious about her work and so allotted little if any time to social or sporting events. There always seemed to be another quiz or examination to study for, texts to be read or another term paper to be done. She had always hoped that "next term" or "after exams" would be better and that she would finally have more time for social activities but the time never seemed to arrive. On the contrary, the work load appeared to increase. After finishing college, she went for an M.A. in Education at the University of Wisconsin, then began teaching. Debbie enjoyed teaching very much and was well liked by students and everyone. She attended committee meetings, went to seminars and did what every good and conscientious teacher was supposed to do. But beneath the professional exterior lay a life stretched thin.

While she was being the good student and the excellent teacher, the years slipped by. Her life, ideas and dreams became more and more creased by the rules of routine and repetition. After she had some experience teaching, Debbie did begin to seek out a more active social life but much to her dismay, she noticed that many of the men her age were already married. Some even had small children. She had also left behind the boys she had grown up with; some had not gone to the university or had moved away. More and more as time went by, it seemed as if only certain types were "left" - the gays, overt and oh, all those latent ones whom one would never suspect, the alcoholics, the gamblers, the mamas boys, the professional playboys, the professional singles events goers and the confirmed bachelors.

The most desirable "catches" had been lassoed long before by some C - student who was really "smart" and had not always kept her nose in the book as Debbie had. She had been too passive always waiting for that "special something" to happen as if it were magic. Like many other bright, ambitious, independent girls, she had put off "that" part of her life until the some vague "someday" when she was finished studying, when she had established herself in her career, when she had done some traveling, when, when, when. And now, like so many other girls, she had come to Israel to find a husband!

March 27, 1981 was the big day! She had broken free - broken out of her small life into the epic of the world. Debbie's parents took her to the airport laden with two gigantic matching Samsonite suitcases. There stood Debbie Warshawsky, perched on the threshold of experience at 31, a girl about 5 feet 6 inches tall, average weight with light brown hair, green eyes, fair skin, a pleasant pretty roundish face with a small smile sometimes clouded by an over serious intellect. Dressed in a new three piece rust colored suit with matching beret, Debbie looked like a medieval knight setting off in search of the Holy Grail. (Debbie did not know that to set off to Israel in search of a life mate was far more difficult than to search for the elusive Divine Cup.)

For Debbie, it was not just an idle pleasure trip but a real quest. She was full of ideals and ready to endure many hardships and dangers on her pilgrimage - even death itself. Ah yes, but the precious jeweled prize - a curly haired, sleepy eyed, commando type Israeli husband was well worth a few risks. Already being conjured up in her mind were visions of the beautiful hills of Jerusalem and the handsome young Tarzans guarding them, their blue black curls glowing like coals in the darkness.

The sound of a crying child quickly jolted Debbie back into reality. She usually did not spend too much time probing such deep questions of identity. They would enter her mind but were just as easily dismissed. It is possible that some more thought about certain situations would have led to greater insight. Yet perhaps she was afraid of an insight too deep or perhaps she instinctively knew that she would have to change her behavior if she looked at her life with greater reality.

This she was unwilling to do. Thus, she was doomed to drift along whatever pathways the torches of life deemed to fire her.

One Friday night, Debbie was invited to a party in the Jewish Quarter of the Old City given by a girl named Eti Rosenbaum. She had met Eti through Shlomo Kantor whom she still knew from tourist days. Eti was a pretty Israeli girl of 31, never married and was hopelessly in love with a middle aged confirmed bachelor, Yossi Cohen. Unfortunately, the feeling was not mutual. In fact, Yossi was becoming increasingly expert at devising methods to escape Eti's pursuit.

He usually ate dinner at the Hebrew University dining room in the evening and often Eti would hang out about outside on the grass or wait in one of the university buildings until he walked by and then pretend that she "just happened" to be in that place. She hoped to have the opportunity of talking with him or more but Cohen caught on to her scheme of running into him and began to plot ways to avoid her. Although he basically thought Eti was a good person, he did not wish to have any conversation with her.

Of course, it was somewhat difficult to have a conversation with Eti. Usually, it was only she who spoke and the topic of conversation always centered on her current problems. This in itself was not so bad but soon the direction of the talk began to flow down divergent pathways unknown to the listener and before long, the listener would be totally lost amid the river Styx of Eti's daily activities and other minutiae. If he endured, he would stand bleary-eyed and exhausted as she proceeded to vomit the deepest recesses of her consciousness and unconsciousness. Cohen did not wish to subject himself to such daily tortures and so escape he did. It was sad though to see Eti lurking about looking for her beloved and to realize that he had once again succeeded in sneaking out the rear exit.

Of course, she invited Yossi to her party and of course, he did not come. It was probably the reason why she gave the party in the first place thinking perhaps he might come for the free food and wine. Had it been any other place but Eti's, Cohen indeed would have easily undertaken such a journey for the sake of the food, but nothing could lure him to Eti's. The thought of being in the least indebted to her filled him with such fear that he wanted to flee instantly. Eti was not overly disappointed in the fact that Yossi did not come to her party since she half expected it.

The party was a fairly pleasant affair with about 20 people present. Debbie had brought a box of chocolate cookies since Eti had asked if she could "bring something" which usually meant some food or drink one had made. Debbie noted, however, that with the sole exception of Professor David Kremetsky who had offered a bottle of wine, she was the only one at the party who had "donated" anything.

Eti had prepared quite an array of food, nonetheless, and there was wine plenty. Debbie observed that people helped themselves rather freely and quickly as if they were in a hurry. Some were dancing; others just remained sitting and talking. The highlight of the evening was a solo performance by her girl friend, Braccha Shapiro, who sang folk and pop songs accompanied by her guitar. A pretty girl, she sang well and everyone seemed to be having a pleasant time.

Debbie was also having a good time. She liked the people who were there having known most of them from the university where she had spent a lot of time. She was somewhat disappointed that there were no new people, however, who might have been more available for her. About 10:30 P.M.. Debbie saw that many people were leaving, in fact, it seemed that most left within about a 15 minute time period. It was quite noticeable as though something had happened of which Debbie was unaware. Perhaps they all had appointments elsewhere, she thought to herself. Only Eti's closest friends were left. Debbie couldn't believe that a party could be over at 10:30. In the United States, parties usually began at that hour.

When she had a chance, Debbie went into the kitchen where Eti had disappeared with some empty dishes.

"Well, how did you like it?" Eti inquired as she was sorting the dishes. Debbie noticed that her cookies were still sitting in the same place Eti had put them when she had given them to her. Apparently, she planned to keep them for herself. No matter, Debbie thought, practically, they were good cookies and she could understand that she didn't want to put them out for the crowd who would devour them in two minutes.

"Oh, fine," Debbie's answer to Eti's question came after a second's reflection.

"Eti, why did everyone leave so suddenly? Did something happen?" Debbie asked looking very somber and perplexed.

"No," she said wearily. "Why?"

"Well," Debbie began again hesitatingly. "Everything seemed to be going well and then suddenly people started to leave."

Eti sighed, then shrugged her shoulders resignedly. "Don't you see, the food was gone." She laughed but it was not a genuine laugh more of a "well, what can you do" act of acceptance. Debbie was shocked; she had never encountered anything like it before. It would be unthinkable in the United States. There people would leave a party when they didn't find anyone to socialize with and felt awkward, of if they saw an old lover with a new friend or because they weren't having a good time and had an opportunity of going elsewhere or... but never, ever because the food had run out. (Israelis would probably consider the other reasons as silly as Debbie thought theirs to be.)

"Are you kidding?" Debbie screeched, still not believing.

"No," Eti stated emphatically. "People come for the food here, that's that. So what can you so?"

Professor Kremetsky offered Debbie a ride back to the New City. He was a middle aged man, divorced, a Biology professor at the Hebrew University. Debbie liked him as a friend because he was truly a nice person, the kind of friend one could rely on in times of need.

"Yossi didn't come," he commented sadly. "I thought maybe he would."

"Poor Eti," Debbie remarked, thanked him for the ride and went upstairs. Such was her first party in Jerusalem.

The next day Debbie thought back over the evening before and how people left because the food was gone. She studied the fact that superficially Israel looked like the United States or any Western country yet the longer one lived here and the deeper one plunged into the culture, the more one began to understand that there were many major differences in the life style, behavior, and value systems of the two countries.

Debbie did not realize that while she was trying to analyze this Israeli behavior, yet another example of cultural difference was taking place at that very moment in her hallway. It was Saturday and she had a date with Shimon as she had had several other Saturdays in the past. She had finished getting ready quite early and was waiting for him in the living room. Last time they had gone for lunch and then for a leisurely stroll in the Liberty Bell Park. She had had a marvelous time and was reminiscing about it when she heard some noise in the hall. Thinking he had arrived, she peeped out the doorhole to see. Instead of Shimon, she saw her next door neighbor, Mrs. Goldenblum, polishing her mailbox.

Mrs. Goldenblum was an attractive woman, about 55 and this day she was decked out in a crisp and daring pinafore, her dark hair done in an elaborate bouffant. She constantly bragged about her son, the PhD in Psychology. There seemed to be no end to the grants and invitations abroad that he received. It was rather strange, her being in the hallway, shining her mailbox on the Sabbath.

Then Debbie heard a noise from downstairs. Mrs. Goldenblum also glanced down. Soon Shimon appeared at the top of the stairs. Mrs. Goldenblum flashed him a warm smile and said something to him which Debbie could not hear. She continued to watch through the peephole as Mrs. Goldenblum chatted with Shimon as though she had known him all her life.

"Why," Debbie thought indignantly, "She's actually flirting with him, the old battleaxe."

Debbie did not wish to see anymore and returned to the living room. Mrs. Goldenblum had probably waited for him knowing that it was likely that he would arrive about that time.

"The old bat," Debbie fumed, "and she's married too and probably wants a young lover. "Don't they ever have enough, these women?"

Finally Shimon rang the bell and Mrs. Goldenblum disappeared into her apartment. Shimon came in beaming and happy as usual. Debbie offered him a Cola and they sat down in her room. After talking awhile, Debbie said as casually as she could, "I heard my nosey neighbor cornering you in the hallway."

"Oh, yeah," he said absent-mindedly as though he had already forgotten or dismissed the incident from his mind. "I was surprised when she started talking to me. I didn't know what she wanted." He started to reach for his pocket, pulled out a small piece of paper and handed it to Debbie. "She gave me the phone number of her daughter in Ramat Aviv. She wants me to call her."

Debbie looked at the phone number written in careful digits with "Irit Goldenblum" printed above. "Why," Debbie asked realizing it was a stupid question but she didn't know what else to say.

"Well, I guess she wants me to meet her. Told me she's 31, a teacher and that she's very pretty and nice, you know, all that."

Debbie was speechless, "the nerve of her" curling up inside her lips but not quite making it to the outside. "Well, you better hang on to it, it might be a real opportunity," she teased, trying to make it sound like a joke but it came out instead with notes of anxiety and anger.

"What, are you kidding?" he cried, tossing it into her waste basket. "There, that's what I think of her."

Wonderful Shimon, thought Debbie admiringly and falling more in love with him every minute. They had a wonderful day together but occasionally visions of Mrs. Goldenblum in her bright red pinafore kept entering her mind like an evil demon.

Three days passed and then Debbie saw her chance. Mrs. Goldenblum was coming out of her apartment. Debbie leaped up from her chair and opened the door. "Hello-o" she cooed in a tone that dripped with a ton of potential fury. She dove right in.

"My boy friend tells me you gave him the telephone number of your daughter. I didn't know you had a daughter. You never speak of her. You just talk all the time about your son, the psychologist."

Mrs. Goldenblum sighed, "I have a daughter also. She's still single, like you."

Debbie thought how pathetic it was that this woman could discourse on the divine attributes of her son for at least an hour but all she could say about her daughter was that she was "still single." The tone in which she said it also indicated that this blessed state of singleness was to be viewed with no less dread than the plague, leprosy or AIDS.

Apparently the woman did not think she had done anything wrong in giving Shimon Irit's number. If she did, she certainly didn't show it. There was no guilt, no explanation, no attempt even to hide it. Finally Debbie could contain herself no longer and blurted out, "I think you have a lot of nerve to give MY boyfriend the telephone number of another girl, even if it is your daughter. He's MY boyfriend."

"Oh, but you are leaving." Mrs Goldenblum said calmly.

"Who says I'm leaving?" By this time, Debbie was really mad. She did not get angry often but when she did, she boiled. "I'm not leaving. I came to stay."

"Oh, come now," Mrs. Goldenblum repeated her logic. "You are a tourist, an American. They never stay long. Life is much too hard for them here. My daughter is born in Israel, like this young man. They have many things in common. He's such a nice young man, an economist in the bank with a good future. She spoke as though they were already planning to be married.

"I am not a tourist. I am an *olah hadasha* (new immigrant) and I am here to stay," Debbie argued vehemently. "Forever" she added confidently as an afterthought. "Besides if you want to know, he threw the piece of paper in my waste basket." Debbie proudly produced the paper and tore it to shreds. "That's the result of your dirty work, hah."

"It's the custom here in Israel. Nobody thinks anything about it." Mrs. Goldenblum, went on still calm and matter of fact. "If one girl decides that a certain young man is not suitable for her, she gives his number to her girlfriend."

"Well, Mrs. Goldenblum, I'll have you know that I think Shimon is very suitable for me." She emphasized the word "suitable" as a British lady might have said. With that she closed the door but her fury had not abated. She felt exhausted. The aggression and desperation of Israeli women for a man was really intolerable. There was more than one kind of war in Israel.

As time went on, much to Debbie's chagrin, Mrs. Goldenblum would continue to ask her "if you are still going with that nice young man." Debbie assured her that she was and that things were progressing wonderfully.

Debbie still had to become accustomed to and accepting of a dominant Israeli trait known as *Chutzpah*. This is an essentially untranslatable word and examples may clarify it better than any definition. Mrs. Goldenblum's action definitely would come into this category, also anyone walking blase ahead in line in a queue or climbing over the fence in the waiting line for the bus. It is to have the "nerve" to do something most people would hesitate to do or would not normally do. Usually such an action would be considered negative or uncouth but in Israel, there is a definite undercurrent of admiration for someone who has such "courage" or "daring."

A good example is the following. As Debbie often walked down Ben Yehuda street or Jaffa road, a young guy would approach, stop next to or directly in front of her to block her way and say with a bright smile and brazen voice, *"SHALOM"* emphasizing each syllable slowly and clearly as though he had known her all his life and now after a long absence he is so happy to meet her again.

At first, Debbie fell for this trick each time and even after she had lived in Israel for a long time, she still occasionally succumbed. She would look at the guy with expectations of recognition of a life long friend. Instead, all she saw was a face she didn't know. She would look bewildered and in a confused state attempt to place the person.

"I'm sorry , I don't remember you. Where do I know you from." she would ask innocently, also often embarrassed.

Ignoring her question, he would pose his own. "Where are you from, the States? Or some other introductory comment like, "Hello, I know you from the Hebrew University."

Finally, some insight would descend on Debbie and she would realize that the guy did not know her at all but just used the big and loud "Shalom" to stop her, secure her attention, and start a conversation.

This infuriated her partially because she was angry at herself for falling into the trap and partially because it was a lousy trick. Debbie was an honest, straightforward person and did not like this approach. "Get out of here, you creep," was eventually her response when it happened again and again.

One day, Debbie was rushing down King George Street, deep in thought, and looking neither up nor to the left or right. All of a sudden she heard one of these big energetic Shaloms to which she responded with a grunt and continued on her way. Then she became aware that someone was desperately running after her. Now she had to look and see who it was when the voice said, "Hey, don't you remember me, Bob Colan?"

"Oh, Bob, I didn't see you," she stammered embarrassed, recognizing one of her former partners from folk dancing and long time friend. She tried to explain the situation so he would not think she had been rude. However, he had lived in Israel for a year and so understood quite readily. Then their conversation turned to other more pleasant things.

Bob was not going to stay for very long, unfortunately. From him, she heard the latest gossip from the folk dancing crowd. So and so got married, had a baby, got a grant etc. etc. It was at times like that when Debbie did think about New York but never did she really wish to go back. "It would just be the same scene again," she thought. "In Israel there is always something new even if the "something" is not always so pleasant. Anything is better than boredom and stagnation."

Often Debbie would go to concerts either at Binyanei Hauma, the largest hall in Jerusalem or to the Jerusalem Theater. The orchestras in Israel were excellent and the concerts were always enjoyable to say nothing of the pleasant atmosphere of the concert halls. Yet, not even here was one immune to strange approaches.

One evening, Debbie arrived at the theater and was waiting in line at the box office when a tall, well dressed although not good looking man about 45 slinked up to her in line and held out a ticket.

"Would you like a ticket?" he said simply.

Debbie thought he meant to sell it as some people often do outside the theater before a performance. "How much is it? Debbie asked as she looked at the ticket.

"Nothing. It's free. I have an extra ticket, that's all. Someone couldn't come." he said non-chalantly.

Debbie looked mistrusting and thought quickly why he would give away a ticket for nothing when he could easily sell it.

"I don't know what to do with it. Really take it," he said, coaxing now.

Debbie felt uncomfortable, but assumed that he was in earnest.

"It's for this concert?"

"Yes, of course."

"OK, if you don't want it." Debbie innocently took the ticket, glad that she would not have to pay the $15-20 entrance fee.

Debbie did not question or even notice why he had approached her and only her although there were perhaps 18 or 20 other people on the line. He left to enter the theater. Debbie took her time since it was still early. When she got to her seat, she was somewhat taken aback when she saw him again in the next seat. Then she thought to herself, "Of course, he bought two tickets, naturally, they would be together."

She sat down and smiled pleasantly although there was something she didn't like about this man. He was really ugly and his face had a kind of perpetual almost contorted smirk on it.

The concert began shortly thereafter so there wasn't much time for a conversation. During the intermission, however, he began to ask the usual questions, "Where are you from? Are you a tourist? How long are you staying. Do you have family here?" Had they come from anyone else, Debbie would have answered briefly and sought to excuse herself. But after all, this man had *given* her a ticket, free of charge. So was she not obligated to be pleasant to him and to have a conversation? Was she not indebted to him? And so they chatted during the 20 minute intermission.

Intermissions are always long in Israel, because many people eat sandwiches, coffee and cake and other goodies and of course, the theater is eager for an extra business. After the concert and the intermission conversation, it also seemed quite natural that they should somehow continue the togetherness that the free ticket had fostered. Debbie still felt turned off by him but the obligation incurred by accepting his gift lingered on.

"Where do you live?" was the next inquiry. He also "happened" to be going in that direction so how could she not allow him to walk with her? As was usually the case, the other person pushed the questions and well-mannered, ladylike Debbie would provide the answers, rarely the other way around. As a result, he soon knew a lot about her but she very little about him, only that he was of Afganistani parentage, a fact of which he seemed to be very proud.

As they neared her house he asked for her telephone number and if he might see her again. By now Debbie had been pushed to the limit of her endurance. She did not even want to talk to this man much less go out with him. So she said, she didn't have use of the phone and the landlady didn't like it if people called and disturbed. He knew he was being put off and whined the usual, "Why are you afraid to go out with me?" At this point, Debbie slowly retreated. "I have to go now. Thanks again for the ticket." He persisted and she walked faster in fear and flight. Finally, she was inside the door and rid of him. Oh he was so ugly, ugly it seemed from a perpetual snarl. Well, it was her fault, accepting that ticket.

A few months later, it happened that Debbie was again going to a concert. She saw the Afganistani but she need not have feared another encounter with him. There he was with another outstretched ticket, this time to another obviously American girl, innocently waiting in line. The scenario was then re-enacted, but perhaps this time with a different ending.

Debbie should not have felt obligated to him. It was a method he used to meet tourists. Perhaps he wanted to emigrate to the United States since he approached only tourists. Or perhaps he wished only a very transitory or "extra" relationship without involvement. Tourists always leave after a few days. Nevertheless, his method was usually quite successful. No one could resist anything free and the acceptance instilled in the receiver a sense of duty and obligation to be nice to him. Debbie continued to meet him during the course of her stay in Israel - always in tourist haunts, sitting by the Windmill, or the Western Wall with a young girl tourist.

In the beginning, Debbie often wondered, "How can the Israelis discern an American girl from an Israeli so easily? But after living in Israel even for a short while, one could see the world of difference. The style of the clothing, the quality of the fabric (Israeli material is cheap looking and coarse.), the hairstyle, makeup - all betray the tourist or new immigrant. Her very shyness, deference, and politeness give her away. So does the facial expression described by one Israeli as "soft and pleasant as contrasted to the hard, sharp and tough look of the Israeli girl." The body movements and general manner were also different: slower and more guarded by the American; fast jerky gestures, more spontaneous for the Israeli. Thus, everywhere, American and other foreign women were easy Red Riding Hoods for any big bad Israeli wolf.

One situation where it is especially easy for the Israeli wolf to stalk his prey is the long distance bus ride. Again, the innocent unsuspecting pre-occupied tourist is the usual victim.

It happens very easily. Usually the first people on any bus will chose a window seat. So any girl may expect a guy to annoy her if he comes onto the bus and plops next to her even though half the window seats are still available.

Or if he chooses her over a seated male.

Debbie remembers the first time it happened to her when she got on a bus in Beersheva bound for Jerusalem. She was the second person on the bus and naturally chose a window seat near the front. Let it be mentioned that this was early in Debbie's Israeli stay, a time when she felt new, hesitant about everything and very shy. She was everybody's compliant tourist. Fourth onto the bus was a big burly soldier, quite fat with all his gear and gun jangling as he boarded, presented his ticket and then moved along. He looked exhausted but not too tired to notice Debbie nor much to her horror, to drop heavily beside her.

It was also a very old bus with hard narrow seats and one third his bulk landed on top of her. She looked around stupefied to see an empty bus. Why had he chosen to sit down in such a narrow place when he really needed two seats? She sighed and tried to extricate herself from his weight. Her "Could you move over please?" fell on deaf ears. She pushed him over and then a spark of understanding crossed his grisly face. He murmured something in Hebrew then made an attempt to move only to glide back conveniently into the same position minutes later.

Had Debbie been more experienced or more aggressive, the time to change seats would have been immediately after he dumped himself. By the time this idea presented itself to her, the bus had nearly filled and besides just getting up and out presented an enormous problem. She was fated to sit next to Benny (for such was his name, he informed her later when he misinterpreted one of her complaints) during the journey to Jerusalem. To make matters worse, this was the slow bus that approached Jerusalem via the Tel Aviv coastal road, hence requiring two and a half hours unlike the bus which drove through the West Bank and required only one and a half hours.

Need one describe what these two and one half hours sitting next to a fat, sweating dirt-clad guy were like. It was not long before he began to put his leg as close to Debbie as possible and his hand kept moving onto Debbie's leg. At first she merely tried to edge closer to the wall but alas there was no space to move. She was hanging so close to the window that it looked as if she were contemplating jumping out. Then she would attempt to push his hand and leg away. But this was to no avail for they would reappear seconds later with even greater intensity. Finally she gave him a strong elbow jab which initiated some verbal response. Perhaps now Debbie thought there might be peace. And there was - for awhile.

But soon, the situation was once again the same. Debbie looked around the bus desperately if there might not be a free seat somewhere but every seat was occupied. The only choice was to stand which on a bumpy and winding road would be just as uncomfortable as Benny. Then she recalled an article in some woman's magazine which dealt with ways of handling unwanted advances. The article promised sure relief if a load verbal comment was made for all to hear. The man would then be embarrassed and rapidly disappear. Debbie was desperate.

So she decided to say loud and clear, "If you don't stop annoying me, I'm going to punch you in the mouth." But her statement loud as it was, had little effect. First of all, it was in English, which probably few in a bus from Beersheva would understand. Secondly, it evoked more a response of annoyance because many passengers had by this time become drowsy; some were dozing already. Thirdly, some smiled knowingly but in an accepting "After all, boys will be boys" fashion. People sealed many an eye to the frolics of a soldier on leave who after all could only be expected to "try his luck" serving all the time with only men and being far away from his wife.

Therefore, advice that would have worked magic on a New York subway was not so powerful on the Tel Aviv coastal road. Then once again there was peace. When Debbie dared to turn to discover why, she saw that Benny had fallen asleep. Weariness had finally overcome him. Debbie was relieved and sat back relaxed in her seat and within a short time, she too succumbed to sleep. When she suddenly awoke, Benny's hand was fumbling and groping in terrain not to Debbie's liking and his heavy leg was resting halfway on her own. "Ugh" was her first response and then she kicked him off with all her strength. This was no small matter.

She looked out the window as though relief lay outside her cramped cubicle. She saw a sign "Doron Junction" indicating that this would be the next crossroads and below it, it said, "Jerusalem - 10 km." Debbie couldn't believe it; they would arrive in Jerusalem in about 15 minutes.

Benny lay somnolent and half smiling when suddenly as if motivated by some ulterior mechanism, he blinked his eyes, sat up in his seat, gathered his gear and got up. He looked at Debbie and said something in Hebrew, then pointed outside the bus. Whatever it was he said, he did so with a friendly and inviting manner as though all the blows and punches she had given him along the trip hadn't happened. Perhaps this had even encouraged him. After all, it was a form of contact.

The bus slowed as it neared "Doron Junction" and stopped. Benny repeated the same thing with a pleading look and motioned his head in the direction of the door. Then suddenly Debbie realized that he was planning to get off at this ungodly place which especially in the dark seemed to be in the middle of nowhere. He started to plod his way to the door. Debbie said "Goodbye" half in relief but half in disappointment too that somehow she would never see him again. In the two odd hours they had spent together, Debbie developed a curious type of attachment to him in the way one develops an attachment to an ugly child or animal when one is with them long enough and has experienced a great deal with them even though it may have been unpleasant. Or perhaps it wasn't really all so unpleasant. Perhaps Debbie was flattered by his attention and enjoyed the physical contact. But of course, she would not admit this to herself.

Benny got off and walked in the direction of another bus shelter. He turned once more to the window and waved with his gun for her to follow. Debbie hesitated for a few seconds.

"Oh, I couldn't," she thought quickly to herself. She raised her hand and waved goodbye to him. He shrugged his shoulders, raised his gun in farewell and walked to the other shelter. The old bus started up again and drove away. Debbie looked to see where she was but saw only a lonely country setting outside, some farms, and chicken coops. Benny was gone.

"He wanted you to get out with him," a voice in the seat behind Debbie whispered and laughed.

"Really, in this wilderness?" Debbie answered.

"It isn't such a wilderness. There are many kibbutzim and moshavim in this area. He probably comes from one of them and has a day or two off. He just wanted to make the most of it. Not an easy life, the army, a reservist he was."

The voice belonged to a man about 40 who had apparently been observing and listening to the whole affair, probably taking his part in the enjoyment also. Debbie didn't answer but just sat back to savor the last moments of her trip in comfort.

When they got out in Jerusalem, the voice in the seat in the back of Debbie attempted to move up a peg. Apparently he had not liked being a seat behind and would not have minded being in Benny's seat.

"What a chap," he started again as they got off the bus. Then only did she notice the British accent.

"Yes, he sure was. Boy am I glad to be here," Debbie said relieved and luxuriating in being in the fresh air outside the small cramped old bus.

"Where are you from?"

Debbie was still answering this question out of sheer habit when suddenly insight illuminated in her mind that this friendly sympathizing stranger was just another Benny, just a cleaner more civilized looking one with an English accent - but a Benny nonetheless.

"I gotta go. See you," she mumbled wearily, taking her bag and made for the bus shelter that would take her home.

"Wait," Benny's successor cried. "I own a toy shop on Narkiss and Herzl Street. My name is Len. Why don't you stop by sometime? Number 12 Narkiss."

"OK" Debbie shouted, no more intending ever to go to 12 Narkiss St. than to the moon. "Goodbye" and she walked away.

"There is no end to these ever lurking, ever patsying guys here." she muttered out loud to herself. "If only some of them would be half way decent, it wouldn't be so bad." But it was like looking into a refrigerator of leftovers and not wanting to eat any of them. What and if you eventually ate anything depended on how hungry you were!

Experiences such as this one continued to plague Debbie's trips on buses. She eventually learned to recognize the possibility quickly and to move immediately. Another problem that a woman may encounter on a bus ride is that occasionally a man sitting in the seat behind her will put his hand through the opening at the bottom of the seat and attempt to feel her buttocks. Many times Debbie would jump suddenly in her seat as a hand made its way over her bottom. Elderly men and very young adolescent boys usually were the biggest offenders in both cases.

All these minor monsters were mulling about in Debbie's confused mind as she walked quickly up Ben Yehuda Street. Her head was cast down so she did not immediately notice the large number of people coming in the opposite direction. In fact, so deeply was she locked in her depressed thoughts that she took no notice of them or of anything else but kept obstinately trudging up the hill. It was not until she felt a strong pull on her arm and a loud voice speaking into a megaphone that she peered up and was jostled loose from her absorption. He spoke in Hebrew and pointed for her to go back in the other direction. Then she suddenly saw the rest of the crowd coming toward her and the area into which she had been going being cleared.

"What's the matter?" she asked somebody but they didn't seem to understand. "Suspicious object," a voice responded from behind who had overheard her question. Debbie looked about her perhaps for comfort or additional explanation.

Some individuals were anxiously staring into the evacuation area but most seemed quite accepting of the situation as though it happened quite often and they had become very accustomed to it. A few looked at their watches and sighed obviously annoyed at the delay in their plans. Debbie wondered if she was far enough away from the suspicious object should it be a bomb.

It took but a few minutes for the special bomb squad to arrive. Debbie could see men with special yellow helmets and masks get out of a truck. They had something in their hands but her nearsighted eyes prevented her from seeing. Five minutes later, everyone was again walking in their original direction. The bomb scare was over and as was usually the case, although not always, it was nothing - just some trash in a bag someone had carelessly left behind. But as the slogan went, "Better suspicious than sorry." Debbie was relieved and continued on her way. An experience like this, especially when it is for the first time, always has a sobering effect.

On the way home, Debbie ate in a cafeteria type restaurant near King George Street in Jerusalem. Sitting across from her several tables away was a man about 40 with a briefcase, obviously a businessman. However, he was dressed in jeans and a faded yellow University of Wisconsin T-shirt. This was Debbie's Alma Mater and it gave her a happy sense of nostalgia to see the T-shirt with the Wisconsin badger insignia in the middle - symbol of the famous football team. She felt so good at seeing it again after all these years that she decided she would go over and speak with him. For her, it was a lifeboat between them in this sea of strangers.

She approached him and said, "Hi, I see a fellow Wisconsinite. When were you there?" He looked up surprised and bewildered. *"Ma?"* ("What" in Hebrew). Debbie pointed to his T-shirt. "Didn't you go to the University of Wisconsin?" Then after awhile he seemed to understand. "No, no," he smiled. By this time Debbie recognized that he was not even an American and that his comprehension of English was quite limited.

"Where did you get the T-shirt?" Debbie queried.

"Oh," he thought for a minute.

"A cousin of mine sent it to me, oh, 7-8 years ago. I don't remember so well now."

On closer inspection, the T-shirt did look obviously well worn. Debbie was embarrassed. "I went there," she explained, "and I thought maybe you did too. Sorry." "That's OK," he smiled again and Debbie sat back down in her seat.

She was disappointed that she had not met a University of Wisconsin alumnus but even more shocked that this man had little else to wear to business than an old faded T-shirt which he did not even buy nor whose message held any meaning for him. After this incident Debbie began to take closer notice of people's clothing in general and then realized that the clothes of this man were the average of an adult male on the streets of Jerusalem. On the whole, people dressed in simple fashion often in worn out-of-style clothing. Girls were in midis, minis, ruffles, shirts, etc. - clothes collected over a period of time. Whatever they had, they continued to wear. New styles did not make easy inroads here. The same was true for men who dressed casually, even shabbily for the office.

"OK. let me ask you just one question: I'm 36, do you think, you know, if I came here to live, do you think I could get somebody?" This was the ultimate question Shirley Glikin hurled headlong at Debbie Warshawsky as they collided one day on one of the small alley like streets in the Jewish Quarter of the Old City of Jerusalem.

Debbie had been in a hurry to meet someone at 1 P.M. when the other young woman passed by her. "Hey," she stopped Debbie and cried, "I know you. You're a folk dancer."

Debbie vaguely recognized and remembered her as one of the regular Tuesday night dancers at Phil Kern's an international folk dance group in New York that she used to attend.

The girl was obviously brimming over in eagerness to talk but Debbie explained she was already late for her appointment, hence the reason for the abruptness of Shirley's dramatic and desperate query. She asked it with such an intense and fierce look on her face like a hungry lion eyeing an unarmed tourist that Debbie felt pity for her and decided to give her a few minutes after all.

"What do you mean by 'get'? she asked, "Do you mean a husband,?"

"Of course, a husband," Shirley answered firmly as if the question had been an absurd one. "What else?"

"Well," Debbie began to explain, there were all types of relationships in Israel and whether or not one could "get" depended on the kind of relationship one was looking for. A lover was relatively easy to find; a husband, well, that was something else. "There are not many single men your age. But give it a try," Debbie waved to Shirley as she tried to start again toward her desired goal. "I'll see you at folk dancing." But Shirley kept talking.

"You see," she continued, "I'll have to give up my teaching job where I have tenure plus my rent controlled apartment." She looked anxious and worn as though this conflict had been plaguing her for some time.

"Think it over carefully before you decide," Debbie offered as though it were an original idea. "But come," she repeated, "you'll never know until you try. You can always leave after awhile. I really do have to go now." Debbie hurried to her destination leaving Shirley to ponder her plight.

At the moment, however, Debbie was continuing her plunge into the inner labyrinths of the Old City. The streets were so small and similar that even a seasoned traveler could lose his way if not careful. Many new and beautiful townhouses had been constructed with the awesome white Jerusalem stones. Debbie threw an admiring and envious glance here and there as she rushed by. Everywhere young mothers, modestly attired, could be seen with happy toddlers playing nearby. Oh, would she ever be like them! They seemed so serene and in place as though they had been there for centuries. Courtyard after courtyard revealed the same domestic scenes until they began to blur into a series of panoramic paintings in Debbie's mind. Only the sharp crevices of the stones on the walk as they dug into the thin soles of her worn shoes reminded her that it was not a clear museum floor she was treading but the massive uneven stones of the Jewish Quarter of the Old City.

Finally after a few minor false digressions down the wrong alleys, Debbie arrived at Hatikva Street. It was a blind alley consisting of perhaps four or five townhouses. The address she had copied down turned out to be a small basement level apartment on the right side. For a minute, it reminded Debbie of similar sunken level apartments in Greenwich Village. But it was only the level that triggered the association; everything else could not have been more different.

She walked down approximately 8 or 9 steps and looked for the name on the bell and rang somewhat hesitatingly. She was more than a half hour late. Debbie had almost given up that anyone was home when a tall thin and very pale looking woman opened the door. "Yes?" she said in a very soft almost belabored voice. "Hello," Debbie chimed amiably. "I'm the girl who called you yesterday about your ad in the *Post*. I'm sorry I'm late."

"That's OK. What was it you were interested in? I got several calls for each item," she explained quickly with an American accent that still had faint traces of New York.

"The toaster," Debbie smiled. "I've been without one so long here. I really miss it. And they're so expensive in Israel - $80 for what you could get for $15 in New York."

"Please come in and take a look at what I've got. Perhaps you might also be interested in some of the other things," she added hopefully.

"Well, I don't know, Debbie stammered, "I live in a furnished room so I have pretty much everything. But there's no toaster."

As she entered the living room, Debbie's eyes lit on a pretty little girl of about 4 or 5 years with a whirlpool of dark hair framing and partially hiding her beautiful face. Large black eyes stared out at Debbie curiously. "This is Shirli, my daughter," the woman stated now smiling weakly for the first time.

"She's gorgeous," Debbie said energetically. "What a charmer." The woman looked away suddenly when Debbie said that as if in surrender. Then she summoned her control and energy and pointed out the items for sale - "all the appliances, the typewriter, these carpets and also some of the dresses - although I think they are a bit too small for you."

Debbie examined the toaster which was still fairly new and in apparently good condition. In fact, the same could have been said about all the things for sale. "How much is it" Debbie asked. "$25" "I'll take it." Debbie agreed eagerly. By Israeli standards, it was a bargain. Debbie was happy and started to open her purse to get the money. It was then that she noticed for the first time the very sad and weary look on the woman's face, especially her eyes. She was only about 35 but her face had already taken on an old and worn aura.

"Here," Debbie extended the money to her.

Then she hesitated for a minute not knowing exactly how to phrase her idea. "How come you are selling all these good things? I don't mean to be nosey but do you think it's wise? Are you planning to return to the States? Where exactly are you from?"

She thought for a minute, looked at Debbie not knowing whether or not to confide in a perfect stranger. But the need to talk and to unburden herself was so overwhelming and Debbie's face so open and honest that she began her story.

"I'm from Connecticut originally and lived most of my life in New York. Yes, I do plan to go back, that is, as soon as everything is settled here."

Debbie looked puzzled so she continued. "My husband and I have divorced or rather I should say my husband has divorced me which is the only way possible in Israel. Do you know the laws here at all? A woman cannot get a divorce here unless her husband grants it to her."

"Well, yes, I know the laws vaguely. I'm not married yet so I guess I never worried about things like that." Debbie tried to explain her ignorance. The woman had by now lost much of her earlier passivity and was aflame with obvious anger and hurt. She laughed in an almost devilish way.

"No, I never thought about problems like this either when I first came. I barely knew they existed. And then I fell in love, oh brother, with an Israeli. He was nice at first, they all are, but then soon showed his true colors. I won't bore you with the details. He grew unbearable and I wanted a divorce. But he refused to give it to me unless I would give him most of my money and property. He had nothing, absolutely nothing when we married. I paid for everything. I didn't even mind then, I was so happy to be getting married. And he was good looking, a real charmer as you said before. So who could think about practical matters. Oh, I was so naive, like a child, it's unbelievable."

"Why couldn't you get the divorce," Debbie asked.

"All marriages are religious and come under the rabbinical laws and court. Only a man can grant a divorce here, if the marriage took place in Israel. Now I understand why he was so anxious to have the wedding here. For his family, he had said and I believed him." She sighed wearily.

The emotional strain wore heavily on the woman and it was obvious that she had suffered a great deal and still did. "Why didn't you just separate?" Debbie suggested.

The woman had to summon her strength just to answer.

"A woman here without a *get* (legal divorce) is an outcast in the society. She cannot marry again and is still considered a married woman by all. So there is no social life for her," she sighed again. "So to be rid of him, I paid him what he wanted and I got the divorce. Sometimes I suspect he planned it so from the beginning. Some do, you know. There have been many such cases. You must be very careful," she warned.

"Anyway, now I am left with very little. I am selling the appliances because I still owe my lawyer some legal fees. Then I will go back to my parents in Connecticut. At least he will let me take the child out of the country. He could prevent me from doing so. Most men have done this and then the woman is forced to remain here or give up the child. Of course, all choose to remain but they are very unhappy." The woman seemed to feel better at this small crumb of consolation.

Debbie's brief happiness at anticipating warm toast for breakfast vanished as the divorcee related her tale. She even felt guilty for taking the woman's toaster away from her and wanted to give it back. But the woman steadfastly refused. "I hope things work out better for you here," she wished Debbie as the latter made move to leave. "And I hope you will also find happiness again," Debbie said earnestly. "Goodbye Shirli," she waved at the little girl who had remained so quiet and serious during Debbie's visit.

As she walked home, toaster in arm, Debbie was disturbed and truly wished she hadn't answered the ad. The woman's pale pinched face would haunt her for a long time. She thought back to Shirley's desperate question of finding a husband in Israel and here she had been confronted with a possible answer of what could happen when one was "lucky" enough to find one. Was there no alternative?

When Debbie arrived home, she found a message left by Mrs. Levinsky, her landlady, on the telephone. A man had called, an American tourist. She wondered who it might be and finally figured it out, Paul Kalish from folk dancing, that's who it must be. She was surprised that he had come to Israel since he had never even expressed interest in doing so although she had encouraged him many times.

Debbie had known Paul for many years but only at folk dancing. She had never gone on a date with him. Once or twice he had offered her a ride home from folk dancing but when she invited him in for coffee, he always had some vague excuse to continue on to his home. Years earlier, Debbie had relegated him to the "lost causes" category - guys who were nice and friendly but somehow not interested in women more than as aquaintances. She even suspected him of being a latent gay. He came regularly to folk dancing and danced with many girls but that was all - that is, until Nurit Levy.

Debbie first met Nurit at folk dancing in Washington Square

Park on a Saturday night in July. One should say, she first saw Nurit since at this time the dark haired Israeli tourist was deeply lost in the arms of Stanley Becker on a bench in the park, not far from the folk dancing. Nurit was visiting in the United States and was possibly trying to snare an American guy so she could stay in the States.

When Debbie went to folk dancing at Phil Kern's the following Tuesday, she remembers a transformed Paul Kalish come over to her panting "Come to the back. There's someone I want you to meet. You'll like her. She's great."

He looked so high as if he had taken every psychedelic drug in the pharmacopoeia. It was unusual that he wanted to introduce the "someone" to Debbie. Never before had he done anything like this. It seemed as if he were bursting to tell the whole world, "Come, meet my wonderful beloved." He couldn't contain his admiration and wonder for this goddess. Debbie was not really interested in meeting another girl but could hardly refuse because it might look as if she were jealous. So she allowed herself to be dragged along by the elated Paul to the back of the hall.

He proudly presented the object of his wonder to Debbie. "This is Nurit. She's visiting from Israel." Debbie could all but hide her surprise at seeing the same girl she had seen buried in the ecstacy of Stan's arms and no less in the same horrendous dress of broad bright yellow and black stripes.

"Hi," she managed. "Hope you like it here."

Nurit smiled a bit and that was that. Paul was so beside himself that he barely noticed the coolness that had passed between the two young women.

Nurit was different to be sure. Apparently she was taking the Ashkenazy men by storm. She was dark, exotic, alluring, something from the Orient, like a model for Sabra liqueur in the Sunday *New York Times*. Debbie noted that quite a few Sephardic Israeli women, especially the Yemenite and Moroccan ones, had succeeded in capturing American men, all of them Ashkenazy. "Opposites attract, I guess, " Debbie told herself. Nurit's grandparents had each come from a different place, from Egypt, Morocco, Iran and Iraq. Such a combination was formidable and could even knock out what had been a hopeless case like Paul Kalish.

Paul kept running around like a crazy man and did not notice that Nurit stuck to the back of the hall where the Israeli guys living in New York usually hung out. Debbie wondered whether or not she should mention it to Paul that she had seen the very same Nurit with Stanley just a few days earlier. But she decided that it was none of her business and again she might be thought of as jealous. "Let him find out for himself," she convinced herself.

A week or two later, Paul again spoke with Debbie and related his desperate efforts to obtain an extension of Nurit's visa which was shortly to expire. Paul was a lawyer by profession and it seemed he was doing all in his power (which was probably not very great) to have Nurit stay in the United States. But it was in vain. When her time was up, she had to leave. Paul was visibly heartbroken and upset, so much so that he again failed to observe the fact that Nurit did not really seem to mind going back to Israel. In fact, in the intervening weeks, Debbie and Nurit had again met at folk dancing and had gotten on a somewhat more friendly basis. When Debbie expressed interest in perhaps settling in Israel, Nurit suggested that they might share an apartment in Jerusalem and gave Debbie her address in Jerusalem to contact when she arrived there. Alas, she did return and Paul obviously had now followed her here. "Oh brother," Debbie mused. "Someone should care for me like that."

Sure enough, it was Paul Kalish on the other end of the line when he called again. "I'm here." he announced as though somehow this was a fact worth taking note of. At first he spoke in the same elated tone as he had in New York but after a while he admitted that Nurit had not given him the red carpet treatment he had foolishly expected. Apparently he had declared the same "I'm here" to her with not the most cordial welcome. He said he had seen her once thus far which had been pleasant but further attempts for her attention had been less successful. She was very busy, her family, her work, blah, blah, blah.

Debbie surmised that he was calling her for help in how to handle Nurit. Or perhaps even to intercede on his behalf. As he spoke, he started to sound more and more upset and agitated. Debbie felt sorry for him. He was a simple timid helpless soul and was certainly no match for the ultra sophisticated and captivating Nurit. Entebbe commandoes and paratroopers would be more in her line.

A few days later, Nurit called Debbie and invited her for Sabbath lunch. Debbie could hardly refuse since she lived only a few blocks away. Saturday came and Debbie made her way to Nurit's parents apartment. She was always a bit apprehensive about meeting parents for the first time. They were religious so Debbie checked her dress for its appropriateness. Would they speak English? How long would she have to stay? These questions went through her mind as she knocked on her door. Nurit opened it and almost immediately Debbie's eyes passed over toward Paul already sitting at the table. She was flabbergasted. "If Paul is here to meet her parents, why did she invite me?" she wondered. It was hard to make small talk. Her parents and brother were nice enough but she was embarrassed at being there. "Of course," Debbie concluded. "She invited me to minimize the importance of Paul's being there. The event, therefore, wasn't the future son-in-law meeting Nurit's parents for the first time but a pleasant lunch for friends of Nurit."

After the dinner, Nurit suggested they go for a walk. So they spent Saturday afternoon walking around the beautiful streets of Rehavia with Nurit dutiful as tour guide, pointing out the President's house and other sites of interest. Paul, miserable but trying to appear cheerful, already recognizing that all was not going well with Nurit and poor Debbie dragging along, pretending nothing was wrong and that they were just three friendly folk dancers. She felt guilty at having spoiled Paul's big day but she knew she was not at fault. How could she have anticipated Nurit's plans.

Finally Debbie suggested that it was getting late and she still had a few things to do. So they started to walk back to Nurit's house. On the way, they would pass Debbie's apartment. When they reached Debbie's door, Nurit smiled and said quickly and unexpectedly with her deep voice, "Well, thank you both for coming. It's been a very nice afternoon. I have to go now and hope to see you again soon." With that she turned and walked away briskly leaving both Paul and Debbie speechless and standing as if electrocuted. Debbie recovered first and motioned to Paul to follow her. Nurit had already gotten quite a way up the block, having walked hurriedly to get away. He hesitated at first then went after her. Debbie went inside her door relieved that the ordeal was over. What a wasted afternoon!

A few days later, Paul called Debbie and asked her when folk dancing was at the university. It was obviously a pretext for a need to talk but they arranged to attend the session at the Hebrew University. Paul didn't dance at all and looked very glum. Debbie suggested that he ask some girls to dance but he obstinately refused. "Some of them are so pretty," she hinted. "What about her" and pointed to Rachel, one of the most beautiful of the Israeli girls.

"Oh no," Paul said dismissing her quickly. "Why not?" Debbie quizzed. "Oh, she really looks unapproachable," he answered fearfully. Finally he asked a mousy looking girl with brown hair and a white T shirt to dance. She had been standing behind one of the poles and seemed eager to dance. They danced for awhile and then it ended. Paul wanted to leave.

When they got back to Debbie's apartment, she proposed they take a short walk and then Paul told her the story. Basically, Nurit was not interested in him and told him so. She had begun to treat him worse and worse as time went on finally making excuses not to see him at all. Debbie could see that Paul was deeply hurt. Apparently he had expected her to welcome him with open arms and instead he found an aloof rejection. Debbie felt sorry for him. He was really a nice guy and Nurit should have treated him better but of course if she didn't want him, then what is the point. What else could she have done? They stopped for awhile and sat in the circle above the Cafe Rendezvous. Paul thanked Debbie for listening to him. She then suggested maybe they might make a tour of the Cave of Absalom, a stalagtite cave which had been recently discovered and had since become a new tourist attraction. Paul was interested and they arranged to go on one of the organized half-day tour buses.

The day arrived and Debbie looked forward to the trip. She had been told that the cave was truly worth seeing. On the bus, Paul and Debbie sat opposite another American girl tourist who was travelling alone. Paul struck up a conversation with her. At first the three spoke together all the way to the cave, the ride of which travelled a lot of narrow winding roads weaving in and out of the rock-laden Jerusalem hills. The scenery was picturesque but Paul and the tourist were not noticing it because they were so busy talking to each other. Finally they arrived and the guide led them inside. At first they were gathered in a small room where a guide told them the history of the cave and the nature of stalagtites while their bodies became accustomed to the intense humidity inside the cave.

Then they went inside. First it was dark and then suddenly the lights were switched on revealing a phantasmagoria about the size of a cathedral. It was much larger than Debbie had expected and what was implied by the word "cave." Hanging oracles of brilliant colors were everywhere. The reds and oranges in particular added a hellish nightmare like quality. It was truly a magnificent sight! They had built small bridges over the chasms and the group slowly toddled after the guide.

In addition to the stalagtites of centuries meeting the stalagmites of a similar number of years, Debbie noticed that Paul was also more and more allying himself to the tourist and leaving Debbie out. "Frustrated love" the guide explained was the name given to the stalagtite that had been growing toward a particular stalagmite and would have eventually touched it. But now since the uncovering of the cave, further formation of stalagtites was made impossible and so alas, the two lovers would never meet.

By the end of the tour, Paul and the tourist had become a twosome and walked on ahead together, leaving Debbie behind and alone. She did not even see them leave the cave. Debbie had lingered awhile with the rest of the group to treasure one more last look at the beauty of a completely natural phenomenon. Then she too left and when she got outside, she looked for Paul and the tourist but there was no sight of them. Debbie walked around anxiously looking for them. The guide had said to gather together and get ready to go back up the hill where the bus was waiting. It was quite a climb and Debbie did not want to go up without her two friends. She considered the possibility that they had perhaps returned to the cave and so she also went back but did not see them anywhere.

She feared that she could not wait any longer. The group had already begun the climb and she did not want to get stuck behind. So Debbie also started to walk back up the winding pathway with tall trees and an occasional bench gracing one side. While she was trudging up the hill she kept worrying what had happened to her friends. When she finally reached the top the point from which they had descended, Debbie was shocked to see a ways off, the tourist sitting in a very sexy pose on top of the fence and an adoring Paul worshipping at her feet.

"What a disgusting sight!" she thought. She was mad. They had gone up the hill immediately and had not even bothered to wait for Debbie or to be in the least concerned with where she was. And all the while she had searched for them, they were sitting here in the cool shade mooning over each other.

"So this is where you disappeared to. I was looking for you," Debbie exclaimed trying not to sound angry as she walked toward them.

"We wanted to get away from the crowd," Paul explained matter of factly without apparent guilt or apology. In fact, Debbie thought he even looked angry because she had intruded on their talk. They continued to drool over each other so Debbie walked away. On the way back on the bus, she said little. She was hurt. Here she had suggested the trip so that Paul might forget Nurit and then he totally ignored her, a friend of ten years, in favor of a complete stranger. Well, she was finished with Paul, that was for sure. She didn't say much, just a quiet goodbye when the bus entered the center of Jerusalem. It would be many years before Debbie would see Paul Kalish again and by then he would be very much married and a father.

The next day Debbie felt she needed a place of solace and a period of quiet so she went to the place where she was always most at home - the university. It was a beautiful warm day and she sat down on the green grass of the Givat Ram campus to drink in the healing balsam of the hot sun. At times like this whenever she was somewhat upset and had sat down in the sun for comfort, she often thought of the disturbed character in the Virginia Woolf novel, *Mrs. Dalloway*, Septimus Smith. Although he often contemplated suicide, he would cling to the few pleasures he could still enjoy murmuring as if to convince himself that "Life is good, the sun hot."

Debbie tried to collect her thoughts and to assess the first few months she had been in Israel. All in all, she had enjoyed them. "I feel comfortable here, right somehow, in a way I could never feel in New York. I want to stay," she admitted to herself simply. She had told many of her friends she would only go for a few months but she had already anticipated that she would like it very much and that the few months would slowly turn into much more.

Her place in the sun had suddenly grown too hot and as if moved by an unseen hand, she got up and began to walk towards the library. She didn't quite know why she was going in that direction since she did not intend to go to the library. As she turned the corner which would bring her face to face with the huge national library, she suddenly saw in front of her, big as life, or even bigger, the object of all her dreams and phantasies - Shimon.

"Hi," she purred in a sexy voice, looking at him in all wonderment, as though he were some kind of miracle.

"Shalom," he said looking somewhat embarrassed. It had been a while since their last date. "I just returned a book to the library.

And of course I voted in the elections."

"Oh," Debbie replied. "Is that what all the commotion is about?" She had noticed many students going around with flyers and others sitting behind long tables distributing leaflets but didn't pay much attention to them.

"Whom did you vote for?" Debbie continued wanting to make conversation.

"Why, right of course," he said confidently, adding "Right is right" as if it were a silly question even to ask.

"Oh, are you a rightist?" Debbie asked. She was in such a state of mixed emotions that she could not really think of anything intelligent to say and was asking stupid mechanical questions. Actually she would been more of the opinion that "right is never right" but now she was not able to argue critically.

"Sure," he declared. "What else is there?"

"Oh, I've always been somewhat on the left," she answered.

"I used to belong to an organization called "Americans for a Progressive Israel" while I was in the States.

"What's that?" he asked, "Something like *Shalom Achshav*? (Peace Now)"

"Yes," she said, trying to appear knowledgeable about such matters. "It's affiliated with *Mapam-Mapai*, the Labor Party."

"Are you crazy?" he cried.

"Why?" she looked at him puzzled.

"Nobody here belongs to that. It's crazy. It doesn't work. Only the Argentinian immigrants go for that. They are still so naive that they don't know any better. They come from governments which were Fascist so they think that left is good and democratic. And they assume that left in South America is the same as left here. But it's not the same. Left doesn't work here, not with the Arabs," he finished authoritatively.

"Oh," Debbie whispered weakly, not being sufficiently political or even informed to argue.

"Well, I have to go. I promised to distribute these for a friend." He flashed a pile of flyers.

"I was just going to get some lunch. Would you like to join me?" Debbie invited.

"Well, I really don't have time. I'm supposed to be working. I just came down to vote and help out a bit."

Debbie was disappointed but smiled cheerfully. "Take care" she called as he ran off energetically.

Debbie went off and now decided to have lunch in the university cafeteria. She went through the self service line and found a place at the back of the hall. She had not yet gotten far into her meal when all of a sudden Shimon also came along with his tray and headed towards her.

"May I sit here?" he asked motioning to the empty seat across from Debbie. "I decided to get some lunch after all before going back to the office," he explained. He had the typical Israeli lunch of humous, tachina, salad and beer. They talked mostly about the kind of job he had and the course of study he was taking, the importance of the student elections and finally, their wonderful night together on Mount Scopus. They had a free and easy conversation, each munching away at his food and each seemed to bask in the other's company.

At one point the conversation shifted to Dorrit. "You know, this girl I dance with sometimes," he said frowning and making a motion with his arm as though he could barely remember her name. Debbie concluded that she had nothing to worry about and barely heard what he had to say about her.

Debbie couldn't believe this was actually happening to her. She still had some difficulty in looking at him directly in the face because he was so beautiful. She was afraid that if she did so that she would be staring or gaping. So she merely took the luxury of glancing at him occasionally, smiling and looking down at her tray or elsewhere. He gobbled down his food, then said, "I really have to go now. I've already taken too much time from my work."

Debbie also decided to go back home and they walked together and headed across the campus again to the main gates where they would get the number 9 bus to the town center.

What a joy it was, thought Debbie to be walking with a guy as tall and powerfully built as Shimon. He looked like a mid western university football hero. All the men she had ever dated in New York had all been schlumpy types - short and skinny. Before he got off at the town center, Shimon asked her if she wanted to go to see the Paris Ballet next Tuesday night when they were performing in Jerusalem.

Debbie was literally walking on air. It was obvious that he liked her. Surely he had come back to the cafeteria because of her, hadn't he? Before meeting her, he had planned to go back to the office immediately. She couldn't wait until Tuesday night. What luck it had been to go to the university today! She suddenly loved student political elections. Life was really looking up for Debbie. She was glad she had made the break and had come to Israel.

Debbie frequently met other American girls in Israel that she had known in New York. A few days later, as she got on the number 9 bus from Mount Scopus and inched her way to the back of the crowded bus, she saw a girl who used to dance regularly at Columbia University on Monday nights. She recognized Debbie also.

"Hi," Debbie called, struggling to move in her direction. "I didn't know you had come here."

"Yeah, I've been here almost four years now," Sheila answered somewhat wearily.

"That's great," Debbie chimed enthusiastically reporting that she had been in Israel almost three months. She asked Sheila what kind of work she did because Debbie had started thinking in terms of trying to find a job now that she had definitely planned to stay.

"I'm a nurse at Hadassah, Mount Scopus," Sheila replied again without much enthusiasm.

Debbie was impressed and inquired how she could manage with the Hebrew and if nursing in Israel was very different from that in the United States. Sheila related that the language barrier presented no problem since all the orders, medications, procedures and equipment were written in English. She knew some Hebrew to be able to relate better to patients.

"The worst part about nursing in Israel is the high turnover rate," Sheila complained.

"Why is that?" Debbie queried as she jerked back and forth each time the bus started up or stopped suddenly.

"Well," she explained, "there are many nurses coming here from Europe, especially Scandinavia, Germany, and England and they want to try Israel for awhile. Usually, after six months or so, they get bored or whatever and go back. Just when you think a girl is broken in well enough to really be of use on the ward, she is ready to leave. It's hard on me too to always be working with beginners. They don't know where any equipment is or which doctor wants what and when. So they are always asking me questions and sometimes I have to show them if we do a procedure differently here than they do it in their country."

"Why, then, do they come if it's so difficult and such a drastic change?" Debbie puzzled.

Sheila laughed. "Mainly I think because they heard that Israeli guys are rated A-1 in bed. So they want to try them out. Then when they find out they are much not different or better than their own guys, in fact, some are worse, then they disappear very quickly."

Debbie wanted to hear more but Sheila had already pushed the hold button indicating to the bus driver that he should make a stop at the next station.

"Come up and see the hospital sometime. Here's my card. I have to get off now. Nice seeing you again." With that, Sheila moved quickly to the door and jumped off.

Debbie thought deeply for the rest of the bus ride. So many girls were coming from everywhere following the myth of the invincible Israeli cock! Once there had been the myth of the invincibility of the Israeli army. That had been dispelled. But the invincible cock was still going strong.

Debbie's next weekend would be spent in the development town of Yeroham. She was not very eager to go having hoped to spend the days with Shimon. However, she had already put the family off several times. They kept inviting her and finally she could not give them any more excuses without offending them. This weekend she had firmly promised to go to Yeroham.

Debbie had met Eran Golan at Israeli folk dancing at a New York YMHA a few years earlier while he was in New York studying for his Master's Degree in Engineering. They had become good friends. Debbie often helped him with his English compositions and had invited him several times to dinner at her parents on the Holidays. They continued to correspond even after he returned to Israel, his wife and four children. Naturally, when Debbie decided to come to Israel she wrote to him. He wanted her to visit Yeroham ever since she had arrived in Israel.

It was a long trip to Yeroham via Beersheva. When she finally reached his house which was not easy, she was warmly welcomed by Eran and his four children, less warmly by his wife who just barely seemed to tolerate her presence throughout the visit. They had a modest one family house comfortably furnished with a lawn in the front and a chaotic wilderness for a yard in the back. Eran apologised for this saying he didn't have enough time to make a garden.

Debbie had brought barbecued chicken for eight with an assortment of salads. Miriam was happy at seeing this and exclaimed in a relieved voice, "Now I have something to serve when the Zudikers come tomorrow night." Each family member came and went about his activities almost as if she hadn't been there. One thing that surprised Debbie was how different Eran was at home. She had known him as the tough hard-nailed commando, the macho male and the super patriotic Israeli. Now she was almost horrified to see him washing the living room floor, bouncing his five year old daughter on his knee or making a barbecue on the front lawn.

At one point, Yoram, his eight year old son came into the kitchen where Eran was working to show his father the drawing he had made. Debbie half expected Eran to glance at it perfunctorily and say, "Yes, it's nice" or something like that. Instead, he took the picture carefully, studied it intensely for several minutes, then offered several comments slowly, "Yes, it's very good, this part is well done and the figures are clear but I think the moon could be somewhat smaller. Is the moon really that big? And maybe you could use more different colors." He took time to point out all these factors to Yoram and waited until the child understood and responded. Content with his father's opinion and interest, Yoram eagerly went off to try again.

"I'm amazed how much time and patience you have with all your kids. Most American parents would just kind of shake them off," Debbie commented to Eran after Yoram had left.

"Well," Eran explained with a wisdom and sense of psychological understanding Debbie did not think he possessed. "You see, Yoram is at best only an average child, maybe less considering his emphysema. If I shake him off, as you say, he will not try again and maybe he will do less than average and less than he can. This way if I take time with him, he will have the strength and courage to try again to make it better because someone cares. And this way, he will at least use all the talent he has. Did you notice how happy he was to try it again? So I think in the long run it will be worthwhile that I take time and patience with him and with all of them."

Just as they were talking, the door bell rang and in bounced a very pretty young brunette in a manner which indicated that she was very much at home in the Golan household.

"*Erev tov*," she said with a pronounced American accent. The new arrival was beautiful, fairly tall with short dark curly hair and a peaches and cream complexion. She had a perfect figure with long slender legs which she exhibited in short shorts. Debbie vaguely recognized her as though she had seen her somewhere before.

Eran was obviously delighted to see her and they began conversing in Hebrew. As if knowing full well what would entice him, Marilyn Krieger put one of her long stem lovelies atop a kitchen chair. Eran began to caress it in rhythmical fashion moving closer and closer to the top. She was bubbling over with happiness. Apparently she had merely stopped by to tell Eran the exact details of her marriage and her plans for the immediate future. As soon as she had finished relating this information, she flounced out in the same way she had come in.

Debbie was curious to know who this magical creature had been. She oozed with so much radiance that Debbie had been nearly blinded, emotionally speaking, that is. She had the self-confidence of a queen and the *chutzpah* of an American Jewish Princess. Eran saw Debbie's querulous look then proceeded to explain in a pseudo angry voice yet glowing with obvious admiration for her.

"This one," he began. "I am so mad with her."

"Why?" answered Debbie as this was the natural response.

"What Miriam and I didn't do for this girl, you wouldn't believe. She came to Israel two years ago from New York into the WUJS* program.

She was a real Zionist then, or so I thought. Miriam and I were her foster parents. She was like one of the kids; she could call whenever she wanted; she was here every Shabbat, everything we did for her." Eran shook his head as if exasperated and obviously disappointed. Debbie breathtakingly waited for him to finish the story. "And now?" she urged him on.

"And now!" he fumed. "Do you know what she did?"

"No," Debbie answered with even greater excitement. "What?" She was making fun of his discomfort but he was too involved and upset to notice.

---

* WUJS - World Union of Jewish Students - a one year program for college graduates situated in Arad where the participants receive an intense 6 month *Ulpan* (language instruction) and orientation to Israel and then are placed in jobs of their profession (when possible) for 6 months. During the year, each person is assigned foster parents to whom they can go for advice and friendship.

"Well," he continued. "She always pretended to be such a Zionist. Now, do you know what she went off and did?" he repeated. "This is getting ridiculous," Debbie thought.

"She's not only going back to the States but she married an army officer and she's taking him with her. What am I supposed to do, fight the Arabs by myself? She just told me now they are leaving next week. I never thought *she* would do such a thing."

"So," Debbie murmured to herself having sized up the situation. "It was all clear now. Here was a queen who has captured her king, a huntress who has lassoed the first prize. No wonder she was radiating all those laser beams!"

Apparently Marilyn had come to Israel immediately after graduating from college as a social worker and after a year at WUJS, had been assigned to Ashkelon which was near an army base. At 24, the rest was easy. She had also been a folk dancer at the YMHA at one time which is why she had looked familiar. Eran sat quietly now, his emotional energy spent.

"Well, what's so terrible about that?" Debbie asked matter of factly. "That's why every girl comes."

"What!" Eran looked surprised. "But she said she was a Zionist," he insisted again.

"Well, probably she is. We all more or less are that. But at the same time, we all think it would be wonderful if we also found a husband here. Can't you understand that?"

He shook his head wearily. "No, either you love Israel or you don't. Now the two of them will sit in New York." The thought was too much for him and he got up and went into the living room. Debbie knew there was no use trying to explain to him. A man could never understand such things.

Anyway, Debbie was happy to have heard Marilyn's story. So it *was* possible to find a husband in Israel. But of course, Marilyn was young, beautiful and sexy and with those ingredients, one could mix a bowl of marriage anywhere. Yet, Debbie was heartened by the news and began to dream of herself in the same blissful situation.

Who was it that came to Israel to lasso a husband. The possibility certainly lurked in the minds of many an American (or for that matter, Canadian, British, South African, Australian, Brazilian, etc. etc. etc.) girl. Usually she was over 28, and perhaps had been less than successful in meeting the man of her dreams in her own country. Or she was not quite satisfied with the men she had been dating - dull, boring, "schlumpy" types who unfortunately sometimes seemed to be the only kind available. She couldn't see wasting her life with a man like that - not yet anyway!

Others were recently widowed or divorced and wanted to begin over again in a new place.

And so their gaze then began to rest on the faraway Promised Land, the Land of Milk and Honey, the Land of the Patriarchs and Prophets and handsome Entebbe Commandos (like in the film). Perhaps there men were still men. Often the girl asking the loaded question had been a dewy eyed two week summer tourist who although spending most of her time whizzing around on her Egged tour bus, had nevertheless stopped long enough in a few places to notice that Israeli men *were* different from the home grown variety she was used to - a direct contrast in fact. They were friendly, aggressive, uninhibited, good looking, and even if they were not so good looking, they exuded an exotic charm that boy next door at home lacked so completely and finally, they were interested in *her*. What she didn't know at that time was of course that they usually showed the same degree of interest in every foreign girl they met. The reasons for the interest were often not social as Debbie would soon find out.

Nevertheless, the first or second tourist impression that indeed Israeli men were a very special breed lingered with many a tourist girl long after she left on her El Al flight back to New York, Los Angeles or London. It haunted her memory every time she went to a party, singles event or blind date and found only bland, passive, awkward, neurotic or "such a nice boy" types, standing idly about. Then the image in her mind of the Israelis with their thick curly hair, their bright darting eyes, confident masculine manner and eager conversations came forth.

It was at times like this that the American Girl starts to think that perhaps if she went to this Golden Paradise not just for a brief summer vacation, but for a lengthier stay, she might be able to snare one of these magnificent specimens for her very own and take him back to her home town as a Grand Prize one wins in a bazaar or as a super duper souvenir. Some more adventurous types might even think of settling down with their Tarzan in the jungles of his native habitat. However, the ultimate details and plans are usually hazy at this time. The focus is on whether or not to take the big plunge at all.

For most girls, going to Israel is a big move, leaving family, close often life long friends, and a routine comfortable even if sometimes boring life style for an unknown, faraway, culturally different and potentially dangerous environment. For others, giving up a challenging, interesting and financially rewarding job or profession is a major consideration. Many have worked hard to find such a job and then to advance in it that they hesitate to give up years of struggle for what may turn out to be a foolhardy and possible empty adventure. For some, the consequences would be irreversible. For example, if a teacher who has obtained the coveted and precious position of tenure in her school or university left her post, she would never be able, given the present job market, to secure another such position should she decide that life in Israel is not for her. For still others living in New York and various cities, who have been blessed with the good fortune of possessing a rent controlled apartment, the move would entail relinquishing this rarest of gifts (much to the immense delight of the landlord who could then quadruple the rent). How sad would be the young lady upon return (should she fail in her quest for the Crown Prince) to discover that the only available studio apartments cost $1300 and up per month! She would be forced to move outside the main part of the city to a remote borough or suburb which in most cases would result in social suicide. Or to crowd together in a small apartment with one or two roommates.

There are many other considerations. The reader is free to invent her own, should this question also inhabit the deepest recesses of her psyche. Note the use of *her* rather than *his* since this is almost exclusively a feminine phenomenon. It is thus understandable that those who jump over these difficult hurdles and race on to the finish line at Ben Gurion Airport are a very select class indeed. They should thus be treated with respect and interest if not with awesome reverence. Some would consider them courageous, adventuresome, idealistic, independent and strong-minded. Others, less kind, might hint that they must be desperate and love lorn. Israelis would merely write them off as just plain stupid!

It should be added, however, that few if any actually admit their true motivations for going to Israel. Certainly, they would never reveal it to others; some not even to themselves. Suddenly, they develop an intense interest in Zionism, in Jewish history, in archaeology, or in the Bible. Others long to search for Jewish roots or a lost Jewish identity. All at once, perhaps for the first time, they are happy and proud to be Jews. In fact, a renewed interest in the Jewish religion also frequently occurs. Some feel a sudden guilt at not having done enough for their people and decide that now was the time they should give of themselves. A few cite their wish for travel, adventure or for new experiences in their professions. What could be more respectable or commendable than a teacher, nurse or social worker who wishes to gain more knowledge and expertise! This list of plausible excuses is endless and so completely credible that most girls succeed not only in convincing others but also themselves. Some begin to bask in the music of their Hebrew names. Janet becomes Yehudith, Ann adopts Hannah and Carol calls herself Shira. If they have no Hebrew name, they search for a middle name or simply add a new one, either biblical or modern.

The phenomenon is not limited only to those of the Jewish faith. Gentile girls from many countries flock to Israel each year to see the Holy Land, to visit Biblical sites, and to work on *kibbutzim*.

From Scandinavia come young students of political science and social science to observe the working of the kibbutz system. From Germany may come young female citizens concerned with making restitution for past history, to improve German-Israeli relations, or just out of curiosity to see what is going on. But it is usually not long before their eyes and flaxen blond hair fall on some Israeli or Palestinian of the male species, after which their vehement anger and dedication to progressive ideals wane and recede into the background or else their political beliefs suddenly become strangely similar to that of the person they find. A girl who today is espousing the virtues of a kibbutz may be discussing the welfare of "victims of military occupation and imperialism" next week.

Finally there are a few girls who come beguiled by the myth of the Middle East male as sexual acrobat and fantastic lover. How could the shy, bland men of her previous experience compare, she thinks, with the throbbing cocks of the Middle East. Unfortunately, many are disappointed when stark everyday reality does not conform to their wildest fantasies and they realize that the men of the Middle East for all their desirable qualities are nevertheless also human and subject to the same foibles and predicaments as men everywhere else.

Usually when they discover the truth, they leave very quickly and head back to the colder climes and to their own species of the male animal.

The spotlight is on the young and often not so young woman whose heart still yearns for marriage, children, and a home and truly believes that this dream will be fulfilled in Israel. There are many such girls - the Judys, Karens, Sharons, Michelles. They come and they go. They are tall, short, thin, plump, fat, very fat, educated and not, intelligent or just average, professionals and secretaries, beautiful and homely, aggressive and shy, ranging in age from 20 to 55 years and even older. Most are perhaps between 25 and 35. From all over they fly to descend on what they perceive to be a Jewish male paradise. For some, it is the last stop after having already tried California, England, France or Italy.

According to some statistics she had read, the average length of stay for an American was two years. Hence the explanation for the AACI newsletter which monthly lists long columns of names of newcomers. However, there is no list for those going out the back door. Were they all to stay, Israel would quickly become just another American state.

The rest of the weekend in Yeroham passed quickly. It was rather a dull life they led, Debbie thought. Miriam remained distant speaking to her only when necessary. She probably took Debbie to be just another one of her husband's "friends." Indeed, she easily could have been especially while he was in the United States. But Debbie never wanted to "waste time" with married men, especially one with four children. Even on this weekend, there would have been a chance.

Debbie was to sleep on the living room couch. Just as she was getting ready to lie down, Eran came into the living room. Miriam and the four children were already in bed. He came up close behind Debbie as she was undressing and put his arms firmly around her.

"Well, little friend," he whispered, caressing her breast. Did you have a good time today?" He started to move towards the couch.

Debbie liked him a lot. He was good looking, intelligent, energetic but also very much married and who could forget the 4 kids running about. And now he wanted to do it with her on the couch in the living room with his wife and 4 kids sleeping in the adjacent three rooms. Debbie tried to maneuver tactfully out of his strong commando type embrace.

"But Miriam and the kids will hear."

"They are asleep."

"But Yoram is always getting up. I heard him last night."

"So what, he will not care. He will just go back to bed. Besides, it's time he learned a few things." So ran the dialogue between them.

"No, Eran, not here, if it were some other place, I'd like to, but not so close. I'm a guest here."

"OK," he said resignedly, not pushing himself on her. "You are a funny girl. Good night." He went off to join his wife in the next room, shaking his head, not understanding her response.

The next morning Debbie rose early because she wanted to catch an early bus to the Central Bus Station in Beersheva where she would then get a bus back to Jerusalem. As she made her way into the kitchen, Eran was already walking towards the front door to his work as an engineer for the aircraft industry. Miriam was busy in the kitchen getting breakfast for herself and the children. She worked as a public relations agent in one of the local hospitals. She offered Debbie some coffee and bread and they made polite conversation.

"So you see what it's like here, huh," she laughed with a kind of "Well, that's life, grin and bear it" attitude. Debbie thanked her once again for her hospitality, ate quickly and was off.

As she waited for the bus, she surveyed the row of small one family houses with their small lawns and gardens, children trudging to school, their schoolbags heavy on their backs like backpacks. She wondered what it would be like to live in a town like this permanently.

Peaceful and happy or boring and confined? She wasn't sure. Certainly, it was no place for a single woman; couples and families were the only viable form of social unit. As far as she had observed, it was that way in most of the small towns in Israel. In fact, she had to admit to herself that it was that way virtually throughout Israel. With the possible exception of Tel Aviv, a truly "singles scene" as one would know it in New York or in any big American city, did not really exist in Israel.

On the long and boring bus journey from Beersheva to Jerusalem, Debbie was already eagerly anticipating with joy her Tuesday night date with Shimon. The Negev desert had already receded to the deeper crevices of her mind.

Tuesday evening finally arrived. Debbie was excited at the

thought of being with Shimon again, this time on a real date. She knew it would be something they would both enjoy, since Shimon, like most folk dancers, also enjoyed ballet and other forms of dance. She wore her light aqua dress with the three tiers of ruffles, then the stylistic rage. But she was careful not to be over-dressed. First of all, Shimon was not one who liked to get "dressed up" even for the most important event and secondly, people in Israel, generally speaking, especially in Jerusalem, did not dress up for concerts, plays or other such events - at least not by American or European standards.

It had been a long time since Debbie had seen a major ballet company and she was not disappointed. The Paris Ballet performed a magnificent new choreography of Ravel's *Daphnis and Chloe* and the traditional *Bolero*. The dancers especially the principals were first class. During the intermission, she and Shimon walked about awhile in the foyer, then stopped for some coffee and chocolate cake. Debbie felt so proud she hoped the whole world would see her. She was glad also that the performance was a good one and that Shimon had enjoyed it because in the beginning, he had grumbled a bit about the ticket price. She noticed that he did not like to part readily with his money but forgave him at the same time since he did work hard for his salary and continued to pay tuition for his studies at the university.

During the second part of the performance, Debbie grew somewhat restless and could focus her mind less on the dancing than earlier. She wanted so much to invite him to stay the night she could hardly contain herself. Would it be like the first time? She noticed that he looked at her several times during the performance when he thought she wasn't watching so she concluded he might be having similar wishes. Her feelings were more tender than eyesight, her love more delicate than the lithe movements of Chloe.

Finally, the dancers took their last calls and the audience began to file out. The audience had enjoyed the performance and so there was more applause than usual. Debbie was often appalled at how stingy Israelis were with applause even for a good performance, many already rudely running off to catch that last bus. But tonight, it took somewhat longer to empty the great concert hall of Binyanei Hauma. Debbie and Shimon were also lingering more slowly than usual within the moving crowd. Then finally they were outside. It was already May but the Jerusalem nights were still veined with cold currents.

Debbie intertwined her arm in his and moved close to him. She thought for an instant that he actually stiffened and moved away. But then he smiled, not looking at her and not saying anything either. Debbie felt somewhat uncomfortable with the silence and so she broke it with a usual dull question, "Did you enjoy it?" "Sure," he nodded with a similar dull answer, "It was OK."

Then finally they came to the end of the road where the buses turned in different directions. "Would you like to come to my place for awhile?" Debbie asked softly with her voice as well as with her eyes.

Again not looking at her and staring into an unknown distance, he said slowly, "Well, I'd like to really, but you know, tomorrow is a work day for me." Debbie was crushed.

"Yeah, sure, I know, Israelis begin work at 7:30 A.M.," she stammered.

"7:15," he corrected seemingly grateful that she had let him off the hook. They walked towards the bus stop and then just as suddenly he changed his mind and said quickly and impatiently almost pushing her in the direction of the bus that would take them to Debbie's apartment. "Oh, what's the difference, let's go." Now he was smiling and blushing at the same time and definitely looking her right in the face. Poor Debbie, her heart oscillating like a pendulum between desire and denial, each time bringing it closer to a yet unknown pit.

The possibility that perhaps something might be wrong didn't occur to Debbie. She was so happy and so eager to be with Shimon that she vehemently blotted out any truth or obstacle that would infuse her Edenic fantasy with painful reality. She wanted this to be perfect and she would not let anything spoil it, even if a wise voice had warned her to be cautious. She would not have listened even to the goddess of love who was already spinning her orbit of planetary woe.

Whatever hesitations Shimon might have harbored before were gone by the time they reached Debbie's apartment. They drank some "Kinley", then there was some more tense small talk. It would seem almost as though Shimon were waiting for Debbie to start. Perhaps there was less guilt that way or perhaps he was just a passive person.

Finally, she stroked his arm and smiled seductively, that is, as seductive as a girl like Debbie Warshawsky is ever going to get. He began to feel her behind. "Oh no," Debbie thought. "He would go for my worst point." Debbie was convinced that her buttocks were far out of proportion to the rest of her body which was actually not the case. From there he progressed to her breasts which were full and round, her best point. Shimon was a considerate lover and a good one but he needed an equally active partner to bring out his best attributes. Debbie still tended towards shyness and inhibition although she had done much to overcome this. A siren or femme fatale, alas, she would never be.

Nevertheless, they enjoyed each other and Debbie was in ecstacy. At last she had what she had always wanted, an emotional and sexual experience with a man she loved. Debbie was an old fashioned romantic type who firmly believed at least at this stage, that love and sex went together for a truly meaningful experience. "Sure you can have sex without love," she would argue, "but it is meaningless, just an act, merely an interlude to the real thing." She would enshroud the idea of sex without love in intellectual or feminist language, calling it an "alienating experience" or "psychologically demeaning" or some such phrase to support her argument

It should also be remembered that Debbie was in love. For Debbie this was the real thing. Shimon filled all her thoughts and fulfilled all her needs. She did not seem to notice or did not care to see that he was less involved than she. They had their arms around each other and for now he was hers. For once, she did not think beyond. They spent a blissful night together.

Debbie lay awake a long time just looking at him and luxuriating again in the thought that this was actually happening to her. She had always hoped it would, of course, but somehow it had always loomed in the "someday" future or had happened to someone else.

In the morning Shimon awoke at 6 and rose immediately. It was truly as he had said the evening before; he was to be at work at 7:15 A.M. He went into the bathroom to shave.

Debbie got up to fix some quick breakfast. As she passed the bathroom she stopped to watch the man she loved shave. Even such a simple everyday task was special to Debbie if it was Shimon who was doing it.

"May I watch?" She said coyly smiling.

"If you insist,"he answered just a bit too gruffly to be a joke and continued to work away with a very serious face saying nothing more. Debbie felt uncomfortable and unwanted and stole away quietly. She wasn't sure if he was angry or not. She decided to let it slide rationalizing with her never ending capacity to do so, that she also did not always feel friendly in the morning.

He didn't stop for breakfast just gulping down a cup of black coffee. Debbie tried to coax him to eat more of what she had prepared but he was literally "running out" fearing that he would be late for work He seemed very eager to get away although Debbie did not note this fact She wondered why love always looked so different the morning after the night before. But again she quickly shrugged off the idea with the thought that evenings and nights are just naturally more conducive to romance. They had had a beautiful time together and she was satisfied with that and with the way things were progressing. She was the eternal hierophant of hope.

Debbie had now lived in Israel for four months the length of time she had originally anticipated staying. However,her plans were slowly changing. She enjoyed living in Israel despite certain difficulties and Jerusalem was a city like no other. And of course there was Shimon! So she decided to stay on indefinitely. Once she had taken this important step, it also became crucial that she find a job in her profession - teaching.

She had already inquired at the counseling services at AACI (Association of Americans and Canadians in Israel) which had given her some leads as to where she might find a job teaching English as a foreign language. There was a greater demand for this than for the teaching of literature or for other foreign languages.

It was not easy. She went from place to place learning that most of the available teaching positions were in the outlying areas such as towns near the Lebanese border or in the development towns of the south or in the *kibbutzim* which were in isolated areas. Well, Debbie knew for certain,"I don't want to be in an area which is far from a major city such as Jerusalem or Tel Aviv. In fact, I don't want to leave the city at all. To do so would be to commit social suicide .I have good credentials and several years teaching experience. Why shouldn't I hold out for something better!" She would of course have to improve her Hebrew so she enrolled in a twice a week evening course at the Open University.

The more she searched, the more she learned just how many jobs there were in teaching English as a foreign language and in how many different institutions. She had always thought of teaching just in terms of "schools", high school, university, etc. but jobs were available in hospitals,in various ministries of the government, in language schools, in banks, even in the Knesset itself. However, most of these jobs were only part time and often temporary. Yet she found that it was not uncommon especially for Americans to have 2 or even 3 part time jobs to make the equivalent full time salary. To stay in Jerusalem, many were willing to make this sacrifice.

Along her journey to find a job, she also learned that very often in the summer when regular faculty in the university teaching English return to the United States or England, there are some basic courses in English language and composition available. Debbie decided to apply for these and went to speak to the chairperson at the Jerusalem University. She thought at least a summer job would be a start. She discovered the summer chairman was a young woman about her own age and also from New York City who had been living in Israel for about eight years. She told Debbie that at the moment there were no courses available but that they often hired teachers just at the beginning of the course, if the student enrollment warranted it. She added that there probably would be a good chance that there would be additional enrollment since many students wish to get their English language requirement out of the way before they begin their studies. She would call Debbie if this was the case.

She continued to search for a full time job and eventually landed a part time job in a high school in a small development town almost a half hour outside Jerusalem. She had had many interviews in different schools but in this school, the chairman seemed to be especially impressed by her qualifications particularly by the fact that she had gotten her "30 plus" credits at the university beyond the M.A. degree.

Debbie was pleased that at least someone appreciated her intellectual efforts and achievements in education. Radu Rubinstein was a friendly person, an immigrant from Romania and did much to make Debbie feel at home in the school. He introduced her to the other teachers and gave her a lengthy orientation to the teaching program itself. The fact that the job was only part time and did not pay very much was of little concern to Debbie at this time. Somehow, she would manage. She would continue to live in Jerusalem and commute the half hour by bus to the school.

Then one day while she was busy washing her clothes in the late afternoon, the doorbell rang and she was surprised to find the chairman of the department standing there.

"I was in Jerusalem visiting my parents," he explained, "and I remembered that you live nearby so I thought I'd walk by and see if you were home. I'm going to the Cinematheque later and I wondered if you would care to come along?"

Debbie invited him in, they talked about a variety of things and found that they shared much in common. Later they made their way down Hillel Street to the cinema which specialized in foreign films and so called "art" films. Debbie liked the chairman and was very happy she had gotten this job. He was good looking, still young, probably in his early forties and very interesting to talk to. Had he not been married and had she not been hopelessly in love with Shimon, Debbie might have taken a romantic interest in Radu Rubinstein.

On the way, they chatted mostly about the coming academic year and plans for the school. He also told her about his wife who, a teacher for emotionally disturbed children, would be taking a year off to study for an M.A. in this field in the United States. This would also provide her with an opportunity to observe new methods and then train Israeli teachers upon her return.

They entered the cinema and the film began. Debbie sank back into her seat for what she thought would be a relaxing two hours. But her comfortable position did not last long. Barely had the light gone out, when suddenly Debbie began to feel something on her right knee. At first she thought she was imagining it, but then she realized that Radu was slowly putting his hand under her skirt and making his way up her thigh. He was gently stroking her thigh up and down.

Debbie was too stunned to react; she did not know what to do. She felt like pushing him away but after all, he was her boss and had given her a very fine job. Finally she gently took his hand in a friendly humorous kind of way and held it until he got bored.

He did not persist and Debbie was grateful for that. So now she knew why she had been hired. Not because she was intelligent and had graduated "cum laude" from college or because she was a good and experienced teacher or because she had published articles and poems but because she was a female, a sex object. This realization left her in a very depressed mood. Would she never be appreciated for her real talents? (The answer is "No", Debbie).

Radu had withdrawn his hand completely now and had even moved over somewhat in his seat in the opposite direction from

Debbie. Debbie hoped she had not offended him. When the movie was over, both pretended nothing had happened. He walked her home and then since he shown no signs of wanting to leave, and because she felt guilty and was afraid of having offended him, Debbie invited him in for coffee. They stood on the balcony making superficial talk. Debbie saw that he was looking at her passionately and this made her anxious. She didn't want an entanglement with her boss or with a married man yet she didn't want to lose the nice relationship she thought she could have with him - a friend and colleague she could trust. She continued to talk, laugh, and keep a safe distance from him. He was a gentleman and took the hint; he did not approach her again. (at least not for awhile).

Debbie was glad that she had handled the situation well or so she thought. Still she had been surprised; she always wanted to think that people liked her for her intelligence and capabilities. She was disappointed to be judged only by her physical appearance and sexual attractiveness. She realized with fear that he had possibly hired her as a potential "fill-in" for his absentee wife. Perhaps now he would change his mind and withdraw the job offer. He didn't, however, and Debbie made preparations to teach at the school.

Then one day in the beginning of July, Debbie got a call from the Jerusalem University English as a Foreign Language department asking her if she was still interested in teaching summer school. Was she? Wow. She had almost forgotten about her application. To teach at a fine school like the Jerusalem University was certainly an opportunity. She was thrilled and excited. Many more students had registered than they had anticipated and so they needed additional teachers. They told her to come in for an orientation and to bring all her academic documents with her. The course would begin on Sunday.

Sunday found Debbie Warshawsky as a teacher in Israel and she felt proud and lucky to have received this course. It felt strange at first to teach on Sunday but Sunday was a busy work day in Israel, the beginning of a new week. She enjoyed teaching her class which was composed mostly of very good students. There were exceptions, of course, but for the most part, they were serious, hard working and conscientious. There were many sections of the same course and the instructors in the various sections met occasionally to discuss quizzes, essays to be discussed, exams and general teaching problems encountered.

The class met everyday from 9 A.M. to 12 noon. One morning as she entered the main gate and walked toward the Perlman Building, she saw a large group of about 50 students kneeling upright on the grass without moving and with huge pieces of white tape pasted over their mouths.

There was a wide area of green grass and they knelt approximately five feet apart, staring straight ahead into the distance. It was an impressive sight, one not easily forgotten. Debbie wondered what it was all about.

Then she noticed Nisrin, one of her Arab students among the crowd. It did not look as though she were intending to come to class. Later, Debbie learned that it was an Arab student demonstration protesting the fact that they were not given permission to publish their own student newspaper in the Arabic language. The rationale given was that there already was one student newspaper in existence and thus another was unnecessary. It had been an extraordinary picture. Rousseau and Dali could not have done better!

The days flew by. Debbie was busy with the course and willingly gave much extra time to students needing help. One day, after the class had already been over for some time and all the students had disappeared, the short girl in the second row with the long Polish name lingered behind, slowly gathering her belongings. Debbie assumed she wanted to discuss one of her compositions as she usually did. Her name was Chava and although she was a very dutiful, hard working student, she was a poor writer and consequently usually received grades lower than she hoped for. Often she would stay behind after class and subtly emphasize how many hours and how hard she worked in hope of gaining Debbie's sympathy and perhaps a better grade. Mr. Shevach, the elderly gentleman in her class had said of Chava that she was probably the only virgin left in the class. Debbie smiled at this thought as Chava approached.

But today Chava had a different mission. With a kind of sly sheepish look on her face, she said softly as if in strictest confidence, "You know you don't *have* to do that."

"Do what, Chava?"

"You know," she said more boldly now, "make things easy for them."

"Them. Who is "them" Chava? And what do I make easy?" Debbie quizzed.

"You know" she repeated, "like when you give topics special just for them."

"Can you give me an example? I'm not sure I know what you mean."

"Well, like when you gave the topic for a composition to be done at home, "The Role of the Woman in Judaism" you put Christianity and Islam in parenthesis. You didn't have to do that." Chava replied like a mother reprimanding a small child.

"But Chava, that's not making things easy. That's just making things fair and equal. Do you think I should make Nisrin, Ruwaida and Faiza write about Judaism?"

"Why not?" she continued pouting like a whiny little girl.

"But they may not be familiar with the role of women in Judaism," Debbie tried to argue logically.

"So let them look it up in the library," Chava retorted angrily now.

"But the purpose of a course in Composition," Debbie explained, not realizing the futility of arguing with the prejudiced Chava, "is not research on a specific topic in the library but to construct, develop and style a theme. I'm not interested in the point of view or opinion the student takes but in how well he presents and supports his idea."

The words fell on deaf ears.

"If they don't like it, let them go to their own universities." Chava was almost shouting now. "On the West Bank" she added thinking perhaps Debbie might not know where "their own universities" were. "They don't have to come here. This is an Israeli university," she declared, flushed and breathing hard.

Debbie finally realized that what were to her logical rational arguments and quite self evident truths were not clear at all to the Israeli girl. She was also becoming exasperated now at the obvious prejudice of a girl she had thought of as a pleasant, plump, plodder type of student.

"Well," Debbie stated, now utilizing her power as instructor. "I have been teaching English Composition for a long time. And I always give a wide selection of themes so that every student in the class will have an equal chance to demonstrate his writing skill. To me, every student in this class is equal. I am an American and as long as I am teaching this class it will be taught in American style - every student has the same chance. That's that!" she concluded with the wave of her hand indicating finality.

Chava just heaved a loud "Hmmmph," took her books and stalked out the door. Debbie would not have thought that the seemingly quiet, unassuming girl could be so fierce. Anyway, Debbie thought she had stood her ground. Absolute equality of all students in the classroom was something she believed in quite strongly.

Later, Debbie wondered for awhile if it was just prejudice against Arabs or if Chava was perhaps jealous of some of the Arab students who were obviously brighter than she and received better grades. Some of the Arab girls were also better looking and sported better figures than the dumpy looking Chava.

Then she recalled the conversation she had had with one of her best students shortly after the Arab student demonstration.

"Why don't they let the Arab students have their own newspaper?" Debbie asked as if it were a logical procedure.

"Why should we?" Ariel answered quickly and matter of factly, as if that opinion were the logical one and Debbie's was ridiculous.

"Well, it seems only fair that each group should have its own medium of expression and in their own language." Debbie argued.

Bur Ariel remained firm, "No, we don't have to give them

anything. And we won't," he added emphatically.

Debbie was surprised at his views because she had been accustomed to intelligent students being tolerant and liberal and the stupid ones as being rigid and narrow minded. For Ariel, a good and loyal student was one who was concerned with what was best for Israel and the Jewish people, even if this meant that another group's rights had to be denied. For Debbie, this was a complete change of orientation.

The course was nearly two thirds over when one day, Salem, one of the best Arab students, a very bright, tall, poetic type, who could already write almost like a professional social science scholar, came up to her desk after class.

"You know," he began quietly, "what you always say in the class, that it doesn't matter what point of view we take in our compositions as long as we can develop our arguments? Well, that doesn't apply to us."

"What do you mean?" Debbie tried to fish for more information.

"Well, haven't you noticed that none of us ever chooses any of the politically or Arab-oriented type topics you give as possibilities for themes?" He posed the words more in the manner of a statement than a question.

"Yes, I did notice and wondered why since I thought you would be able to write very well on such a topic with which you are very familiar," Debbie declared, noting his use of the word "us."

"We would never dare to write on any political theme because we can get into a lot of trouble. We are not permitted to write on what is considered inciting or inflammatory material," he explained in a matter of fact way as though he had been living with this reality for so long that he had grown accustomed to it.

"Even just in a classroom composition?" Debbie asked in disbelief.

"Yes, in anything, it doesn't matter."

"But I wouldn't show it to anyone."

"I know, but perhaps someone could come into your office and see it."

"That's really awful. It must make things very difficult for you. I wish you had brought up the matter sooner," Debbie said sympathetically.

"Yes, but that's how it is here. We see that you do not know so that's why I tell you now," he concluded.

"Yes, OK, thanks." Debbie was at a loss for words. "I'm sorry."

She really did feel sorry for his plight, their struggle. And Salem was so bright. At first Debbie had thought that he might be getting outside help since his compositions were written in a kind of sociological jargon. But then he wrote in the same manner in class. Apparently he had done much reading in the social sciences and had imbibed their language. He was truly talented and such a nice person too. And yet the future and its prospects were bleak for him in Israel.

Debbie thought about their situation for awhile but then felt powerless to do anything about it. Besides she had concerns of her own. Shimon had gone to *miluim** for four weeks to Ashkelon and Debbie did not expect to see him until it was over. She missed him and thought about him constantly. Before he left, she had given him a poem she had written about him, a drunk articulation of her soul. She was surprised when he turned a deep beat red after she had given it to him. He even seemed somewhat upset and ill at ease.

He did not read it all immediately, just glancing at it and indicating that he wanted to read it when he was alone so he could better concentrate on the meaning and structure. Debbie took this to be a compliment. Quite possibly he was afraid to read it, thinking it would require some commitment on his part which he was not ready or able to make.

Debbie was so happy these days, happier than she had ever been before in her entire life. She had a job she liked at the

---

* *miluim* - army reserve duty. After the basic three years of army training, Israeli men continue to serve 6 weeks - 2 months per year in the reserve army until age 53.

present, a contract for another in the fall, a good relationship with the man she loved which had all the prospects of becoming a serious bond that would end in marriage and she lived in the beautiful city of Jerusalem. Who could ask for more? She was so glad she had come to Israel and merely regretted that she had not done so sooner. Dissonant echoes faded into the background.

CHAPTER 3
THE DESCENT INTO THE UNDERWORLD

The course was already in its fourth week when Shimon returned from his army duty. Actually he had already been back more than a week but Debbie had not heard from him. She was so busy and involved in the course that she did not notice or think to check. Sunday evening she quite naturally went to Mount Scopus for folk dancing as usual and would see Shimon there as soon as he returned.

She wasn't certain whether or not his duty was over but was happy as he came down the stairs to the basement of the twelve and a half building in the Resnick students dorms. He had a very serious face as he got in line behind Debbie to buy a ticket to enter the hall.

"Welcome back, hero," Debbie called smiling. He smiled back suddenly blushing profusely. Debbie looked at him admiringly as usual thinking how wonderful it was the way ruddy complexioned redhaired people could become suffused with life at a moment's change.

He looked anxiously at how long the line was and cranked his neck to see inside. He seemed somewhat impatient to get in. Debbie remarked about this and he said that he had not danced in a month. "No dancing on a military base," he laughed.

The line was moving very slowly and Debbie tried to make conversation. "Well, I guess congratulations are in order," she announced happily.

He looked surprised and answered, a bit embarrassedly and at a loss for words, "Well, maybe," and smiled.

"Sure is," she continued. "An M.A. in Economics is a valuable thing to have and you did it all yourself too. That's reason to celebrate."

"Oh, you mean the university," he said only now understanding her comment.

"Sure," she repeated, so eager to please him with her laudatory,

"Didn't you say you didn't accept any money from your parents. You worked full time all the way through. It's not easy to work and go to school at the same time. And a degree in Economics is a difficult one."

He raised his head again to see why the line was so slow in progressing. He was serious now and anxious. Then Debbie began to think out loud, "Well, if you didn't think I meant the university degree when I said 'congratulations' what did you think I meant? Did you win some prize or scholarship or get a better job?"

"Who me, for sure, no," he laughed nervously.

Instinct warned Debbie at first to "leave it," that is, not to press or probe further in the direction the conversation was going and she was silent for a minute or two. But then it bothered her. "What did he think I meant if not the degree?" Somehow she didn't want to find out. She sensed there was something to fear. Yet her curiosity was strong and she thought it might be better to know. It was probably nothing. Yet she listened breathlessly weighing his every word on the scale of infinity.

"What's the matter with this line. Why aren't they letting people in?" he was getting exasperated now.

"It's moving," Debbie encouraged, "you see" and she moved ahead a foot.

Then she plunged in, "Oh, come on, tell me," she said in an anxious high pitched voice, "What did you think I meant when I wished you 'Congratulations?'"

"Well," he answered sheepishly looking into the ground and blushing again, "some other happiness."

Now Debbie became very panicky and unconsciously was holding her breath as if in self defense for somehow she felt something terrible was going to happen. "Oh yeah," she said with a shaky voice, "happiness like what?" Her body was rigid with fear and she looked at him with vast pleading eyes.

"Uh," he said weakly, first looking at the line again, then at the ground, "I'm getting married next week."

Debbie's life came to an end with these words.

She was silent for a minute trying to comprehend the enormity of what he, the man she loved, had just spoken. For awhile she stood as if suddenly paralyzed, unable to move or speak.

Then she finally managed a "You're kidding." He didn't say anything just taking a deep breath. "When did all this happen?" She began to feel wild. "Who are you going to marry?" she went on quickly, looking at him in disbelief.

"Why, Dorrit, of course," he answered emphatically as if the question were an absurd one.

Before Debbie could answer again, the line had by now advanced to the table where the tickets were being sold. It was her turn to buy. Her mind was racing. "Let's go somewhere and talk," she whispered quickly to him. She wanted to say more but the words stubbed on themselves as they tried to leave her mouth.

"Later, I want to dance now. I haven't danced in a long time," he declared definitely pulling out money to pay for his ticket. Debbie saw she had no choice but to spend the evening folk dancing pretending for three and a half hours that she was having a good time.

It was hard even for an expert dancer like Debbie to dance while her head and heart were spinning. She did the dances mechanically. The room was too crowded and too noisy to be able to talk when she had a million things she wanted to scream. All the people around her were acting as though nothing had changed. Didn't they realize the world had stopped?

While they were dancing, Debbie gradually gained control of her rationality and began to think if there was anything she could do. There wasn't. Time was too short. "When did you decide?" she asked as he twirled her around in the Israeli mazurka. "Last week," he responded.

"Why so quickly?"

"Dorrit wants it that way. We're not going to have a big thing."

"Does everybody know?"

"Who is everybody? Just our parents and a few relatives.

You know, if it's any consolation, no girl can turn like you can in the Israeli *mazurka*, so easy. You are really the best. Dorrit has trouble turning. I have to push her."

Debbie looked at him to see if that was supposed to be a cruel joke but she saw that he was in earnest. He was like that, very literal and factual, sometimes. "Well," she thought, "perhaps this is what one must expect from an economist." For her, what would have been a compliment at any other time now just added more flames to the stake where she was being scorched.

For one time in her life, she couldn't wait for the folk dancing to end. Debbie who loved to dance so much - wanting to leave! Finally it was over and they went to the snack room in Building nine of the Resnik dorms where Shimon had his room.

They had a long talk; it was almost three A.M. when Debbie finally left. They spoke amicably. Debbie could never really be angry with Shimon. He told her how he had first met Dorrit in the folk dance course when the teacher had partnered them off. "I didn't like her at all at first, thought she was snobbish and you know, thinks she is a queen, but she lived in the same building of the dorm as me so I often ran into her." He continued about his first girlfriend, Shira, whom he really loved and dated for three years but who wanted to remain a virgin and eventually he couldn't bear this situation any longer. "So well, when Dorrit came along, she was very experienced and willing, so . . . And now, she has given me an ultimatum! 'Either we will marry next week or I do not wish to waste anymore time with you. I am 27 and want to get married.' "

That was the situation. "And you are going to let her push you around like that?" Debbie cried hoping he would see his folly. This tall husky ex-football player and soldier was going to cower in front of a girl half his size.

"No," he said bravely. "I'm willing. It's time I got married. I'm 31; some guys get married at 21. And she's OK. She's a teacher and we get along and all that."

She questioned him why he had bothered to date her at all. He told her that he wasn't sure at the beginning but that now he was. I don't want to break off with Dorrit," he went on.

"Why not?" Debbie coaxed, "You could find a million girls to go with." Debbie countered.

"Well," he thought for awhile. "If you start with a new girl, in the beginning you don't know what she is like. It takes time to get to know her. And then after all that, she may not want to do it, like Shira. Or it may not be good. So it's better to stay put and keep what you have, you know, if it's OK." Then as if he suddenly realized what he had said, he stopped embarrassed and red-faced leaving Debbie to come to the logical conclusions.

Alas! So Shimon, like so many men who marry, sold his freedom for sexual security and availability. The cock had done him in. With this girl the noose would be a tight one.

To say that the days, weeks, months following the wedding of the man she loved were difficult ones for Debbie would be a gross understatement. She felt as she never felt in all her life - totally despairing and abandoned. It seemed as though her life had completely ended. She went about daily life like a zombie. She looked like a desert - silent, barren, and empty.

She started her job in the school but even there she did only the bare minimum of what was required and did not approach her teaching with enthusiasm and challenge as she had previously. Yet still her classes and the energetic and demanding students provided a strong diversion from the constant thoughts of Shimon and "what might have been" as well as the terrible reproaches which she cast upon herself. She felt she was to blame for everything. It was the times outside the school and job that were the most painful. The nights, Sabbaths, the long rides to and from the school were often the times when she would allow the tears to flow. She told no one about what had happened and so was totally alone in her all-enveloping grief. Even her wonderful Jerusalem had now become a diary of painful memories, each site a monument to where she and Shimon had done this or that.

One time her chairman asked her if she could try to put on a more happy face when she entered the classroom. He explained that the students did not know she was sad and might interpret her overly serious face with the fact that she was angry with them for not doing an assignment correctly. But she could not scrub the pain off her face.

On another occasion she was sitting in a cafe having coffee and cake and an Israeli girl came over and invited Debbie to join her and two guys at her table. "You look so sad," she said, "come" but Debbie did not go. She did not want to speak with anyone. Life itself had become unfamiliar and she spent much time groping around its darkened alleys.

Yet we do not wish to dwell on these times in Debbie's life since it is not our intention to sadden the reader nor to create sublime Aristotelian tragedy. The art of poetry is to entertain and to enlighten. Suffice it to say that it was a period which lasted far too long. Who was it that said, "There is not a man alive that is worth one tear."? Her mother, perhaps.

All the activities into which Debbie threw herself with an almost compulsive abandon offered at best only a temporary relief. She was still ill with love and desire. There would be periods of forgetting and then suddenly a relapse when she would whip herself with the memory of each event and how it went wrong. "How love could have been if only I had been clever enough or quick enough, if only I had come to Israel sooner, if only I hadn't spent so many days in touring, if only I had told him at the very beginning how I felt, if only that stupid Shlomo hadn't interfered that night with his offer of a ride home." Oh, the aching ideas that tore through her mind like an idee fixe!

"How clever Dorrit was to have given him an ultimatum. 'Either we get married next week or it's all off.' If only I had known about it, perhaps I could have prevented it," she chided herself again and again. "And of course, he had fallen for it. How smart Dorrit was not to tell anyone! After all, it was getting the husband that counted not the dress, or the reception or the flowers on the car.

Why do I always learn everything too late? Perhaps the day he had come to my room, he really wanted to unburden himself about Shira." Thus, the guillotine fell continuously on her mind but without bringing the relief of oblivion she so desperately sought.

She would never know, that was the hardest part. She kept ruminating trapped in the now turbulent sanctuary of her own thoughts. If only she could get them out of her head. It was like a crippling plague for which there was no remedy and from which there was no recovery.

Everytime Debbie thought of them together, she experienced excruciating pain. One day was an especially depressing one. It's strange how some were so much worse than others. She went to Tel Aviv in the morning because the flash on her camera was not working. To complicate matters, she also got her monthly period, a time when she usually felt more depressed anyway. She became so despondent that she started to cry. "Life will never be any different for me. I will always love Shimon," she concluded helpelessly. Everything seemed so bleak and hopeless. Her whole day - the time in the taxi, walking around the city - she spent thinking about him. Her mind was in complete chains. Even her dreams were infected with Shimon.

When she finally located the camera repair shop, she was told it would cost about $80 to fix her flash. She informed the clerk that the flash had only cost $60 but he did not believe her and held firm to his price. Too weary to argue, Debbie decided life could continue without a flash. The repair shop for a broken love was also difficult to find; once found, it was even more expensive!

In the evening, the loud ringing of the telephone finally interrupted her obsessive thoughts. It was someone whose personal ad she had answered on one of her "better days." He asked her to go out with him. Friends had been advising her to go out with other men as often as possible. Hence she had responded to several ads listed in the *Jerusalem Post*. It had seemed to be the easiest way to meet someone and now she was grateful for the possibility of a change.

His name was Larry and he was from Toronto, Canada. They went to the Notre Dame Hotel but just sat, had coffee and talked for awhile. Debbie was not particularly attracted to him and he was half bald but she liked him and trusted him. The Notre Dame Building, now a hotel, is a magnificent white Gothic structure. Its elegance affected her and she felt stronger. She noticed that she often felt better when she could talk with somebody else or when she had a change of atmosphere. Guessing that this diverted her mind from the problem, she resolved to try to keep busy.

A few days later she saw Larry again and this time they went to the Rockefeller Museum. Debbie expected that she would again have a fairly nice time. They did enjoy themselves while they were inside the museum. After walking around viewing the various archeological exhibitions from different epochs of ancient times, they sat down in the courtyard by the pond and took photos like tourists. But then Larry became very serious and said he wanted to talk. They returned to her room and immediately he started in .

First he stated somberly that he realized things couldn't "go anywhere" between them and so wanted to inform her of this and not to expect anything from him. He went on as though he had prepared a long speech, a long list of complaints which he spouted out like a Juvenalian ode.

He insisted also, "God is not as important in your life as He is in mine." Well, yes, he was right. It seemed to her that God was almost an obsession in his life. From this point, he became progressively nastier, admitting he didn't like her hairstyle which he felt was too elaborate and overdone. He also did not hesitate to criticize her clothes, including what she was wearing, "I think they are too loud in color and also you have a very loud voice which is very irritating."

Almost as an afterthought, he then added that she looked as though she cried very much, another negative quality. "I can see it in your eyes which are sad and dreamy - definitely not my type. I would like a more lively girl."

Then he confessed not surprising in the least that he had a

problem with relationships. He had had a steady girl friend in Canada but could not bring himself to love her because she was too short. She was perfect in every other way but he could not accept her height. Thus, they broke up although both were saddened by the parting.

At first, she was so surprised by his unexpected outburst that she couldn't respond. Then later, as they walked down King George Street, the full enormity of the whole scene descended on her and she became upset. She had only dated him twice and already he was acting as if he owned her. It was not difficult to understand why he was not married at 42. He probably behaved in the same way with each girl in his search for perfection. What else could one expect from a "leftover"? Besides she would never want to be married to such a religious person. "Just the nerve of him! Such a creepy looking guy," she fumed to herself, "making such criticism. He should look at himself." She wailed that he had given her a kick and had made her feel bad. Then his anger reached the boiling point and he preached accusingly, "You brought it on yourself."

Debbie was relieved when he finally left. She was so fed up with getting kicked about by these guys. It seemed the nicer one was to some men, the more they would take advantage. When she used to be oblivious to men during her 20's, they would come after her. Now that she wanted them, it was just the opposite. Strange psychology! she thought. "Ah, Debbie, you must learn to play the game called "Relationships."

That very same evening, Debbie went to the folk dancing group at the Hebrew University Beit Sprinczak because she anticipated that Shimon would be there. There had not been any folk dancing on Sunday and Monday so for sure he would go on Wednesday instead.. She knew he loved dancing so much that he would not do without it for a whole week. She rushed to get there for the first couple dance. One had to be there at this time to secure a partner for the evening. Otherwise, one would have to sit all night. Sometimes girls even asked guys outside or even earlier to make certain they would have a partner.

She had calculated correctly. He was there and without Dorrit. What luck! Debbie became very nervous and hesitated but then desperation gave her courage. She tried to appear non-chalant and asked Shimon to dance. He said, "OK, sure." While they were dancing he seemed to enjoy it although he kept glancing anxiously around the room. Perhaps he was fearful that one of Dorrit's girl friends would tell her he had danced with "the American girl."

All Debbie could think of was how wonderful it was to dance with him. Obviously, she idolized him; there was no end to the list of superlatives she would apply to him. He was so tall, so strong, his thick red blond hair glowing in the light. He looked like a hero from some ancient Teutonic mythology. How wonderful it would be to have a man like this for always! She couldn't fathom being so lucky.

She felt her sense of loss even more strongly because had she been quicker, more clever, maybe she could have gotten him.

Then for the second round of partner dances, he started to avoid her and moved far away to the other side of the room and picked other partners even though it was the custom to remain with the first partner throughout the evening. He even chose girls who didn't know how to folk dance at all. That hurt Debbie a lot - that he even preferred to dance with a girl who didn't know any of the steps to dancing with her. She watched him struggle to push the girl in the right direction and to try to call out the steps. He had a rough time and she was glad. "Serves him right," she grumbled.

When the dancing was nearly over, she plotted to walk out at the same time as he. She was lucky again and got a *tramp* (lift) in the same car. Oh, how exciting it was to sit close to him! The car was small and packed with people, therefore, providing a good opportunity to actually touch him. She was so nervous that she sat almost paralyzed next to him although she tried to make small talk about the dancing. Then just as quickly, they reached the main campus gates and the ride was over.

A few lucky moments like this or a few stolen seconds in some of the dances would be her only chance to ever hug the man she loved. The enormity of this truth was so heavy to bear that she found herself breathing heavily as if to compensate.

The pain rained over her until it filled her entire being, From the wonderful warmth of his body she was vomited out of the compact car with the others into the cold empty night. The others ran quickly to catch the last buses and to other destinations. Debbie stood alone for awhile before moving on. She wanted so much to die as she stood there in the dark emptiness waiting for the last bus to the city center. But death did not come; only the number nine bus swung fast around the circle and came to a sudden stop. She dragged herself on and it drove off into the night.

One day as she sat on the bus on her way to the university, Debbie was thinking that she was really going about everything in the wrong way. She found it was sometimes helpful to just sit quietly and ponder the totality of the situation. The swaying movements of the bus as it turned all the corners on the number 9 route had a tranquilizing effect. The beautiful scenery of the Israel Museum, the Knesset and the Monastery of the Cross was breathtaking and always offered a small source of pleasure and comfort amid the sea of pain in which she was continuously engulfed. Sometimes certain insights would emerge at these times which unfortunately never lasted very long. It was too easy to fall back into the old feelings and patterns.

A friend once suggested that she be less romantic and sentimental and more opportunistic. "Perhaps he was right" she thought to herself. "You are wasting time running after Shimon. You are almost 32 and have had little experience from life. You should try and get something yet before it is too late. At the rate you are going, you will wind up with nothing. You don't have much time and choice left. You are a very nice and deserving person, more so than many others. Why should you not have a nice husband, children and home like other girls? You have to take some action now and try to lift yourself out of this slush pile of pain." This was the speech she often made trying hard to convince herself of its inherent wisdom. But the head and the heart are far apart; reason and feeling rarely meet.

Every now and then she would make an attempt to escape this prison of suffering. Her placing an ad in the matrimonial section of the English language newspaper, *The Jerusalem Post* which would automatically also appear in the leading two Hebrew dailies, was one such attempt.

She had written: "Attractive American teacher 31: 170 seeks to meet sincere interesting mate, P.O. Box   Jerusalem." In Israel, almost all ads are short mainly due to the high cost and because Israelis generally expressed themselves in the most direct and succinct manner. Too much indicated neediness and desperation. They were also not completely accepted by the public.

Debbie wondered whether or not personal ads in the newspaper really were a good way to meet somebody nice. Many people were dubious. One man advised her that only people who were unable to make contact in any other way would resort to this. Any normal healthy guy could meet a girl in a million places. The replies are probably as different as there are varieties of people. One had to have patience and meet everyone who appears to be suitable with an open mind and heart.

Out of all the replies she received to her ad, Chaim Sokolov's letter seemed to have been the most interesting. She agreed to meet him in Tel Aviv at the *Sherut* station for Netanya. They planned to spend Shabbat at the beach of this small beautiful resort town on the Mediterranean. The beach there was less crowded than the one in Tel Aviv.

Debbie was still emotionally raw from her recent experiences so her mood was not very conducive to having a happy day. She had taken a *sherut* to Tel Aviv from Jerusalem but when she arrived, she could not remember the place for the *sherut* to Netanya. She knew it was only one block away but was unsure in which direction to walk. She asked a parked taxi driver where it was. Taking her for a tourist, he said he would take her there in his taxi, most likely adding an expensive detour on the way. "It's only a block," she sneered at him.

Debbie's pet peeve were taxi drivers who "took" tourists counting on their lack of knowledge of an area to make money off them. She herself had had many negative experiences with them and so became enraged very easily whenever they tried their tricks on her, now that she was wiser.

Unfortunately, she was still stewing about the taxi driver and of course everything else when she met Chaim. He noticed and commented, "Oh, you are so nervous," then adding sensibly, "You should not get so upset. It is not good. You should be more quiet." She didn't realize it then but later she thought perhaps this angry "hyped up" tense feeling which she had apparently communicated to Chaim might have been a real turn-off for an easy going doctor such as he. And then what luck! He would have to be a neurologist. Anyway, it seemed as though she had lost him before the date had even begun.

Nevertheless, when she saw him, she too was disappointed, He was relatively short, shorter than Debbie, pathetically thin and he had red hair of which only two small sprouts over his ears remained intact. "Nothing like Shimon," was Debbie's first reaction. He was 41 but looked older perhaps because of the lack of hair. Born in Bulgaria, he had spent virtually his entire life in Israel. He seemed very interested in the United States and asked Debbie many questions about life there. At the time, he was an intern and looking for a residency in neurology at one of the Israeli medical centers. This would be difficult to accomplish since there were many more doctors seeking positions than there were places available. Thus, many sought to go abroad.

When they finally reached Netanya beach, Debbie tried to relax. It was a caressingly warm day and the sparkling water looked so inviting. The beach was beautiful - clean sand and the wonderful hot sun beating down everywhere. She loved to sit in the sun no matter how hot it was. It gave her a feeling of security, protection and warmth like a Benevolent Deity watching over you. She tried to pretend she was having a good time but her eye kept roving around the beach if it might not catch sight of Shimon. He came from Netanya and his parents still lived there. She wondered which part of the beach he went to; it was so long and winding that she couldn't possibly check it all, although she had so often tried. She wanted so much to comb the sand and look for him but Chaim was an obstacle to this. He kept straining to make conversation but she barely heard him. Every few minutes, her eyes would search the crowds for Shimon.

Chaim was a nice person but he just wasn't Debbie's type. She tried, (she really did) to convince herself to like him especially when she saw all the families and kids on the beach but it just didn't work. His words knocked on her sore psyche. He was bald and short and skinny, all no-no's on Debbie's shopping list. Even when he spoke, his dead-pan face never changed its expression. He was quiet and unassuming which is a nice way of saying "blah" not the dynamic ambitious type of man she admired. She tried to emphasize his good points, that he liked books and music and that he was very well educated, a doctor but somehow she could just not bring herself to like him - at least not as a boyfriend or lover. "Why was it always that way," she complained, "the ones you want are unavailable and the ones you don't want are left?"

Debbie saw Chaim again on another Saturday when they took a drive and then a walk in the Liberty Bell Garden. She noticed that he had asked her several times when she was going to return to the United States. At first she told him she would go back after a short while.

Friends had warned her that some Israeli men are looking to emigrate to the United States and so seek to become friendly with American girls. They told her the best way to test a guy for such intentions is to tell him very emphatically that you want to make *aliya* and intend to say in Israel forever. This is usually (although not always) enough to chase this type away. So when Chaim again questioned Debbie's plans to return to the United States, she summoned all her acting skills and declared, "I really love being in Israel and have decided to take a job at the Aleph School in Jerusalem. I also started a course in Hebrew at the local Ulpan. I may even consider selling my apartment in New York and buying one in Jerusalem." Debbie never saw Chaim again.

So much for personal ads. They very frequently brought Chaim types but Debbie was not ready to give up. The next Friday found her once again eagerly reading through the lists of people searching for a partner. She checked several that were appropriate and eventually wrote to three of them.

On the weekend, Debbie thought she needed a change of scene and made the rather lengthy and rocky trip to Tiberias and the Sea of Galilee. It was three and a half hours each way but Debbie was a seasoned commuter and distances did not scare her. Besides she preferred swimming in sweet water and green grass was a welcome change to sand.

She stayed overnight in a large youth hostel near the central bus station which was also walking distance to the lake. Debbie did not mind staying in youth hostels since she often met university and adventuresome people there. This time she struck up a friendship with a tall young woman from Zurich, Switzerland who was visiting Israel for the first time. Her name was Sabine von Wagenfeld and she was a fifth year medical student at the University of Zurich. She was part of an exchange program which her university had with Ben Gurion University - Soroka Medical School whereby Swiss students would come to study for the summer at Soroka and Soroka students would go to Switzerland.

She liked the experience because it enabled her to do things such as, holding the retractors during surgery that only a much more advanced doctor would do in Zurich. And of course in her free time, she could tour the country.

There was not much to do in the evening and when Sabine suggested that they "take a look" over to the Galilee Plaza Hotel Debbie readily agreed. This was a five star hotel a few streets from the hostel. After entering the hotel and brousing in the shops, they discovered the hotel's nightclub which had a singer and several musicians. Sabine was delighted and said, "Oh let's see if there is dancing." Debbie was less enthusiastic but allowed herself to be persuaded to enter.

The two young well dressed women sat down at one of the still empty tables. They ordered drinks and before long two young Israelis between 25 and 30 came over and with a great deal of self confidence asked if they could sit down at their table, already partially doing so before the surprised Debbie or Sabine could answer. They were quite good looking in a strange and sophisticated way. After the usual "Where are you from? How long are you staying? "one of them asked Sabine to dance while Debbie chatted with his friend.

Soon afterwards the one who had invited Sabine to dance quite casually asked, "Are you two girls staying here at the hotel?" Sabine who had obviously enjoyed the dancing was excited and talkative. "Oh no," she answered as if it were a total impossibility, "We are staying in the youth hostel just a few blocks over in that direction. It's a really nice place."

The looks that appeared on the two men's faces when Sabine happily voiced her information are beyond description. Immediately, their eyes shot back and forth messages between them. Before long, one of them arose, the other quickly following and said, "Well we have to be going now. Nice to meet you." As quickly as they had come onto the stage, so rapidly did they exit.

The two girls were shocked, Sabine the more so. Apparently no one had ever treated her in this way before. "Did I say something wrong?" she asked several times hardly able to believe what had happened.

"No, of course not, but it was wrong for them ." Debbie explained. They are probably looking to meet a nice rich girl here and obviously if we are staying in a youth hostel, we are most likely poor, not rich. They are not going to waste their time on us."

Debbie saw that Sabine was upset "Don't worry. We are best rid of them. They look like trouble to me. It's good that they left." Finally she was convinced but the evening had been spoiled. Not long after, they left and slowly walked back to their hostel. The next day passed uneventfully; Debbie went swimming and quickly the weekend came to an end.

After such disappointments, it was time again for Debbie to seek solace as she always had in the past - in the intellectual sphere. Here at least she felt comfortable and there was less chance of being hur' 'Vhenever she had the time, she would attend lectures or worksh ps at the university or at various cultural centers often regardless of the topic.

So when a three day writer's conference was advertised in the *Jerusalem Post* to be held at Tel Aviv University, Debbie decided this might be a good way to forget past events and at the same time to break into the Israeli literary world or at least the English division of it. Several foreign lights would also be present, among them a Library of Congress poet and a *New York Times* literary critic. Debbie was determined to attend as much of the conference as her teaching schedule would allow.

Arriving late on the first day (it was a two hour trip from Jerusalem to Ramat Aviv) she entered in the middle of the keynote address by the *Times* critic, Stephen Bismuth-Cayne. Next on the program was an Israeli novelist speaking on "The Writer's Function in Israel," a speech which evoked much discussion. Then came the coffee break, the time for which many people waited eagerly as a chance to meet people and to make new and important contacts.

Debbie looked around the huge auditorium, lounge and lobby for a familiar face but found none - none at least that she might approach. She saw several people from the Israeli Writers Association but after their rejection of her membership application for no apparent reason, she was in no mood to seek them out. She stood by herself and began to eavesdrop on a nearby group of three young American women speaking quite loudly.

The focus of the discussion seemed to center on one of them, a woman about 35, dressed in a very chic 3 piece suit, spiked heels and a truckload of rings on each finger tapering in coral red nails of one and a half inches each. She was quite attractive in a very made up sort of way utilizing all the tricks of modern fashion and cosmetics. Debbie strained to overhear what wisdom she was spouting forth.

In an impassioned voice guaranteed to convince anyone, the fashion plate was promulgating her plans to initiate a new cultural channel for Israeli Television. It was a tragedy indeed, she thought, that Israel had no channel such as Channel 13, National Educational TV and many others in various cities of the USA which brought free or relatively inexpensive cultural events, such as, concerts, operas, ballets, lectures and discussions of an intellectual nature to the masses. She had been a volunteer for several years in one of these stations. Well, Isolde (for this was her name) would now provide the same service for the culturally deprived and downtrodden of Israel.

The fact that she had only been in Israel for one month did not seem to be a deterring factor to her. The jungle of Israeli bureaucracy also did not loom as an obstacle. She continued with her speech for such it sounded as if it had been rehearsed and performed many times. While she was thus professing, Isolde continuously glanced about the room as though looking for someone. Was she perhaps looking over the crowd for that Special Someone.

At this point Debbie entered the conversation with her usual remark, "Do I hear American English?" The theme of discussion then shifted to the writer's conference specifically the two lectures of the morning and the proposed workshops for the afternoon. It turned out that the other two women were hopeful writers, one a poet, the other, a writer of children's stories but as yet undecided.

Yet beneath all the idealistic and humanitarian rhetoric lay ever the same hope and wish, maybe to find that illusive Prince Charming. This is not to imply that Isolde did not bear good intentions in bringing culture to the underprivileged; she probably believed that she actually could and that her desire was sincere.

Debbie predicted failure for Miss Joan of Arc in both spheres. What many experienced and professionally trained Israelis had already tried to accomplish in raising the level of Israeli television, certainly an inexperienced newcomer would not be able to do. It was also unlikely that a girl of this type would be able to find a suitable mate among the Israeli population. *Vogue* magazine and daily life in Israel were two different worlds.

Debbie remembered the formula proposed once by her friend Aaron regarding American girls. One could predict with reasonable accuracy how long an American girl would stay in Israel by the length of her nails. The longer her nails, the shorter the stay. He dared to say this to Debbie after viewing her chewed off stubs. The coral daggers ending Isolde's fingernails thus indicated a brief stay. And so it was! Isolde left Israel two months later without having inaugurated a new cultural channel. She explained that the government would have erected too many barriers to the ultimate realization of her goal. Prince Charming did not accompany her.

The next session of the conference proved to be fairly interesting but as writer's conferences go, there were no intellectual earthquakes. The poet from the Library of Congress spoke on "The Writer's Craft: Was It Really Necessary?" The audience sat dutifully spellbound by his words of practical advice.

In the afternoon, individual workshops were held whereby the audience broke into smaller groups according to genre: poetry, fiction, non-fiction etc. each led by one of the speakers. A person could choose whatever area of writing he was interested in or he could elect to go with a particular leader. Debbie chose the poet's workshop still somewhat naively believing that the Great Poet would notice her immense talent and eagerly make her into another Sylvia Plath.

This was the myth or energizing force behind most Writer's conferences and workshops. Organizers would invite big name writers (or often only minor writers as long as they were published) in the hopes of attracting young inexperienced usually beginner poets, short story writers, and non-fiction writers to come, pay the often high registration fee and attend a "workshop" with the Great Personage. Ostensibly one attended such a workshop to learn the craft of writing from the utterances of the Great Master or to have him make a pronouncement over one's work. One would "work" along with him.

Yet this was rarely the only reason people went to Writer's workshops (since many believed that they already knew everything that was to be known about writing). The hidden reason which no one was willing to admit is that the would be writer hoped to make such an impression on the Master that he would then arrange to have his work PUBLISHED. Yes, that was the magic word - PUBLISH. After all, the only difference (so many believed) between the Great Master and themselves was the mere fact that the former had his work in print for all the world to read while their masterpieces lay unrecognized and unpraised in the desk drawer. Others had dabbled in several media without success and waited for the Great Master to tell them that they were really born poets or brilliant dramatists and their problem lay only in finding the right genre.

And so they would come, the naive and innocent would-be writers in droves to sit at the feet of the Great Master, And sit they did, not at the feet as they had expected but in large uncomfortable classrooms containing as many as 60 or more "participants." Sometime one did not have even a chance to speak with the Great Master. There would be apologies of course on the part of the organizers but what could they do if Mr. X was in such demand by everyone. This was the penalty one had to accept to sit within hearing distance of a truly "great" person. Almost always the books written by the Great Master were offered for sale. Some young innocents would dutifully purchase at least the latest book (stating that they were already proud possessors of his other works) thus affording them the opportunity to speak a few precious words with the Great Master as they asked for his autograph. Some a bit more clever would merely bring along an old copy of an earlier work for him to sign.

Many hopefuls would wait until the end of the workshop before approaching the Great Master with any additional manuscripts. Little did they know that being deluged by neatly typed manuscripts in brown manila envelopes and being barricaded into a corner to "discuss" it was the thing the Great Master most dreaded and most carefully planned to avoid. He had no intention and no desire whatsoever to "help" anyone of the numerous worshippers at his feet to publish his work. Great Masters were usually interested only in continuing to publish their own work. They merely consented to lowering themselves to giving such workshops because they were a major source of income for many writers especially poets and minor writers for whom the sales of their books were not enough income.

The trick was to arrive as late as possible (for some more aggressive hopefuls would attack *before* the workshops began), get the mechanics of the workshop over with as quickly as possible (the bare minimum he had to read to conduct the workshop), be as professional as possible (be aloof and distant) and above all, disappear at the end before the hungry hopefuls would quietly, shyly, secretly, aggressively or in any other way, manage to approach with the manila envelopes. Even one desperate Tantalus, stretching out to devour the Great Master with his word-drunk poems must be escaped at all cost.

"Would you have the time just to glance at my novel? I've been working on it for five years and don't know if it's any good." "Since you said in the workshop that my poem was interesting, I thought you might want to look at the other 75 poems I've written since I once took a creative writing course in high school." These were typical questions. Therefore, preparation for a quick exit with necessary excuses, airline or train deadlines, etc. was an absolute must for the Great Master if such a disaster was not to befall him.

The now starving hopefuls would go home frustrated and disappointed because they had spent their time and money and had received little or no attention. Once again, they drowned in the sea of rejection. Often all they had gotten from the conference was another autographed novel or book of poems to put on their already cluttered shelves. They would blame the particular Great Master thinking only he had been snobbish and unwilling to help not realizing that most Great Masters and Writer's Conferences function that way. Many would try again with different Great Masters ever hoping that perhaps the next one would somehow be different and notice them. On the way home from the conference, Debbie pondered the fact that in many respects, writer's conferences and singles events had much in common.

After the conference was over and Debbie was once again home more often, she received a telephone call from another one of the ads she had answered from the *Jerusalem Post*. He said he had called twice before but no one had been at home. Over the phone, he sounded nice and intelligent and they agreed to meet at her place at 6 P.M. after he had seen his last patient. Kurt Nowozek was a psychiatrist in private practice.

About 6, the phone rang. It was he saying he would be late; he had an unexpected patient who was quite disturbed and he felt he had to stay. Debbie had been ready and hated the suspense of waiting even longer. She was still nervous to meet an unknown stranger for the first time. She always wondered, what would he be like, would he like her?

Finally he arrived quite late but she was surprised when he walked in. He was breathtakingly handsome, very self-confident in his walk and manner, charming and well-dressed. She knew immediately that she could like this man very much. She grew excited and tried to be her charming best. Although she would have preferred to go out somewhere, she acquiesced easily when he suggested that since it was so late, why didn't they just stay there and talk.

She offered him a soft drink and he laughed, "Don't you have anything stronger?" She felt embarrassed and unsophisticated because she did not. Israelis usually didn't drink liquor so she was surprised that he would have wanted vodka.

"Are you Russian?" Debbie asked Kurt.

"No," he replied quickly. "I am from Czechoslovakia but I

have been in Israel for 10 years. I am 41 years old, divorced for three years and have one son, age seven. Anything else you want to know?"

He was fairly tall and sported an athletic build. His hair was full, dark blond with soft curls that hung loosely on his forehead. His eyes had that sleepy dreamy quality she liked so much. At first they got along very well, chatting very quickly. It was obvious that he had a sharp mind and a persuasive manner. He spoke about his practice relating that he had at one time been a neurologist but found that too depressing. "Very few patients ever get well," he explained. Now he was engaged in the use of behavior therapy in the treatment of various conditions, such as, overweight, smoking, obsessive behavior patterns and depression. It was easy to see that he was very successful. Debbie wondered whether he had mostly women patients and he answered that he had both but yes, most were women.

The interaction moved rapidly; Debbie liked him and felt she was making a good impression since she understood something about his work and was able to make intelligent responses. He spoke in a charming manner and could easily hold someone's attention; Debbie found him to be an interesting and fascinating character. She asked him the usual questions, how he liked it in Israel and so forth. In Israel, everybody has a story to tell and usually will tell it to anyone who happens to fall into their pathway. Kurt Nowozek was no exception so slowly he unfurled his story to Debbie's willing ears.

He seemed to be full of a kind of nervous energy and began immediately "As I have told you already, I was born in Czechoslovakia to a Czech mother and a German Gentile father. When I was five years old the Nazis came into my town. My father had instructed me to point to a Gentile woman as my mother when the soldiers came thereby saving him and me the fate of most European Jews. In the meantime my mother was taken to Auschwitz where she died. I always hated my father for tricking me and not staying with my mother." Kurt was still visibly upset by this memory and began pacing around the room.

Then he continued, "After graduating from medical school, I applied for an exit visa so I could emigrate to Israel. It was denied and I was told that since I had received eight years of university education to be a doctor for the Czech people, I would first have to work eight years as a medical doctor in Czechoslovakia. I was certainly not interested in remaining eight more years in Czechoslovakia. I had decided to become the most loyal and hard working supporter of the Communist Party, so much so that I was invited to an international conference in East Berlin. As the train pulled out of the Vienna train station, I excused myself from my colleagues, left the compartment where we had all been comfortably seated and jumped off the train. I travelled through Austria, Italy and arrived in Haifa via a boat from Naples. There I was greatly aided by the Jewish Agency in establishing myself as a doctor. Before long, I met and married a Hungarian immigrant and had a son."

He stopped for a minute as though he had just thought of something important. "Are you Hungarian by the way," he questioned. "No," Debbie answered somewhat puzzled. "Good," he sounded relieved. "Because I would not want to have anything to do with you if you were." Debbie was surprised but said nothing.

He went on, "After several years, the marriage went wrong, I don't know what happened. Anyway, we divorced. Unfortunately, I had to give her the apartment and all the furniture and she also gained custody of the child. Then there is the monthly child support payments, the "proper" education of my son and related expenses. What it all means is that I am not in a financial situation to marry again. This should explain my ad in the newspaper."

Debbie recalled the nature of the ad which was now more understandable. "Doctor, 41, handsome, sporty seeks, rich, young and beautiful for marriage. P.O. Box 261, Tel Aviv."

"I was in a very playful, dare-devil mood, rare for me when I answered your ad. What did I write, something like 'I am rich, young and beautiful and waiting for you. Come and get me.' I thought perhaps you were joking or exaggerating. After all everyone dreams of marrying a young, beautiful and rich partner," she confessed.

But Kurt had not been jesting. He explained quite clearly and matter of factly to Debbie that when he arrived in Israel from Czechoslovakia, he had nothing, "only the clothes on my back. I cannot begin again that way. I am too old for that now."

Romantic Debbie immediately countered with, "But don't you want to marry someone you love?"

"Well, sure," he thought for a second but then quickly added, "Ten years ago, I would have married you just for your body but now I have to be more practical. I am an established doctor now with somewhat of a reputation. So I need a nice house and then suitable furniture to go with it. Also I want to be able to go abroad at least once a year and take vacations in Eilat."

"You will have to find a millionairess for all that. I won't suffice," Debbie chirped sarcastically," an oil heiress, maybe."

"Of course," he added as if it were an afterthought, "I have only myself to offer." It was apparent that he did not anticipate this to be a big obstacle. Debbie also estimated that there were so many women in Israel from all over looking for a husband, he could probably have his pick of young, beautiful and even rich woman, especially since he was a medical doctor and a good looking and charming one at that.

At this point, Kurt started to put his arm around Debbie and grew very affectionate. They were sitting on the sofa in Mrs. Levinsky's salon. When Mrs. Levinsky heard that Debbie was going to entertain a doctor, she offered, "You cannot receive such a man in your room. You may use my salon for the evening and I will go into the other room."

And then he wanted sex, right there on Mrs. Levinsky's couch. Debbie explained the situation, upon which he continued, "OK, let's go into your room." Yet, Debbie had been turned off by his materialism, his too crude approach and his total lack of romantic feeling. Even now, he probably wanted sex from Debbie not because he had any positive feelings for her but so that his trip from Ramat Gan and his giving up an evening of his time would not have been a total waste. He did not call again.

It might be added here that not all Israeli men are interested in money. We do not wish to create a false impression. Another ad that Debbie had answered called and inquired as to the size of her bust. She decided to spare herself this one.

Debbie found a very interesting book in a shop, "Married Men Make the Best Lovers." What a different way of life it described compared to her meager love existence. She wondered sometimes if most people really do have exciting lives like that or if that's just what they write in the books in order to sell them. It was very depressing to realize how many wonderful chances she had missed.

She didn't know quite what to do. Whatever, she knew she must act quickly or she would have nothing at all when she was old. Now she still had a chance because she looked young, sexy and pretty. Yet the spector of middle age steepened each year that went by. She must do something before she would journey into the horror of old age.

The next weekend, the urge to "do something" led Debbie to visit the large sport center at the Technion University in Haifa. Her teacher's ID card was sufficient for her to gain entry although with a fee. It was a huge new center with all the latest facilities including an Olympic size swimming pool and a surrounding green lawn dotted with white lawn chairs.

Debbie used the pool which she found marvelous for swimming then sun-bathed on the green grass. She saw many interesting men but they were all attached, chained or otherwise fused with wives and kiddies. It was impossible to make any contact. How alone she felt when she saw all of them! To be one of those women, she thought would be the greatest prize in the world - to have a desirable man for your very own; that was worth struggling for. She realized that if she met a really nice man here that was good looking and interesting, she could forget Shimon or at least he would not bother

her so much. A lot of men gave Debbie the eye but dared not do more because their wives were with them. Such was the nature of the Daedalian labyrinth which engulfed Debbie and rendered her helpless. She wondered if there would ever be a way out?

Debbie had hoped that Kurt or Chaim would call again despite the negative beginnings but they did not. Instead yet another candidate called to present himself for Debbie's affections. She fantasized what was hiding behind this personal ad. After the experiences she had had, anything was possible.

Ariel was from Haifa, a sabra, 41, an engineer, divorced with one child. He delivered all this information over the telephone in a very flippant tone as if he couldn't care less whether he met Debbie or not. He definitely refused to come "all the way" to Jerusalem so Debbie agreed to compromise and meet in Tel Aviv in front of a well known photography store. She rationalized his unwillingness to come to Jerusalem with the fact that Israelis do not like to travel long distances.

He was already waiting there when she arrived. To her dismay, he was quite a bit shorter than she with thinning straight blond hair and a very round, almost fat face. They went to a cafe and had coffee. They got immersed in a very interesting conversation and Debbie began to like him better as they talked. He seemed like a nice guy. The fountain of hope inside Debbie spurt forth again - a mistake she would always make.

He invited her to a party at his house that Friday night and thinking it would give her an opportunity to meet some singles in Haifa, she said she would be happy to come. Debbie made the trip to Haifa (distances were not a problem for her) and went to the party. There were about 25 people there, all of them arriving at various intervals during the evening. It was fair as far as house parties went. She danced with several men but they were all dull types. The girls were better, some even very attractive. Ariel danced with most of them.

Since it was too far to go back to Jerusalem and to save her the expense of a hotel, Ariel suggested she could spend the night in his apartment. If she wanted, she could use the guest room. She replied, yes and he said somewhat sarcastically, "Even if you wanted to sleep with me, I would be too tired." Later, as she thought back on that entire incident with him, she could remember again that distant and basically hostile "oh, I don't care" attitude all along the way.

The next morning, he was very brisk and efficient. "We'll clean up first and then have breakfast." He thrust a big soggy mop into her hand and a pail and commanded, "You do the living room and I'll do the kitchen." Debbie was somewhat taken aback at the way he pushed her to do it. Had he asked in a more polite manner, she wouldn't have minded. But he left her no choice. She was also hungry and accustomed to eating breakfast first in the morning before working. Nevertheless, she did it without complaining; after all, he had let her spend the night. He warned her to "be sure and look behind the couch, radiators, etc. for stray glasses. It's amazing where they will put them."

He worked quickly and so did she. Then they had breakfast during which he stated in a matter of fact way. "We will clean up some more, have lunch, then I'll take you to the Haifa Museum and then to the Central Bus Station. About 3:30 P.M. the buses will start running." She agreed looking forward to walking around with him in the museum. She didn't quite notice or perhaps she refused to see that he was "telling" her his plans not "asking" her if she wanted to participate or not.

During breakfast, he told her some more about himself. His ex-wife had been from England. He bragged, "I taught her everything when she first came to Israel" never quite defining what "everything" was but one could easily tell that he felt himself quite put out by the effort. "We were married eight years, have one son, then just like that, she met someone else and wanted a divorce. Now she lives with the other man and her child in Tel Aviv."

He related all this in the same kind of flip manner in which he had said everything else but Debbie could plainly see many open wounds which hurt very much and the volcanic rage that lay underneath the "I don't care" surface.

Then suddenly he changed the direction of the conversation and began discussing the idea of women working and going on for advanced education. He voiced a vehement opinion. "I really dislike women in the business word especially if they are in high positions. Women like this think only about themselves and don't concern themselves with their family."

Debbie tried to mention that there are women who manage both very well but he grew more agitated and she saw that this was truly a big problem with him. Then he started in on a triage against American women whom he obviously hated very much. He shouted in a very savage tone, "They're all a bunch of spoiled, egotistical brats and care only about the status of the man, nothing else." By this time it was not an exaggeration to say that he was foaming at the mouth. One cannot convince or even sway someone with feelings as intense as his. She tried to calm him but without success.

Apparently meeting with American Debbie had unleashed all his fury against his English ex-wife and unearthed some bad memories of other American girls. He told her the story of his first visit to New York where he had attended a discotheque which had been rented by a Jewish organization for the evening for Jewish singles. He related that the first thing girls would ask him was where he had gone to school. When he answered the "Technion" they had never heard of it or were not impressed. " All they want is a Harvard or Yale man." This night seemed to have been a harrowing experience for him. Debbie tried to explain and to present a different viewpoint but succeeded only in getting him into an argument.

Then he decided, "I'll fix lunch" which turned out to be some soup from a package. He seemed very surprised that Debbie did not recognize the soup. He devoured his very quickly almost as if she had not been there. He then proceeded to clear the plates just as fast barely allowing her to finish.

"And now I'm going to drive you to the Central Bus Station," he said sternly. Debbie was shocked and reminded him, "But it's only 12:30 P.M. and the buses don't start running till 3:30 or 4."

She didn't even bring up his earlier promise of a trip to the museum.

"I said I was going to take you to the Central Bus Station, so get ready," he thundered. Debbie understood that she best not argue any further.

On the drive down the Carmel Mountain, he said very little except, "Don't worry, this won't be the worst thing that ever happened to you." The beauty of the landscape, as they sped around and around the winding road leading to the foot of the mountain and to the Central Bus Station was a direct contrast to the ugly mood of the driver. Towering new buildings were perched on the slopes defying the rocky terrain. They seemed to stand alone against the wind bravely keeping watch over the big circular harbor and the glistening blue Mediterranean.

Debbie was not at all familiar with the Haifa Central Bus Station and when they arrived at the deserted station, she broke the silence that had developed between them and said almost to herself, "I hope it's safe to sit here for four hours,"

"It's just a few hours," was the cold matter of fact reply. He stopped the car at the front entrance, motioned for Debbie to get out and drove away.

It was unreal. Debbie couldn't believe what had happened. She sat down on the bench in one of the empty queues and looked around the huge bus station to see if there was anyone else there. Of course not, who would be in the Central Bus Station on the Sabbath at 1 P.M. with no buses operating?

She began to think about what had changed his mind. It seemed to be related to her not recognizing the soup or perhaps with the morning's discussion. He had unleased all his hostility toward his ex-wife, the girls in the disco and probably all the other women who had rejected him, on poor unsuspecting Debbie. He was full of hate and anger and Debbie became his powerless victim.

Well, Debbie was angry too. "I wonder if I am the only one who always winds up with guys like this. Or are all the men over

40 problematic? They are, after all, the leftovers, the rejects of the mating game. Or did the fault lie with the fact that I had met him through a personal ad?" Ah Debbie, maybe it was an unholy alliance of many factors all operating together to condemn a single woman over 30 to such a miserable fate!

These thoughts pounded her mind as she sat there dwarfed in the large empty hall with so many silent buses. She felt anonymous, alien, and alone. Suddenly, she was walking down the long empty corridors of Kennedy Airport on her very first tourist trip to Israel in the summer of 1978. She was late and everyone else had already boarded. She had been so young then, so eager, so naive. A three week United Tour to Israel - two weeks guided and one week on your own!

She had such a wonderful time that she stayed the entire summer. (of course, she lost her three week budget air fare ticket necessitating her loyal mother to dish out an additional $600 for El Al). But what is money when you are having the time of your life! For this is how Debbie interpreted it.

Compared to previous summers spent taking courses for that "30 plus" credits that would earn her more status and money, studying for comprehensive exams or taking a third foreign language, this was heaven. It was her first big trip so everything she saw and everything that happened or more importantly, everyone she met was glorified and magnified out of proportion. All of Israel wore a misty pale halo.

Debbie also had the unique quality of seeing and remembering only the positive elements in a situation and completely ignoring or forgetting the negative. Therefore, she had memories of that first trip to Israel which were unrealistic and not quite in keeping with what actually took place. She was a summer tourist in a rosy dream. Seeing only superficial realities, she failed to penetrate their true meaning.

The one thing that seemed to impress Debbie most on this momentous journey was how friendly, pleasant and eager to help everyone was. Everywhere she turned, people spoke to her with interest. If she looked puzzled even if only for a moment, someone would immediately jump out of the walls or so it seemed, approach and ask her if she needed any help. (Literally, this was the case; guys would often appear out of nowhere). Sometimes men would even run after her on the street asking her to "drink coffee with me." This was very new to Debbie, who being very shy, had never had a very active social life and lacked practical experience dealing with the opposite sex. It was also new to Debbie who was from New York where one wouldn't dare talk to a stranger and he not to you unless he had shady intentions. She still remembers one guy, Michael, who seemed to turn up everywhere and "just happened to run into her." And yet another, Ilan, also ubiquitous and ever asking her to join him in a cup of coffee.

One day, as she waited to cross on the corner of King George Street and Jaffa Road, two men came up on either side of Debbie to begin a conversation. She felt like a queen!

Like most tourists, Debbie was slow in picking up the real reason for their interest. She was in a heightened intensive period of trying to tour and having a good time so she was not given much to depth psychologizing of others' motivations.

She did not realize that most of the guys who approached were alas not so enamoured of Debbie's charms, many though they were, as they were of the possibility that through her they might "go to the States" - that magical place where the dollars flowed like waterfalls and where one did not have to work very hard, and where there was no compulsory military service. Debbie, like most Americans, took her citizenship for granted and having been imbued with the idea of *aliya* found it difficult to understand anyone interested in *yerida*. People were supposed to come to Israel, not leave it.

Yet Debbie's worst recollections were not of this type. While staying at the Great Shore Hotel in Tel Aviv, she was looking for a place to folk dance. After questioning the entire concierge, they finally relegated her to the bell hop who had at one time been a folk dancer, Eli Altoni.

Eli not only knew the place, a very good one in Jaffa, but offered to take her there. She was delighted but somewhat shocked when she discovered that the mode of transportation was to be by motor scooter. It was a little bit frightening as our heroine had never been on a motor scooter before but it was exciting to wizz through the streets of Tel Aviv into the artist's quarter in Jaffa to the WIZO building, on the rooftop of which would be the folk dancing.

It was a beautiful place outdoors with brightly colored lights around the side of the roof. The dancing was excellent. Debbie danced a lot with Eli and all in all had a wonderful time. The sultry languishing warmth of a summer night added to the effect. When it was all over, Eli invited Debbie to his place in Jaffa for "coffee." She went; after all, he was a nice Jewish boy. Little red riding hood rides again!

But there was much more of course than the proffered cup of coffee. Eli wanted to go to bed but Debbie had never been to bed with a man on a first date. And then it was not even a real date. Eli had just showed her where the folk dancing was. When she squeamed out of the situation Eli quite efficiently said he would call her a taxi. Riding back to her hotel in the taxi, Debbie felt badly and thought perhaps she had hurt his feelings. She asked the taxi to turn back. The driver was surprised at the request but did so. When she got there she rang the bell; Eli answered and said, "I knew you'd come back. They all do." Debbie was in such a turmoil that she did not notice this statement. She had hoped that they could be close in the big double bed but Eli coldly got a blanket and motioned that she could sleep on the couch. Debbie was hurt but spent the night on the couch.

For Debbie, Eli was something special - handsome, dark, very masculine of Indian origin with blue black curls worn in a bouffant style. What Debbie didn't know was that for Eli, she was just another tourist, one in a steady stream. He met many each day and whenever possible tried to seduce them. If they yielded, fine;

if they didn't, that was OK too. Debbie, a very sensitive girl continued to feel guilty and thinking she would try to smooth things over, talked with him in the hotel and asked for his address. When they had been together, he had mentioned the possibility of her coming again to his place and their spending more time together. So she happily made plans to visit him bringing along some candies and chocolates either for him or for the many nieces and nephews of which he had spoken. He told her Street #75 in Jaffa.

On one Saturday when she knew he would not have to work, Debbie set out for Jaffa in a taxi, telling the driver the address. She herself could not remember the way to his house, recalling only flying down innumerable dark labyrinthine streets and curving around many turns on the scooter. She could visualize only the poor one story cave houses on one side of the street where Eli lived and the row of new eight story apartment buildings with yellow panels on the other side.

The driver remarked that numbers for streets were no longer being used; all the streets had names now. The numbers were in use in the beginning days of the State. But Debbie insisted that a friend had given her this address so the driver persisted, asking again and again for street #75. She gave him a description of the yellow paneled buildings on the one side and he in turn related the description to several passersby. Debbie knew for sure it existed since she had been there loud and clear once upon a summer's night. She prodded the driver on. It was not a dream or fantasy!

Finally the driver stopped, exhausted and said he would go no further, at the same time pointing to the police station across the street, "You ask there; they know everything." By now the bill had reached $35, an enormous amount by Israeli standards and for 1978. Debbie paid.

She went in hesitantly, looked around and asked the secretary for information. She in turn called one of the men who spoke some English. Debbie related what had by this time become a saga and was assured again that numbered streets were in use a long time ago but now all the streets in Jaffa had names. Debbie, so trusting in the truth of what Eli had told her, clung to her childish faith. After all, had he not even written it down ? At that moment, a very good looking man with a powerful build enhanced by his uniform entered. He was smiling at Debbie, feasting his eyes on her, obviously delighted at what he saw. The man who had been advising Debbie turned to the newcomer and asked him in Hebrew about Street #75. The man who had entered was the captain of this unit, Itzhak Kadoni. Since he spoke little English, he motioned with his hand and head for her to go outside.

Once outside, he again jerked his head in the direction of a police van and nodded for her to get in. She got the message that he would willingly help her to find her destination, He drove around for awhile and asked a few times but nobody knew of the infamous Street #75. Then he turned off the main road and drove to the shore of the Mediterranean and stopped the van. "Beautiful," he managed to say gesturing toward the expanse of the sea. They got out of the van and walked for a while. It was pleasant and Debbie liked being with this tall handsome police captain. She almost began to forget about finding Street #75. They sat down on a bench and started to kiss. At first Debbie was somewhat anxious in a foreign country with a strange man on a lovely dark shore. But he soon made her forget her fears.

Afterwards, they drove through a squalid section of Jaffa. She saw poor huts, old people lingering about the steps, children in rags sitting in the middle of the dirt roads, still outside at this late hour. Apparently not many cars came to this area for everyone stared as they drove by. All had hungry big-eyed looks. At one point, the street was so narrow that Itzhak had difficulty in turning the van around. "Indian Jews," he said, "very poor. I show you because no tourists ever come here to see all of Israel." Before they departed, he gave Debbie his card from the office and they agreed to meet again.

Still she wondered about the elusive Street #75 and where it had disappeared. She went to the hotel to look for Eli but the senior bell hop said that Eli would not be on duty until the following evening. She thought of trying once again to find his house, this time perhaps with a more knowledgeable taxi driver. But the threat of repeated failure and the heavy cost of the taxi dissuaded her. She couldn't wait for the next evening to uncover the secret of Street #75.

Finally Eli arrived looking well as usual. Smiling, she said to him, "I came to visit you yesterday but couldn't find the way. I couldn't remember the streets we drove through that night; it was too dark to notice anything. Tell me, where is Street #75 anyway?"

He smiled knowingly and answered nonchalantly, "It doesn't exist. They used to use numbers but gave that up when they named the streets."

"Then why did you give me this address?" Debbie asked still puzzled.

"I thought you might come so I gave you that address to prevent you from finding me. I always give it to tourists. I don't want people to come. I want my peace and privacy so I need to protect myself."

Debbie was speechless! All that sweat and heartache to locate this fantasy address and it didn't even exist. He had given it to her on purpose. The enormity of this understanding was staggering to her. This incident would serve as the beginning of the education of Debbie Warshawsky.

For a few days, Debbie was still reeling from the blow she had received. Yet gradually the general positive atmosphere of a summer vacation and the adoring eyes of Itzhak helped her to put the escaped Eli into his proper place in the background.

She adopted the philosophy that the best way to forget a handsome bastard is to replace him with an even more handsome bastard.

She went riding about in Itzhak's police van which was a very exciting experience for her. Another police officer from his precinct also rode along, presumably Itzhak would drop him along the way. He knew so little English and she so little Hebrew that conversation and communication were almost non-existent. Then he drove into a very poor and dirty section of South Tel Aviv, near the Central Bus Station. It was virtually a slum and Debbie wondered if perhaps he hoped to apprehend a criminal there. But then he stopped the van, they got out and walked a short distance in an overgrown field and went into a small one story house. "Shack" might be a more accurate description of the run down dwelling which after an initial surprise, Debbie understood to be Itzhak's home. While they were eating, Itzhak, in his halting English, told Debbie that he was divorced and had a five year old daughter. A beautiful portrait of an angelic looking girl with golden hair was on the wall - perhaps the only outstanding feature in the otherwise bleak room.

Debbie felt uncomfortable in this strange apartment not knowing even where she was and wondered what his real intentions were. She noticed a woman's face cream and several other feminine items in the bathroom. Did he have a wife who was conveniently away or perhaps a live-in girl friend? Why had he asked her questions such as, "How much does a police captain earn in the United States? and other such inquiries into American life. Perhaps he too had his eye perked for an American tourist to take him to the Land of Plenty! Nevertheless, the evening eventually followed the same pattern as the one with Eli, although Itzhak proved to be more kind and easy-going.

As part of the organized tour Debbie had been on initially she went to visit a kibbutz in the northeastern part of Israel, a very popular and rich kibbutz with a beautiful guest house to which most tourist groups were taken. Debbie, as usual, was very enthusiastic and determined to see more of the kibbutz than the ordinary tourist film which they had shown the group. She wandered about and eventually struck up a conversation with one of the gardeners. She thought she was being very clever and sophisticated asking questions about kibbutz life and activities. He told her, "After I finish my work in the evening, I will give you a "special" tour of the kibbutz." Debbie was delighted and agreed to meet him.

He kept his promise and showed her the swimming pool where they sat for awhile, the children's house, living quarters, even the bomb shelter. While they were sitting by the pool, she heard something that sounded like shots in the distance and was informed that the kibbutz was near Lebanon and that what she heard were Arab soldiers practicing target shooting. It did not even occur to her to question the truth of his statements. Then he invited her in to his place for a soda and in order to see the average living quarters. Debbie went innocently oohing and aahing all the way, even when he pulled out the machine gun he had under his bed. "Most people have one in their houses," he explained. And then very matter of factly as though he were still talking about the machine gun, he told her that he wanted to go to bed with her, just like that as though that were his payment for the "special guided tour." When Debbie was surprised at his quick and brusque change and politely told him that she barely knew him, he said disdainfully, "OK, so you can go." Debbie was hurt by his curt dismissal of her; she had wanted to be friends.

She couldn't understand that if you didn't "give" immediately that was the end. She still had to learn this lesson and also an ever bigger one. Even if you *did* give, most likely it would still be the end. What she didn't realize once again, that in the tourist sites, people like the gardener found an endless flow of young Debbies. He would try each one in turn. If they went with him, fine; if not it was OK too. The next one would. Debbie was one of a thousand tourists who would come, spend their one day at the kibbutz and leave the next morning. She hoped to see the gardener at breakfast the following morning, and looked everywhere in the dining hall to see if she could catch a glimpse of him but he was nowhere to be found. After breakfast, her bus was scheduled to leave. Debbie quickly rushed to the grounds where she had met him but again she was disappointed. Just as quickly as men appeared in this exotic land, so did they disappear! Debbie was the last to board the tour bus. For the gardener, Debbie's departure passed unnoticed.

One of the things that Debbie looked forward to most on her tour of Israel was to go Israeli folk dancing in the *real* place. She had been Israeli dancing at the university and at the Jewish community center for about five years but surely that was nothing compared to dancing in Israel itself. Debbie would race through dinner in the hotel often foregoing several courses in order to rush to the folk dancing.

One night on the Mount Scopus campus of the Hebrew University, a young Israeli, about 35, asked her to dance. She was happy to do so, since he was tall, good looking and a very good dancer. At that time she did not yet know that it is the custom in Israel to dance with the same partner all evening. For example, if a man asks a girl for the first dance after they call out "*Zugot, zugot*" (Pairs, partners), he almost always stays with her for all the couple dances. This is in direct contrast to the custom in the United States where partners separate after each couple dance and seek new partners for the next dance.

In the United States, to stay with a partner even for two dances is to indicate considerable interest in that person. Even very close pairs do not stay together all night. Since Debbie was unaware of the difference in dance etiquette, she interpreted the young man's continuing to dance with her as genuine interest in her rather than merely as a routine practice. Although she was not particularly attracted to Arieh Atar, she found him interesting to talk to. He had been in the army for five years, had originally studied history but now decided that he could do more for Israel through legal means rather than through the military. He was just finishing his last year of law school and would soon take on a one year apprenticeship in the appellate court which was required for his final law degree. All this appealed to Debbie's idealism and her Jewish girl's heart began to throb. To her, he appeared as Hosea himself, fresh from the pages of the bible.

They got along very well and found that they had much to discuss. He was a vivacious energetic talker, his eyes wide awake at all times. After the dance, it seemed quite natural that they should continue this rapt conversation over a cup of coffee and since all the student canteens were closed at that hour, it also appeared quite natural that the cups of coffee would be prepared in the student dormitory kitchen and consumed in his room.

After they had exchanged some more brilliant conversation, he came over to the bed on which Debbie was sitting and started to put his arm around her. He began to fondle her and caress her shoulder, then slowly worked his way down her arm. He had been operating very nicely saying "Sweet nothings" into her all too willing ear when in the same tone and pitch, he murmured, "I think I should tell you that I have a wife and three children in Ashdod," Debbie wasn't sure if she heard correctly but she perked up after having been lulled somewhat by his deep undulating voice. She was taken aback and instinctively began to move away from him. "Are you kidding," she cried rather loudly to which he responded only with "shhhhh."

Debbie certainly didn't want or need a married man with three kids. She was annoyed too at having spent so much time with an ineligible man. Or perhaps she was also seething with fury that all attractive interesting men over 30 were already married. She said as politely and calmly as she could although she was raging inside. "Well I don't want to become involved with a married man so I'd better go." But it was past two and the buses had stopped running at 12 and it would even be difficult to find a taxi, assuming one could find a phone booth, (the only telephones at the time were in the basement of building 5) knew the number of a taxi service and had the necessary telephone tokens in their possession to make the call.

Debbie was stuck and had to spend the night in his small dormitory room. She slept unsoundly feeling out of place. In the morning he offered her a meager breakfast of coffee and corn flakes from the box. He was curt and cold and said he wished to study so she would have to leave immediately after eating. It was hard for her to believe that the harsh efficient snappy person eating on the other side of the small table was the same happy folk dancer, dedicated lawyer and smooth talker she had met the evening before. It was truly an amazing transformation. Debbie ate slowly hoping somehow that he would again become the nice person he had been but just the opposite occurred. He became increasingly impatient and annoyed that she was not eating as quickly as he. After it was over, he hurriedly rinsed the few dishes and made preparation to study.

A more sophisticated and clever lass would have made a beeline for the door but alas, our good-hearted Debbie who wanted everybody to love one another kept trying to reconcile an impossible situation.

"About last night," she began and he loudly interrupted yet trying to maintain some semblance of control, "Look, I want you to go now. I have work to do."

"But I just wanted to explain," Debbie wailed.

At this point, he lost control and started to scream. "There is nothing to explain. I have had enough of you." He stood up and towered over Debbie who stood speechless and transfigured in space like Lots' wife in the desert. "If you don't get out of here right now," he stormed, "I'm going to call the guard." He began to move towards her.

Hosea had become Cheribus, mad dog guarding his room like the entrance to the underworld. His movement towards her initiated a reflex action in Debbie to move back. She managed to turn around and run out She kept running without looking back and soon heard a loud slam of the door. She did not stop running until she was far away from the building. "Oh God," she panted, surprising even herself at the invocation since she wasn't quite sure if she believed in any higher being. The normality of the morning air and sunlight brought back a sense of reality and balance as though what had happened inside the tiny room was something out of a Kafka novel.

Debbie thought about this event for a long time. Here she was in the land of her people, where there were supposed to be all nice Jewish boys, so how could such a thing happen? How could he be so cruel, so unfeeling? One would think that events and incidents such as have been described would linger in Debbie's mind but as we have said in the beginning, Debbie had an uncanny quality to remember or at least to emphasize the positive and to blot out the negative elements of a situation. This was both a good quality and a bad one; good - because it enabled her to go on without becoming depressed and sad but bad - because she would continue to fall into similar hurting situations. She would repeat the same mistakes of being too trusting, too giving and too good. Nice girls like this, unwary and unsuspecting, fall an easy prey to guys out for a quick lay, a good time and a rite of passage abroad!

The bark of a stray dog transposed Debbie back into the pain of the present. By the time the buses came back to life at 4 P.M., she was very tired of the whole situation. She was convinced that there was no fate in the whole world worse than being single.

Quite naturally, after her recent experiences, Debbie hesitated to try another ad. Yet she kept hoping that someday one would be OK. But of course, they just keep getting worse as though that were possible. Unfortunately, each time she discovered that indeed, it was!

Although Debbie's social life left much to be desired, her professional life was improving. The chairman of the summer session at the Jerusalem University where Debbie had taught English the previous summer had been very pleased with her teaching. So much so that when the Director of Internal Development of the Bank of Israel, Boaz Sharir, called her and declared his interest in having an instructor from the university come to teach a few courses in the bank, she thought immediately of Debbie and called her. Debbie was delighted to accept since her job at the high school was only part time. It also sounded like a challenging new experience to teach in the central bank of Israel. It would be equal to teaching in the Federal Reserve Bank in the United States.

Debbie was happy to begin her job in the Bank of Israel.

It was only a few courses in business and technical English but the students were well motivated since they needed to know English on the job. The atmosphere was exciting and the pay excellent by Israeli standards. The new bank building was beautiful and spacious, a huge inverted pyramid and she felt important just to enter it. And with so many men working there, who knows, it might be an opportunity to meet that Special Someone.

One day Debbie ran into her boss by accident on Jaffa road. She thought it would be a good time to ask him about the ordering of texts to be used for her courses. It would be wise to order them now so they could arrive in time for the beginning of the classes. As she approached him and began to talk, Debbie noticed that he was very uncomfortable and squirmed around a lot. At first she didn't realize anything was wrong and continued to speak about the books. He started to look about him uneasily as though he had just committed a terrible crime. At that point, he looked so anxious and became so agitated that Debbie stopped talking. She truly thought he might be in the beginning stages of a grand mal seizure.

Finally, he managed to blurt out amid gasps, "We have time yet to discuss that. I must go." He sighed and turned about quickly as fast as his condition would let him. He walked toward one of the cars standing in the parked lane. In the parked car honking her horn sat a woman, obviously his wife and three children. She looked furious and he was petrified. He ran the latter part of the way to the car and hurriedly got in. She drove away.

Debbie watched the scene thinking how sad it was for him to be henpecked and yet marveling at the power she had over him. What a contrast to the relationships Debbie had with men where she was always the powerless one. She wondered why this was so but could not arrive at any answer. It was unusual for an Israeli to be so henpecked although he was part of the religious community where the women often dominated, especially those of European origin.

Debbie knew she had to be careful when associating with married men even in harmless innocent situations. One never suspected if an irate wife might not be lurking and looking nearby.

On the whole though married men in Israel seemed to be quite free. She noticed in the bank once she began teaching there that quite a few married men visited their "friends" regularly for a leisurely lunch. Office hours are much less rigidly kept than in the United States and it is not uncommon for one to disappear for a few hours.

One time when Debbie was folk dancing in a circle dance, a dark haired, good looking guy moved in next to her and said simply, "Do you want to go for coffee afterward?" By this time, Debbie had learned that "going for coffee" means "sex"". She answered that she had planned to stay for the advanced group. Then when they called out for "pairs", he chose another girl to dance with. How clever he was to pick up a "suitable" girl during the circle dances. How terrible it would be indeed if he selected a girl for the partner dances who would not go with him afterward. And then he would be stuck with her for the whole session. He didn't waste time; he checked first and made sure.

A few weeks later, Debbie saw this same dark haired folk dancer in the immigration office while she was renewing her visa. He was sitting on a crowded bench waiting in line for some reason. Debbie went over and said cheerily, "Hi, what are you doing here?"

He smiled sheepishly almost meekly. At the same time, the woman sitting next to him who was about seven months pregnant shot Debbie a severe dirty look, said something to him and intertwined her arm in his thereby telling Debbie and the whole world that this was her property!

In the *Jerusalem Post*, Debbie had seen an announcement for a singles party at the Triangle Hotel organized by an American psychologist, T. Gordon who had supposedly run successful singles parties at the Hotel New Yorker in New York. There was to be a lecture by a woman psychologist on "How to Find a Suitable Partner for Life." The entrance fee was $6. Debbie decided it was worth a try.

Alas, the Triangle Hotel was not the New Yorker and Jerusalem, the holy city of three faiths, was not New York. Debbie knew she had made a mistake the minute she paid her entrance fee. Had she been a more aggressive girl, she would have immediately taken a long look at the sparsely filled ballroom and the many heads with kippas that passively sat waiting for all the fun to begin. Instead, she stole a shy hopeful glance at the potential mates of the Promised

Land and let the six dollars slip into the hands of the ticket seller. She walked in slowly.

A large ballroom full of tables for eight greeted her. Here and there, a few brave souls sat huddled together. An old white haired man about 70 called out to her revealing several missing teeth, "Hey honey, over here, there's plenty of room," motioning her to join him and two other equally enticing friends. She smiled weakly and pretended to be looking for someone. She peered around and each alternative seemed worse than the next.

Finally, her searching eyes landed on a relatively young woman sitting by herself at one of the tables. Debbie asked, "May I sit here?" The woman, weighing about 300 pounds and wearing a bright red tafeta dress, nodded absent-mindedly. She sat almost motionless, like a Buddha in meditation. Debbie was relieved just to be sitting down and therefore to be less conspicuous. Why is it always so difficult to walk into a hall where there is a singles event? Since there were so few people present, the entrance of each additional person was viewed with great interest and hope that the evening might still be salvaged.

As she began to relax somewhat, Debbie sneaked a look around the room. What a motley crew! She had been to really bad singles events before but the souls assembled here seemed to be not only the bottom of the barrel but the barrel positively stripped of its insides and turned upside down. She saw at a glance that no one there was even worth talking with. The Saturday evening was already shot, however, she didn't have anywhere else to go and in Israel, $6 is a lot of money to waste. Debbie did not know that there were specific singles events for "religious" singles nor that the Triangle Hotel was a religious hotel.

She still harbored hopes that perhaps the lecture might be interesting but this too proved to be a disaster. All Dr. Gordon did was bemoan his losses of the evening. How he had paid so much to rent the ballroom and how he couldn't understand why his single events in Jerusalem were not successful. The lecture too was brief and contained the superficial how to do it recipes typical of such singles events. No depth psychology here.

Debbie thought of leaving but there was still the food spread out at the back of the ballroom apparently to be savored during the intermission. She might as well get her $6 worth, she rationalized. She kept her seat and watched the others as they headed back for the food thus hoping to make one more assessment of the men there. Fat, stodgy, slow moving and old. One small person struggled his way slowly in between the tables. He tottered now and then making grimaces of all types to accompany each step, not necessarily in harmony. "Oh my God," Debbie muttered to herself, "a man with cerebral palsy at a singles event." She felt pity for him and guilt at the same time at her own horror but this was really too much.

She was just preparing to leave when the old man who had called to her at the very beginning passed by and then suddenly stopped and sat down at one of the vacant chairs at her table.

"Where you from, honey," he asked, his eyes bright and leering, grinning again with his toothless mouth.

"Let's get some food, while it lasts" Debbie cried, leaping up and back to the long table at the end of the hall. There really wasn't much choice of food either, just coffee, some buns, a few cheeses, some raw vegetables and cheap wine. She filled her plate and went to sit down again.

The fat girl at her table who had scarcely spoken all evening although she was American and therefore, spoke English, had now come to life. She was busy gathering as much food as possible and piling it high on her plate. As Debbie started to choke down a cheese bum (she really didn't like eating anymore), Gordon, the organizer came over to her and began chatting. Soon it became clear that he wanted Debbie to help him advertise these events to her friends and to anyone she met.

"We all have to help to make these a success," he pronounced with a broad flashy confident smile. "Oh, I'm not staying very long," Debbie lied. The thought of any further contact with this group filled her with nausea. When he heard that, he walked away quickly looking for another prospective victim to help him with what was definitely an impossible task. Debbie could stand it no longer; she took her bag and hurried from the hotel.

She wanted to run also from her plight but from this there was no escape. She decided to walk home partially to sort out her thoughts and to clear her head of the hotel's atmosphere. Jaffa Road and King George Street were still swarming with people, mostly teenagers but even at this hour, couples with strollers could be seen parading their numerous offspring down the street. Sometimes it seemed to Debbie that Jerusalem was composed mainly of pregnant woman and strollers. There was some truth to this, of course, but in Debbie's mind, with its ever ticking biological clock, the impression was perhaps exaggerated especially on this particular pathetic evening. She was further than ever from her goal, which was to become one of those pregnant women with a stroller. The clock ticked loudly. When she got home, Debbie sat down on her bed and cried like she had not done in a long time.

CHAPTER 4
IN CIRCE'S CAVE

Because the room at Mrs. Levinsky's had become too small for her accumulated belongings, Debbie wanted to move into her own apartment. It was still difficult for her to find an apartment since she was not well enough acquainted with all the neighborhoods of Jerusalem to make the best decision. She was also not well enough versed on prices so landlords could quote fees that were beyond what the apartment was worth. Americans usually had to pay more than Israelis for the same flat and landlords preferred them because they would pay in dollars. Some landlords also required payment of rent as much as a year in advance; many wanted six months.

It was also difficult to find a place that was adequately furnished. Usually apartments had old furniture, old meaning beat-up, used and worn, not antique and even that was often sparse. Someone had warned her to always try the bed, advice she followed, and which often led her to reject the apartment. Finally, she rented a two room apartment which was scantily furnished for a price that was too high, but time was passing quickly. "I don't want to continue teaching and be running around the city searching for a place to live at the same time. It was hard enough hurting and hunting at the same time," she explained. In a way, the sparse, odd, and tired looking furniture of her new apartment echoed the meager and out of place furniture of her life.

After Debbie lived in this apartment for some time, she discovered another American girl from New York City living two floors above her on the other side. At first Debbie thought that Judy Parker might become a girl friend for her but then she learned that Judy was living with an Israeli guy. She was a pretty friendly type but kept her distance as every girl with a boy friend will do in the presence of a single girl without.

Slowly Debbie learned that Judy was a college graduate in

sociology and had been a graduate student for a short period, after which she spent several years as a California hippie. Now at 32, she had come to Israel determined this time to get her man. She had been in Israel for one year and had met Avi while waiting to have her bicycle repaired. He drove up to the same mechanics shop and the conversation about bicycles led to more.

Avi was only 27, a factor which bothered Judy somewhat, a Sabra from a large Iraqi family (8 brothers, 3 sisters). He had only a high school education and worked in a real estate office. He was quite good looking, well built and seemed like a really nice person. Debbie wondered how well they really communicated since his English was quite limited and Judy's Hebrew was equally sparse. However, she attended an intensive Ulpan and worked at her Hebrew eagerly, almost desperately, Debbie thought. They lived in a one room flat which was all they could afford. Judy didn't seem to mind. She was an easy going type of person, the kind that would always be ready to volunteer for something and to pitch in and help regardless of the situation. Debbie occasionally met them as they were coming or going. They always seemed to be very happy.

One day about a month after Debbie had made the great quest for an apartment, she was walking down King George Street, one of the main streets in Jerusalem and a tall man about 35 came running up after her.

"Hello," he boomed panting as he started to stride next to her. At first Debbie thought it was just one of the regular guys that did that to her on the street and ignored him. "Don't you remember me?" he continued looking at her intently. She looked and didn't recognize him; she kept walking. "You looked at my apartment and thought to rent it for this year on Aza Street, don't you remember?" he repeated.

Then the scene came back to her: a faded harried blond woman about 7 or 8 months pregnant, two little devils chasing each other around the small living room, toys cluttered everywhere and he trying hard to make it seem like a palace. Yes, now she remembered. "I decided not to take it," she explained, "because it was too far from the town center. I need to take a bus from there to the school where I teach."

"I understand. And where do you live now?" he questioned further.

"Oh, about three blocks from here. You see, it's close to everything here."

He was a good looking man, tall, dark hair with fair skin, a lawyer with a big office on one of the main streets of Jerusalem. Debbie had often passed by and seen the shingle hanging outside. Now he was again intently staring at her. She was not prepared for the next question and it took her awhile to comprehend it.

"May I visit you there?" he asked as non-chalantly and matter of factly as he had posed the other questions. Debbie looked for a minute and was silent. Then she stated nervously. "Well, I'm hardly ever home. I teach during the day and go out almost every night. so I don't see how it would be possible."

"OK," he whispered smiling. "I wish you luck here in Israel," and then he took off quickly.

Debbie felt some regret as she watched him hurry down the street but then she remembered the pregnant wife and the kids and thought, "No, I couldn't do that to anybody. If I were pregnant, I sure wouldn't want my husband with someone else." She dismissed him from her mind as being not very different from the many other although less important, guys that frequently stopped next to her on the street or on a street corner waiting for the light to change and asking the infamous question, "You want to drink coffee with me?" - the "drink coffee" of course translated as "going to bed." How long it took Debbie to learn that! It would take her even longer to realize that choice opportunities such as the one she just cast aside do not happen very often and that it could be a very pleasant and productive way to spend the time while waiting for Mr. Right (who may never come).

Although it was only part time, her teaching job was very demanding. It was in a large development town which had been established as housing for the many workers that had been brought to the area to toil in the automotive industry. There were problems of course, which were often reflected negatively in the students' behavior and attitudes. Yet Debbie was a good teacher and when she was in the classroom, she became more forceful and confident than she was in social situations. She had decided to give her "all" to these children and it was paying off in the positive response she got from them.

The chairman of the literature and language department was pleased and went out of his way to make her feel comfortable and at home in the school. Eventually he learned of her recent disappointment and tried to match her with one of his life long friends from Rumania, who was an engineer in the school. In Israel, everyone occasionally plays the role of matchmaker.

They were walking one day around the school grounds, Debbie thinking that he wanted to give her a tour and acquaint her with all the facilities. On the way to lunch, he mentioned he just wanted to stop by one of the offices. It turned out to be Eddie's. He asked Eddie to join them for lunch in the school cafeteria, an invitation he eagerly accepted. During the meal, they chatted about his work as engineer in the school and how many responsibilities it actually involved. Eddie was about 45, a tall good looking man in a rugged masculine way. His English was somewhat halting but he communicated well. Debbie would have liked him but she noticed that he was really just pushing the food around on his plate and when he said after they had finished that he had to return to work, Debbie saw that he had eaten virtually nothing.

She commented on this to the chairman and he just sighed and shrugged his shoulders. "He is always like that at this time of the year," he explained. "Why," Debbie said simply. "Well, his two sons were here for the summer and they just returned to Rumania. He had been married for many years to a Rumanian Gentile girl who came with him to Israel when he came on *aliya* 17 years earlier. They had two children; she had wanted to come to Israel and liked it here at first. Then the Yom Kippur War broke out in

1973. Eddie was called to go to the war leaving her alone with two small children. She had been very frightened not even knowing where Eddie was stationed and decided she didn't want her sons to also grow up and die for what was "not their business." She picked up a Rumanian tourist and went back to live with him eventually marrying him. Every summer, the two boys come to Israel and stay with Eddie. The only problem is that during this time he becomes very emotionally attached to them and after they leave, he always sinks into a deep depression."

It was a sad story and Debbie felt sorry for him understanding from her own experience how he must feel. She concluded, however, that this was not a person who was ready for another relationship. But she would be friendly and keep him very much in mind.

One day after her class, Debbie decided to go to Yeroham once again to visit her friend Eran Golan. She had not been there since the time that Marilyn came to tell her good news. It always made her feel good to see Eran since he was such an outgoing positive personality.

She planned to surprise him and just walk into his folk dance session. His eyes lit up as he suddenly saw her dancing in the crowd. But of course, he was busy teaching a few dances and playing the music so it was not until quite late in the session, when Debbie crept over to the stereo equipment and cooed, "When am I going to have the honor of dancing with you?" that he finally grabbed her, swung her around and leaped with her in the old familiar way.

As the dance neared its end, Debbie expected to leave with Eran. However, she noticed a chubby blond about 30 hanging around by the stereo as if waiting for something. When Debbie went over to Eran at the end as if to say "Are you coming. I'm ready" she again saw the blond standing there and realized she was waiting for Eran.

"Are you going with her?" Debbie whispered.

"Well," he answered hesitatingly, "but what will you do?"

"Oh, no bother," Debbie replied somewhat embarrassed. "I'll

just go to the Yeroham Hotel."

"Do you know where it is?"

"Sure, just a few blocks over. Don't worry. I know my way."

Eran seemed grateful to be relieved of having to make a choice and left with the blond who was by this time losing her patience.

Debbie headed over to the Yeroham Hotel somewhat disappointed at not being able to have Eran for herself. She entered the hotel and was already in the process of filling out the registration form when a young guy about 16 came running in. "Don't" he cried motioning with his hand that she should stop writing. Debbie looked confused.

"Don't" he repeated. "Don't stay here at the hotel. Come with me."

"Who are you?" Debbie quizzed although she recognized him as one of the folk dancers that had been at Eran's session.

"Eran sent me." he explained. "Come, you can stay with me. I live with my mother in a house not far from here. We have a place for you."

Debbie had stopped writing and considered him for a moment. He looked harmless enough - thin, pale, somewhat gawky in his manner. She believed him when he said that Eran had sent him. It seemed logical enough that he might have had guilt feelings at sending her off alone. After all, it was obvious that she had come to the folk dancing because of him. Also, she was pleased at not having to pay for the hotel. She decided to go with him. After all, this was Yeroham, not New York City and he was a folk dancer.

"OK," she said with a smile, "if you're sure you don't mind."

"Come on," he motioned and they left the hotel and went to his car. After a short drive, they did indeed arrive at a small stone house surrounded by a small plot of unkept overgrown greenery. They entered the house. A woman's voice said something in Hebrew. The young boy poked his head into one of the closed rooms ostensibly to explain the situation to his mother. After he did so, he motioned to Debbie, "Come" and led her to a small room with two small beds, standing opposite each other against the wall.

Debbie was disappointed to see she would have to sleep in the same room with him. Yet she reasoned with herself that a guest room was a luxury one didn't find in Israel. Anyway, it would only be for a short time.

He began to undress, eyeing Debbie appraisingly.

"Do you go to school here in Yeroham?" she asked trying to divert his attention.

"School" he shrieked with a flash of anger. "I'm a soldier in the Israeli army. Second year," he added emphatically.

"How old are you?" Debbie asked surprised because she had taken him for 16 or 17.

"19" he answered proudly baring his chest. "You like?" he continued expanding his thin bird like chest until she thought it would break.

"It's nice, huh, you want?"

Debbie smiled weakly not knowing quite how to handle the situation. She was already very tired and this was just an added nuisance.

"You know," he boasted, oblivious to the fact that Debbie was not even remotely interested. "For nice lady like you, I don't ask much."

At this point, Debbie grew suddenly awake again. She couldn't believe she had actually heard those words. She decided to play his game and chirped, "Really, how much is 'not much'?"

He thought for a moment, obviously in love with his own importance as a desirable male. His face was thin, bony even and it was an unhealthy pale framed by dirty blond hair, which hung limply and without style.

"Oh, for you, I do it for only $100."

Debbie laughed at the ridiculousness of his proposition but then stopped when she saw his eyes darken in extreme intensity and anger.

"Perhaps some other time, tonight I'm tired from dancing. Besides I'm not a rich lady like you suppose."

"$100 is not much," he argued.

Debbie lay down on the bed with her clothes on and closed her eyes wishing she were in a nice private room in the hotel.

Fortunately, he relented. "OK, if you don't want." He had begun to lie down when as if he suddenly remembered another argument, he jerked up, "Girls like me, they say I'm good."

Debbie sighed having thought that it was all over, "I'm sure you are," she soothed his bruised ego. "Another time I will find out." "OK, OK" he answered in a disgusted tone of voice and lay down again.

Debbie did not sleep much during the night. There was no heat and it was cold. She was grateful when morning came. He brought her coffee and some bread and by seven, he dropped her at a local bus station where she could catch a bus to the central bus station of Yeroham and then another to Jerusalem. It had been a long trip.

"Thanks a lot," she smiled. "I appreciate it," she lied.

He just made a motion with his head indicating acknowledgement and she was relieved when he drove off, thankful that things had ended as pleasantly as they had.

She called Eran that evening and told him the story. She thought that he would be surprised but he wasn't at all. She also did not receive the sympathy she had expected.

"Well, why shouldn't he try and get money," Eran argued. "Soldiers don't get paid much and he and his mother are poor people. Another girl might have taken him up on it." In the last statement, Debbie even detected a hint of chiding almost as if she had done something wrong by not paying $100 for him. "The American is always supposed to pay, I guess," she muttered to herself. "One Israeli male sticks up for another, I should have known."

"He said you had sent him into the hotel to get me, is that so?" Debbie added out loud.

Eran shook his head. "No, I didn't send him."

Again, Debbie was taken aback at the ease with which this puny devilish teenager had taken control of her. "I'll have to be really careful from now on," she promised herself gravely. "They will try anything here." The worst part was that in Israel, he would have received praise for being so clever and acting quickly to make the most of an opportunity.

After this incident, Debbie thought back to just a few weeks earlier to an American girl at folk dancing. One evening at the Hebrew University folk dancing session on Wednesday, her friend, Shoshi had brought over a young shy girl to where Debbie was sitting.

"I'm sure Debbie knows," Shoshi told the girl confidently. "She's a teacher and went to the university for many years. So she knows all about it."

Ever eager to help others, Debbie perked up and said, "What's the matter?" The American girl was quite awkward and sighed nervously as she sat down. She had never attended college so she felt somewhat out of place. "Well, I met this really wonderful Israeli guy and we really love each other very much. He's in his second year at the Hebrew University but he wants to finish his third year of law school in the United States. So we want to get married and then go there for awhile and then come back. Do you think he can do that, finish law school there?"

Debbie didn't know whether to laugh or groan at the ridiculousness of the idea. "Law school in the United States is three years in itself - *after* four years in the university proper. It would be totally impossible for anyone with only two years of university to be admitted to any law school, much less into the third year. Either you boy friend is grossly misinformed or he is pulling your leg."

"Why do you say that? He's a wonderful person. We're going to get married," Jody (such was her name) came to his defense.

Debbie winced at her naivete only to painfully remember in the not too distant past when she too would have believed such a story.

"It's not possible. And surely he must know that if he's inquired. The fact is that many guys want to go to the States and so marry an

American girl that they can get in easily and be able to stay. My advice would be to pretend like you have decided to stay in Israel. Emphasize how much you love it here, job, life, music, archeology, politics, religion, etc. and that you want to live your life here. It's so much more exciting, etc. etc. If he stays, he really loves you. If he disappears, then you know the truth. That's how I always test the fellows. It works. Most vanish immediately. They don't waste time."

Jody looked puzzled and hesitant. Debbie did not think she would have the courage to do it. But she was mistaken. When Debbie saw Shoshi again, she inquired about Jody and how she had fared in handling the situation. Shoshi related how the girl started to tell the guy about wanting to live in Israel and that she was interested in learning Hebrew, in getting a job, perhaps even becoming a student in the university eventually. "Well, you were right," she admitted.

"It was really sad. I felt sorry for her. I don't think she expected it. After she told him, he didn't say much but that same night at folk dancing, he didn't even look at her and started immediately to talk to another American girl. So he is just interested in going to the States."

"Yes, I knew in this case, I was right. First of all, an Israeli guy doesn't "fall madly in love" so quickly, if at all. She must be very inexperienced with men not to have recognized that. And then the business about finishing law school. Well, that was absurd. And he knew it. He must have thought she is very stupid.

"Yeah, probably," Shoshi sighed, "She really feels bad."

Debbie kept thinking about Jody and her shattered dream of real love. She estimated that situations like this must happen every day to innocent unsuspecting young American girls. Only most are too embarrassed to tell of their experiences, ashamed of the fact that they were gullible and stupid. And instead they boast of the "wonderful times" they had with the A-1 men. Debbie recalled the time when Shimon had told her of the Junior Year abroad student who had approached him with, "I'll bet you can do it five times"

Myths like this are easily perpetrated.

About a week later, Debbie met her Israeli friend, Aaron as she was sitting in a cafe on Ben Yehuda Street. He came along and sat down next to her.

"What kind of place is Ohio?" he asked abruptly with an intense look on his face although he tried to appear casual.

"Ohio?" Debbie sighed at the thought of such a question but in her typical trusting and literal way, proceeded to give an answer as though she were in a grammar school geography class. "Well, it's a very large state in the Mid West. It has several big cities but most is farm land and small towns." Then she began to analyze him more carefully, "Why do you want to know?"

Ignoring her question, he continued, "What kind of people live there? Rich people? Is it an interesting place?"

She repeated her question with the implied impression that no more information would be forthcoming if he did not answer. "Why the sudden interest in Ohio?"

"Well, a friend of mine, Sephardi like me, has a chance to get married and go there to live. He met a girl, you know, one of those "one-year program types"[*] and her parents will pay for his university and all. Her father's a judge and they live in a big house. But he's a little bit worried, you know, that if they pay for everything, they will also tell him what to do. And he's afraid of that. He doesn't know if he will like it there or not."

Debbie was shocked at the logical. rational way Aaron was dissecting the guy's offer. The fate of the girl in question was not even mentioned. Women obviously were meant to be used by men; they were willing vehicles through which the man could carve his destiny.

"What about the girl? Does he love her at all? Debbie cried exasperated.

Aaron looked baffled as though wondering why this should even be a consideration. It certainly hadn't occurred to him.

---

[*] Junior year abroad program at the Hebrew University in Jerusalem (for foreign students, very popular among Americans)

"Well, she's you know, the type that comes to the one year program. A typical American Jewish girl. They're all the same," Aaron explained laughing, obviously pleased with what he thought was an exact description.

"What?" Debbie screamed now. "What do you mean, they're all the same. How can you say something like that?"

"Well. you know," he added still smiling, "kind of this high, (he made a motion with his hand to indicate about 5 foot 3 inches) a little bit fat, dark curly hair, you know, they're all like this."

"They are not," Debbie screamed enunciating each word. "Every girl is different in looks and personality."

"Well, yeah, sure," Aaron agreed not really wanting to discuss this point. "So you think Ohio is OK for him?"

"I think he should decide if he really loves this girl and wants to be married to her. He will have to live with her." Debbie tried to emphasize the seriousness of the proposed step.

Aaron failed to grasp her point. "It's a real chance for him. If he stays here, he will not be able to go to the university and he will be nothing. But, it's nice in Ohio? he asked again.

Debbie saw that she would get nowhere with him. It was a different mentality, a different value system, a different way of thinking.

"I've never been to Ohio, just to pass through on my way elsewhere. If her father is a judge and they are Jewish, they probably live in one of the big cities. But I can't say for sure if you don't know the name of the place."

Aaron seemed satisfied with her answer. "Well, I'll tell him. He has to decide soon."

"Tell him to think carefully about it," Debbie tried once more to warn.

"Well, I think he will probably go. But thanks anyway." Aaron finished his coffee quickly and left Debbie sitting as he had found her. She felt oddly used, an information dishrag that had been squeezed dry.

After Aaron left, Debbie pondered his own situation. He

himself had never told her the story but she heard from a close friend of his that he had once been married to an American girl and lived for some time in New York City. Debbie wondered whether he also married her just to get into the United States. Since he lacked education and had no usable skills, her father had set him up in a business. However, in New York City, one must work very hard to make any business succeed and Aaron was not especially inclined towards hard work. Even in Israel, he held only part time and temporary jobs. Thus, in time, there was a divorce and Aaron returned to Israel. Every now and again he could be seen walking about with an American girl. Debbie concluded that he was probably also "looking." Perhaps he had even been asking for himself, not for a friend.

It should be mentioned, however, that sometimes women quite stupidly put themselves at risk. In other words, they are asking for trouble. Frequently, large ads for matrimony appear in the English language daily, the *Jerusalem Post* as well as in the Hebrew newspapers, such as: "Wealthy industrialist's daughter, 31, seeks Israeli for marriage. West Berlin," or "Divorcee,42+1, attractive, slim wishes to meet Israeli for life abroad. Oyster Bay, Long Island, New York."

There is no end to these tempting ads. Is it surprising that so many respond? There are also organizations offering matchmaking services specifically introducing Israelis to "foreign" visitors and to Jews living abroad. It is a very popular and widely used service among all ages.

Exploitation is by no means confined only to the male half of the species although it is most predominant there. Israeli women can also be predatory and the number of examples is increasing. One day as Debbie was waiting for a bus at the Central Bus Station in Jerusalem on her way to school, a young woman about 30 approached her.

"You are American, no?" she asked in a quick efficient manner. Debbie was so accustomed to this question that she no longer exhibited any kind of response when she heard it. "Can I ask you something?" she continued not waiting for Debbie to answer. "I want to go to the States. Can you tell me, it's easy to get a job?"

"Well," Debbie replied slowly not really interested, "it depends on what your profession is. What kind of work do you do?"

"I'm a masseuse," she said proudly.

Debbie was somewhat startled by this admission and didn't know how to reply.

"I work at the Marriott Hotel, in the Health Club," she went on.

Do you think I could get a job in the United States?"

"I suppose so, Debbie replied. "I don't know much about that."

"And what about American guys. I heard they are easy to get. Is that true? I could get one, yes?"

Now Debbie was flabbergasted. "The nerve of her" she fumed. "Coming to the United State to take our few eligible men away." It was true though, many Israeli girls have married American men and the number is increasing.

"No, it's not so easy as you think. Of course, some have but these are usually the Sephardic girls, Yemenites and Moroccans who attract the men because they are so different both in appearance and in behavior from the Ashkenazy women. You know, opposites attract. Since you are obviously Ashkenazy, it will not be so easy. There are plenty of Ashkenazy girls."

She seemed unconvinced as though she knew better, and smiled smugly.

"Oh, there's my bus. Thanks a lot." she rattled off quickly and ran.

Debbie's head whirled. There was so much to know, so much to watch out for. Whom could one trust? She turned her attention to her lesson plans for the day and began to review.

Debbie also made friends with other teachers in the school especially with two American women. One was Barbara Segal, the history teacher who was from Connecticut, single and had lived in Israel for five years. She was 31 and as they said "looking" - quite aggressively so.

Once the chairman asked Debbie, "Why do you always sit with Barbara in the dining room?"

"Well, we have a lot in common. We are about the same age and come from the same area. She's from Connecticut. Why?" Debbie asked.

"Well, she is well known among the men as, you know, "an easy lay." And if you are always seen with her, they may assume this about you also. For example, shortly after Miri Graetz left her husband, Bob Kaplan, Barbara made an unannounced visit to him asking him to go to the cinema with her. It seemed, however, she also wanted something more. Unfortunately, he did not like her and found her visit very intrusive. Well, you have to admit, she's not very attractive and she's somewhat overweight." he estimated as though he had been evaluating a product and was now rejecting it.

"I think that the men are misinterpreting Barbara's actions. You present her as a "bad girl" but possibly she is only desperate for a husband and in her panic gives men a false impression. I know she confided to me that she was very eager to marry because she wanted to have at least three children and she feels time is getting short." Debbie explained as best as she could without offending her boss.

It was true. Barbara was desperate. Debbie recalled how willingly she had been to share her ideas and tricks by which she hoped to meet and keep eligible men. One way she had discovered to do this was to be a volunteer for AACI in assisting new immigrants.

"That way," she informed, "you have first crack at the men and at a time when they are new and needful of you. They don't know anything and are very dependent on you and very grateful when you offer help and advice." She had rented a large apartment presumably for a good reason and often offered them a temporary place to stay while they were looking for their own place.

However, she told Debbie the story of a recent experience which had boomeranged on her. "I had been helping this new immigrant from England. I thought he was really nice so I said he could stay with me until he found a job. After a while, we became lovers and things seemed to be going well between us. I thought this time it would work out. I told my family and the situation had progressed so far that many of my relatives and friends were planning their vacations so they could come to my wedding."

"So, what happened," Debbie asked eagerly.

"Well, we had been living together for five months when I thought it was time to give him an ultimatum. I told him I felt uneasy about the way we were just living together and that I wanted to get married and make it legitimate. I made him the proposition that either we should get married or that he should find his own place to live. Much to my surprise and horror, he moved out the next day. I didn't expect it; I thought he liked me. My mother cried on the telephone when I told her the news. Well," she concluded, "some things blow up in your face."

It was doubtful whether this experience would prevent Barbara from attempting a similar stunt again but perhaps next time or the time after that, she would win.

The other woman she became friends with was an American from Florida by the name of Lisa Schultz, the school's only French teacher. At first Debbie assumed that Lisa was a married woman because there was always much mention of picking up kids from school and similar domestic concerns. As time went on, however, Debbie learned from others that she was a divorcee.

Lisa had come to Israel at the age of 26 after receiving her M.A. The job at the Bet Shemesh school had been her first and only job. She soon married another teacher also an American who taught at the Jerusalem University high school. It was like a fairy tale. They were thought to be an ideal couple and all seemed to be perfect.

She had one child, then another. Each time her mother would come from Florida to help out with the new baby. Finally, her parents decided to sell their home in Florida, her father gave up his business and with the money they purchased a large flat in Bet Shemesh and furnished it completely allowing also for the presence of the two grandchildren. Given the prices in Israel, this was financially depleting. Nevertheless, they were happy to be with their daughter, although they missed the Florida seashore and found the semi-arid climate of Bet Shemesh unpleasant. To add to the difficulties, her father was unable to succeed at beginning a new business since he did not know Hebrew and found it hard to accustom himself to the ways of the largely Sephardic population of the town. It was a culture shock for both parents. Yet if Lisa was happy, they were content also.

For about eight years, everything was wonderful. They got along well, the children were healthy, Lisa received tenure at the school, her parents were close by. Then she began to notice that her husband, Robert, was spending more and more time with his male friends. Since many of them were teachers, he explained this by saying that through their discussions about intellectual and pedagogical topics, he would often receive ideas about which to write and hopefully to publish as articles. Robert hoped in the future to be able to teach on the university level. Lisa was very busy teaching full time and caring for a household and two children, so she did not give it much thought.

Until one day, the storybook romance came to an end when Robert asked Lisa for a divorce. He wanted to move in with his lover, his male lover. Lisa was not prepared for such a shock; she had not even suspected. But then when she began to put all the pieces together - coming home late, frequent telephone calls, his frequent impotence. She had always worried about another woman. This was actually worse; she could not begin to compete. They were divorced, he moved in with his gay lover and became a gay activist - a phenomenon unheard of in Israel - at the time and unacceptable as well. He would go on television, radio, give lectures, everything to try to obtain legal and political rights for gays. This was of tremendous embarrassment for Lisa and she worried about the welfare of her children in school. Would the other children make fun and ask if their daddy was "queer?" Children could be so cruel. And this was how she lived from day to day. She once warned Debbie never to sell her apartment in New York. "Don't burn your bridges behind you."

Day to day life was also difficult for Debbie. Although she tried to use her work as a diversion, there were many days when she would slip back to her thoughts of "what was" and to feelings of guilt and regret. Pain lingered on her face, well dug into its trenches; hope fumbled to hold on.

To lift her spirits which had plummeted pretty low at this time and to try and get out of the rut she had fallen into, Debbie thought about becoming involved in some new and different activities. Folk dancing was fine but it involved too close a connection with Shimon, at any rate, in Jerusalem. Seeing the happy couple dancing together was too painful for her. And there was the problem of getting a partner without having to sign one's life away. This had been a big disappointment for her.

Israeli folk dancing in Israel was quite different from how it was in the States. The main difference lay not with the dances themselves. These tended to be essentially the same although most groups did not play the dances of the *yordim* - that is, those Israeli choreographers who had left Israel and were now residing in the United States. It was the values and attitudes surrounding the dancing that made it different. For example, one danced with the same partner all evening or at least for the duration of one session. Most persons also danced with the same partner week after week, month after month. In fact, some pairs had been together for years. Many were just "dancing partners" - not involved in any other way. Often they were dating or married to non-dancers. Of course, it occasionally happened that the dancing partnership evolved into something more.

This was contrary to the policy in the United States where one usually danced with a different partner and therefore had much more opportunity to meet and chat with many types of partners throughout the evening. Israeli folk dancing was a social event. Many individuals could be seen standing rings around the hall talking; some never even danced at all. The noise from all the chatter was sometimes greater than the music being played. Instruction in folk dancing was provided at the beginning of the evening although it was not considered very important except for beginners and was even avoided by the regular dancers.

In Israel, on the other hand, Debbie noted that teaching was very important. There was quiet in the room while the teacher demonstrated and at other times also. Folk dancing was not so much a social scene as a gymnastic one. People performed each dance almost compulsively as though it were all part of a series of ritualistic tribal dances. Few people could be seen standing about idle or merely talking; all were dancing.

Debbie did not like the Israeli atmosphere in folk dancing. The idea of having only one partner all night and each time one went to dance was ideal for those who had a partner whom they liked very much and for those who were not interested in meeting anyone or for those who really wanted to perfect a dancing style. For a newcomer who wanted to mix and mingle, it was lethal because there simply was no mixing and no mingling. Everyone was coupled off and the entire dance floor seemed to be sealed off like a frozen pond. The only people standing around were a few unfortunate women who did not get partners and usually they did not stay very long since it was almost useless to wait for anyone to become free. Or occasionally, there was a man or two who were already known to everyone as being "hopeless" dancers and that all one would gain from one of these would be mutilated feet.

To make matters worse, this led to a fierce competition for partners, all of course, to the male advantage. Almost always, there were more women than men. Since the men were at a premium, they had a choice and chose the youngest and prettiest they could get. Left by the sidelines then were the "older" women and those who were overweight. The interpretation of "older" depended on the individual group. In a university group, 30 could be considered older whereas in a community group, the over 40 year olds might be the out-group.

The women often devised ingenious ways to capture a partner away from another woman. One could look for a couple who were not yet cemented for life, perhaps a couple dancing together for the first time. Then when a "change partner" dance was played, the aggressive woman would enter the dance at the moment of change (even though technically, according to the dance, she was not supposed to) and take a man. Somewhere else in the circle, there would be a woman without a partner. Usually this was done so quickly and smoothly that the perpetrator went unnoticed. The unlucky woman without a partner was then alas deported to the sidelines.

The "change partner" dances were deadly and of course the women who had partners hated them because they ran the risk of losing their men. So one way to avoid this danger was simply not to change partners when it was time to do so. The women would say to their partner, "Let's not change," and then simply stay in place. It happened once to Debbie that her partner had moved on to the next girl and as she was about to smile to welcome the partner who should have moved on to her, she saw that he was staying with the girl he had. So Debbie stood there without a partner and soon found herself out of the dance.

Perhaps the fierce resistance to change and the desperate attempts to hold on to one's possession signals a characteristic of the Israeli mentality in general. It is a kind of insecurity that pervades the entire culture. It seems that since there is so much insecurity from the external political situation, Israelis seek to maintain a high level of security in internal domestic matters.

Another method that women without partners would use to gain this cherished object is simply to wait for a moment of weakness or hesitation in any one pair and then move in quickly and GRAB. That is literally what was done!

One evening Debbie had been dancing all evening with her partner. (needless to say, one must do *every* dance; one *dare* not take a break). Then a record came on to which she did not immediately recognize the music. She hesitated not more than a second before getting into position to see if she could pick up which dance it was going to be. This moment of hesitation cost her her partner. While she was intent on listening to the record amid the noise of the room, another woman moved close from behind and from the other side of her partner. She motioned only with a toss of her head indicating that she knew the dance and beckoning with him to join her. By the time Debbie recognized a different version of *Chen Zelo*, she was horrified to see her partner walking off with the new woman. By the time she could say anything, they were already dancing.

It should be explained that Israelis very often speak via head movements. These are so subtle and quick that outsiders are completely unaware that any communication has gone on. One of the most common is the toss of the head to the right or the left which means "Come on along." Still another which Debbie had encountered was the nodding of the head up and down. She had once asked someone to dance and he shook his head up and down yet didn't move from the place leaning against the wall. Debbie had misinterpreted his nod for an affirmative response and was bewildered when he refused to budge. Later she learned that this particular head movement signalled a negative answer. Quite often Israelis would also use the head to point to a specific place or object.

Debbie was no match for the clever, aggressive Israeli woman. Her beloved hobby of folk dancing had turned into a jungle where only the strongest and most clever survived. No one could ever miss a session. If one did, another girl would grab her partner and next time claim that he was HER partner.

Once Debbie spoke with a girl who was really very ill. When Debbie asked her why she didn't go home she seemed surprised at the question. "Oh, I would lose my partner," she answered matter of factly. Women without partners would even advertise in the "Personals" section of the newspaper. "Tall partner, 30+, for Israeli folk dance wanted, intermediate to advanced,for session at Tel Or

Mondays" would be a typical ad.

Debbie was disappointed because she had looked forward to doing Israeli folk dancing in Israel. Still she was determined to stick it out and see if she could snatch a partner.

The most difficult place of all was Shira's international folk dance group on Sunday night at the university because 95% of the dances played were couple dances. Debbie remembers with pain the very first time she went there, not knowing the system. The dance started like a typical international Balkan oriented group. The leader played several Rumanian circle dances. What Debbie did not know was that these few circle dances at the beginning were to be the only ones of the evening; the rest would be couple dances.

It was summer and the session had been moved to the gym. Debbie had sat down on the first row of the bleachers, not knowing one of the Rumanian dances. Then after this, Shira played a waltz type couple dance. Debbie saw a young man about 30 begin crossing the gym and heading in her direction. Suddenly she heard loud thuds behind her as if heavy crates were being dropped on the benches. Before she knew what happened, Debbie saw the girl take the arm of this young man, shout "Let's dance" (in Hebrew) and lead him out to the dance floor. The girl must have seen the man moving in Debbie's direction, stalked her prey and then quickly jumped down from a high place in the bleachers to capture the desired object.

Debbie was really surprised. "She must want to dance with him very much," she concluded. "Well maybe I will have someone for the next dance." Yet when the next dance was played, it was another partner dance. No one moved! Everyone stayed with the same partner. It soon dawned on poor Debbie that this was how it would be all night. Everyone had grabbed their partner and she was without! Of course then she understood why the jumper had been so desperate to snare the fellow who had intended to ask her. If one does not succeed in securing a partner for the very first partner dance, she will sit all night. In this particular group, the dancing was on a very high level but extremely regimented. Everyone did every dance like clockwork. Debbie would have to find a group that she liked - and a partner - or choose another activity!

She discovered that there are English language poetry groups that meet in every major city in the country. They vary in size and in the quality of talent but the atmosphere is usually an intellectual and friendly one. The meetings are held once a month at one of the member's house or apartment. Everyone reads a maximum of three poems orally (copies of which he has distributed among the members) and then receives comments, positive or negative, from any individual in the circle. To join is simple. One pays a minimal fee of approximately $15 per year to the organizer in Haifa and then receives a monthly newsletter about the time and place of the meetings, recent publications or prizes won by members and names of journals which might be receptive to the writings of group members.

Debbie was somewhat apprehensive as she went to her first meeting, three of her very best poems in hand. There were about 25 people packed into the living room of one of the members. The ages and cultural backgrounds varied greatly but this seemed to add to the total wisdom of the group. There were a few girls in their 20's, many in their 30's and 40's and several older women over 50. Most were American with a sprinkling of English and South African immigrants. Quite a few of the older women were of German and Austrian origin and wrote in their native language as well as in English.

Many had university degrees and held professional jobs.

Debbie noted immediately, to her dismay, that there were only a few men, most in the older age group. There was one younger Israeli poet, who did translations for the group but of course, he was married. One evening, a visitor came from Beersheva who was approximately 45 and divorced but during the intermission he made a beeline for the pretty one in her twenties. Debbie rationalized that she had come for intellectual stimulation and critical commentary, not for match-making.

Debbie was introduced and read her poems which seemed to be well accepted. She was a talented poet and quite possibly could have been truly outstanding had she devoted more time and energy solely to this one activity. Gradually she made friends with one of the English girls who was also single, in her late thirties and had a pretty daughter of 10. Debbie began to attend regularly and enjoyed the meetings immensely. She always felt better and more energetic after having spent several hours with this small close knit group of English speaking writers living in a culturally different environment and constantly surrounded by a harsh and difficult language.

Debbie also ventured to try another new activity - Bridge.

She had noticed from advertisements and flyers that there were several bridge clubs in Jerusalem, one meeting once a week at the Hebrew University, another in a 5 star hotel and a third at a community center or *mercaz*. One evening Debbie stayed late at the university library and then peeked into the hall where they were playing duplicate bridge. She looked around the room quickly and liked what she saw. There were more than one hundred people there, they looked very serious and seemed to be deeply involved in what they were doing.

Most of the people were in their fifties or more but a good percentage were still in their late thirties. Debbie also knew that this game attracted very intelligent people since it was difficult and required much concentration and cleverness, The people she observed looked like a nice group of people - the kind she would want to meet.

Debbie decided to enroll in a beginner course for bridge at the YMCA. She liked the course very much; it was interesting and there was a good teacher. Yet she found she had much difficulty in concentrating on the game and each player's bid and move - a crucial factor in the game. As the other players went their turn, Debbie's mind began to wander to thoughts about Shimon and the other problems in her life. The effort to figure out who had the Ace of Clubs or the Queen of Diamonds or to remember if the King of Hearts and the Jack of Spades had gone out, was just too great and somehow it didn't really seem important at all. She even found it surprising that people could become so excited over these things. She continued in the course because she had paid a large sum of money and she thought perhaps things would get easier as time went on.

Only they didn't! Debbie just couldn't concentrate more than five minutes on bidding rules in bridge. She felt embarrassed and thought she must look like an idiot to the rest of the group. However, she persevered and finished the course eventually learning the game even if she still had far to go to develop expertise. She had to recognize the extent to which her recent emotional upheaval had affected her general well being.

Then when she attempted to join the organized groups, she was told no openings existed and if so each "table" (group of four players) was looking for an experienced player, not a beginner. Since bridge depended on partnership, naturally no one wanted to be at a disadvantage by being paired with someone who had just learned the game. Debbie was so disappointed.

"How am I supposed to get "experience", she cried, "if no one will accept me into their group?" At one place, the leader suggested she join a private group and get experience there. "Very often a member quits and the other three are looking for a fourth. Occasionally, there are notices up on the bulletin board at the faculty club," he advised her. She knew what he said was true because one of the girls from England in her course had learned bridge just because her boy friend was into it and wanted her to play with him and his friends.

But somehow to search for such a group seemed too much of a chore for Debbie now. She was busy at the school and finally had the honesty to admit to herself that she didn't really like bridge at all. It was the kind of activity one really has to be crazy about and to do it several times a week. Since she had a job that required a lot of concentration, she decided that her recreational activity should not also be of the same type. What she needed was a physical activity like folk dancing had been. Yes, she thought, folk dancing, that was what she really loved. She had stopped going lately because she was afraid of running into Shimon and Dorrit. "Why not attend groups that were further away from Jerusalem?" she argued with herself. "Sure it would take time but I could see different faces, meet new people. What more perfect place than Weizmann Institute in Rehovot; they have an excellent group there on Wednesdays."

It was a long trip by bus from Jerusalem to Rehovot, although the two places were not far apart. A direct bus operated only twice a day at 10 A.M. and 5 P.M. So Debbie had to first go to Tel Aviv, then take another bus to Rehovot - about one and a half hours each way. Coming back, the trip was even more difficult. She would have to catch the last bus to Tel Aviv at 11:20 P.M. then take a sherut to Jerusalem. Yet Debbie did not mind or even notice the time and hardship involved. It might prove to be a very sound investment! There was hope for her.

The first time Debbie went, the group still met outdoors in the area of the swimming pool and tennis courts. The guards at the gates advised her she would have difficulty in finding the place in the dark if she was not acquainted with the institute grounds, She could wait at the gate until a car drove up which was going in that direction. None came quickly so one of the guards offered to take her in his van.

Debbie saw that it was quite a distance and that several streets inside forked in different directions. He dropped her in front of the entrance to the sport area. She thanked him and went inside.

It was a beautiful place. A large swimming pool surrounded by green grass dotted with white lawn chairs and cots greeted her. As she walked past the pool, she heard folk dance music coming from beyond the tennis courts. She naturally chose the route which seemed to be the most direct one to the music. But just as Odysseus was tempted by the beautiful music of the Sirens and would have fallen prey to their beguiling charms, had not one of his men tied him to the mast, so too Debbie, in her eagerness to embrace the bewitching music suddenly felt the earth give way under her.

While walking in a very dark area, she had stepped forward

and much to her shock there was nothing but air and then the hard impact of the concrete pavement. She heard herself screaming. She lay still for awhile not certain if she was in one piece. A young man came running from the tennis courts, having heard her screams.

"Are you alright?" he asked in Hebrew. She understood that much, thought for a second and nodded. She had broken only her new glasses and skinned her left knee. "Wow" she exclaimed, "somebody should put a light here. That's quite a height."

"There was one," he said guiltily, pointing up at the wire" but it burned out. Where are you going anyway?"

"To the folk dancing," she replied breathless from her shock.

"Well," he answered again pointing, "You have to get there on the path over on that side.

"Oh, she started to explain, it's my first time here."

"Come on, I'm going to meet someone there anyway. I'll show you the right way," he smiled good naturedly.

They started to walk. "Are you sure you're OK?" he asked again. "That was quite a fall."

"It was the fright of suddenly not having anything under my feet more than anything else," she observed. Then they began to chat. He asked the usual things, where she was from, how long she was staying, if she worked at the institute and so on.

Debbie, having recovered completely now from her traumatic fall began to look more curiously at her brave rescuer. "My God," the thought cometed through her mind, "he's absolutely gorgeous."

His name was Toby and he was about 35, tall, with an athletic build crowned with the most magnificent head of hair she had ever seen. A mass of thick long curls the color of burnt crimson hung over, almost hiding an equally handsome face, friendly smile and blanched white skin with the usual freckles common to natural redheads. Deep set sleepy blue eyes peered out sheepishly from under the hair. Certainly such a face would make the heart of any young girl flutter and Debbie was no exception. She became acutely aware of his presence as a man as they walked down the dark path to the folk dancing area.

Finally they arrived at the stagelike area where approximately 150 people were actively dancing. She planned to ask him to dance with her and was more than willing to show him how, When they put on a very slow melodic couple dance, Debbie asked cheerily, "Come, let's give it a try."

"Oh, no," he retorted quickly and defensively, actually moving away from her, "I never dance. I don't like it at all."

"It's really much easier than it looks. Everything just repeats. I will lead you." Debbie tried to sound encouraging.

"No, please, I really hate it," he said more strongly now and cringing away.

Then suddenly, while Debbie was trying to pull him into the ring, a frail, bony, washed out looking blond girl broke away from her dancing partner and darted over to where Debbie and Toby were talking. She had a hawklike look and a commanding air. Ignoring Debbie, she spoke directly to Toby. Although Debbie did not catch the Hebrew, she could tell that this thin haggard girl had tremendous power over her rescuer and she soon learned that this power was called "Wife."

After she had defiantly established her "claim," like Pluto guarding the entrance to the underworld, she gracefully pranced back to her partner and continued dancing. Debbie watched thinking that she was definitely one of the best dancers in the group. It was obvious that they were unevenly matched, she being the stronger of the two. Debbie knew that he had a large ring through his nose and that this girl was the bearer of the sole key. And of course, she mused further, she should have expected that a good looking, well educated and intelligent scientist like Toby would be married. All the good ones are married, how true, she thought to herself remembering the title of an interesting book she had recently read.

Debbie decided to dance since after all, she had come a long distance to do so. At the same time she looked over the crowd. They were older than the university group she had been used to. She soon discovered that most of the people were unfortunately not connected with the Weizmann Institute. The folk dancing was open to the public and most came from the outside. A few were from the institute but they were firmly lassoed by their spouses.

Debbie should have known better than to think that the scientists of Weizmann Institute would be folk dancers. When she decided to leave, she again sought the help of Toby and inquired where she could find the bus to Tel Aviv. His wife was also ready to leave and they said they would show Debbie where it was.

The three walked together to the main gate of the institute. They looked at the different signposts for the correct one. The wife went to investigate one of the far distant bus shelters thinking that was the one for Tel Aviv. While she was gone, Toby used the opportunity to invite Debbie to come and visit him. He pointed to the building saying, "That's where we live, apartment 28. Come in the morning and visit me. Corinne goes to work in Tel Aviv at 8 and I don't usually go to the lab until 10." He smiled with his smouldering eyes.

Debbie laughed nervously trying not to show how surprised, even shocked, she was. By this time, Corinne had come back with the information that the place she had selected was indeed the correct station for Tel Aviv. In the meantime, Debbie and Toby had gotten into a discussion on the nature of creativity and how the essential process was the same for both scientific and artistic creativity. It would have been a fascinating discussion, had Corinne not intruded with her scowling eyes and shrieking high pitched voice.

"Science, science, science, that's all you ever talk about." she shouted. Toby looked crushed and laughed as though it had been a joke but it was clear that this was a typical attitude on her part. His seeming hunger for conversation even at 11:30 P.M. and his aggressive but perhaps really desperate, invitation now became more understandable. Corinne started to walk away in the direction of their apartment with a sigh of exasperation. Toby, with a look of resignation, tagged along after her but not before he again turned to Debbie and whispered, "You know where I am - 28."

Although it was a long and difficult trip, Debbie was firm in her resolve to continue going to the folk dance group at Weizmann. She hoped that as she got to know the people better, some of them would turn out to be brilliant physicists or biochemists actively engaged in life-saving research. The heart and mind of a 33 year old American Jewish girl searching for a mate have an infinite capacity for such virtues as faith, hope, perseverance and long suffering. Reality, no matter how convincing and obvious, often has difficulty in changing this viewpoint.

Instead of meeting the men of Weizmann Institute, however, Debbie was to encounter the women. On her very second time at the folk dancing, a string of four women about age 40, approached her, one of them obviously being the leader, the others following her. It was immediately evident that this was not to be a welcoming committee. They all looked at her with a mixture of anger, anxiety and hostility.

"Are you here again?" the leader harped in a tone of disbelief. "You come all the way from Jerusalem?" the second one added before Debbie had a chance to answer. She noted that they were all plain and dumpy looking. They stared at her glaringly and came very close almost as if to block her way onto the dance floor.

"Why?" the first one continued in a loud bossy voice. At first Debbie had remained silent having been surprised at the attack. But now, she surged with self confidence and totally disregarding them all, she pushed between the two who were physically barring her from the dance floor. She broke into a forward dance leap and shouted with an abandoned haughty toss of her thick hair, "To dance, of course." From there she moved into the dance circle itself with wide sweeps of her arms and legs in "At va Ani" (You and I). She made a special effort to be graceful and sexy.

Yet as far as groups went, this one was similar to all others she had attended. It also followed the pattern of circle dances first, then an hour of partner dances. And as everywhere else, people were partnered off for all eternity. Debbie thought herself lucky to get a partner in this group where there seemed to be many married couples. He was tall, fairly good looking, and danced well. They danced together for the first session from 8 to 10 P.M.

But then, unexpectedly for Debbie, came the payoff (although she should have known by this time). He asked her to "come for coffee." She said in as pleasant a way as possible that she would like to but she had come such a great distance for this group, she really wanted to stay also for the second session. He tried to convince her otherwise but Debbie remained firm. He left and need we add that the following week he sought someone else to be his partner.

"What a racket the men have," Debbie muttered to herself. "They exploit the lack of partners to their advantage." He had probably approached Debbie because she was a newcomer and hence would not realize what type he was or that he was a heavy drinker. She saw little chance of securing either a dancing or marriage partner and began to doubt the wisdom of continuing to attend this group.

One evening at the folk dancing, Debbie had been listening to a conversation between two very young Sephardic types. She understood that one of them lived in Tel Aviv. In the United States, it was perfectly natural among folk dancers to give one another lifts. The bond among folk dancers was strong and Debbie assumed this to be true also in Israel. One should never assume anything, especially in Israel. So she asked the one who apparently lived in Tel Aviv if he would mind giving her a ride when the dance was over. He agreed casually, not however, making too firm a commitment and Debbie was not certain whether or not she could rely on him.

The last bus had long left, nevertheless, and she was dependent on him. She had to continue to search for him in the crowd since she was afraid he might leave without her. This is exactly what would have happened if Debbie had not kept such a close eye on his whereabouts. He was about to leave and Debbie ran after him reminding him of his promise to give her a ride. "Oh yeah, that's right," he remembered, "OK, let's go."

Debbie had been told many times that Israelis make many promises but unlike Americans, take them very lightly and think nothing of the fact when they ignore or forget about them. One of the reasons for this is that there are so many problems and difficulties in the daily lives of people that only the most urgent and important occupy their minds and attention. Anything less so is easily dismissed.

He was average height, very thin and dark, about 22 although he looked even younger. They got into the car and drove towards Tel Aviv, about a half hours ride away. At first they talked about different folk dance groups but then as they drove further away from the towns, Rehovot, Rishon Lezion and out into the wide open country area, he began to look at Debbie with interest.

He would look ahead at the dark road and then he would stare at her for just a few seconds too long. Debbie became uncomfortable and continued to talk about anything just to keep his mind occupied. Then suddenly he said, "I'm going to stop over here" and he slowed the car down. "We can go into the woods."

"Oh no," Debbie cried, "not here."

"Why not, it's nice," he argued.

Debbie began to panic because she saw he was really serious. The thought of going with him into that dark woods filled her with real dread. She looked at his thin body and estimated that she might be able to fight him off. But then remembered that he had had three years of Israeli army training and probably knew all kinds of combat fighting tricks against which she would be helpless.

"It's awfully late. I have all the way to Jerusalem to go," she said as convincingly as she could. "Maybe some other time."

"No," he stated matter of factly, "it won't take long." He was silent for a few minutes and Debbie hoped that he might have changed his mind. But again suddenly, he looked and said, "Here is a good place" and started to slow down the car and swerve somewhat off the road.

"I don't want to," Debbie told him firmly but with a slight smile.

"Why not, it's nice," he said again with his simple English and equally simple logic.

Then Debbie thought of a different strategy. "Well," she

debated. "I can't understand why *you* would want to - with me. Surely someone like you must have plenty of beautiful girl friends, dark exotic Yemenite girls" and she made a few Yemenite hand gestures to try and convince him.

She made her voice sound as pleasant and logical as possible and it seemed to have its effect. At least he was still driving. "Or maybe you have a steady girlfriend?" she inquired hoping to keep him talking.

"Oh, I have three," he boasted, "one in Rishon, and two in Tel Aviv."

"Don't they get jealous of one another?" Debbie asked as if it were the most interesting thing in the world.

"Oh, they don't know one about the other."

"They must be very beautiful" Debbie commented as if only beautiful were suitable for him.

"Oh, sure, of course," he answered. "But still, you know, you always think, maybe with American, maybe it will be different."

"Oh no," Debbie tried to laugh matter of factly, "A hole is a hole. Every girl is the same."

He looked somewhat satisfied for the minute, then suddenly changed his mind and again began to search the road for a good place to stop. "Yeah, I guess," he agreed, the darkness flashing from his eyes, "But I just want to try anyway."

Debbie grew exasperated and tried still another way to ward him off. "But oh, I don't see at all why you would want me," she argued. After all, I'm old enough to be your mother. See, I have so many gray hairs already." She pointed to some light strands in her hair which in the dark could have been almost any color. "You don't want to fuck your own mother, do you? she questioned him in a tone and language that would be easy for him to understand.

He turned to her with a look of horror. "Oh no, of course not," he exclaimed.

"Well, that's exactly what it would be," she declared.

"Well, yeah, I guess so." He finally seemed convinced and continued to drive. Debbie sighed and relaxed for the first time since she got into the car.

But this respite was also to be short lived. They were nearing Tel Aviv and he said, "I will leave you at the Holon - Tel Aviv Junction because I am going to Holon and so I do not enter the city center. You can go from there by foot or take a taxi."

Debbie couldn't believe it. The thought of standing on this dark deserted highway crossroads at 12:30 A.M. and of walking down the dark highway to Tel Aviv was more than she could bear. "But you said you were going to Tel Aviv," she cried almost hysterically. "I am," he answered. "Holon is Tel Aviv."

"No, it isn't," Debbie argued, "It's a suburb." He didn't understand this word and just shrugged his shoulders.

"Please take me to Tel Aviv. It's not safe for a girl alone on that road." Debbie pleaded.

"But it will take an extra half an hour if I have to go into the city."

"OK, Debbie answered trying to keep calm although her anxiety was increasing with every moment, "I'll make it worth your while, I will give you $10."

He didn't say anything for awhile and then they were coming close to the junction. Debbie wondered what he would do but was afraid to ask. Debbie saw huge signs in Hebrew and English, "Holon, straight ahead, Tel Aviv - turn right."

"See, this is the way to Holon," he pointed and then began to swing the car into the right lane in preparation for a right turn.

He drove fast down the straight road leading to the main city of Tel Aviv and Debbie dared to relax again. Soon they reached the Central Bus Station where Debbie could get a sherut to Jerusalem. He left her at the edge of the big complex because traffic regulations did not permit him to enter the main part. She thanked him for going out of his way and offered him the $10. "Oh, no. I don't want it." No matter how hard she tried to give him the money, he adamantly refused to take it. "Good night," he said apparently glad to be rid of her and drove off. She never saw him again.

The next day in a calmer moment, Debbie thought back to the

previous night's adventure and concluded that she had been lucky indeed. Actually, the guy had been a fairly primitive, but not a mean person. She decided that she would not return to dance. It was too difficult a trip and the chances of meeting someone suitable were minimal.

Not long thereafter, Debbie thought of all the people she had met at Weizmann Institute and recalled meeting Mikhail Galin at the university. She had not seen him since that initial meeting on the campus grass and had dismissed him from her mind when she saw him meet the other tourist. But then during the summer, she had received an unexpected tourist card from him from southern France. Why he had sent it she didn't know but thought he probably wanted to maintain connections with all Americans, no matter how tenuous they might have been.

Now she thought about him again. "Perhaps I will go to Weizmann and venture to see him. I could make the pretence of visiting someone else and say I wanted to drop in and say hello and thank him for the card, ask how was his vacation and so forth. Who knows through him, I might be able to meet other scientists at the institute." For Debbie anything and everything was worth a try!

As soon as she could manage an entire afternoon free, Debbie trotted over to Weizmann Institute and "just happened" to be walking past the Physics Building. She went inside and after some inquiring, located the office of Dr. Galin.

He was sitting in his office writing when she poked her head in the door. He remembered her, of course, and greeted her warmly. She thanked him for the card and they chatted first about his European trip and then about her activities since they had met that day on the campus of the Hebrew University.

Then he asked her, "Have you seen the Weizmann House?"

"No," she lied since she had seen it briefly on an organized tour years earlier.

"Let's take a walk back there. It's a very beautiful area," he invited. So they went stopping here and there to admire a sculpture or pay homage to a grave. Finally they came to the house itself, a large white old fashioned type house surrounded by a neat lawn and professional gardening.

However, as one walked some distance from the house, the landscape seemed to be less cared for. The shrubbery became wild and unruly, the trees dense and thick. On the ground heavy and cluttered lay the fallen leaves of the season. It was a direct contrast to the well kept appearance of the house. In fact, it was even difficult to walk in this part and Debbie's high heels were certainly not the best footwear for such a thriving thicket. She couldn't understand why Mikhail was leading her more and more in this direction away from the house.

When they were some distance from the house but still in full view of it, he stopped rather suddenly and with a very firm movement turned to kiss Debbie very passionately. She was taken off guard and at first resisted but then yielded to the urgent pressure of his body.

They kissed and embraced for awhile and then he pulled her down on the ground. It was hard and dirty and Debbie was uncomfortable; it was hardly an idyllic place for lovemaking. He began to loosen his belt and undo his pants and she realized what he was intending to do.

"Oh no, not here, in front of the Weizmann House," Debbie exclaimed.

"Why not," he snapped. "No one will come."

"Tourist groups often come back here," she argued, "and besides we are in full view of the house. Mrs. Weizmann could even be looking out." She tried to say all this playfully but he wasn't listening and continued to embrace her aggressively. Debbie struggled to be free and finally succeeded in pushing him away. He was angry and kept insisting that no one would see them. Yet Debbie was firm that this was not the proper place for a love tryst. She had too much respect for a scientific institute to defile its grounds in such a cheap way.

When he saw that there was no chance of seducing Debbie

Warshawsky on the fallen fall leaves of the Weizmann Estate, he decided to end the tour hurriedly and returned to his office. She was surprised that he even bothered to take her phone number and promise to call her when she knew he probably had no such intention. Yet she really did not care for him and had merely tried to talk herself into liking him. She discovered that under his delicate blond appearance lay a certain coldness, toughness and authoritarian quality. A few years later, she heard he had taken a position at a university in California.

One day as she was on her way to work, the girl upstairs called down to her, "Hey, can you talk a minute?" Judy was matchmaking again. This time she wanted to introduce her cousin to a girl friend of hers at a Sabbath lunch. Debbie was to come also so it would not be so obvious. "Just come upstairs for awhile, you don't have to stay if you find it too boring."

Then she couldn't resist relating the saga of her wonderful cousin. "He is 35, has been in Israel for 11 years and works as a statistician at the Bureau of Statistics. He has never been married but he's a really nice guy, the kind that would give you the shirt off his back, you know," she tried hard to convince. "The only problem is that he's the type that doesn't pay much attention to dress, appearance, things like that. He would wear a red sock and a navy one at the same time and not even notice it. And sometimes, he's a little dry, you know what I mean," she concluded. Yes, Debbie knew the type all too well. But she promised to come. Who knows. Sometimes frogs can turn into Prince Charmings. Or was that just in fairy tales?

Saturday arrived and at about noon, Debbie walked up the two flights of stairs that led to Judy's apartment and knocked on the door. The others were already assembled. Debbie was introduced to Judy's cousin, Steve, who looked exactly as she had pictured him - average in every way. He was pleasant looking, fair with reddish blond hair and freckles. His worst characteristic was perhaps a midwestern twang and nasality in his speech and a choice of language that belied his high level of education. But it was obvious, as Judy had told her, he was a "nice guy." He was the type of person most girls would pass over in a singles crowd in search of a more glamorous, dynamic man.

Unfortunately, the latter would usually turn out either to be a selfish bastard or a so called "difficult" type or one who would pass her over completely whereas Steve would make a good loyal loving mate and dutiful father. What simple logic! Yet each girl keeps hoping that this time it would be different. Logic would bow to love and the beautiful bastard would become a nice guy. (P.S. He doesn't ever!!!)

The girl Judy had invited was truly ugly. She was short and skinny and had a bird like face. She talked (which was most of the time) with a savage New York accent and with an authoritative air on all matters - a perfect mis-match for Steve.

Judy in her usual friendly way succeeded in keeping a happy mood as she served the simple but pleasant lunch. She had even baked a cake for the occasion. Everyone spoke English, so Judy's boy friend did not participate much in the conversation. His English was so limited that Debbie wondered how or if he and Judy ever had a deep conversation. Judy tried to help occasionally translating the gist of the conversation for him with her limited Hebrew.

Debbie liked Steve. After all the high pressure Israelis, it felt good to talk with someone who was easy-going and low key. As the conversation continued, it became apparent that he knew much more and was interested in many things besides statistics. Then the "lunch" was over and each guest slowly said goodbye. Debbie went downstairs to her apartment. Sparks had not flown and heavenly matches had not been made.

To supplement her earnings at the school and bank, Debbie decided to offer some private lessons in English and to do some editing and translation work whenever she could. So she went around and put up notices in the university, in Hadassah Hospital, the consulates and other places where people might be interested in utilizing such services.

Much to her surprise, each of these places already had several such leaflets hanging from its bulletin boards. As she tacked hers on the same board, she couldn't help reading some of them. Several she saw at Hadassah Hospital seemed strange because they emphasized the fact that the teacher was a girl and a "recent graduate" from a university. Debbie wondered why anyone would admit that they were a recent graduate (sometimes even a year was given) rather than an experienced teacher. It took Debbie some time before she realized that these had been written by English speaking girls whose true intention was to meet a doctor or other professional through her lessons, hence the real message comes through: "I'm a recent graduate, therefore I'm young." Debbie had to admit that she too had entertained the thought that a handsome ambitious intern or resident might want to improve his English. But she would not have been quick or clever enough to advertise her availability in this respect. She still had a lot to learn.

She received a few responses, two to teach English and one for editing. One of the callers was a secretary in the university who had seen both Debbie's ad to teach English and the one to do English German translations. She assumed Debbie must know German very well and asked her if she could teach her husband English in German. She herself was an American who had lived in Israel for five years. They were planning a tourist trip to the United States and therefore he wanted to learn some English before the journey.

When she went to the apartment in Talbia, a fashionable area in Jerusalem, Debbie was surprised to find a fairly attractive energetic woman of about 40 married to a distinguished looking but white haired old gentlemen of about 70. He had come to Israel from Germany in 1931 and had been a widower for three years when Glady's met him at a friend's party.

"How could such a vibrant woman marry such an old man?" she asked herself. "He is not rich, a celebrity, or even a professional man." She tossed this about for some time and finally reached the sad conclusion, "For a woman in Israel over 40, there is no other choice but to marry a much older man. Men of 40 prefer a much younger woman and can get her also. Even men of 50 wanted a woman about 30 or younger. Many are divorced and bitter and don't wish to marry again at all."

Debbie gave him many lessons and found him to be an interesting intelligent man. She could understand why this woman had probably chosen to marry him rather than be a single woman of 40 in a family orientated society. Unfortunately, the "tourist trip" turned out to be a permanent one, so she never saw them again.

Debbie also taught a professor at the Jerusalem University who was from Russia. He was handsome and interesting but happily married with two children. The other was more of an editing task also for a professor of mathematics at the Jerusalem University. He primarily wanted someone to correct the grammar and spelling in his letters and manuscripts. He was still very young and looked more like a student than a full professor yet he had already attained a high and tenured position at the university. He also had recently married.

One day he asked her to check a letter he had written to the University of Chicago replying that he would not accept the position they had offered him. The letter consisted of two short sentences, "Thank you for the invitation. I am sorry I cannot come. Sincerely,"

"Is it OK?" he asked already in the process of taking it away as finished business. Debbie was horrified at the terse and cold quality of the letter but didn't quite know how to broach the subject in a tactful manner.

"Well," she answered slowly, "the grammar and spelling are OK, but. . . well. . . do you ever want to go to this university maybe at a future date or do you not care about it at all?"

"Oh yes, sure," he answered puzzled. "Why do you ask?" She tried to explain to him how his letter which seemed correct and efficient to him, would appear impolite, snobbish, disdainful or just plain careless in Chicago. She apologized for having to point this out but he welcomed it saying, "No, that's what I want you to do - to correct whatever is wrong."

Then Debbie composed a very nice letter. "Thank you very much for inviting me to come to your university for one year. I am greatly honored that you have considered me for this position. However, I deeply regret that due to previous commitments, I shall be unable to accept your kind offer. Hopefully, I shall have the opportunity of working with you sometime in the future. Once again, thank you and regards to all from Israel. Very truly yours, Avrahm Rossinsky."

When Professor Rossinsky saw it, his eyes opened wide and he remarked shaking his head, "So much, oh, you Americans have so much time. You know, I was now two months in Lebanon on *miluim*. When I came back, all this (he pointed to a huge pile of work) was waiting for me. Nobody did anything. We in Israel have no such time for all this fancy stuff. After all, I said what was necessary, no? - that I wasn't coming."

Debbie couldn't answer right away. "It's just a different place with different problems and different expectations," was all she could think of to say. "OK, I will send it," he decided quickly and handed her the next paper, obviously not wanting to waste more time on the matter. The longer Debbie was in Israel, the more she became convinced of her own response. It was a different place from the United States with a culture and mentality of its own.

By this time, Debbie had recovered sufficiently emotionally from her encounters with all the negative men she had recently met that she was willing to venture meeting another reply to her original ad in the *Jerusalem Post*. She had always put this particular letter aside from the more interesting ones because the handwriting was scrawled like a very small child and because he was a Russian from a very obscure province. But he was a doctor she reasoned and perhaps might be interesting to meet. One could never know.

He came from southern Russia, near the Iranian border and had been in Israel for three years. He was a specialist in internal medicine at Maimonides Hospital in Haifa. Since he also gave a course once a week at Tel Aviv University Medical School, he suggested meeting in the lounge of the main library on the Ramat

Aviv campus. Debbie waited in the assigned place but he arrived late excusing himself that the exam he had given had taken longer than expected.

They talked for a long time in the library lounge although Debbie would have preferred to go elsewhere since others sitting close by were eavesdropping and others were being disturbed by the noise. But he made no leave to move. They spoke about many things but Debbie noted immediately that he always tended to steer the topic of conversation back to the United States and how life was there. One of the first questions was, "What type of work does your father do?" and "Does your mother work also?" He did not seem impressed when she informed him that her father owned a small restaurant in New York.

"Why don't we go down to the student cafeteria. It's not far and not expensive," Debbie suggested finally.

"No, it's not a nice place," he offered dismissing it quickly.

"Well, let's go for a walk." And so they began to walk around the very dark streets of Ramat Aviv, a suburb of Tel Aviv.

Debbie was getting somewhat tired and bored. Also she had not eaten dinner and little lunch and so was violently hungry. It was hardly a date and resembled more an information getting session with his asking all the questions. "How much does this and that cost in the United States? What is the average rent, cost of house, apartment? What is the average salary? What does a doctor in private practice earn a year, in a hospital?" Debbie kept trying to orient the conversation to other topics so she might find out something about him. But it was impossible. He pretended not to hear her and just continued asking the questions he wanted firmly and demandingly.

Debbie looked at him after awhile and wondered why she was wasting her evening with him. He had given his age as 45 but he looked at least 55 and he was swarthy in every sense of the word. He was shorter than Debbie, overweight, had a round face and straight sleek black hair. There could be no doubt about the fact that he was truly ugly. And he had warts - big, black, thick warts on his face and neck. "Sleezy" was the word which best described him.

Then she heard him asking, "Jews in America, they are mostly rich, yes?"

Debbie was getting increasingly exasperated by such questions and merely answered, "Well, it depends."

"Almost all the doctors at my hospital have married American girls and they are all rich," he continued to argue.

"Well, it depends on what you call rich," Debbie exclaimed.

"Well," he retorted angrily and with disdain, "There are those who are small restaurant owners and then there are those whose income is $200,000 a year." He looked at her as if she were some lowly worm to be stepped on and he debating whether or not to dirty his shoes.

Debbie was hurt and confused; she had never met anyone so crude and crass in all her life. She looked around her and wanted to run away from him. But the street was dark and tree lined, a residential street she did not recognize. She had no idea where she was, they had been walking a long time, and she did not know how to return to a main street to secure a bus home. It was not a place for a girl to be alone. She would have to be nice to him.

She rehearsed the words in her head, "Do you think we could go back now? I still have to go all the way to Jerusalem and I must teach early in the morning." She was about to voice this to him when he dictated suddenly, "Well, that's all. I must return to Haifa. I have duty at 7:15 in the morning." Relieved Debbie followed him as he started to walk in the direction of the main road. They found a bus which took them to the Central Bus Station in Tel Aviv.

"Well, goodbye," he mumbled quickly without much looking at Debbie discarding her as one would throw away a used match or wilted flowers. "Yes, it was nice meeting you," Debbie responded perfunctorily.

He walked away, ostensibly to the queue for the buses to Haifa. Debbie went to buy a ticket for Jerusalem and luckily one bus was waiting to be filled. She climbed aboard and took a window seat. She looked out at the alley next to hers where stood the waiting bus to Haifa. Her eyes searched for the doctor but they did not see him. "That's strange," she mused, "He was in such a rush to catch the bus and now he's not even in it." She began to consider that perhaps his entire story had been a hoax and that he was not at all a doctor in Haifa.

She examined each seat in the Haifa bus and in the queue outside but caught no glimpse of him. She looked around the Central Bus Station in general as far as she could from her limited vision of the bus window. "Well, who cares," she sighed and relaxed back into her seat. Her bus was filling fast and would soon leave.

After about three minutes, out of the corner of her eye, she saw a bulky figure approaching the bus queues from across the street. She sat up straight in her seat and stared. There he was shuffling along with a huge felafel[*] sandwich in his hand greedily munching and chomping his face into it. He headed towards the Haifa bus and got on pulling his ticket from his pocket with one hand while balancing the felafel in the other. He walked down the aisle, dropped down heavily into a seat and continued to eat without looking out the window. Just then Debbie's bus driver ignited the engine, closed the doors and drove the bus out of the queue and on its way to Jerusalem. Her stomach tightened with hunger; her whole being throbbed with a pain far deeper.

Evenings such as the proceeding one always exerted a depressive effect on Debbie and she would stew about it for a few days even though intellectually she knew he wasn't worth the trouble. It was just so disappointing. She wondered how many guys like this existed, just wanting to take whenever and wherever they could. She would have to be careful. It seemed she had warned herself of this many times before.

---

[*] felafel sandwich - a very popular food in Israel consisting of balls of fried chick peas, salad, and dressing, all contained within a pocket of pita bread. The cost is about $1.

CHAPTER 5
SCYLLA AND CARYBDIS

The next Saturday was still a relatively warm day for the time of year, a kind of Indian summer. The sky had burst into bloom again. Debbie decided to take a walk in the Liberty Bell Garden where a blizzard of flowers greeted her jangled self. She settled down on a bench alone and tried to relax in the warm sun. She wanted so much to have a long "think" by herself reassessing her stay in Israel and making tentative plans for the future.

She compared men like the Russian with some of the men she had dated in New York. Which was worse? Was it really better here? Once comfortable on her bench, she started to recall the singles life she had led in New York.

Debbie had tried computer dating but without much success. This approach fit in with her intellectual orientation toward life thereby exerting a tremendous appeal for her. "It sounds OK, a scientific and rational way to meet the right person, so much better than blind choice," she argued when her mother expressed skepticism. "Just money making" her father had echoed in the background like an ancient Greek chorus commenting on the action yet being ignored by it. She decided to give it a try.

A representative from the "organization" came to her apartment to interview her. An endless array of questions about life style and personality both her own and that of her dream man made Debbie anticipate possibilities. She had been promised a list of "up to 10 names a month".

Debbie was a bit worried about how she would cram all these wonderful men into her busy teaching career. She waited eagerly for her first list of names. Well, her concern about having enough time was in vain. The first month brought only one name written on what looked like a computer print-out sheet. In the second month, again only one lonely name stood at the top of the otherwise blank sheet. The third, fourth and fifth month - the same story.

Debbie finally decided to phone the company - "Operation Marriage" to find out what was wrong. She was told very curtly that she was "difficult to match" but no explanation was offered as to why. Debbie grew angry and said she had been promised ten names a month. "No," the voice responded smugly, "if you read the contract carefully, you will see that you have been provided with "up to 10 names" which of course could indicate only one all the way up to a maximum of ten. Debbie knew she had been cheated. When she complained angrily, the man on the phone intimidated her stating that perhaps she was neurotic and not really suitable at all for any names. He repeated that she was very difficult to match and after all, they don't want to pair people that might be completely incompatible (or problematic, he continued after a pause). It had all sounded so nice and scientific. Then she thought that perhaps she might truly be hard to match but her mother had greater practical sense and knew that the company (indeed if that is what it was) was probably operating with very few subscribers, especially men. After all, with so many opportunities for men to meet so many girls everywhere, who would find it necessary to pay the registration fee of $200.

Well, yes, there were actually a few; those lonely robot looking names on the computer sheet did mushroom into real people. Debbie wanted to meet them anyway even if there was no choice. The first candidate ushered forth by the infamous computer was a nicely dressed 34 year old executive with a major insurance firm on East 58th Street and Madison Avenue. He was a few inches shorter than Debbie, and chubby although not grossly fat. Fair and pleasant in appearance, he seemed to be friendly and cheerful also in personality. He took her to dinner in a good restaurant and then to a concert at Carnagie Hall. In the beginning, because Debbie was naturally shy and didn't talk much, she didn't notice, in fact, she was glad even relieved that he was doing all the talking. She listened at first, then, grew gradually less interested as he delved into minutiae and eventually was bored as he droned on and on. By the time they arrived back at Debbie's house and were sitting in her kitchen drinking coffee, Debbie's eyes were glazed and she felt as though hypnotized or perhaps she was just falling asleep. Derek, on the other hand, his face now bright and perky, grew more energetic with each passing sentence. He was soaring on at lightning speed about what Debbie had lost track of long ago. She finally made some excuse about getting up early in the morning but it took him quite a while just to stop long enough to listen to what she was saying so drunk was he with his own words. He finally left and she never saw him again.

Debbie didn't remember anything he said except during the course of the evening, he confided that he had until recently been very overweight. His company had forced him to lose 80 pounds in 6 months or else he would be fired. He described in detail the tortures involved in the losing of the 80 pounds - pound by pound and the difficulties of keeping it off. He told her that he could easily regain the weight in three weeks if he let himself. He agreed to lose the weight because he did not want to lose the job and also because he was afraid he might not be able to secure another. Slimness was a must for a New York executive. Debbie imagined how fat he must have been with the additional 80 pounds since he was still quite overweight.

When the second month of her one year subscription came, another lone name appeared on the computer like sheet. Debbie was still curious enough to try again. The next "match" for Debbie according to the wise and all knowing computer of "Open Marriage" was a short, shy and thin engineer from Long Island. Again he was shorter than Debbie and his thinness made him even more frail. He had never been married and lived alone in a house, the son of a distinguished New York University German professor, well-known critic and scholar. Debbie was impressed and delighted at this since she too loved literature. She had often wished that her own parents had been educated and so envied Dan his good fortune of having grown up with educated parents.

However, much to her dismay, she soon discovered that Daniel Mayer did not share the views of his patrician father. In fact, he was a vehement rebel against the "system" which he perceived as hostile to him. Slowly he revealed that he hated "academics" who, in his opinion, did nothing but "write stupid articles that nobody ever reads" and in general disliked anything formal.

He took Debbie to a restaurant that required "jacket and tie" and no sooner had they closed the door upon leaving when Daniel ripped off his tie and opened his shirt as though he had been strangled all evening. Debbie was eager to make a good impression and to please (a girl desiring to find a husband often tries too hard to please and thus defeats her purpose) so she said nothing and even went along with his anti-establishment views. She also complained about the "publish or perish" philosophy in the universities and that she only wrote because she was forced to in order to receive her degree. (Ah, Debbie, how we women foolishly squash our own talents and aspirations and humble ourselves before some faltering schmoo in pants one calls a man!) This was a lie, of course, since Debbie loved to write and do research and indeed had many bright and original ideas. But since she agreed with or acquiesced to Dan's ideas, quite naturally, Dan continued to ask her out.

One woeful day, Debbie's natural love and enthusiasm for literature and research asserted itself and she began to enthusiastically tell Dan some of her ideas. Thinking that Dan would be interested, she forgot herself and her mother's ever repeated injunction to "act dumb." The bubbles on her flushed happy face burst when Dan scowled, "Hey, so you do like it, after all - just like my father." Debbie was crushed when she realized what she had done; she had committed the "Unpardonable Sin" of the Single Girl - to appear brighter than her date or to reveal one's hidden skills. "You're one of them," he cried disappointed.

Debbie finally had to admit her guilt. Yes, the verdict was correct, she did like to write scholarly articles, she did like to get "dressed up" in nice clothes and no, she really didn't like country and western music or folk songs from the Appalachian mountains. The truth had come to light with all its ugly consequences. The punishment was inevitable and severe. Loss of the man and with it loss of meaning and hope in life. Each time it happened, a little more was eroded from Debbie's soul. It took a long time for her to see that Daniel Mayer was not worth the money or energy

Match Number Three arrived as usual on the first of the month. By now, Debbie realized that she would never receive more than one name a month. They arranged to meet, as usual, for the first time - at a public place. Debbie arrived on time but there was no sign of anyone who might be her mysterious knight. She waited more than an hour then finally left disappointed. She couldn't imagine what had happened but vaguely remembered a grossly obese man in a phone booth watching for a very long time and wondered if that had not been her date, only perhaps he had lost his nerve to approach her. And then there was George, whom she had met at folk dancing.

They had planned to go to the Turkish night club Hagi Baba on Mac Dougal Street, not far from Feenjohn, the Israeli night club. She had been looking forward to it and was disappointed when George suggested they go to Atlantic City instead. Yet she had never been there and it intrigued her to go to a big gambling casino. She worried somewhat that it was already too late to go since it was a two and a half hour bus ride each way. George asked how much money she had. She said "$50" "That's OK then," he estimated. "I also have only this much. An hour will be enough." Debbie and George set out for what would be her first gambling adventure.

When Debbie first entered one of the "rooms," she was amazed at the massive size of the halls. Miles and miles of spinning roulette wheels, backgammon tables, whirling wheels of fortune and numbers games. George's eyes glowed when he saw the sight and he smiled. He started in immediately by changing some money into the casino's money. Then to Debbie's surprise, he proceeded quickly to the slot machines showering them with coins until they were gone. He conducted himself as a professional, one who committed the crime often. Although he lost all the money rapidly, he was not unduly upset by it. Then he switched to the numbers tables and kept playing number 22, his lucky number. Only tonight it wasn't so lucky. Still he kept playing number 22. Debbie wanted him to stop since he was losing so much so quickly. He did not even hear her so engrossed was he in playing number 22. It seemed to be a matter of life or death to him. It was at this point that Debbie realized that there was something very wrong with George.

He had finished with the money that he had brought and started to play with hers. Debbie foresaw that the same fate awaited her $50, only this time at the roulette wheel. She excused herself and went to the ladies room and put $8 in her bra - enough for bus fare back to New York. When she returned, George was deeply in the throes of watching the wheel slowly winding down to another number, not the one he had played. Debbie suggested they stop for a soda in the nearby snack bar. George did not want to leave the hallowed aisles of gambling but finally after having lost everything, he reluctantly dragged along like a dog on a leash. He had been right about the time though. It had taken them less than an hour to go through $100. It was obvious that he came here often and lost just as often. She remembered now he had sometimes mentioned he had been with his friends in Atlantic City but never having been there, it didn't bear much significance for her.

They left and walked back to the bus depot. George was broke and dejected. Debbie took the money from her bra and went to the window to buy tickets. George's eyes flashed angrily at her. "You still have money. You said you didn't have any more money," he barked in a loud angry voice. "George," she whined shocked, "We have to get home. Where could we go if I hadn't put the money aside?"

Well, we could stay at one of the hotels," he waved his hand at the strip of swanky 5 star hotels. Debbie sighed and was quiet.

The bus left after awhile and they were both silent on the trip back. Now Debbie knew why George was still available at 31. She had wondered each time she went out with him why some girl had not already grabbed him. He was average in looks, not gay or impotent, had a friendly easy going personality, at least away from the roulette wheel. Well, now she knew. Certainly every girl would run from this. He would lose everything; all she and her parents had worked so hard to attain could be gone in one evening. It was a frightening thought.

In New York, it is called making "the rounds." Debbie tried singles dances in an endless variety of places, including Jewish community centers and the Unitarian Church (where almost everyone was Jewish), singles discos, lectures on various topics in various places, alumni parties, parapsychology meetings, the Scandinavian Society (where virtually nobody was Scandinavian), the Wagner Society (where not everyone understood the *Ring),* the Appalachian Mountain Hiking Club (where some even hated walking) and numerous places for folk dancing, indoors and outdoors. The list was endless!

Every week she dutifully purchased the *Metropolitan Almanac*, the Bible for all single people in New York and carefully read it from cover to cover scanning all the events and happenings that might prove interesting and of course fruitful in meeting that Special Someone. She went to each event with this secret hope that was hidden so deeply inside her, sometimes it did not even rise into her consciousness. Yet each time she returned home vaguely disappointed even if the activity had been entertaining and otherwise enjoyable. Time passed and discontent grew.

To add to her dismay, most of her friends had already married, some had a child or two. They slowly began to stay away from the old places and activities and new younger people filled in the spaces. Debbie began to feel out of place. Perhaps for her also, it was time for something new.

It was not that she did not have many friends. She did; everyone liked Debbie. She was always one you could come to ask for advice or consolation. She was popular at folk dancing and rarely lacked a partner. But that's all there ever was. After the dancing was over, many said, "Well, that was a good session. Are you coming next week? Good, see you then . So long." And that was it. Few dancing partners ever advanced to the stage of dating partners. She had seen the same faces for almost ten years. It was time for something new!

Debbie's reverie was suddenly broken when a dark haired girl sat down on the bench next to her. Debbie was disappointed since she had hoped to have the bench to herself. It was especially irksome since there were so many other benches she could have chosen. Debbie thought for a minute about the famous bench scene in *The Zoo Story* and the tense interaction between Peter and Jerry but then dismissed it. The dark gloomy warty bulk of the Russian doctor still loomed in her mind.

She was half lost in her thoughts while the other half was watching the cars drive by. The girl on the bench had an Israeli magazine and was leafing it through. She was turning the pages slowly. After a long time, Debbie finally got curious enough to glance at the magazine. When she disengaged herself from her own thoughts and did look, she saw there were only photographs of nude women together. Then she looked at the girl more closely. Who would be reading such a magazine?

The girl looked at Debbie intensely, then flashed her a smile full of erotic alleys inviting her to trespass. She pushed the magazine closer towards her pointing to the picture of two women making love. Obviously knowing no English, she pointed to Debbie and then back to herself, meaning "you and I"? Debbie just shook her head and muttered, "No time for such things. Sorry." Then, feeling uncomfortable, she got up from the bench and walked away.

It was another *Zoo Story*, Like Peter, Debbie relinquished the bench to the strange Jerry. Like Peter, she was unable to accept or even speak to a person so different from herself and thus rejected her and retreated from the scene. It was the only such encounter that Debbie experienced in Israel.

Occasionally a Hassid[*] would stop her on the street and ask

---

[*] Hassid - a member of the ultra Orthodox branch of Judaism. They are easily identifiable by their nineteenth century mode of dress, such as long black coats, wide hats, etc.

for the time or for street directions. Then suddenly and without any transition, he would blurt out, "Are you married?" and try to get friendly. Debbie was polite but always maintained some distance.

A tall blond German Gentile girl studying for an M.A. at the Hebrew University related the story of the Hassid who approached her at the Central Bus Station. "Are you Jewish?" he asked.

When she answered "No," he looked happy and declared, "Oh, good, then I can do it with you." Having never seen Hassidim before, she was quite surprised by his statement and didn't understand what he wanted. When he made it more clear, she threatened to hit him with her backpack. He ran.

In a recent symposium on AIDS, one of the panelists, a medical doctor offered the point that perhaps there might exist a mode of transmission of the disease other than sexual contact or blood transfusion since after all, Hassidim also get AIDS. Debbie provided some useful information.

Once a Hassid wanted Debbie to act as a spy among the Christian missionaries operating in Jerusalem. Since she did not look Jewish, he thought she might be able to move freely among them and to uncover their plans and activities. Debbie refused because she disliked sneaky work and betraying people regardless of who they were. Besides she was not in Israel for such purposes although she wondered at times if her real purpose would ever be fulfilled.

All around her she saw some examples - American women married to Israeli men but of course, there were many more examples of single American women "without" plus all those who had failed, left the country and never spoke about it. Worst of all, she thought, were those who returned to the States and boasted about what a "marvelous " time they had with all those A-1 men.

Although the newspapers and newscasts were filled with political, social, and economic happenings, these events only lightly impinged on the mind of Debbie Warshawsky. She was busy thinking of other ways to meet people besides personal ads and folk dancing. The one singles group she had been to had been such a disaster she couldn't bear to think about it anymore. But she swallowed her disappointment (There is no end to what a single girl can swallow) and decided to investigate some other groups and give them a try at least. In this way, her life stumbled on.

The first one she went to was a regular Friday night group in Kiryat Yovel, a suburb of Jerusalem. Usually, there was a lecture, a singer or singing group or some other "program" followed by refreshments and open dancing by the audience. There were about 100 people attending from the 25 to 35 age group, most being in their mid to late twenties. Debbie recognized several faces from the folk dancing groups. She spoke with some people and danced a few times but she was not really interested in anyone there and no one seemed interested in her. People attended because they had nothing else to do, not because they genuinely wanted to meet someone.

Then she tried a group in Tel Aviv at the Z.O.A. House (Zionist Organization of America) sponsored by the British Olim Association (British Immigrants Society). This was not a regular group but they had frequent events and dances especially around holidays. Here there was a much larger crowd but the age grouping was about the same. The guys were mostly Israeli but the girls were predominantly British and American.

One thing she noted were the large number of truly fat girls that were present. At least they are dancing, she thought to herself. Again she did not see anyone who even remotely appealed to her. Most of the men were quite short, she observed. One guy invited her to dance several times; he seemed pleasant and for want of a better choice, she did so. He was shorter than she and very thin with red hair that was already beginning to thin although he was only about 28. After the dance, he walked her to the bus station and made a date for next Saturday night.

Debbie was rather looking forward to her date with Ami. They decided, or rather he decided that they would go out in Tel Aviv where there would be more of a selection of open restaurants and cinemas, etc. than in Jerusalem where she lived. At least this is what he told Debbie. However, this was OK with Debbie who wanted a chance to see more of Tel Aviv.

They arranged that he would pick her up at the Central Bus Station when she arrived there from Jerusalem. He did so but instead of driving into Tel Aviv for something to do, he drove to his apartment in Holon, a suburb of Tel Aviv. This was also OK with Debbie because at this time she still very much wanted to see how Israelis lived from day to day. Debbie did not understand that he had had no intention of taking her anywhere.

They went to his flat and talked. He served some Cola and potato chips. Time went by quickly and then he started to fidget about. "Well, let's see which cinema we could go to." But it was already past 10 o'clock and the last showing was at 9:40. "It's too late now," he pretended to be concerned. "Oh, we must find one that has later showings. I'll look in the newspaper," he offered with all sincerity. But of course, he couldn't find any. The paper was in Hebrew so Debbie couldn't check.

"Well, do you mind just staying here?" he asked to which she replied, "No, not at all." He started to move closer to her on the couch and began to kiss her. Becoming passionate very quickly, he explored first her breasts, then the rest of her body. "Let's go to bed," he whispered.

Debbie moved back somewhat and sighed, "No, I don't think so. I like you but I want to get to know someone first very well before I become intimate with him."

"So you want, like a boy friend, you know, for a long time?" he asked surprised.

"Sure, don't you?" Debbie inquired as if it were the only possible choice.

"Well, if I had known that that was what you wanted, I wouldn't have asked you out." he stated matter of factly.

"Why not?" Debbie looked puzzled.

"Sure, I want a regular girl friend, but for that you are too old for me. Just to have a good time, well, it doesn't matter so much if you are older or not, you see?"

Debbie saw! With the speed of a comet, she saw! "How

could I be so stupid and not recognize that all he wanted was sex and even without spending a dime?" she berated herself.

Furious, she wanted to leave the apartment immediately but by this time it was almost 12 and she did not know exactly where she was. It was a residential neighborhood and there did not seem to be any taxis about. Even to get a sherut to Jerusalem on a Saturday night would be difficult with so many people coming from concerts, theater and all. He said she could sleep on the couch and she gladly acquiesced. It is amazing how much anger can be stilled and repressed when practical matters of comfort and safety intervene.

The next morning, he drove her early to the Central Bus Station on his way to work. He told her that he had had a girl friend for quite a long time and he really liked her very much but she was very fat and he couldn't accept that. He blahed blahed about her attempts to diet and promises to lose weight and how they eventually broke up but Debbie was not listening anymore.

The innocent trust that American women of all ages and educational levels place in the simplest Israeli male is unbelievable. A put-down she would not tolerate in the United States is somehow OK when it is made by even the most primitive Israeli macho. Would she ever learn?

Yet, she was ready to try again. A friend told Debbie about a private singles group that she might join. He himself was a member, knew the leader well and felt it was an interesting group of people with various activities each week. The organizer was a 38 year old divorcee from England.

Nevertheless, when Debbie called, she was told quite curtly and in a brusque manner that, "There is no opening at present for a woman. You will have to wait until a woman leaves before you can join. However, I think that I should warn you, there is a waiting list and there are many women ahead of you Besides, I think you are really somewhat too young for the group." She then abruptly ended the conversation and hung up.

Later, Debbie learned the real story from the friend who had told her about the group. "I'm not surprised she said that," he explained. "Marsha only started the group so that she could have "first crack." at the men who wanted to join as well as control the kind of women who came into the group. She never chose anyone younger or more attractive than she. The result is that most of the women there are fat, forty and dumpy."

He also confided (whether it is true or not, no one knows) that this very same respectable lady made frequent trips to the Dead Sea where she slept on the beach. Nearby there was an army camp and occasionally it just happened that she would pitch her tent very close to where the soldiers had theirs. What transpired shall be left to the imagination of the reader!

By far the worst singles event Debbie ever attended (it was even worse than the Triangle Hotel) was at the Dorrit Hotel in Herzlia. She had seen an advertisement in the *Jerusalem Post* and like all advertisements of that type, it had an interesting, alluring approach promising fun, excitement and romance to those who would come. It had looked inviting to Debbie and she fell victim. "I think maybe since Herzlia is a rather well to do neighborhood, the group might also be a high level well educated group." Thus, she reasoned with herself. "Then too, there will be new faces since Herzlia is about 80 kilometers north of Jerusalem."

So, as usual, she set off on her journey with high hopes. First, she took a bus to Tel Aviv and when asking for information at the Central Bus Station, she discovered that she needed a special bus that traveled along the shore, a bus which she could only get at a certain point in the central city. After some difficulties in reaching this point, Debbie found herself walking down a rather dark sleazy street she had never been on before. It was then the red light district of Tel Aviv. When she finally reached the end of the long street where the number 93 bus would stop, she was forced to stand in front of a very cheap hotel which was obviously for prostitutes and the like. To make matter worse, she then learned that the bus stops only once every hour.

She considered returning home but the thought of walking down that dark street again repelled her. Besides, she had come so far already, she might as well find out what kind of place the Dorrit Hotel was and meet the exciting people at the singles gathering. Several men walked by and leered at her; a few spoke but she just pretended not to notice. Two soldiers hung around the area, seemingly on duty since Debbie saw them using their walkie-talkies. It was uncomfortable to stand there alone in the cold and Debbie cursed her single state. "How much longer will I have to go to places like this?" she kept asking some unknown Deity.

The bus finally came and a short while later, Debbie got off at the Dorrit Hotel. It was a beautiful 5 star monster standing on the shores of the Mediterranean. Inside it was equally glamorous but it looked as if it were completely empty. She found the place where the party was supposed to be - the Jordan Room which sounded very elegant but turned out to be the hotel's bar and lounge.

The two organizers sat outside behind a long white table. Debbie tried to smile in a carefree manner as she paid her seven dollars but didn't think she was too successful in convincing anyone she was happy. It had been an ordeal to get there and now she awaited an even bigger ordeal to enter behind the dark curtain covering the entrance into the promised land of love and romance.

She took a deep breath and went in. Several people were standing at the bar. Most were seated in living room fashion, circles of 4 to 5 people facing each other. It was the worst possible arrangement in which to meet anyone. She headed to the bar to get her "free" drink which turned out to be a very weak and watery punch. As she sipped the dreadful stuff, she dared to look around the dimly lit room. She couldn't believe her eyes. There were about 35 lonely women and two men present in the room. Most of the women were between 30 and 40 and not very attractive. They sat there passively, hungry and disappointed, like reapers at a barren harvest. She felt like going out and demanding her money back but then decided a scene would only make matters worse.

After awhile, she started to talk to the girl next to her who was from England and had been in Israel seven years. Then one of the two men began speaking to the English girl and she gratefully turned her attention towards him and away from Debbie. Debbie had observed him speaking with many of the women and assumed he must be a hired "mingler" or one of the organizers. Her hunch was correct as later in the evening she saw him conversing with the two women outside who had taken her money. After an appropriate time of about an hour, Debbie realized no one else was coming. All the love-worn singles were still sitting there nursing their wounded stumps like drinks. She quietly and unobtrusively sneaked out the door and went home. Somehow the journey back was less problematic perhaps because she knew what to expect. It was a night she would not forget so quickly!

In reconsidering all the singles events she had attended, Debbie wondered why they were all so uniformly disastrous. Surely there must be more people "out there" who were single especially men. To be sure, the divorce rate in Israel was low but that alone could not account for the sad situation in singles places. She elected to ask some other Israelis what they thought about the matter. She had questioned a few friends once before but now hoped to find different answers. But their opinions were similar

A married girl friend expressed surprise that Debbie would even consider going to "such places". She said, "I can understand why women would have to go to "such places" because there are so many available women, but a man who would need to go there must be really terrible, not the kind you would want." Each time she mentioned the term "such places" her face would twitch into an ugly scowl as though she were referring to some medieval torture chamber.

A bachelor friend offered the same advice, "In Israel, it is not really acceptable for a person to go to so called "places for 'single people'. No one would admit he had to go to a special place to meet someone. No decent guy would go to such a place. I wouldn't. Why should I? Pay $8 to $10 to meet a girl when I can just go out on the street or to the cinema and meet plenty of girls. The only type you will meet there is someone who cannot make contact at all in any other way. Or somebody who is not doing any activity like a hobby or sport. There are a million places to meet girls. I know in the United States, people are going to such places. But here, no."

Debbie put the psychological pieces together. An Israeli male would not compromise his masculinity by admitting publically that he needed an external aid to find a partner. It would reveal that he was needy searching for love and romance (which did not really exist in Israel as in the United States), that he was lonely and desirous of such a lowly item as a mere woman. These things an Israeli macho would never admit even to himself much less to others. It would be a disgrace. And it was true, there were plenty of women everywhere. The society was free and open. It was not New York City. In Israel, one could easily (and relatively safely) open a conversation with someone in a cinema, park, beach, cafe, public gathering or just on the street. The relatively warm weather for most of the year was also conducive to people being out of doors more and hence being available for contact to be made. Yes, if one thought about the nature of Israeli society, one could understand why a singles dance could not possibly succeed. It simply was not necessary!

Well, if the men were not at singles dances, where were they? Besides the exchange rate of the shekel to the dollar and for how long they would be sent for army duty, what else were Israelis interested in? The third most important male preoccupation in Israel after money and the military was football. This football in the United States is known as soccer.

Debbie actually enjoyed soccer so it was no sacrifice on her part to attend a game. She went to several on Saturday afternoons either at the YMCA in Jerusalem or at the stadium in Netanya. The one glaring difference between soccer in the United States and in Israel was immediately obvious. There were no women! Football games were a male phenomena. She felt strange at the first game when all the men stared at her. After awhile she noticed a few more feminine souls amidst the sea of angelic male countenances (perhaps "demonic" would be a more descriptive word for their behavior during and after the game) but even they were firmly attached to a man and son.

Going to a soccer game in Israel is more than just seeing an athletic event. It is an experience in itself. To buy a ticket alone requires Herculean strength and Odyssean cleverness. The queue is unheard of. Instead, a "huddle" of approximately 25 to 40 men crowd around the box office window each trying to be first or next in line. The pushing, shoving, shouting is unbelievable. For the weak and the old, the atmosphere is dangerous. Therefore, very often one can find certain men who have bought many tickets standing about one to two blocks away from the stadium. They will then sell those tickets at a slightly higher price to those who are unwilling or unable to fight in the huddle.

On one particular day in Netanya, Debbie was determined to buy her own ticket and to push and shove her way like the others, no matter what. It was an incredible experience unparalleled in the United States. People actually physically elbow their way in, maneuvering an inch here, pressing another inch there. The progress anyone makes must be measured in inches since people are already literally on top of one another. Everyone must behave in this way merely to maintain one's position. To be idle even for a second would soon result in being outside the huddle.

Debbie once saw a man try to climb over the huddle from the back into a front line position. He was stopped by a policeman or he might have been stampeded by the mob. Many police stand guard at any soccer game, should the enthusiasm of the spectators get out of hand as well as to prevent some football lovers from entering without a ticket - a not uncommon occurrence since tickets cost about $7.

Debbie pushed, shoved and elbowed her way to the window. Several of the men smiled approvingly even admiringly. Pushing and shoving are not viewed as negative behavior in Israel; on the contrary, they are indicative of strength and prowess. To out-maneuver the others in a crowd is a sign of cleverness and intelligence.

Finally, she secured a ticket and jumped into the mainstream of the crowd thronging into the stadium.

It was a huge stadium. The seats were not numbered so that many of the best seats in the center had already been occupied. Her eyes scanned the stadium for a good place to sit. She felt strange with so many male eyes staring at her. After settling in a place, she began to look around at the audience. Men of all ages, all types, some with children, comprised the crowd. After an initial glance of surprise, they ignored her.

These men had come to see an exciting football game, not to meet a girl.

Several times, she searched through the maze of faces if she might not see Shimon among them. He was a great football fan and attended games quite regularly, having once been on a team himself. She did manage to locate him at two games she attended in Netanya. Yet each time he was with another guy and all he did was smile and wave hello.

Some of the games were quite exciting especially if both teams were good. The fans cheered and booed and on the whole there was much tension and excitement. The big problem came when the game was over and the entire stadium would descend at once upon the few small exit ways. Again there was much pushing and shoving as each person planned to get out quickly preferably before all the others. One had to move along with the crowd. There was no letting the others pass. The thrust of the crowds to the exit was like a deluge of water after the breaking of a dam. Occasionally before they reached the final exit, some of the men would urinate against the wall of the stadium.

As far as meeting someone was concerned, Debbie thought soccer games might be a good place but one would have to go regularly. There were many men but the opportunity to meet them was limited by time and place. Probably almost all were married, so a single girl looking for a husband would have to search out the single men which would not be easy to do in such a short time. If a girl wanted merely to have an affair with a married man, the array and choice would be limitless and probably many would be willing. At any rate, the men were at least *there* in the stadium. Debbie concluded that the best opportunity to strike up an acquaintance was before the game and during the intermission. After the game was more difficult because everyone rushed home. One had to select a seat carefully since this area would constitute the realm of people one would be surrounded by during the game. Changing seats was impossible at a crowded game which most were. Debbie became quite involved in the games themselves and liked them immensely. She decided to continue attending them whenever her schedule permitted.

Before Debbie came to Israel, she belonged to a group in New York called "Americans for a Progressive Israel" affiliated with the Labor Party and espousing essentially liberal ideas. Actually Debbie's interest in Israel was of long standing and she often attended lectures in various places on topics or problems that dealt with Israel. This particular group sponsored meetings, discussion groups, lectures, trips etc. and Debbie attended fairly regularly. Of course, it might also be possible to meet a nice Jewish boy at one of these functions which was no minor reason why many girls attended. In Israel, API was affiliated with the *Peace Now* movement Indeed, Debbie remembered one of the best functions in New York was a joint meeting of Peace Now and API hosting many well known speakers.

So when Debbie had seen some days earlier an announcement of a *Peace Now* demonstration to be held in front of the museum in Tel Aviv on Saturday, October 21st, she felt eager and interested to participate. Usually she did not like demonstrations and protests but this one could be an interesting diversion and a political event in Israel was surely to be exciting. "And who knows," she debated with herself, "I may meet some people with whom I would have something in common." It was easy to strike up a conversation with a person over a query regarding some political point or to say something about the demonstration - a conversation one might not be able to initiate in another setting. In the milieu of a demonstration, all are united by a common belief and this is certainly a cementing factor among the members. The ad in the paper had promised that buses would leave for the Tel Aviv Museum from the Jerusalem Theater at 1 P.M. and would return at 11 P.M. - free of charge. They expected demonstrators from all over Israel; some two thousand were awaited. Debbie decided definitely to go.

She arrived early at the Jerusalem Theater. Only the organizers were already there sorting the signs, shirts and other paraphernalia to be used. Debbie sat down nearby where the organizers were working. "Hi, " she said quietly. "Hi, hey, how about giving us a hand? We need to get these various areas organized," one of them shouted. "Well, OK," Debbie answered. "I'll do what I can." She was willing but not overly anxious to please people she barely knew.

Debbie worked hard for almost an hour, unloading large signs, piles of handouts and other equipment. Slowly people arrived, but it was barely enough to fill the bus. Debbie noted immediately that it was not a crowd conducive to finding the one and only. Many were young students, some were single women over 35 with the same idea as she, many were hippie types and a few were elderly idealistic ex-Europeans. She even considered backing out but the hope that those coming from other areas or from Tel Aviv might be more promising goaded her on to stick it out.

Finally the bus left and about an hour later arrived near the Tel Aviv Museum. There were more groups there, each loosely organized. Debbie chose to carry a huge sign, "Katamon, not Hebron" which seemed to her not to be too politically radical while at the same time espousing humanitarian concern., Basically what the sign meant was that instead of pouring money, energy and effort into the Israeli settlement of Hebron, an Arab city, the funds could more wisely be spent on improving the conditions in a poor Sephardic Jewish neighborhood in Jerusalem called Katamon.

Debbie walked around the demonstration area smiling at the other participants; she felt part of history. Yet she did not see anyone she might find interesting. The few times she tried to initiate conversations were without success. They seemed to be so deeply involved in the political issues that they had no time or interest in having a flirtatious conversation with a new girl. Anger, frustration and tension put a damper on the emergence of any romantic feelings. Guys who came to demonstrations, demonstrated; girls came to look for guys.

At one point, the television reporters and cameramen came, also radio personnel. One of them caught Debbie's eye but by the time she figured out a course of action to get his attention, the moment had passed. They all moved about very quickly. At one point, the camera lights focused directly on Debbie's sign and held it there for what seemed to be ages. Debbie wondered whether or not she would appear on television. Would Shimon see her perhaps? He would not approve of *Peace Now* nor of her demonstrating from a leftist point of view. From their discussions, she had learned that he was very patriotic and definitely on the right. Later Debbie looked for the cameraman again but failed to see him. Apparently the press had zeroed in quickly, taken their shots and left just as fast.

Surrounding the square had been police cars and vans, army jeeps and scores of plain clothesmen. But there were no incidents of violence; it had been a peaceful demonstration and a moderately successful one. Finally the crowd began to thin and the organizers went around to gather the equipment. The bus would leave for Jerusalem at 10 P.M.

Debbie felt somewhat disappointed that the demonstration was over and nothing exciting had really happened. She didn't know herself what exactly she would have wanted to have happen. She grumbled, "It just seemed like a lot of work instead of fun." Surely, a demonstration is not meant to be fun but to make a political statement and to let unheard voices be heard. But let us not be too hard on Debbie!

Then she remembered that she was not far from the Municipality Building in Tel Aviv - where they have outdoor folk dancing on Saturday nights in the warm weather. It was only 10 P.M. and it lasted at least until 11 P.M. She could go back to Jerusalem on a regular bus, she reasoned to herself. She grew excited at the prospect because she recalled having had a great deal of fun there when she had been a tourist. Yes, she decided she would go; she had had enough of this group. No one would even miss her if she didn't return on the organized bus. She put down her sign on the disorganized pile where the others had thrown theirs and walked out to the street. So much for demonstrations!

Debbie walked down Shaul Hamelech Street and asked one of the people standing at the bus shelter in which direction lay the Municipality Building. He seemed to know and pointed south, told her to walk about 6-7 blocks and then turn right for two more streets and that is where it would be. He spoke with such assurance and gave such details that Debbie trusted his judgment completely. She hurled a cheery "thank you" and hurried on her way hoping still to get in quite a bit of dancing. She walked swiftly 5-6-7 blocks but somehow it was not the area she remembered from her tourist days. Still she thought she might be mistaken. After all, the person she had asked was an Israeli and seemed to know. She walked the two streets to the right and looked about like a new tourist. The neighborhood was becoming increasingly shabby and the Municipality Building was nowhere to be seen.

Finally in despair she asked another passerby for the Municipality Building and he replied, "Oh, it is fairly far, perhaps you should take a bus." He proceeded just as methodically and with just as much enthusiasm to outline an itinerary which would put her in exactly the opposite direction of which she had just come. Debbie was furious with the first direction giver and numb in disbelief at the same time.

Hesitating at first, she began to walk back. By this time, it was getting late; she was tired and it seemed that she was nowhere near her destination. Since she had been led astray so completely by her first set of directions, she doubted the second also. Deciding to ask once again, she was amazed when the third informant offered still another map to the Municipality Building. Although Number 2 and 3 differed in some respects, they both led back to where she had come from and then to the North.

Finally she arrived back at the Tel Aviv Museum area and then asked once again. The fourth explanation corroborated with the third so perhaps, Debbie concluded, it could be accurate. As it turned out, the Municipality Building was a mere four blocks from the Tel Aviv Museum. Had she received proper directions the first time, it would have been so easy to find.

There is a joke told among Israelis that if one needs to find a place, one must ask at least three different people for directions. If two are the same, he may be reasonably certain that they are correct. It would take Debbie awhile to learn this even longer to laugh about it. "Why don't they just say they don't know," she would fume, "instead of giving false directions with such detail?" Ah Debbie, you must understand, it is difficult, perhaps impossible, for an Israeli to admit that he doesn't know something, no matter what it is - but especially when it concerns his own city.

Debbie did finally arrive at her destination and saw a huge crowd of people filling the square. They were of all ages: children, teenagers, young adults, parents with strollers and senior citizens. It was a chaotic scene, but a happy one. It was difficult to determine where the dancing began and ended. Here and there was a circle of dancers with spectators so close by almost obscuring them. Sometimes the line of dancers would break through the huddle of onlookers. Many of the circles were very young teenagers; however, Debbie finally found a group of people closer to her own age and joined in. After all that trouble, she was glad at least to do a few dances.

They started to play *Hine ma tov* and Debbie leaped into the circle. She knew this dance only to be a circle dance and was surprised when after the first chorus of the dance, the circle suddenly split and everyone coupled off except of course, Debbie who was once again without a partner. She watched the Israelis do a chorus of the dance in a couple choreography then revert back to a circle dance alternatingly. She wondered whether this was the correct version or the one done in the United States. Perhaps the Israelis had added the variation. Anyway, she had felt stupid suddenly standing by herself on the dance floor. Soon it was 11 P.M. and the crowd dispersed.

Debbie had to ask again which bus went to the Central Bus Station where she could get a sherut to Jerusalem. They told her #26 or #9 and pointed the direction to the appropriate bus shelter. When she arrived at the shelter, she again asked people waiting if the #26 would go to the central bus station. They nodded. When the bus came, she queried the driver also. What she didn't know was that this bus did not actually enter the bus station but made a stop one block away on its way to Jaffa. For someone not watching carefully it would be easy to drive right by the central bus station.

Fortunately Debbie was looking out the window and suddenly she saw the big bus terminal one block away. The driver was about to shut the door. Debbie shouted quickly, "Tachina merkazit?" "Ken" was the answer and he left the door open another two seconds. Debbie hopped off in a panic. What a fate it would be to wind up in a new place like Jaffa late at night and after such a day. "Whew, thank God" she whispered as she walked briskly to the sherut station. "Yerushalayim?" the driver asked as she approached.

"Ken" she answered and got into the car. It was not a long wait.

Every Wednesday night, Debbie continued to go folk dancing at the university. It was the one activity where despite the social atmosphere described earlier, Debbie still found some satisfaction. Then one evening, she heard the name Moshe Maoz being mentioned in an announcement. When she went to inquire and much to her surprise and happiness, she was told Moshe was in Israel and would give a dance workshop the next evening. Moshe was a terrific personality and one of Debbie's favorite people and she liked the dances he choreographed. While in New York, she always attended his folk dance weekends. And so the next evening found her eagerly heading to the YMHA in Katamon where Moshe would teach. It was there that she learned about the proposed weekend at Kibbutz

Machanayim in the north of Israel. It sounded like real fun and if it was like Moshe's other weekends in New York, it would be a wonderful experience. She informed Moshe she wanted to come and he promised to secure her a room on the kibbutz.

Friday afternoon, Debbie boarded the bus going to Tiberias in the Galilee region of Israel. The bus station had been mobbed as is typical of early Friday afternoon. The bus too was crowded, filled with many soldiers going home for the Sabbath. The bus would not go directly to the kibbutz but would only make a stop along the road and Debbie would have to make her own way to the kibbutz. They said it was not far from the road. It was a long ride, about three and a half hours. As the bus moved more and more to the north, the road became more primitive until finally it was only a dirt road with wide open fields on each side. There was not a house or sign of civilization anywhere, just rock laden fields with fledgling specimens of agriculture here and there struggling to survive.

This rural scene was alien and somewhat frightening to city "born and bred" Debbie. She began to wonder if she would really find the kibbutz and feared being stranded on a lonely dirt road with no one for miles to ask for directions. She looked around her on the bus and tried to determine who would be most likely to speak English. But she did not see any promising candidates. Actually, by now more and more soldiers had gotten on the bus and she was surrounded by them. She asked them about the kibbutz and they knew enough English or perhaps they just recognized the name "Machanayim" to convey to her the notion that they would tell her when the kibbutz came. One motioned with his hand that all would be well, don't worry but only said "OK."

Then suddenly as the bus trudged along the small dust tormented road, one of them pointed to a sign on the road that said something in Hebrew. Debbie looked but of course not knowing Hebrew well enough, it had no meaning for her. She looked at him puzzled and he said "Machanayim - po" (Machanayim - here) and he motioned for her to get off. She looked again at the sign but the magic letters eluded her. She looked out of the bus expecting to see the kibbutz but all she saw were more broad expanding fields on either side of the road. "Where" she cried frantically and by this time another soldier was also looking. He pointed to the far distance on one side of the dirt road, but all Debbie's near-sighted eyes could see was a small dot of something on the distant horizon. One of the soldiers had gotten up to pull the string that would signal the bus to stop. Debbie was afraid to move, afraid to leave the warm womb of the bus that had been cradling her back and forth for the last three and a half hours, afraid to go out into the lonely dirt road with the threatening lonely fields on each side with only the assurance of strangers that this was indeed the place for her to get off and that the tiny speck in the distance was really a gathering of human life. "Are you sure?" she pleaded again and exasperated by her confusion, they again pointed to the sign not realizing that what was clear and intelligible to them could not be deciphered by Debbie.

The bus stopped but Debbie was still in her seat deliberating whether or not she should get off. This bus was no different from the city buses described earlier. One must be ready by the door and jump off quickly before the door slams. Debbie was just about getting up from her seat more out of automatic response than out of conviction when the door slammed shut having been open for perhaps seven seconds. "Rega". the soldiers screamed sounding like a very dissonant chorus and Debbie pushed her way to the door, dragging her heavy overnight bag along behind her. She looked once more at the distant dot but realized she had to jump out if the door was not to slam again after which the bus driver's patience would be at an end.

She jumped out as if she were parachuting for the first time wondering what would await her as she landed. She felt like a newborn that was bewildered by the strange place into which it had half unwillingly come. The door slammed immediately and the bus plodded on to its next destination. Debbie looked after it almost nostalgically as it disappeared into the distance. Then she was alone in the silence standing on a dirt road in the upper Galilee near the Lebanese border with only an unintelligible sign and the directions of strangers to guide her. She squinted to determine if she could somehow make the speck hazily hinting at something in the distance more clear but it was to no avail. She lifted her heavy bag and began to walk in the direction of that something that she hoped and prayed (that is, she would have prayed if that's what she did) would be Kibbutz Machanayim.

They said it was not far from the road. Ha! Debbie soon learned that "not far" meant something quite different to an army trained long distance marcher Israeli than to a taxi- taking and subway riding American city girl. She began to wish she had stayed home and was angry with Moshe for not having told her how difficult it was to get there.

She walked what seemed to be at least an hour when finally the speck began to emerge as a series of tiny one story huts scattered over an acre or so of land. She felt better at the promise of some sign of life there even if it was not the kibbutz. After what seemed to be an eternity, Debbie arrived at the small speck in the distance and it was indeed Kibbutz Machanayim, a small kibbutz of 100 members near Rosh Pinna. At first she walked around awhile and it looked completely deserted. She entered what looked like an office and found a young man about 18 sitting leisurely in a chair. She started explaining who she was and what she was doing there but soon saw that he understood no English whatsoever. He motioned, "Wait a minute" and went to call someone else. He came back with an older man who apparently knew some English and Debbie explained again.

Moshe had promised to make a room reservation for her but obviously had forgotten since the man informed her he did not have one. By this time Debbie was tired from the trip and the anxiety of finding the right place had left her drained. He thought for a minute, then asked if she would mind sharing a room with a 15 year old girl who had also come for the folk dance weekend. Debbie said she didn't mind at all and a few minutes later was ushered into a wooden cabin with one sparsely furnished room. She met a thin freckled faced girl of 15 with two long braids, a long thin face with bright eager eyes named Serit Rosenfeld. It was a girl she would meet many times during the next six years.

They looked each other over for a minute. Then Debbie said, "I hope you don't mind my sharing your room." "It's not mine," she answered, "I came from Safed to the dance." They got along well from the very beginning and later went for a walk around the kibbutz.

Machanayim was one of the poorer kibbutzim, not one they usually show to tourists but it had a pleasant country atmosphere. Rows of attractive little bungalows formed the western side of the kibbutz. Each house was separate with a small area of land surrounding it. Here and there small children could be seen playing on the grass, rocking on a wooden horse or pedaling around on their tricycles. A few adults also were sitting in front of their homes, although it was still somewhat early for relaxing. Usually later in the evening, most adults would enjoy the cool country air and twilight stars. They also passed the children's house, a school, tennis and basketball courts and something that might have been a bomb shelter.

Soon it was dinnertime and Debbie eagerly looked forward to going to the common eating hall and seeing all the other persons from the kibbutz. Probably at no other time and place is Kibbutz Machanayim so united as at the evening meal held in the gym size dining hall. Dinner was served cafeteria style; there certainly was plenty of food and one could take as much as one wanted. Debbie noticed, however, that everyone took only an average amount; no one took advantage of the opportunity to take an excess. Soon the dining hall which had long rows of tables was filled to capacity. Everyone was busily eating and chatting away happily with the others at his table. The kibbutzniks ate quickly and left the hall immediately when finished. Soon others came to their place, then they too departed quickly. It was obviously a way of life with which they were very familiar.

In the evening, the kibbutz members and those who had come for the workshop gathered again in the dining hall for Israeli folk dancing. Debbie joined right in and had a good time. She was disappointed in that she didn't have much chance to talk to Moshe Maoz. He was with his wife and child and remained distant. What a difference the presence of a wife makes, Debbie thought. Usually Moshe was so friendly and talkative with everybody when he was by himself. Now he was like a man on a chain, dutifully obeying his master. It was a factor she hadn't counted on. Moshe had always made her feel good somehow; maybe his enthusiasm, energy and outgoing personality helped to lift her out of her usual quiet, overly serious and somewhat inhibited self.

The workshops started the next morning after a hearty Israeli breakfast in the dining hall. Salads and fish of many kinds had been offered as choices, a new experience for Debbie who like most Americans did not eat very much for breakfast. The workshops were like many others she had attended in New York City, at hotels and at folk dance weekends in upstate New York. People had come from the surrounding areas, mostly from Haifa and other places in the north of Israel. Debbie scanned the crowd but did not see anyone she found interesting or wanted to talk with. She concentrated on the dances being taught first by Moshe and then by Noam Levy, the famous and perhaps also the best Israeli choreographer who had come in from Haifa. First there were circle dances, then couple. Fortunately, people were not as paired off as they were in the regular weekly groups and Debbie managed to get a partner for the couple dances. It was a good looking young Israeli from Tiberias, about 25 years old. Debbie like him and they had a good time while dancing. Unfortunately he took off rather quickly when the couple dances ended and they reverted to circle and line dances. "Oh well," Debbie thought, "he was probably too young anyway." She saw Serit dancing with one of the younger boys. Debbie thought back to when she was that age, a time when any and every boy on the horizon was a possibility. Only she didn't appreciate this fact then or utilize it to her advantage. Now at 32, Debbie found that most men were either married, too young or presented some other problem which would be a barrier to a relationship. Serit seemed to be as oblivious as she had been. She treated the boys who had stopped by the room with a minimum of interest, certainly not with encouragement and spoke eagerly of her plans to become a medical doctor.

In the evening, there was open dancing although the dances taught during the day were reviewed. The next day passed in a similar uneventful way until suddenly at 3 P.M., it was all over and people started to leave in the same quick way in which they had filed out of the dining hall. Debbie was accustomed to people lingering on and talking with friends after a dance session but in Israel when something ended, it ended rather abruptly. She had already observed the same quick emptying of a concert hall or theater immediately after the performance.

She had hoped to secure a ride back to Jerusalem with someone but had not been able to find anyone in the crowd from Jerusalem. She had not yet learned that in Israel, people do not travel great distances for folk dancing. The high cost of petrol and the sheer amount of driving would put it beyond the realm of consideration for most Israelis. Moshe did not have the following in Israel that he did in United States where many, usually women, adored him. The fact that he had left Israel many years earlier and now lived in California also caused him to be viewed with some criticism. By the end of the last workshop, she would have settled for a ride just to Haifa or Tel Aviv but even this proved to be impossible. People had come together and they were now leaving together and Debbie was again by herself. She went to Moshe to ask him how she could get back to Jerusalem but he too was busily in the process of leaving. His little girl was crying and having a temper tantrum at the same time and he seemed to be engaged in domestic squabbles with his wife also. He suggested maybe she could go to Haifa with Noam Levy, if not, to ask in the office, they would know when were the buses to Tel Aviv.

Everyone left quickly and before she knew it, she was the only one still hanging around. Serit had gone with some people to Safed. She decided to look for the kibbutz office but when she finally did find it, after much asking and walking about, it was closed. One kibbutznik just bringing in a truck saw her walk dejectedly away from the office and yelled, "Segur?" (Closed?). "Autobus, Tel Aviv?" Debbie questioned. "Ah", his eyes lit up in understanding . "Po" (there), he pointed to a time schedule of buses to Tel Aviv posted on a nearby pole. To Debbie's dismay, it was in Hebrew and very confusing. The kibbutznik came to look at the schedule with her and pointed out that a bus had passed by 15 minutes earlier. Indeed, at 1:15, there had even been a bus to Jerusalem. It was her fault; she should have checked earlier instead of being so embroiled in the dancing. There would be another in 50 minutes. "Efo?" (Where?) Debbie asked worried now about how she would find her way out of the kibbutz again. He pointed to the road in the distance and made a motion with his hand of a bus shelter like in a game of charades. Debbie knew she would have to go back to the road where she had gotten off two days earlier. Well, it didn't seem so very difficult; once she would be on the bus, it would be OK. "Toda" (Thank you) she smiled. At least he had tried his best to help her. It was after all, a kibbutz, not Port Authority Bus Terminal in New York.

She had almost an hour to wait. She began to walk toward the entrance of the kibbutz which would lead to the road going out to the main road. On the way she again had to pass the dining hall which seemed to be the focal point of the entire kibbutz. She was intending to pass by but saw four young people with snow white hair hanging around the water cooler. She looked again; she had never seen such a dazzling platinum color and it was obviously natural. Their faces were also the same hue. Debbie wanted some company and decided to go in and find out who these beautiful creatures from outer space were. She approached with "Hi, were you here for the dance weekend?" She knew they hadn't been; they would have stood out like torches among the relatively dark Israelis.

"No," they chimed together, "We just got back from an outing in Tiberias."

Three were from Sweden, one from Denmark. All were students

of social science at the university who had come to serve as volunteers on this kibbutz and to study it as an experimental phenomenon of socialism. They were very friendly and urged her to drink some of the cold water. "You have to drink a lot here," "You can get dehydrated very quickly." They asked her what she was doing at the kibbutz and she explained about the folk dance weekend and how she was now going back to Tel Aviv by bus.

"In fact, " she looked at her watch, "I'd better be going. I wouldn't want to miss it." They said a cheery Goodbye and Debbie walked off. Somehow their energy and enthusiasm had had a good effect on her and she felt better and stronger than she had before she saw them.

She started to walk down the road which then seemed to lead into another. It all felt very confusing and as though an eternity had passed till she finally saw the bus shelter. "Whew," she sighed as she plopped her heavy overnight bag on the bench. "Just in time," she murmured to herself as she checked her watch again and sat down.

She waited and waited. No bus. She thought she must have missed it and grew very anxious. She looked around at the wide expanse of fields and wondered what on earth she was doing there. She hated to admit even to herself that the weekend had certainly not been worth the amount of effort that it had taken to get there. A half hour went by and she was certain that she must have missed it. She didn't know what to do, to continue to wait or to return to the kibbutz and ask for a room for the night. Neither alternative was appealing especially the latter since she envisioned already the difficulty of making this request understood in English and a halting Hebrew.

As she continued to waver in her decision and looked down the long road for the bus that would never come, she became aware of a truck coming from the road where she had just walked. As it drew close, she saw even with her near-sighted eyes the same four volunteers with whom she had spoken. Their hair glistened in the sun like a transfigured apparition. She vaguely saw that they were making some gestures in her direction but couldn't make them out. She ran quickly in the direction of the truck which at this point symbolized life to her.

"Whatcha sitting there for?" one of them called.

"I'm waiting for the bus to Tel Aviv but it hasn't come or else I've missed it," she explained.

They laughed and said, "You'll wait forever there. That's not the place for Tel Aviv. That's the bus to the Golan Heights and it only comes once a day at 10 in the morning." Debbie was ready to give up! She then noticed a schedule in the shelter but since it had been only in Hebrew, she had not even bothered to look at it. In the cities, some things were also written in English but she supposed few tourists ever came here to warrant an English version.

"Come on, get in," one of the Swedish girls motioned, moving over to give her room in the truck. Debbie was not used to riding in trucks and it was all she could do to get into the highly placed seats. "We'll take you to the right place," the driver, the boy from Denmark offered.

"Gee, thanks," Debbie said gratefully but embarrassed by what was apparently a stupid mistake. The truck drove on quite a distance before it turned onto the main road.

"This is the main road," they explained and Debbie looked but they all seemed the same to her. Apparently she had greatly misjudged the distance she had walked two days earlier after she had been catapulted off the bus. She couldn't believe that she had actually walked so far. That "speck of something" had goaded her on so strongly that in her anxiety she had under-rated the distance. Now, on the other hand, in her eagerness to get home, she had over-rated the very same distance.

"We're going up to the market in Rosh Pinna" they said stopping the truck before another bus shelter. "Here is the right place for Tel Aviv and there are buses going every two hours or so. Don't worry."

Debbie thanked them. "I would have sat there until tomorrow morning if you hadn't come along," she joked. They turned the truck in the opposite direction and went cheerfully bouncing along the rocky road. Debbie thought how much they seemed at home there.

This time Debbie looked at the schedule and although it was also only in Hebrew, she could make out that she would have about a half hour wait before the next bus. She sat down somewhat relieved and looked around again at the lonely landscape on which she was a mere dot. She felt unsafe somehow but tried to convince herself that it was not New York or New Jersey where a girl sitting alone on a deserted country road better say her final prayers. After a half hour, an old bus come rattling along the rocky dirt road. It stopped, the small narrow single door opened and Debbie hurriedly climbed aboard. "Tel Aviv?" she asked hopefully. "Ken" the driver nodded.

It was 12:30 A.M. when the rickety old bus finally made its way into Tel Aviv's Central Bus Station. It had taken what seemed to be a century to get there plodding along slowly and stopping everywhere. But Debbie was relieved at any rate to once again be in the center of civilization, in a big city even though it was only at the Central Bus Station, certainly not a desirable place for a young woman alone at 12:30 A.M.

Debbie hurriedly hunted around the bus station looking to see if there was still a bus to Jerusalem. She was so happy to be back in the city and not among those empty fields and dirt roads that she just wandered aimlessly about the station. After awhile she noticed a soldier looking curiously at her. Then she saw he was walking after her. She started to feel uncomfortable and went to one of the stands still open to buy an ice cream. Much to her dismay, he stopped also and studied her more closely. "Please stop following me." Debbie implored him in a nice way.

"What are you doing here?" he asked.

"I'm trying to find a bus to Jerusalem," she answered curtly not now in the mood to be polite and answer dumb questions.

"Buses finished at 11:30. Sherut now" and he pointed across and up the street to the parked Mercedes limousine waiting for seven passengers necessary to begin the journey to Jerusalem.

"Where are you coming from?" he continued suspiciously eyeing her heavy traveling bag."

"Kibbutz Machanayim," she returned.

"What did you do there?" he persisted.

"Hey, why all the questions?" Debbie was getting tired of answering what to her were now boring and silly questions. She wanted to forget about the weekend. Besides she had no interest in him whatsoever.

"Security," he finally said looking very serious and efficient now.

"Oh, so you think I'm a terrorist?"

"Why you are walking around the bus station alone 12:30 at night when there are no buses going?" he threw the question at her now with a stern tone to his voice that meant business and was even somewhat accusing.

"OK, I'll tell you. I was at a folk dance weekend at the kibbutz and she showed him the little flyer in Hebrew she had gotten at the workshop advertizing Moshe Maoz and Noam Levy as the guest teachers. Since nobody bothered to show me the correct bus shelter for the bus to Tel Aviv, I waited at the wrong one. It took some time till I finally got on the right bus and I'm glad to be here in the city not out in the sticks. I didn't know there are no more buses. In New York, buses go all night."

"This is not New York," he said.

"It sure isn't," Debbie retorted, angry now at having to justify her presence and actions at the bus station to this skinny young teenage looking kid just because he had a uniform and gun. The suppressed anger she felt at having been forgotten and ignored by Moshe, at not having been offered a ride by anyone, the general frustration of the journey and the unfulfilled high expectations that she had for the weekend - all rose to the surface now and were displaced on the soldier. She threw the rest of her ice cream into the basket, adjusted her traveling bag and walked away to the waiting sherut without looking back at the soldier.

Debbie approached the sherut hoping that she would be the seventh passenger and it would speed off into the night to the eternal city. But such luck rarely occurs in Israel and Debbie was only the second to arrive. Only an elderly Hassid sat in the front seat . After 15 minutes, a couple with a baby came. The baby girl did not stop crying for the entire trip.

Another 20 minutes passed and a thin young man opened the door and questioned "Yerushalayim?" "Ken" was the chimed reply of the other four who felt relieved that soon the car would move. At this point, the driver came over and asked the waiting five if they would be willing to pay the additional fee for the missing two passengers and then they could leave immediately. After all it was late and at this hour, persons came only rarely. All agreed happily to pay except for the gruff Hassid who staunchly refused.

Their elation quickly ended and they sat once more in the still darkness. Debbie had an idea and relayed it to one of the men who spoke English. She would be willing to pay the extra fare for herself and the Hassid if the others paid for the seventh person.

The man quickly called the driver and before long the Mercedes swung onto the highway leading to Jerusalem. The sherut sped along at what seemed 100 mph and 50 minutes later, it was swirling around the curving lanes entering the city. The driver began asking where each person had to go once inside the city, hoping to make extra money. Once he reached the main sherut station, the taxi became a "Special" and the prices climbed.

He queried Debbie also and she just shook her head. He didn't believe that she didn't need additional transportation and asked once more (few people lived in the center of the town). Besides, from a foreigner, he could always command a higher price especially at that hour.

Debbie shook her head again and said , "I can walk." "I take you," he offered with a smile. Debbie already knew it would cost plenty and got out without looking at him. Debbie was learning that the only way to get rid of potential salesmen was to ignore them completely. It was not far to walk and this was the prime advantage to living in the center of town and near everything. When she finally got home, she sat down on the bed, dog tired and wondered why the folk dance weekend which had sounded like such fun, turned out in the long run to be an ordeal instead. Well, she would think about it another time. She lay down on the bed, her thoughts slowly began to sag and soon she drifted off on a rocky dirt road to sleep.

CHAPTER 6
PENELOPE UNRAVELS THE BRIDAL GOWN

Soon the soccer season was at an end and quite suddenly winter descended on Jerusalem. Winter was usually fairly cold in Jerusalem with much rain and even an occasional snowfall. This year was no exception. It was also time for the yearly Israeli Medical Week to take place. This was always a big event with many conferences, exhibitions and social events with international representation. Debbie hoped to attend as many of the events as her teaching schedule would allow. Unfortunately this was not as many as she would have liked but she went with her dauntless enthusiasm thinking it might be a good opportunity to meet someone interesting.

And so in the bite of a Jerusalem winter morning, Debbie found herself heading for the Hilton Hotel and the adjacent Congress Center where the conferences and exhibitions were being held. An exhibition of military medicine was also on display outside. The days passed quickly and one day she arrived at the conference about noon and entered the lounge of the hotel. She immediately noticed a very handsome man sitting on one of the corner sofas eating lunch. She recognized him as having given one of the lectures on neurological disorders two days earlier. He had curly dark hair. a very white complexion with deep dreamy eyes. He could have passed for an Israeli but his expensive dark suit was a better indication that he was a foreigner.

Debbie sat down on a sofa near him, at least within talking distance, hoping perhaps to find some excuse to start a conversation. Just as she was about to order some coffee and cake, Debbie saw, much to her horror, that the dark woman who had been sitting on the sofa in back of the handsome stranger, had begun to speak to him. Debbie had not paid much attention to her because she was ugly with harsh deep lines, not so young and the kind of Israeli that frequented the hotels in the hopes of ensnaring an unsuspecting tourist. Or worse, she could have been a prostitute. There had been some operating in the Hiltons. But now that she had dared to move in on Debbie's territory, Debbie became acutely conscious of her presence.

Before long, the handsome man and the "prostitute" were engaged in an interesting and lively conversation. At first, Debbie was ready to give up but she could not bear losing this brilliant beautiful man to such a lowly creature. Much to her own surprise, she heard herself saying, "I really enjoyed your lecture on Monday. You must have been working a long time on that project."

He looked pleased that she had spoken to him and suggested smiling, "Why don't you turn your chair around and I'll move in this direction, then we can all talk together." The Israeli woman smirked obviously annoyed at Debbie's intrusion. Debbie quickly turned her chair in his direction and soon they were a triangle.

He got up and introduced himself, "I'm Gregory Roth from the U.K." "What a beautiful accent and just the right amount of nasality," Debbie thought admiringly. Debbie introduced herself; the woman did not. Debbie probed at her, glad that she had registered for the conference - a factor which put her in a superior position.

"Are you also with the conference?"

"No," came the grudging reply.

"Oh, then you must be a guest in the hotel?" Debbie continued mercilessly hoping to expose her intentions.

"Well, no, " the woman admitted. "I just came in for a cup of coffee."

"Wow, this is an expensive place to come for a cup of coffee," Debbie remarked sarcastically, again surprised at the tone of her own voice and at how cruel she could be. Usually she was so kind and passive; now she was like a lioness with her cub. But whom was she protecting? Gregory from the clutches of a prospective money seeker or herself?

"It's no more than downtown," the woman retorted, trying desperately to defend herself.

"Oh, sure it is, it's double, in fact," Debbie contended with the voice of authority, then turning to Gregory, posed another question, "Will you continue with your research on cerebrospinal fluid or will you turn to something else now?" As he finished his reply, the woman realizing that she had been defeated, got up and said, "Well, I really have to be going. Enjoy the conference."

At last, Debbie had the doctor to herself. She was so proud of herself that she had been brave and had the nerve to talk to him too. From that point, Gregory and Debbie fell into an easy conversation so natural between two very intelligent, very educated and very dedicated people. He asked Debbie about her work and life in Israel. Debbie spoke happily but it was not long before he casually mentioned his wife and two sons. Debbie was actually not surprised. She knew only too painfully by now that men such as Gregory Roth were no longer available. She took it in stride and would enjoy his company as long as she could.

By this time, he had finished eating his huge Hilton type lunch of fried fish. "It's good but just too much," he commented, suddenly looking at his watch. "Gee, it's just about 2. I'm sorry I have to go. I've booked this tour to Bethlehem for this afternoon. Some of my friends suggested it and they said to be in front of the hotel by 2. Sorry to run off like this. It's been nice talking to you. Maybe we'll run into each other again sometime." Debbie was kind of stunned since she assumed this wonderful conversation would go on all afternoon. He got up, smiled, and ran off.

As she sat there by herself, she realized just how lonely she was. Sure she had friends and a job and activities. But it was not enough. She was only kidding herself. She needed a partner, a soulmate, someone just like her with whom she could talk easily and who would understand her. She had become so used to being alone or with people who did not satisfy her, that it was not until now having been fed just a little that she understood its magnitude.

"Hey, I could go along on that tour to Bethlehem," the thought suddenly popped into her head. She jumped up and ran wildly to the front of the hotel. Only the doorman and guard stood there.

"Did the bus to Bethlehem leave yet?" she asked breathlessly.

"Yes, Miss, it left about five minutes ago." Debbie looked longingly down the road into which the bus and Gregory Roth had disappeared. "There will be another tour tomorrow, miss," the doorman said, sensing her disappointment.

Debbie wanted to attend the conference the next day in the hope of seeing the interesting Doctor Roth again but it was one of her fullest teaching days and it was impossible for her to take the day off. She thought about it all day long - the crowds of people at the Hilton, the interesting lectures, the sophisticated, educated participants and of course, Gregory. She felt very frustrated being stuck in the classroom with a horde of kids. It was also the last day of the conference and her last opportunity to meet Gregory again. She tried to rationalize, "Oh well, he is married anyway and will return to England."

Was it really Gregory himself that she wanted to see again so badly or what he represented? It was probably a combination of both. Then just as suddenly as the idea of going on the Bethlehem tour came to her, so did the thought that she might indeed see Gregory again by going on one of the post-Congress tours the next day. It was Saturday and she was free. "Why not?" she thought, "It will be a chance to spend a pleasant day. I haven't had a really good time in so long." Most of the seemingly "good time" events she had attended only succeeded in making her even more depressed and in heightening her awareness of being alone and single.

She remembered that Gregory had mentioned something about going on a tour but she could not recall if it was to Masada or to the Galilee. When she arrived on Saturday, there were several buses already waiting. She quickly walked by each one scanning the seats for his familiar face but she did not see him.

The various tour guides saw her looking and kept asking, "Which tour do you wish to go on?" How could Debbie answer! So she tried to avoid them and kept searching around. Precious minutes passed and still she did not see him. Could he have changed his mind? Perhaps he had already seen these places.

"Madame, the buses are almost ready to leave. Would you

please decide which one you want," one of the guides pleaded. Debbie felt panicky. Now she didn't want to go at all. Yet since she had gotten up so early and had come so far, she reconsidered and decided to board the Engligh speaking bus to Masada. As she sat on the waiting bus, more and more people continued to climb aboard. Then suddenly she saw him come into the bus. But her instant rush of joy was frozen as she saw him busily talking to the blond woman who had entered immediately behind him.

Debbie had hoped that he might sit next to her and left her bag purposefully on the seat to discourage anyone from taking the place. Once she had even told an elderly woman who wished to sit there that she was holding it for someone. Now she was dismayed as Gregory and the blond got into the seat directly behind her; they acted like a happy couple eager to be with each other.

After awhile, Debbie turned around and as if she had seen him by accident, she feigned surprise and chirped, "Why, hello again. Are you coming on this trip too?" He looked surprised at seeing her again but certainly not displeased.

"Oh, you're the one I spoke to the other day in the lounge."

"Yes, how are you? How was Bethlehem?

"Oh, it wasn't much. I was sorry I went. There wasn't much to see."

By this time, the blond next to Gregory had leaned forward in her seat with a concerned and somewhat annoyed look on her face. Debbie was telling him that Masada and the Dead Sea were far more interesting, the reason why she was making the trip again. He spoke lively and energetically perhaps flattered at having two attractive women adulating him. Yet he seemed genuinely happy at seeing Debbie again. The seats in the bus were high and it was difficult to carry on any lengthy conversation comfortably with someone sitting in front or in back. So out of sheer discomfort, both Gregory and Debbie sank back into their respective seats and the bus drove off.

For Debbie, the landscape along the way to Masada Mountain and the Dead Sea were familiar territory. For the post Congress tourists, the view was new and breathtaking. Heading out from Jerusalem into the Judean Desert, the bus traveled through hills and valleys of tan colored sand sparkling in the rising sunshine. Soon stone mountains with an amber glow appeared in Debbie's bus window. Proud and mighty they stood there in the sand and sun chained to each other for centuries.

Finally, they arrived at the majestic Masada Mountain, the jewel of the entire range. Many other tour buses were already parked in the large lot at the foot of the mountain. The guide purchased a group ticket for the cable car to the top of the mountain and he waved the group past the long queue of individuals that had gathered. Finally the cable car came and they all went in, some reluctantly as they anticipated the sharp lift.

On the ride up to the top, the tourists oooh'd and aaaah'd and shared a fantastic panorama of the Negev Desert and finally the surrounding stone mountains and the distant Dead Sea enshrouded as if in a royal blue haze. Cameras clicked constantly like a mini symphony inside the tiny capsule.

Finally the cable car arrived near the top of the mountain after which the tourists were required to climb an additional 200 sandstone steps to reach the actual top. Gregory continued to walk next to the blond as the guide led the group around to examine what was left of the famous Zealot stronghold. The group was fairly large so it was possible for Debbie also to walk close to Gregory and occasionally as circumstance allowed, to whisper some comments to him about the oh so interesting ruins they were viewing at that particular moment.

When they entered the remains of what had once been Herod's Roman Bath House, Gregory started to talk more with Debbie than with the blond. As the guide explained the method by which the steam entered the room from below and then rose to the floor level situated on pillars, Gregory stood next to Debbie on the gangplank. From that point on, they were together. The blond strangely went off and began to walk with others. Debbie never knew why.

After they descended from the mountain, the group went to eat in the restaurant nearby. Gregory and Debbie sat in a separate part of the restaurant and resumed the conversation they had begun in the Hilton lounge. They spoke easily and freely with each other as though they had known one another for many years. Both talked about their work, aspirations, and activities. So engrossed did they become in their togetherness that they forgot about the time the tour guide had instructed the group to be back at the bus. Suddenly, Gregory looked at his watch and said, "Hey, it's 10 to 1, we're late. They'll be waiting for us." They hurried back to the bus where indeed the group and tour guide had already become anxious about them.

From there, the bus drove down the sunlit road leading to the Dead Sea, the lowest point in the world. It was a beautiful day and warm despite the fact that it was December. The sea glistened in the sun and from afar the salt crystals sparkled like diamonds. The surrounding stone mountains had taken on a red-orange glow in the afternoon light. All together it was an awesome sight and the tourists couldn't wait to become part of it.

The guide instructed them above all not to allow the salt water to get into their eyes because it would burn terribly and to remove all metal which might be corroded by the high concentration of salts. Anyone could float in the Dead Sea and he encouraged all at least to try. There were also thermal and mineral baths indoors one for men and women and one for women alone and finally, there was the famous Dead Sea mud with which they might coat themselves. The latter was supposed to have beneficial effects for the skin. They would have three hours in which to partake of all the facilities.

The group began to disperse into the various activities. Gregory and Debbie decided at first to take a dip in the Dead Sea itself. The water was warm but unlike any other sea, it was thick and lush to the touch. Gregory attempted to swim but discovered that the water kept buoying him up to the surface and therefore making deep strokes impossible. Debbie floated which required no effort whatsoever. Her feet were sticking out of the water and Gregory began to play with her toes.

"Do you like that?" he asked. She giggled because it was ticklish. They had a marvelous time putting the black health-giving mud on each other playfully and for awhile they looked like two Negroes. They lay in the warm sun and let the mud perform its beneficial actions. Finally they sampled the indoor mineral baths which proved to be very enjoyable and relaxing. How easily one could fall asleep in these hot thick waters. The three hours flew by. No one wanted to leave but at 4:30 P.M., the bus would depart for Qumran and Jericho. This time Debbie and Gregory were there.

The tour made a short stop in Qumran to see the place where the famous Dead Sea Scrolls were found and to view the remains of the Essene community that had once flourished there. How exciting it was to see the huge caves in which the little Bedouin boy had discovered the scrolls; from afar they looked like mere holes in the mountains.

Then it was on to Jericho where they saw the ruins of what was once a great city. Like Masada, it also contained a Herodian palace. From here, the guide pointed to the Mount of Temptation where Jesus was tempted by the devil. On top of the mountain today is a Greek monastery only men may visit. The last stop was the Hisham Palace. The tourists expressed surprise at the stark contrast between the lush jungle-like greenery in the new city and the arid desert immediately surrounding it.

On the return trip to Jerusalem, most of the tourists were very quiet and tired, Debbie and Gregory included. Although she had taken a good fresh water shower, Debbie still felt the salt on her body and especially in her hair which was sticky and matted. As the bus neared Jerusalem, Gregory asked Debbie to join him for dinner at his hotel. She was overjoyed but wished to go home first to freshen up and change her clothes. They agreed to meet at 7:30 P.M.

Debbie rushed home, showered and washed her hair. There was not really enough time to fix her hair properly but "better wild hair than sticky hair" she reasoned. By this time, it was 7:15 and she knew she couldn't make it in time so she called Gregory to tell him she would be a little late. She hailed a taxi to the King Saul Hotel where she found Gregory waiting outside. He looked somewhat worried but happy to see her.

"When you called, I thought you were going to say you weren't coming," he said anxiously.

"Oh, no, " Debbie answered, surprised that he should have said that. "I wanted to very much."

They went into the hotel dining room and ate a very leisurely dinner. It was an elegant place and the food was excellent. But more wonderful was to share it with such an attractive interesting partner. Debbie mused how blissful it would be to always share ones meals with such a partner. She could barely fathom such joy!

After dinner they went for a walk near the hotel. It was a beautiful evening and it seemed as though it would last forever. They got to know each other even better and there was a perfect harmony between them. When they returned to the hotel, they went to his room suddenly tired from their long walk. They started to talk again but somehow both knew that the time for talk had passed. There were a few moments of awkwardness then Gregory said quite naturally, "Well, shall we take our clothes off?"

She smiled delighted at the thought but remained self conscious. "Here, let me help you," Gregory offered. They discovered each others bodies and made love late into the night Gregory was an experienced lover and all flowed smoothly and heavenly. Debbie's awkwardness, fears and hesitations all melted into ecstasy with Gregory's touch. She fell asleep more relaxed and happy than she could ever remember.

When she awoke the next morning, Gregory was already awake. Debbie was still in the same blissful state as the night before but Gregory's mood had definitely changed.

"Good morning," she whispered dreamily.

"Good morning," he answered politely but with a sense of urgency. "I have to get down to breakfast early so I will still have time to get my things together. The taxi to the airport will come at 10:30." He seemed anxious and hurried, not at all like the Gregory of the evening before.

She had not wanted to remember that the conference was over and that Gregory would be leaving today for England, his wife and children. But now she was forced to recall. She took the hint and got up quickly. As though he realized that perhaps he had been too brusque, he said, "You know how it is in these dining rooms, they have set hours and you have to be there, or you don't get anything."

Debbie hurriedly used the bathroom and she threw on her clothes. What a difference from how lovingly they had been taken off!

"You can stay here until I come back," Gregory's rushed voice broke into her thoughts, "But please don't answer the phone. Sometimes my wife calls to find out when I will arrive at the airport."

He went downstairs and Debbie sat down alone. She had been so happy but of course it had to end. "Perhaps a few day like this will be all I will ever have," she thought pessimistically. "I wonder if it will ever be any different." Her experience with Gregory had taught her one thing though, that she could care for someone else besides Shimon. When Shimon had gotten married, she did not think she could ever love anyone else again. No man she had met since then could measure up to him. But now she had and she realized that there were probably more men out there waiting to be discovered.

Gregory did not take long for breakfast and then Debbie knew she had to go. She moved close to him, "I had a wonderful time with you these past few days." They kissed but it was brief.

"I hate goodbyes. I always think it's better if it's done quickly," he announced suddenly upset and agitated now.

"Well, does it have to be goodbye? Perhaps we shall see each other again. Will you be returning to Israel in the future?" Debbie asked hopefully with her never ending optimism.

"Yes, I'll be coming in July for 2 or 3 weeks."

"Well, why don't you give me a call. I'll probably still be at the same number."

"No, I'll be coming with my wife and probably one of my sons and I certainly wouldn't want to see anyone else then." He added the last fact with a certain amount of definiteness that it rather surprised Debbie. She had thought him to be a very easy-going person but where his wife and family were concerned, he was quite firm.

"Well, I guess I'll be going and let you pack and do the things you still have to do." she sighed mustering up all her strength.

Then he mellowed somewhat and said, "I wish you much luck here in Israel. I hope you meet a really nice guy and when you do, he'll be a very lucky fellow. You'll make somebody a very fine wife." He kissed her again lightly and then she found herself outside the door.

Debbie walked away from the hotel but could not bring herself to leave. She hung around the area until she saw the large Mercedes airport limousine shoot by her. It went so fast she could not see the passengers but assumed that Gregory had been one of them. Only then did she begin to make her way home. Her rich experience only made her more acutely aware of how lacking her life really was despite all her activities and attempts to keep busy. Slowly she sank back into the humdrum of her daily life.

But something had happened to Debbie as a result of her experiences with Gregory which she did not even fully recognize as yet. Up to this point, she had always thought of herself as a young girl even though she was already 33, that is, "a young girl who would fall in love with a wonderful man, get married, have children and live happily ever after in a nice house in the suburbs." Now she was beginning to accept the gruesome fact that this might very well never happen to her. If she were going to have any life and love experience at all at her age, she would have to broaden her horizons to include married men. She would have to accept opportunities as they presented themselves.

Debbie thought it best to become involved in some activity so she would not dwell unnecessarily on Gregory's leaving. She had noticed an announcement in the *Jerusalem Post* about a 3 day seminar on Theodore Roethke to be held at the university.

She was not especially fond of Roethke's poetry but convinced herself that it might be important to meet people in her field.

The seminar was poorly attended, unfortunately, perhaps because of the timing or the location; however, it was interesting, well organized and well presented. Debbie had a chance to meet and to become acquainted with Alan Kaufman, the organizer, who was an American and professor at the Jerusalem University. He seemed pleased by Debbie's interest in what was obviously his life-long project. He in turn expressed interest in Debbie's writing of poetry and in her academic background. Due to her teaching program, she was only able to attend parts of the seminar yet on the whole, she enjoyed it and thought it worthwhile.

Her thoughts turned once more to Gregory so she decided to go folk dancing at Weizmann Institute to divert her attention. Perhaps some new faces had appeared. She planned on going to Rehovot after her early morning class at the bank and arrived at the Central Bus Station about 11 A.M. just in time to catch the direct bus.

Standing in the queue was Mrs. Braccha Kaplan, who had been a frequent visitor of Mrs. Levinsky's when Debbie had lived there. She was a nice lady but like most women her age, she was nosy and forever asking questions. Today was no exception. She opened fire immediately but Debbie was prepared for her. The experience with Mrs. Goldenblum had taught her a vital lesson.

"Where are you going?" she began.

"To Rehovot."

"Oh, really, so am I. Where in Rehovot?"

"To Weizmann Institute."

"Oh really, what are you going to do there? Do you know anybody there?"

"Yes, I have a friend there and I'm going to visit him."

"Oh really, who is it?"

"Oh, you wouldn't know him."

"He is Israeli?"

"Yes, but he studied abroad and his parents are from England."
"Oh, what is his field?"
"Molecular Biology."
"Is he divorced?"
"Yes"
"What does he look like?"
"Tall, black hair, very handsome."
"Well, you are very lucky."

Debbie smiled to herself. She enjoyed telling this nosy biddie a bunch of lies although she wondered why she was interested in such exact information. As far as Debbie could remember, she had only a son.

On the bus, however, she told Debbie about her son who had divorced his wife to marry another younger woman. Nevertheless, she stayed very close to her daughter-in-law, who was a wonderful person and the children, blah, blah, blah. She kept talking about her family until finally the bus arrived in Rehovot and each went her own way.

Debbie spent the day at Weizmann and was just about to leave at 5 P.M. for a bite to eat when she passed the Ullman Building for Biological Sciences and found none other than Mrs. Kaplan and a short scrawny dark haired woman with a bird like face about 35 years old sitting on its steps. Debbie couldn't believe she was meeting her again.

"What are you doing here?" This time Debbie asked the first question.

"Oh, this is Miriam, my daughter-in-law. She was visiting some friends here. Where is your boy friend?" The young woman with the bird like face perked her eyes and ears.

"Oh, he went to a lecture at the Agricultural Campus across the road. Well, I'm late, so please excuse me. Hope to see you again." Debbie said quickly and walked away.

"What a woman, unbelievably desperate," Debbie muttered to herself. "She probably thought she could just wait until we came out of the Biology Building together. Then, of course, I would have to introduce her and she would know who the eligible man was and proceed to try and take him away from me. Very clever." An eligible scientist was indeed a rare jewel in Israel. Almost non-existent. Debbie laughed at the joke she had played on the two women and felt somehow she had gained revenge on Mrs. Goldenblum. She would also have to remember that should she ever be so fortunate as to have such a boy friend, she must keep silent about it. Slowly Debbie was becoming an Israeli.

When Debbie arrived at the dancing that evening, there were only the same old faces who were fused with their partners for life. She did the circle dances and only watched the partner dances although she didn't mind very much since she was quite tired. About 11:10 she left unnoticed and hurried to the main gate to catch the 11:20 bus to Tel Aviv - the last one. She had forgotten what a long walk it was from the folk dancing place to the main entrance and was afraid she had missed the bus.

When she got to the bus shelter, there was no one there, in fact, there was no one anywhere. She waited patiently for the bus to come, every now and then straining her near sighted eyes in the direction from which it should come. It was 11:20 and still no bus. She was becoming anxious and already thinking what she might do if she had missed it - stay overnight in a hotel or take a special taxi both of which would be expensive. It was a chilly night; winter had come even to the center of Israel.

She had walked away from the bus shelter toward the direction in which the bus was to come as though somehow it would bring her closer to it. Then upon returning to the bus shelter, she saw a young guy about 22 standing there. She was rather surprised as she did not see him approach from any direction and wondered how he had gotten there so suddenly. He was almost like an apparition. But Debbie was glad to see him having interpreted his being there as an indication that a bus might still be forthcoming.

He eyed her carefully as though he were appraising her value. Debbie dismissed him as just another young guy looking her over and made little notice of him. Still there was no bus. Finally , she asked him casually if he knew whether or not there would still be a bus to Tel Aviv. He seemed to do a double turn when he heard the English language coming from Debbie . He answered that he didn't know and he also seemed not to care very much.

"Did you happen to notice that car there when you came?" he asked calmly.

Debbie looked in the direction to which he had pointed and for the first time became aware of a rather large car parked by itself close to the entrance of the institute.

"Gee, I don't know," Debbie replied, "I just took notice of it now that you mentioned it. My eyes have been looking for a bus so I wasn't particularly interested." His gaze was fixed so intently on the car that Debbie thought he might be contemplating stealing it or going for a joy ride. She was still judging by American norms.

"You didn't see anyone park it there? It's standing in a strict 'No Parking' area close to the main entrance," he asked again, his voice now becoming more urgent.

"No, really, I just noticed it for the first time when you mentioned it. Why are you so interested in this car anyway?" He didn't answer and only kept staring at the car. Debbie continued to assume he was planning to steal it and hence inquiring whether the owner might possibly appear. She began to be afraid of him and wished the bus would come.

"What are you doing here at this time of night?" he asked now in a friendly way.

"Oh, I was at the folk dancing at Weizmann but I had to leave to catch the last bus to Tel Aviv." He seemed surprised at Debbie's answer.

"There's folk dancing at Weizmann Institute?" he asked in disbelief as though somehow such a scientific institute should not lower itself to have folk dancing.

"Sure, back by the swimming pool and tennis courts." Then she looked at her watch. "In fact, it's still going on, till 12. It's a very good group, many excellent dancers. You should try it some time, it's open to the public."

Debbie looked at her watch again and shrugged her shoulders. "I think we missed the bus. What are you going to do? Do you want to share a special?" (private taxi) Debbie asked hopefully. But his gaze remained fixed on the lonely car parked outside the walls of the institute.

"You didn't see anyone come or go from the car, are you sure?"

"You really like this car, don't you? What's so special about it?" Debbie laughed nervously.

He remained deadly serious. "Well, often cars standing where they shouldn't be, have something in them," he informed her as though this was something she should have known. Debbie looked at the car again. She was puzzled at first by what he meant but its lonely presence there in the dark on the otherwise deserted street suddenly assumed new significance.

"You mean, it could have a bomb in it?" she asked horrified and retreating almost automatically in the opposite direction.

"Well, it has happened. I'm the security here. I was standing behind the wall when I saw you coming."

Debbie then realized that he had thought and perhaps still did, that she was somehow connected with this car. "Maybe he thinks I will set the trigger or timer for the explosive to go off." Just then, miraculously, Debbie saw a bus approach that she prayed would be the Number 200 to Tel Aviv. It was! - about 10 minutes late. It had seemed like an hour.

"Well, I'm getting on here. I hope everything's OK with the car." Debbie had never been so eager to board any bus as that one. She was grateful for the warmth therein. It drove off quickly. She looked out the window and watched him walk back to his hiding place behind the wall.

Incidents such as this made Debbie realize that there are many other problems in the world besides her own. She was also reminded that there was much going in Israel of which she was totally unaware. But as always, the surge of daily life and hassles continues unabated, no matter what other problems might exist.

One of the first things Debbie had done shortly after her arrival in Israel, was to join the ACI - the American Club of Israel.

She had been advised by one of her best friends at folk dancing who had spent one year in Jerusalem that this was the place to go if she had any questions or problems and that this is where she would get the most complete and accurate information as an American. It was an organization with branches in each city and offered many different services including free counseling to immigrants regarding their status, laws, jobs, schools, language courses, etc. They also sponsored many social activities for different age groupings such as: the young adult, single parents, Haemtsaim (mid-lifers, age 40-60) and senior citizens. Each group had its own activities, such as, lectures, outings, pot luck dinners, sports, folk dancing and support groups. For example, one of the newest support groups that had rapidly become very successful was Anglo-Saxon women married to Israelis. Other activities, such as the annual Thanksgiving Day dinner was open to all age groups.

It all sounded so nice and inviting; Debbie could hardly wait to join and participate in all those "wonderful " activities. But like many potential "singles" oriented events, the promises made on the advertisement or announcement in the paper were rarely fulfilled in reality. The first event Debbie had attended was a lecture sponsored by the young adults group. When she entered the hall at the ACI headquarters, she was shocked at how few people were there. Only five or six persons were in the audience, a few young girls and two middle aged women. Later a few more arrived but no one Debbie found interesting.

The next event had been a Spring party where again there were many girls and only a few guys. When she arrived, the group was already sitting in somewhat of a circle. There was one chair empty. Debbie was relieved and quietly slid into it. But her relief was short lived as a rough mechanical voice next to her on the left said, "Hello, where do you come from?" She turned and from his looks and the sound of the question, she perceived immediately that he was mentally retarded or disturbed in some way. Then she understood why the seat had been empty. She was uncomfortable and tried to look in the opposite direction but these people were engaged in a conversation and she could not seem to break in. All the while, the retarded one kept talking in a slow monotone voice, deliberately over-emphasizing each word. Debbie looked around and appraised the group.

As she would learn in the future, this had been a typical ACI singles group. There was one girl about 26 with a harsh grating nasal voice who was dominating the group. She spoke with an air of total knowledge and sophistication, a type that would have made a good rival for Brenda Potemkin in Philip Roth's *Goodbye Columbus*. The other girls were like herself, girls who had developed a special love and interest for Israel while at the same time hoping to find a happy social life.

The guys, on the other hand, although there were only a few, so it was difficult to judge, seemed to be a totally different breed. Even as she began to meet more single American men in Israel, the vast majority seemed unfortunately to fall into a definite category - very "schlumpy" types. (The word is difficult, if not impossible, to translate). They were ineffectual as individuals and probably had for a variety of reasons not been able to "make it" in the United States or wherever they came from. Many were non-conformist types, those that would not fit in readily into a corporate structure or into any 9-5 reality - perhaps because they were abrasive personalities or just couldn't cope with authority. Others were just plain "weirdos" - grossly obese or obviously neurotic - the kind one would avoid in the United States.

Many of them came to Israel and were able to create a relatively normal existence in a society where the standards were lower, competition less and where just the fact that they were American gave them a first class superiority in Israeli culture. Here they could assume a status in the society they could not possibly attain in the United States where achievement is the criterion of judgment. It was often just this type of misfit who later became involved with

Kach, Meir Kahane's group. There were exceptions of course but Debbie had not yet met them. This was a revelation and a disappointment for Debbie as well as for all the girls who had joined ACI with the hope of meeting potential dates.

Yet, despite the initial negative experiences she was willing to try ACI again. Now at 33, she felt too old for the young adults group which was designated for ages 20 to 35 but whose members were mostly in their early twenties. For the *Haemtsaim* - or Mid Lifers group, ages 40-60 she was still too young. So she decided to join the Single Parent group telling them that she was planning to have a child and wanted to speak with other single parents about the problems involved in raising a child alone. Since the group was small and they were eager to have members, they allowed her to come to the meetings which were held every Sunday evening.

She went one Sunday evening just to see what kind of people attended. About 10 women and 3 men stood about idly with their coffee cups trying to pretend they were having a good time. They had planned a speaker who would lecture on "Body Language." The minute Debbie entered the room, her eyes landed on Arieh Atar. She remembered him immediately. There could be no mistake even though years had gone by. He was the same arrogant disdainful type he had been years ago on Mount Scopus.

Debbie glanced at him and quickly looked away. Arieh noticed Debbie also and vaguely seemed to recognize her but in a way that indicated he no longer remembered the circumstances. It appeared as if he almost wanted to talk with her. Debbie wondered if he were really divorced or if he was just coming to prowl around, the way he did years ago. She tried to put him out of her mind as well as the hurtful experience she had had with him.

It was a motley group on the whole. The men were schlumpy blah types and the women were barely average or unattractive. The speaker was on par for what one could expect from such a lecture. Debbie spoke to one of the men and several of the women. At the end of the meeting, the leader of the group asked Debbie how she had liked the evening. She took the opportunity to mention something about Atar in the hope of preventing another woman from "falling in" with him. She briefly related her encounter with him and also the possibility that he might be married. Sandy told Debbie that he had only come a few times and that "Yes, I thought he might spell trouble, he looks like it. I'll keep in mind that he could be married. Thanks." She seemed grateful for the information. Arieh perhaps witnessed Debbie's talk with Sandy for he never came to another meeting. Debbie continued to attend because some of the programs were quite good, there was always a chance to make some friends in general and just because it was something different to do.

The group did not always meet at the ACI headquarters; sometimes it gathered at one of the members homes. Debbie was surprised at the difference in attendance, so many more people coming to the home meeting, especially the men. In fact, at the homes, the number of men and women were about equal.

One Sunday evening, the meeting was at Nomi's house in the southern part of Jerusalem. There was a nice size crowd of about 15 people. There was no special program organized so various individuals took the opportunity to tell something. One of these was a handsome lawyer from Argentina who had been in Israel about five years. He was about 35, fair and well built. He related the story of a case he was currently working on.

"It is an important one because it will set a precedent. There was a Jewish man in Argentina who was married to a Gentile woman and had three children. Then he decided to leave his wife and children and emigrated to Israel where he was married again, this time to a Jewish Israeli woman. Naturally, the Argentinian wife was angry and followed him to Israel, demanding that he support the three children. I am representing the Gentile woman.

The husband claims that Jewish law, the law of Israel, does not recognize a marriage of a Jew with a non-Jewish partner. Since the mother was not Jewish, the children also are not Jewish, since children follow the maternal line. His marriage to the Argentinian was invalid, hence he had the right to marry again and that this marriage was the legal and proper one. Thus, he had no responsibilities except to his Israeli wife."

Debbie was shocked at the story and immediately sided with the victim, the deserted wife. She was amazed that the general feeling of the group was with the man and the Israeli woman. Later, she remarked to Nomi, who was herself divorced and struggling to raise a child alone, "Gee, I feel sorry for that poor Argentinian woman and the three kids."

"Why, she's a *goya*," Nomi declared, emphasizing the last word with a frown and smirk on her face to indicate an inferior and loathsome being to be discarded as quickly as possible.

Unfortunately, the lawyer did not return to the group and so Debbie never heard the outcome of the case. She feared that most likely, the man got off scot free.

Debbie was still teaching English as a second language in the Bank of Israel and enjoyed it very much. Most of her courses were for the management but there was one for the clerks and secretaries of the foreign exchange division of the bank. The basic purpose of the course was to improve the employees' spoken English , therefore, Debbie tried to arrange the class so that there would be optimal time for all the students to speak and practice what they already knew.

One day, Debbie asked each class member to relate an unforgettable experience of the previous summer. Some narrated fairly interesting experiences and were corrected if they made a grammatical error. One woman offered to tell a very negative experience that had happened to her the previous summer. She seemed to be visibly upset by the very act of recalling the unpleasant occurrence.

The woman, Sarah, a middle aged clerk, had taken an American girl into her home for the summer as part of a program for young Americans to live with an Israeli family for the summer enabling them to learn about Israeli culture at first hand.

"I was so disappointed in this girl. She had no manners at all," the clerk moaned. She needed no prodding from Debbie to elaborate on her comments.

"Every five minutes, she was going to the refrigerator and taking what she wanted. I never saw anybody eat so much. One time I made a cake and my daughter hid it. When I asked her why, she said, 'So the American won't eat it all.' She made, how do you say it, you know, telephone calls abroad, without asking. Every night she went out, never said where she was going, nothing. Oh, it was terrible. I treated her like my own daughter." She went on and on painting the girl as some kind of monster. Debbie felt ashamed and remarked, "It's unfortunate that you have had this experience after you had been kind enough to open your home." She then called on another student to narrate his experience.

After the class was over and Sarah had left, two of the clerks were still standing in the hallway. Debbie commented again on Sarah's experience with the American girl. They both laughed and the man confided, "Don't worry about Sarah. We've heard that story many times. Do you want to know why she is so upset about the whole affair?" Debbie's interest flared and she quickly said, "No, why?"

"Well, Sarah has a son about 21." He sighed as though a long story was going to follow. "He's finished with the army but he's just kind of hanging around, not knowing what to do. She wants him to go to the university but he is not interested. So she thought it would be a good opportunity if he met a nice American girl, you know, who might take him to the States, maybe her father could set him up in some kind of business or something like that. What happened was that the girl didn't give the guy a second look and starting going out with guys she met at the Jerusalem University. So Sarah's plans were foiled and she got upset."

"Yes, I remember the day when she went down to the office to pick out the girl," the woman clerk chimed in. "She said she would only be gone a little while but she didn't come back until late in the afternoon, leaving me with all the work. I could barely manage. Then when she came, she was all excited."

"I found a rich one, she's 18, her father is a doctor and they live in Marchmont," she told everybody. "That's a beautiful neighborhood, some people told me, big mansions. I went through all the applications until I found the best one. I only hope she comes." "Sarah could hardly finish her work; she kept running around telling everybody. That's why she so disappointed, because it didn't work out, at least not how she wanted it."

Debbie listened attentively to this story since she was unaware of such a program or that people harbored such complex plots and plans under the guise of cultural exchange and understanding. American girls best beware of friendly invitations with ulterior motivations!

Sarah's story made Debbie suspicious and she began to wonder if there were not similar motives behind the frequent Sabbath invitations she was receiving from an elderly teacher she had once met at an ESL conference. At first she thought the teacher and her husband might be lonely and just wanted her company or perhaps felt that she Debbie, was lonely.

Once mention was made of a son living in Denmark who was also a teacher but only gave private lessons. The mother complained that he had some difficulty getting residence permission and was forced to leave and re-enter the country periodically. She asked Debbie if she was a "qualified" teacher. The husband entered the conversation and honestly admitted that their son was not. The old man was about to explain why when his wife kicked him hard under the table and shot him a deadly look. He jumped up startled. Perhaps Debbie surmised now that the old woman had hopes that "something" might materialize between Debbie and her son thereby solving his problems. She recalled now the woman's many questions about her apartment in Manhattan, her parents and their occupations and her future plans. Once her consciousness was raised, she could remember many examples.

Her thoughts then flew back to a time when she first arrived and dated David Shuretsky. He was a similar type, had no steady job and just gave private guitar lessons. Once when she had gone to his place, she encountered his mother and how the old lady had flashed questions at her. Even before Debbie had a chance to sit down, she had declared quite defiantly, "But, of course, your father will buy you a flat?" Debbie was bewildered not understanding her question.

"But I already have an apartment," she explained. David finally came to the rescue chiding his mother for being so quick. He tried to make a joke of it. "She likes you and is trying to match us. She means if we got married." Debbie then realized that she better disappear from this scenario. "Oh well," she mumbled to herself, "I guess everybody is trying to find a place in the world. But I don't want it to be at my expense." She did not want to marry him. She also did not want to waste any more time even thinking about these nosy old biddies with their endless and boring questions.

The holiday season was coming and each day the streets of Jerusalem were filling with more and more tourists who had come either for Christmas or Hanukah. The atmosphere was always more exciting and pleasant at the high peak tourist times. Tourists were happy, idealistic and eager and conveyed this feeling to others around them.

It was Debbie's second winter in the Holy Land and she rationalized that she might as well make use of the opportunity and attend the big Christmas celebrations which were being planned in Bethlehem. Like most Jews, she had always felt left out of the biggest splashiest holiday of the year. She probably would feel alienated in Bethlehem as well but curiosity was a powerful motivator. She began to collect information and schedules for transportation and the planned activities. Since a record number of tourists were expected, Debbie hoped that going to Bethlehem might also provide some opportunity to meet people. It would be a festive friendly atmosphere conducive to incidental conversation and casual acquaintances.

Christmas and Christmas eve fell on a Wednesday-Thursday that year, teaching days for Debbie. However, most of the activities and happenings were scheduled for the late afternoon and early evening on Christmas eve. Debbie concluded that there would be enough time to attend events after school.

On Christmas eve, about 5 P.M. Debbie took a taxi from her school to Bethlehem. The tourists were in the process of coming. Tour buses, municipality buses, taxis and private rented cars with large Budget or Avis stickers visible on the windshield poured into the relatively small town from all sides. Debbie recalled three and a half years earlier when she spent a day here with her tour group. The town looked exactly the same except for the large number of security personnel stationed everywhere. Starting from the entrance to the town to the center called Manger Square, army jeeps filled to overflowing with soldiers were parked along the road. All entrances to Manger Square were closed off and booths with examining soldiers were erected, one for men and one with female soldiers for women. All bags and purses were carefully checked; everyone was bodily searched. For pilgrims coming to Bethlehem for the first time, it must have been a scary sight.

Once one had passed through the booths, the atmosphere was more cheery and festive. A huge Christmas tree decorated with colorful balls and lights towered over one side of Manger Square. People flocked around it taking pictures. Shops and restaurants bustled with eager shopkeepers and tourists. Everywhere people were walking usually in groups so Debbie felt a little strange by herself.

She started to walk around looking into all the shop windows. She saw many interesting things but resisted the temptation to buy. Then, while sauntering down a side street, she came across a small chapel called the Milk Grotto. It looked inviting and curiosity drove her inside. A richly decorated but small chapel with many altars and sections, each blazing with candles greeted her eyes. Large colorful statues loomed everywhere. Here and there, people knelt in prayer in the dark brown pews. She looked around and stayed awhile since it felt good to bask in the warmth of this small cozy place. It had grown chilly outside.

By the time she walked back to Manger Square, the procession of the Patriarch to the Church of the Nativity had already begun. Altar boys in flowing red and white gowns followed by rows and rows of scouts in uniforms of various colors marched around the square, all eventually entering the Church of the Nativity.

At the point, Debbie looked around her at the crowd of people if there might not be someone interesting to talk with. The crowd could be grouped into three main categories: older tourists in couples and groups, young hippie types with bagpacks and young male Arabs from the local areas. As her eyes wandered about, they fell upon a tall towhead about 30 leaning on the railing that had been erected because of the procession. He was good looking, probably Swedish, nicely dressed and seemed to be alone. Debbie tried to think of an excuse to start a conversation. She saw he had the leaflet for the schedule of events in his hand. So, having hidden hers deep in her pocketbook, she ventured closer to him summoning all her courage, plaintively and nervously asked him,

"Excuse me, but is that a list of the Christmas events here?" She had surprised him. He had been lost in thought.

"What?" he answered not immediately comprehending. "Oh yes, it is. Would you like to see it?"

"Yes, if you don't mind," Debbie replied smiling her prettiest smile. "But where did you get it?"

"At the Government Tourist Information Office, right there ahead," he said eagerly pointing out the direction.

"I had wanted to know when the choirs would start singing," Debbie continued.

"Well, I think at 7 P.M., according to this list," he pointed to the information.

"Do you know if they are any good? Have you been here before? Debbie tried to initiate a real conversation.

"Uh, no, first time." He began to look anxiously at the leaflet and then at the stage and other people and Debbie could tell that he was feeling uncomfortable in her presence.

Suddenly, a pretty pink skinned blond approached and excitedly gushed forth in a torrent of Swedish. Apparently she had managed to buy tickets for the Midnight Mass at St. Catherine's, a very important event. Ordinarily tickets were free but had to be obtained far in advance from the Franciscan Office in Jerusalem. In this case, a "scalper" had made money. From the way she spoke to him and from his response, Debbie realized that the young woman was his partner, perhaps even his wife.

"Well, nice meeting you. Have a good time and Merry Christmas," he called as they walked slowly away.

"Merry Christmas, oh brother," she muttered to herself wondering if she had been right to come. Very few people were alone.

She decided to make the best of it and at least see what there was to see in Bethlehem. The exotic architecture of a Syrian Orthodox Church caught her attention as she walked by.

She hesitated at first then peeked in through the open door. Only a few worshippers were inside scattered here and there in the pews and kneeling in front of the numerous altars. An array of golden lanterns with flickering colored lights hung everywhere from the ceiling. The smell of incense filled the room. One felt as if transported to another world. The overall effect was definitely Eastern. Even the devotional artwork had another-worldly quality to it, very much like early Christian or Byzantine art with its strange proportions and perspectives. She stayed awhile then moved on and visited the "Christmas Church" or Weihnachtskirche as it is called in German, a Lutheran Church.

Here the atmosphere was quite different and definitely western. It was a small church with an austere Puritan decor - hard wooden benches, no statues or elaborate architecture, no artworks or incense. Simplicity was the keynote. There was a huge decorated Christmas tree in the front of the church. Pilgrims were beginning to enter for the late afternoon service so Debbie did not stay very long.

By this time, the crowd inside Manger Square had become immense and more and more people were queuing up outside the booths and pouring into the square. Young adults with bagpacks were sitting about on the steps eating the sandwiches and drinking the liquids they had brought with them, much to the chagrin of the local restaurant owners. Debbie began to feel hungry just watching them and finally stopped at a nice restaurant for a bite to eat.

However, on Christmas eve in Bethlehem, even a bite is expensive. It is the one night a year when the restaurant owners and shopkeepers are in a state of sheer bliss at the amount of business transacted. They wait all year for this heavenly night.

After she had eaten in a large crowded restaurant called "Four Arches," Debbie strolled over to the Post Office where large crowds of people were filing in and out. At the entrance, two youths were selling postcards and envelopes with the special *Christmas in Bethlehem* stamp on it. Debbie bought several of each, some to write to friends in New York and some to keep as souvenirs. Then she went downstairs to write and mail them immediately. One could also use regular postcards upon which the special postmark from Bethlehem would be placed.

Also downstairs were the special international telephone booths where long lines of people had queued up to phone relatives and friends in their own countries Debbie considered for a minute the idea of telephoning her parents then dismissed it because of the cost. She was already halfway up the stairs when she thought to herself, "Oh, what the heck. I'll wish them a Happy Hanukah a little bit late or Happy New Year." She got in line, waited patiently and then a "Hello, guess where I am?" greeted her mother's surprised ears.

By the time she went back outside, the choirs were already singing. She hurried toward the huge crowd that had now gathered in front of the bleachers and again scanned the sea of faces for interesting possibilities. Couples and groups prevailed everywhere. Arabs with carpets, jewelry, Christmas tree ornaments mingled with the crowds hoping to sell their ware. She watched as one young Arab skillfully sold a *kefia* (Arab head dress) worth about $1 to a young innocent looking bagpacker for $7. Well, she had been dumb once too.

The choirs came from all over the world as well as from the

local Christian Arab villages. Sweden, South Africa, France, Germany, and the southern part of the United States were well represented on the makeshift stage. Each choir, composed of approximately 35-50 people, sang several songs. Some were truly good, even excellent; one could see that much preparation had been put into the performances. There was considerable variety in the songs and uniqueness in the presentations.

It had grown quite cold and after listening for an hour, Debbie grew restless and returned to the post office to warm up. Along the way, she took some more photos of interesting sights. An Arab tea peddler caught her attention as he poured hot tea from his huge apparatus which resembled Scottish bagpipes. Arabs and tourists alike warmed themselves with his tea.

Later she returned to the choir singing presentation which was rapidly coming to an end. A long line had already formed by 10:30 P.M. outside St. Catherine's Church, adjacent to the Church of the Nativity, where the midnight Mass would be held. This seemed to be the main event of the evening. Dignitaries, media people with their television cameras and security personnel thronged into the church in one swoop. Debbie would watch the services relayed over closed circuit television on a large screen stationed at the entrance to Manger Square. Many without the precious tickets would watch from this point.

Time passed slowly and Debbie was not really so interested in the Mass despite its pomp and decoration. She continued to probe the crowd for any " possibilities" and had a few brief words with people here and there but no fires were kindled. She decided to stay till the end and watch the people come out of St. Catherine's. She had noticed some elegant people standing on line with their tickets and so thought that perhaps the evening might still prove fruitful.

Finally the Mass was over about 1:45 A.M. and the crowd poured out of the church. They all came so fast, being tired and in a hurry now to catch some bus or taxi home. It was thus very difficult to see everyone and Debbie soon gave up trying. It was now possible for anyone to enter the church and Debbie decided to utilize the opportunity to look around. She walked down the long corridor leading back into the church. People were coming in the opposite direction and eyed her with curiosity. She came to the beautiful Roman style courtyard, snapped a photo and quickly entered the church, fearing that custodians would soon shut the doors.

Inside, the church was dazzling bright like a flash of heavenly light. But the Mass had been televised and Debbie soon realized that the brightness was due to the television equipment. There were still quite a few people in the church, mostly gathered in clusters and talking. She walked about looking both at the altars elaborately decorated with thousands of bright red poinsettas and at the people still lingering about. Cameramen were gathering up their equipment and several Franciscans were also nervously running about as though they didn't wish the night to end.

Debbie returned to the back of the church after having come full circle and suddenly under one of the vaulted archways near a side altar, she came upon four men still busily talking and slowly collecting their coats and belongings.

She stood still for a minute hardly daring to believe her eyes. After an entire evening of viewing only uninteresting people, she suddenly stumbled into the Garden of Eden. These men were absolutely gorgeous. They were between 35 and 40 year old, blond and red haired with ruddy complexions, tall and well built and most of all, they seemed to be unattached. Debbie shyly looked about for some potential females that would crawl out of the crevices to claim their men the way it usually was. But there was no one else about.

Debbie had to think fast. How could she make contact with them? What could she say as an opener? She was still shy and somehow their handsomeness made them somewhat forbidding. She lingered close by tongue tied pretending to be looking at the altar. They did not notice her. Finally she pretended to look about her concerned with whether or not to go.

"Excuse me, do you know when they are going to lock up the

church?" she addressed one of the Hercules.

He looked up from having put his coat on. "Well, pretty soon, I imagine," he said swallowing the words in a typical Australian accent.

"I wanted to stay a little longer," she explained. "It was such a beautiful service. I can't bear to leave. Isn't it wonderful to be here where it all happened?

"Yes, it was nice," he answered simply.

"Did you come a long way to be here tonight?" Debbie pushed on.

"We're all from Melbourne and we'll be here a little while longer yet. Where are you from?"

Finally some sort of conversation had been ignited and by this time the other three had also taken an interest in the newcomer that had broken into their midst.

They continued making small talk about the service, the crowds and the town of Bethlehem when they noted that almost all of the people had left and the custodian was walking about shutting doors and gates.

"I think we'd better go," one of the men declared worriedly.

"Are you going back by bus?" Debbie queried one of the two she had by now selected as her favorite of the lot. Yes was the answer; they were going back to Jerusalem. "So am I," chimed Debbie and they left the church together and headed down the road where all the buses were waiting. There was a special bus service that night until 3 A.M. As each bus filled, it would leave Bethlehem.

There were so many buses standing everywhere, tour buses, private buses and municipality buses, that they had to inspect carefully before boarding that they were indeed on the right bus. Jeeps filled with soldiers continued to linger about making traffic in the small town difficult. Finally they located the string of municipality buses that were waiting for the remaining tourists. Although many people had already left, there were still large crowds flocking to those buses. Just as they approached one bus which was already filled to capacity, the doors closed and they had to wait for the next. This one too filled quickly. By the time Debbie and the four Apollos from Australia boarded the bus, there was standing room only. Minutes later, it left the little town of Bethlehem.

Because the bus was so crowded with people, it was difficult for Debbie to converse with more than one of the men, the one next to her. She liked him and he seemed to enjoy talking with her also. He became especially interested when he learned she was actually living in Jerusalem and not just visiting as a tourist. She discovered that he too was a teacher in a boy's school and the conversation turned to topics common among those involved with the education of the young.

Yet Debbie's mind was also plotting to invite this man to dinner and was concerned if it was polite to invite one and not the others. She didn't know how to manage the situation and thought she would wait until they reached Jerusalem and got out of the bus to see how things would progress.

Debbie chattered on, suddenly very awake and happy that her trip to Bethlehem had not been in vain. She really liked these people, friendly, kind and available. They were deep in conversation and by the time the bus neared Jerusalem, Debbie had decided only to invite the one to dinner with whom she had been speaking and she would ask after they got off the bus. She assumed they would get off in the town center, the hotel area.

The bus was heading towards the Old City of Jerusalem and suddenly one of the men cried, "Oh, we're getting close. Guess we'll have to get off at the next stop." Debbie was puzzled.

"Why are you going to the Old City at this time of night? Everything will be closed." she warned.

"Well, that's where we're all staying," her new friend informed her.

"Really," she said surprised, "Where, at the Petra Hotel?"

"No," he seemed a bit embarrassed now and looked away, "at the *Fathers of Zion* house."

Debbie had a quick urge to ask why they were staying there. After all, that was a house only for Catholic priests, wasn't it. The truth suddenly darted into her mind paralyzing her for a few moments. The words stuck in her mouth and she felt as if she could hardly breathe. She must have looked horrified but then remembered to smile. The bus passed the Citadel, the Tower of David and stopped at Jaffa Gate. "Jaffa Gate" the driver called out loudly.

"That's us," one of the gorgeous men shouted and they all made a move to get off. They all said goodbye, good luck, nice to have met you, good luck in your teaching and blah, blah, blah. Then they were off. The bus drove off quickly and Debbie waved from the window cramming another smile against her teeth. They waved back and started to walk towards Jaffa Gate. The next stop was the New City and Debbie's body dropped off the bus at King George Street and she slowly dragged it home. The streets were dark and empty as though they had never heard of Christmas.

CHAPTER 7
FIGHTING THE SUITORS

The next day Debbie was tired, physically and emotionally, as she made her way to school. The shock of the priests had affected her deeply even though she tried to shake it off as unimportant. It was like being shot by an evil Cupid and she sought a way to escape. There was a conference going on at a nearby university which she had hoped to attend at least partially. It was on William Faulkner, one of her favorite writers. But a hectic day of teaching and the shocking disappointment of the night before left Debbie numb and exhausted by the end of the day.

The next day, however, found Debbie on the Bus to Golda Meir University and the William Faulkner conference. It was half over but she was still able to enter and listen in on the lectures. As far as small conferences like this go, this one was fairly interesting. There were quite a few "bright lights" but only one or two interesting specimens from the husband huntress point of view.

The chairman of her department was also there and eventually asked Debbie if she would like to go along on the Masada-Dead Sea post conference tour and serve somewhat as a tour guide answering any questions the guests from abroad might have. He himself was unable to go and thought it would be nice if someone living in Israel would be present. Debbie was happy to accompany the group and looking forward to having closer contact with these important people.

Early Saturday morning, Debbie waited outside the Negev Hotel for the group to assemble and then proceeded to spend an uneventful but pleasant day at Masada and the Dead Sea. The one man she might have found interesting and attractive of course, turned out to be married with two grown sons.

On the trip home from the tour, the group in the car were in high spirits, having had a wonderful time. They began to discuss possible sites for future conferences which might provide them with other beautiful places to see while honoring the birth or death of some important or even not so important author.

"Well, next year, it's Zurich for the Frost conference. That should be great, a beautiful place," one of the professors from the United States enthused happily with all the others readily agreeing.

"1985 is Goethe year in Stockholm," another chimed in "You're the organizer, aren't you?" he queried the American.

"Don't forget to invite me to give a paper. My university won't pay for the trip unless I read a paper."

"What about 86? Who can we use then?" the lecturer from England looked worried. They all thought for awhile. "Surely it must be somebody's birth year or the anniversary of something . Don't worry, we'll find something," another American said encouragingly.

"And in 1987, we can always resurrect Walter Conway. Will you give a paper then? Do you know anything about him," he pointed the last two questions at the young woman instructor from Yale.

"No, I don't, but you can bet your life, I will make it my business to know by then" she answered emphatically. They all laughed knowing only too well what she meant.

Debbie had remained silent during this conversation, being very surprised at their flippant attitude toward writers she held very dear. It bothered her to hear that these so called "scholars" and professors of literature were only using the authors as an excuse to get a free trip to a beautiful exciting place and to have a good time. Academia was a racket like everything else.

For about a week thereafter, the conference and its participants were the main topics of conversation among the teachers at Debbie's high school, many of whom had attended. International happenings were rare in the area so when something was taking place, many availed themselves of the opportunity.

Not long after the conference, Debbie again met Judy Parker.

"Oh, I'm glad I ran into you," she said excitedly.

"Avi and I are getting married and I want to invite you to the wedding." Debbie was not surprised and asked where and when and all the usual questions. Judy seemed happy and talked endlessly about her plans. They would continue to live in their one room apartment but perhaps would buy a few more pieces of furniture. Avi had a fairly good job but was in danger of losing it because of the layoffs in private service jobs. She also had no job but was still studying Hebrew at the Ulpan. Judy didn't seem to be too concerned about this quite possibly because there was always the option of returning to the States. The main problem was how to snare the guy and get him under the huppa. The rest could be handled easily. But how to accomplish this?

Then Debbie's mind dove back to a conversation she had overheard in the Hilton Hotel lounge during Israeli Medical Week. Two middle aged American doctors were talking and one was bragging how he managed to get his future Israeli son-in-law a residency at his hospital. He explained how so and so owed him a favor and therefore, he, the chairman of the department was able to get the desired appointment despite the fact that the son-in-law was in a different branch of medicine.

Well, Debbie certainly could not rely on her father for such a maneuver. And she too held no important position by which she could encourage someone to marry her in this fashion. She had some money but money was not the main factor for an up and coming ambitious professional man, the type she admired so much. They wanted connections - important ones.

Another alternative was the possibility of taking a chance on some poor guy, usually a Sephardi, and provide him with an opportunity for an education through which he could make something of himself. She remembered Sheila Katz from Columbia folk dancing. Sheila was a PhD in mathematics, an assistant professor at one of the city colleges and a consultant to many firms. Professionally she was a big success but like many girls of her type, she had been unmarried at 32.

The story goes like this. Sheila went to Israel for awhile, met an Israeli from Petah Tiqua (an area that had been settled primarily by poor Iraqi Jews) and brought him to the United States. She sent him to engineering school. They got married, had two children and moved to the suburbs. She continued her work, her mother helping with the children. After getting his degree, he was offered a very good position with a leading engineering firm on Long Island and eventually continued for a masters degree. It worked!

Or so it seemed at least. One never knows what is really going on behind the picture window. Yet Sheila appeared to be happy and content . Again Debbie envisioned the possibility of a similar pattern for herself. But the thought of reliving another "school " experience with never ending exams and term papers filled her with anxiety and weariness. She had had enough of that! No, she would have to find her own way. It was frustrating for her even to think about this subject. There were always such feelings of futility since it seemed that little could be done, if anything, to change the situation.

It was also difficult to ignore the "problem" since different aspects of it surfaced here and there under various guises. Even in the work world, it was impossible to escape. For example, quite often Debbie would go to the Jerusalem University to do research, prepare classes, participate in activities or just to sit and drink coffee in the faculty lounge.

Several times she had met Dr. Alan Kaufman, who had been the organizer of the Theodore Roethke symposium she had attended. He was always very friendly in a kind of grandfatherly way and they had had several pleasant academic discussions in the faculty lounge. The white haired chairman of his department and amateur bard was married for the second time and had several children about Debbie's age.

One particular day, they had met again and were engaged in a discussion about publications. Debbie expressed interest and mentioned some of the articles she had published and what she would like to write about if she had sufficient time. Professor Kaufman then casually suggested, "There is a research position open in my department at the university for the next year. Perhaps you might be eligible. Would you please bring some of your published articles to my office so I can determine whether or not you are qualified."

Debbie was excited at the prospect - a research appointment at the Jerusalem University ! Her mind quickly began to fantasize how she would go about her important scholarly work in a very solemn and dignified way as though it were of earth-shattering significance. She thanked Professor Kaufman, promised to gather her momentous documents and fly them to his office as soon as possible.

As soon as possible was the very next day. Debbie had ransacked her entire apartment to assemble a complete collection of her work, published and unpublished. She thought to herself how lucky she had been to run into Professor Kaufman. Towards midmorning, she waited outside his office door while he was speaking with a student. Finally he finished and Debbie went in.

"Well, well, come in, come in," Professor Kaufman greeted her warmly. "What a nice surprise."

"I hope I'm not disturbing you from your work," Debbie said apologetically.

"No, I was just preparing some of those symposium lectures for publication. But it's a boring job and I am glad to have an excuse to stop. Please sit down," he answered smiling.

They continued to make small talk and then Debbie showered upon him two huge manila envelopes filled with her scholarly writing. He promised to "look" at them and give her an opinion in about a week. Debbie was going to leave but Professor Kaufman continued to talk.

"You don't have to leave already, do you?" he pleaded.

Debbie thought that he must not have much opportunity to speak with people and perhaps he was lonely. She eagerly returned the following week to hear the verdict about her work.

This "interview" began much like the previous one with Professor Kaufman going out of his way to be charming and Debbie trying to be polite and not appearing too overly eager. Several times she tried to steer the "small talk" type of conversation into more serious discussion about her research articles and the position. But the professor refused to be budged. Debbie would have to wait.

At one point, he wanted to show her an early edition of a novel they had been discussing. It necessitated Debbie's getting up and approaching the bookcase. As she leaned down to inspect the book, Professor Kaufman took her arm and kissed her full on the mouth at the same time pinning her against one of the hexagonal walls composing his office. She could not escape his grasp.

"Always knew these walls were good for something," he smiled as he gently released her.

Debbie, on the other hand, had been taken off guard and was shocked at his pass. She had thought him to be a gentle grand fatherly type, not one still interested in women. Her feelings must have showed deeply in her face and response because he became embarrassed and apologetic, his smile and obvious pleasure disappearing completely. Debbie tried to laugh now but it only emerged as a weak grin, a second thought where only first thoughts count. She had missed her chance and now he would take his revenge.

"Is that why they made the rooms hexagonal? she tried to joke but the joke was over. He became very businesslike then and she followed suit.

"Did you have a chance to look at any of my work?" she inquired.

"Oh, yes," he replied reaching for the brown manila envelope that contained Debbie's scholarly life. It was in the same place he had put it when she submitted it and in the same form obviously untouched. He handed it to her perfunctorily without intending to comment.

"What did you think of them? she pressed him.

"Well, you know," he drawled, "very nice up to a certain point but we're looking for some highly intellectual material. Yours is somewhat superficial. You know, nowadays, it has to be so no one understands it. Then its presumed to be profound."

"Yes, I know what you mean, far removed from literature it is too," she remarked but he was no longer listening. "Well, thank you anyway for thinking of me for the research position." She took the envelope and left.

His small hexagonal box office had made her feel so claustrophobic. Angry with herself for having fallen for his obvious trap, she decided to go home immediately. "Research position," she muttered to herself. "There probably hasn't been a research position in that department in years. How could I have been so stupid?" She walked down the stairs and through the long dim corridor wondering why there were always so many ugly old frogs and so few handsome princes!

And yet in the ensuing months, several girls she knew did manage to find handsome princes. (Well, would you believe, average princes?) Sharon, the leader of the ACI single parent group married Aaron, one of the American members. Both were divorced, in their thirties, with children. Debbie noted again that being short was certainly an advantage for a girl in the mating game. Aaron was about the same height as Sharon, about 5 feet 5 inches and had never even given tall Debbie a glance!

One day as she was walking down Balfour Street on her way to the Jerusalem Theater, she heard someone calling her name. As she turned to find the face that accompanied the voice, she saw Nurit Levy sitting in the front passenger seat of a white car. The car stopped and Debbie went over. After the initial "How are you's" and "You look so wells" Debbie asked her if she had come back to Israel.

"I am here to visit my family, for two weeks," she chatted happily. "I'm still living in New York, in Brooklyn. I'm married now," she added holding up her hand with a thin gold band

"Did you marry an American?" Debbie asked interested.

"No, an Israeli who had already been living in N.Y. a few years. We bought a two family house in Brooklyn, very nice, all brick. You must come visit us some time. I see that you are still here. You must like it very much. You remember my brother, don't you?"

It was then that Debbie saw the young man who was driving the car and had up to this time remained silent. Debbie wished her well and they drove off. It was then that the doubt again seared through Debbie's mind as it had about two years earlier when Nurit had made the statement that a girl over 28 had no chance to marry in Israel. Perhaps she was making a mistake in staying. She hurried on her way to the Friday afternoon cinema but felt vaguely uneasy.

Then she remembered the rich young Australian girl who married an American. She was 22 and had lived in the same building as Debbie on Pa'amalot Street. What a beautiful wedding she had at the Hilton Hotel Shortly after, they went to the States where he would finish his Masters degree. Here again, height was a factor, both being less than average. The girl was pretty although somewhat chubby.

"Short slim girls seemed to have the easiest time in attracting a mate while tall heavy girls should head immediately for the nearest convent," Debbie concluded.

Also from Australia came Victoria, the pretty Gentile girl with the long red hair and peaches and cream skin. She too was petite in stature. It was not long before she succeeded in beguiling Harold, a good looking American about 32 with an MBA in Finance from NYU to fall in love with her. Shortly thereafter, she moved in with him.

Vicky had only completed two years of high school and hoped to obtain free schooling in Israel. However, she discovered that this free education was not available to her. She did not come under the law of return because she was not Jewish. She was advised to attend the Anglican School in Jerusalem or some other private school, however, she could not afford the necessary tuition. Harold offered to pay for her education but she did not accept it. Eventually, she returned to Australia.

And finally there was Judy Parker who married her Avi in a Sephardic synagogue in the Jewish Quarter of the Old City of Jerusalem. It was a nice wedding except that Judy had so few guests. Her parents came from Long Island, New York with a few friends. Two girls from her Ulpan, her cousin Steve and Debbie were the remainder. On the groom's side stood Avi's parents, his eight brothers, their wives and children, three sisters, their husbands and children and friends.

The ceremony was beautiful with Judy and Avi beaming under the huppa and her mother besides herself with joy. "Thank God, at least one is married. Now I have only one more to worry about." she said with relief shortly after the ceremony. A sister, several years older than Judy was still unmarried.

The reception was held as is often the custom in Israel in the adjoining room of the synagogue. It is much less expensive than hosting a similar event at a hotel or private hall. There was a splendid array of food arranged in buffet style and a singer with a portable piano who provided the music. This music was nevertheless almost exclusively of Sephardic origin, the singer being a relative of Avi's. At one point, Judy's mother said to her daughter, "Judy, dear, why are they always playing that awful Arabic music? Can't you ask him to play a waltz or something else." Judy tried to explain that it wasn't really Arabic but Jewish music from the Eastern tradition but her mother was so excited that she was unable to comprehend. Judy requested a waltz and the singer-player looked bewildered at first but finally managed to play something acceptable to her parents. Soon people were dancing to "Smoke Gets in Your Eyes" and "Under Paris Skies."

There was little communication between the two sides. Each gathered on a different side of the room. Avi's family knew little if any English . Judy's family knew only a minimal Biblical Hebrew. Judy desperately ran back and forth between the groups translating and speaking with her limited Ulpan Hebrew trying to keep everyone happy and to create at least an atmosphere of harmony. Generally speaking, everyone seemed to be having a good time.

Debbie was somewhat disappointed at the lack of "possibilities" at the wedding, nevertheless, she was happy to have the opportunity of meeting Judy's cousin, Steve again. This time she had a much better chance to speak with him during the reception and truly found him to be an interesting and sincere person, just as Judy had described him.

Finally, after the reception drew to a close, it was with Steve that Debbie walked the lonely dark streets of the Old City to the once-an-hour number 48 bus and it was Steve who had earlier checked the timetable when this bus would arrive so they would not have to stand alone for a long time waiting. As they approached the shelter, the bus could be heard rattling up the narrow street. They boarded and ten minutes of small talk later, got off in the New City Steve said goodbye, took still another bus and Debbie walked the rest of the way to her apartment.

And so with these events and experience, Debbie had sunk into the swamps of Israeli life. Would she be able to extricate herself? She had taken many courses in college, but she couldn't remember any as rigorous and difficult as her first survey course in "Everyday Israeli Life." It had often been a painful process and learning had taken place on a trial and error basis - with a seemingly ceaseless array of trials and an equal number of errors.

To the tourist of a few weeks, Israel seems like a very modern country with western comforts, conveniences, customs and attitudes. Yet closer inspection and repeated exposure reveal this first impression to be a false one. Perhaps the complaint one hears most frequently from an immigrant to Israel is the failure of Israelis to observe the queue. Of course, this might also be interpreted as the failure of the westerner to learn the phenomenon of the "huddle." The "huddle" is the type of formation popular in the Middle East - where all the people crowd around the window regardless of order of arrival. Everyone fights and pushes to be next. Aggressiveness prevails and strength is the criterion of success.

Few westerners see beyond their ethnocentricism and pronounce quite boldly that the "queue" formation is the only civilized one. Therefore, waiting in line at the post office, bank, or supermarket is an ordeal and necessitates one's full attention. One cannot allow oneself the luxury of daydreaming or reading while waiting on a long queue (as Debbie loved to do) but one must maintain constant vigilance against the aggressive person who disregards the sacred phenomenon of the queue, ignores the waiting line and proceeds immediately to the front of the line already beginning to state his business loudly and firmly even before he has reached the window. One dare not leave even a trace of a void in the line since it would be immediately filled by someone, on line or not. Meanwhile the blood pressure of those patiently waiting in line begins to rise and there are mumblings of "chutzpah" and other less flattering comments. Needless to say, sometimes rather wordy and loud altercations ensue

One might assume that trips to the post office are a rare occurrence. However, Debbie soon discovered that one needed to make such a journey for each item since the 300% inflation rate (then in effect) changed the prices of stamps every week, sometimes within a matter of days. Gone was the luxury of buying a convenient roll of 100 50's and using them for the entire year. Such small at first unnoticeable details gradually emerged and multiplied as minor annoyances in the daily life of the person settling in Israel.

Another example of situations one has to accustom himself to might be in the supermarket where it sometimes happens that a few women would park an empty or near empty wagon on line for the cashier and then proceed to go around the supermarket and collect the items they want. By the time one has finished the collection, one's wagon would have moved by invisible hands fairly near to the front of the line. This irritated Debbie especially when she, after an hour of marketing, found herself at the tail end of a line of empty wagons occasionally visited by its harried owner. Frequently Debbie pulled out the wagon in front of her and put hers in its place only to be faced with a fight when the irate woman returned. Very often it came, to a physical fight between wagons because the woman would not yield her precious place. One time Debbie remembers a particularly tough fight in which a woman about 8 months pregnant fought wildly for her place. Debbie had to yield to the woman's condition. Could not Debbie do the same, you ask, place her wagon on the line and shop? Well, it would take time for her and other immigrants to abandon ways of doing things they had done all their lives.

Customs were not all negative, however. For example, to return to the supermarket, the customer brought her own bag or tote and packed her own purchases. Thus the line moved much faster. Even here, however, a problem occasionally arose if the person packing were not quick enough to gobble into her tote all the items that were being digested through by the cashier. Woe to the one who was not finished packing and the next woman's items were already flying through and landing on her purchases thereby mixing the two. Looks, sighs, and utterances of annoyances manifested themselves against the shopper who was slow or dallied too long. Debbie simply learned to pack quickly. She also remembered to take along two bags to the market necessary to carry the loads so she would not have to buy (yes, buy) a new bag each time. Yes, even a trip to the Supersol could be an adventure.

The longer Debbie lived in Israel, the more she realized the sharp difference between it and the United States.

In addition to clothing, other items were also at a premium in Israeli society. Things Debbie had always taken for granted - heating, hot water, paper were now considered a luxury. At first she had thought it merely an old lady's idiosyncrasy when Mrs. Levinsky complained that Debbie was using far too much toilet paper. Debbie couldn't understand how a woman who had been a pharmacist could be so concerned over a roll of toilet paper. Yet this is daily life in Israel where even a few shekals count and people are very careful with what they spend.

It was annoying never to find toilet paper in any bathroom even at the university and good restaurants. At first, Debbie thought this was due to a lackadaisical attitude on the part of the cleaning personnel. But one time she saw the cleaning woman at the university putting several rolls in each booth. Yet before two hours had passed, the toilet paper situation was again critical. Then Debbie realized with horror that the Israelis were actually stealing entire rolls of toilet paper and that this was the reason there was never any paper, not the paucity of trees. At any rate, she soon learned to always be prepared by taking some of her own tissue paper with her.

American "plenty" certainly did not exist at least not for the general public. Fabrics were unbelievably expensive and of poor quality. When Debbie tried to ascertain the reason for the poor quality since she knew that certain *kibbutzim* made fine quality material, she was told that the good quality fabric was exported and a very cheap, coarse South American material was imported for internal use. Appliance prices were exorbitant. Refrigerators, stoves, living room sets were at least $1,000 each. Even a simple $15 GE toaster in the United States sold for $80 in Jerusalem. Luxury items such as, perfume, cosmetics, jewelry were also two and three times the price of those items in the United States. It was understandable that people were ultra careful with their purchases.

Another problem was the heating and hot water. Some apartments contained no heating at all and others only a small electric or gas burner which was also to be used sparingly. In Mrs. Levinsky's apartment, heating had been only for a short time in the A.M. and for a short period in the evening. On the occasion of very cold rainy days, Debbie had been allowed to supplement this with a *short* period with an electric burner. Short must be underlined here for it seemed no sooner had Debbie turned on the burner than Mrs. Levinsky would come in and say, "It's like Tel Aviv beach in here now. Turn it off" after which she would take out the plug.

A similar situation existed with the "boiler" - a rather primitive phenomenon by American standards but still ubiquitous in Israel. If one wanted hot water for a shower or washing, one had to put on the switch for the boiler at least one or two hours before. To make matters worse, one had to use the hot water sparingly. After all, both the electricity and the water were expensive. (Water is metered as is all television in Israel). So gone were long luxurious showers and worst of all, Debbie was accustomed to using much water to wash and rinse her long thick hair. This eventually had become a continued source of contention between her and Mrs. Levinsky. The latter felt that Debbie was using far too much of everything.

Although most things in Israel are expensive, one thing is cheap - public transportation which costs approximately 90c per ride within city limits and about $7.50 round trip, Jerusalem - Tel Aviv. This is a blessing, that is, if you survive the ride!

Getting "on" the bus is the biggest hurdle, especially if there is a huge crowd waiting and the bus is already full. The same phenomenon of the "huddle" exists; people will push onto the bus regardless of whether they have just arrived or have been waiting 20 minutes. People try to sneak in from the sides; others put their arms onto the railings to prevent it. It helps to be short and small. Often an innocent and helpless looking elderly woman will be the biggest elbow-er and most aggressive pusher. There is an enormous amount of tension to get on because everyone who has been even a short while in Israel knows that the death sentence is coming and woe to him or her (especially a pregnant her) who is standing on the bottom step of the bus - not quite in or out. When the bus driver sees that the bus is filled (or when he is tired of punching tickets and sees that the oncoming mob is not decreasing) he will pronounce like God Almighty in a loud voice "Efshar lisgore" and suddenly the automatic doors and the side railings close in on whatever is in the way. There are screams, curses and moans but the bus speeds away. If one were on the inside of the closing doors, he now finds himself jammed against the door breathing a sigh of relief which is short lived because the same scenario will be repeated at the next stop.

People usually remain packed in the entrance way because those comfortably entrenched in the body and back of the bus rarely move on even though more energetic bus drivers repeatedly scream "Efshaly koness kadima" (move forward). Some move an inch or two with apparent exertion; no one wants to be moved from the little safe nook he has found for himself to hold on to while the bus flies, lurches and breaks on its way. It is very important that one hold on to something at all times or else he will surely go flying down the aisles or fall against someone. Meanwhile those in the front entrance way have nary a pole or a railing to hold onto. So they jerk back and forth according to the stylistic whims of the driver. (It is no fun to be an Egged bus driver but it is one of the best paid jobs in Israel.)

Then there is the ride itself. It never ceases to amaze tourists how fast these buses go - even through narrow or crowded city streets. It is also no small credit to the Egged bus driver how well he can manipulate such a large and seemingly clumsy bus. They wind in and out of cars and other buses with the ease of a Volvo and with the grace of a Cortina racing car.

Let us also not forget the hilarious (to observers, not to the driver) figure of the new tourist who climbs aboard with a big bank note which after a huge sigh the bus driver changes while using one or two fingers and half an eye to weave the massive bus in and out of city traffic. Accompanying the big bank note is often an even bigger and dumber question such as, "How can we get to the Knesset?" or "Where is Number 30 Tchernikovsky?" (which would be sufficient to weary a tour guide). Often the driver does not speak English very well or the question is so complex, it requires an answer that the driver, changing money, punching tickets, screaming to the passengers to move to the back and flexing the bus to the acrobatic swirls of Jaffa Road, cannot begin to tackle. Sometimes he will mumble to the tourist, "I will tell you" meaning where to get off waving them to move on into the bus. Sometimes he does; other times he forgets. They may be lucky and find another American or English speaking person as they plow their way through the bus who may help them further.

Even in the rough and tough society of Israel, there is bus etiquette. The first seats are usually reserved for the elderly or handicapped. Obviously pregnant women and women carrying small children have highest priority in obtaining seats and almost always even the most macho Macho will rise for these ladies. Women with strollers getting on in the back exit of the bus while their husbands pay in the front, also illicit much tolerance on the part of the bus audience despite the inconvenience they usually cause. Very often, other persons will assist in the lifting of the stroller and child in and out of the bus. Israel is a child oriented society and this is manifested in the daily behavior of all concerned; allowances people will make for the sake and benefit of children are limitless.

Finally, it is time to get off! Well, Debbie had learned soon enough that one must prepare for alighting in advance - especially if the bus is crowded. A similar scene prevails as did in getting on. People tense and anxious begin to push in the desperate attempt to get off - in time before the driver shuts the door - something he does very quickly, usually too quickly. Drivers have closed the door on pregnant women, women with children and elderly ladies stepping off or just in the middle of the crowd. Shouts of REGA go up either singly or by the entire group standing about the exit especially if a child or pregnant woman is involved. REGA is probably the second most important word tourists learn after *Shalom*. It means "wait".

Debbie had once found herself almost at the end of the mob getting off. The driver slammed the door with her shoulder bag still inside the bus. The bus began to drive off as Debbie tried to hang on to her bag containing money, passport, keys, etc. Fortunately, a few loud "regas" from persons inside the bus forced the driver to reopen the doors and Debbie's bag came flying out. This is not an unusual occurrence. If one finds oneself at the end of a large group of people getting off, it is best to holler "rega" in anticipation of the door slamming shut in one's face or worse with one being only half way out. Only it must be said loudly and with force or it will escape the attention of the driver. Learn this word if you learn no other Hebrew; it could save your life!

In this way, Debbie had slowly become acquainted with the daily life of Israel. It was a trying and sometimes annoying lifestyle but Debbie had been still too idealistic and eager to mind even the greatest inconvenience. She had thought that all the wonderful things that were going to happen to her in Israel were well worth a few hassles of living. It was like the first quarrels young couples have; no matter what the problems are, they are easily overcome because the love between them is still so great.

One day when Debbie arrived at the school, she found a notice for an organized tour of several sites, including settlements on the West Bank in her mailbox. The tour sounded fairly interesting and it was designed for visiting academics and teachers, very often those on a sabbatical or on a grant. She decided to go thinking it might be an opportunity to meet someone.

Her enthusiasm was short-lived. First they visited a religious settlement. She didn't bother to catch the name. They were shown around the grounds which bespoke hardship and struggle everywhere you looked. The settler acting as guide glowed with importance as he explained the harsh conditions under which they lived so heroically. Yet the people seemed content and obviously felt that were part of some Divine mission.

What struck Debbie the most were the tiny living quarters and the way as many as four children were herded into one room with sparse furniture, including the ubiquitous bunk beds. Later, in the "dining hall" which also had an unfinished look; there was a discussion session. Some people in the audience asked questions about the settlement's safety regarding their relationship to the neighboring Arab population. They reassured the group by pointing out the large military base nearby which provided ample protection. No one questioned the safety of the local Arab villages from the new settlements.

The most memorable question - memorable because to almost everyone in the room, the answer was obvious - was asked by a tall, very blond woman with a Swedish accent. "Do your children here in the settlement play with the Arab children in the nearby villages?" She had obviously not been in Israel a very long time and to her strongly democratic Swedish mind, the question was quite logical and innocently asked. Apparently, she had not yet picked up the subtle and not so subtle nuances of hostility and aura of disdain that the settlers felt for their surrounding Arab neighbors.

A hush of silence settled over the room and all eyes focused on the young, tough ultra rightist American woman of about 30 who stood in front of the room addressing the group. Her eyes flashed in horror and she snorted as if the question were too ridiculous even to consider. Finally she dismissed the naive inquiry with a "No, of course not" and immediately moved on to another question.

The Swedish woman looked startled and baffled by the curt dismissal of her question and said something to the woman sitting next to her, as if seeking an explanation. Then she knew enough to be silent.

By the time they left the kibbutz, Debbie had had enough. She hated the air of superiority the settlers exhibited toward those around them as though an advanced technology gave them the undisputed right to be there and take over. By this time, she had also assessed her follow academic travelers for "possibilities." Most were on sabbatical and had brought their spouses along. There was one man alone but he stayed aloof and uninterested. Debbie wrote him off as a "hopeless."

The next stop on the tour was on a hill upon which stood the unfinished structure which King Hussein of Jordan had built intending it to be his summer palace. The view from that high point was breathtaking; one could see the surrounding landscape dotted with clusters of white stone houses here and there representing Arab villages.

Suddenly the guide whipped out a Bible and his position, voice and entire countenance took on a preaching quality. Gesturing dramatically, he would read a passage from the Bible which mentioned a particular place which had been inhabited by Jews in ancient times. He would then point to a particular village in the distance and scream,"That is the village of _____ today where Arabs are living on Jewish soil. Do we want strangers, pagans living on what is rightfully ours according to the most sacred text?"

With the last statement, he would always hold up the small Bible as though everyone watching would be able to read the minute print from where they were standing. The fact that the name mentioned in the Bible and the name of the village it was supposed to represent often bore little resemblance to each other except perhaps for the first letter or first two letters did not seem to be of concern to the guide. Debbie wondered how many in the group caught on. She looked around but all seemed to be listening intently; none questioned its validity. "Some academics they are," Debbie sighed to herself.

He went on and on; the list was endless. He tried desperately to whip up indignation in the group that someone else was unjustly living on their land. But the small crowd looked at the simple houses and the rocky arid land and did not seem particularly incensed.

Debbie stayed as far apart from the guide as possible frequently walking away to express her anger and rejection of what he was saying. As time wore on and it became obvious that he would go on indefinitely, others also began to fidget.

Finally, he finished probably more because he had run out of biblical passages than the fact that he realized the group was running out of patience. When they arrived back in Jerusalem, it was already dark. Most of the group, although not overtly enthusiastic tended to accept (or perhaps swallow would be a better word) and to blindly endorse what had been offered. Perhaps they did not care enough to argue or to get involved. Debbie was quite surprised since they were all academic people whom she assumed would automatically be questioning, critical, and broad-minded. She noted that in a political situation, as in the case of the naive American girl tourists trusting every Israeli male, where Israel was concerned, people hesitated to criticise or suspended the critical faculty altogether. It seemed as though people wanted to believe that Israel could do no wrong.

A few days later, Debbie related her experience to a fellow teacher. "Boy, I'll never go on one of those again."

"Perhaps you went with the wrong people. There is another

group with a similar name that makes trips, sponsored by *Mapam* (Labor) or *Peace Now*. I'm not sure which, but you might enjoy those more," he suggested helpfully.

"So you mean there's a rightist and a leftist 'Academics for Peace in the Middle East'?" Debbie analyzed the situation in amazement.

He laughed, "In this country, there are as many opinions as there are people, even more."

Later that day, Debbie again checked the schedule for next year to find out what courses she would be teaching. She had hoped to be assigned more advanced literature courses instead of the ninth year English grammar sections. Much to her surprise, her name did not appear on the list at all; moreover, another woman's name was posted next to the courses that Debbie was now teaching.

"We've had a cut in the budget for next year, so we won't be able to rehire you for another year," the new chairman for the current year, Shai Dubner, informed Debbie curtly when she inquired.

"But there is a new name on the list where mine is supposed to be, so you must have hired someone else," Debbie argue. "Besides nothing was said at the teacher's meeting last week about any budget cut."

The new chairman had never like Debbie. He had been forced to keep her on another year after the outgoing chairman had offered her another contract. Radu was now in the United States on a sabbatical. Dubner had given hints of his hostility but Debbie had been too preoccupied and too naive to notice. When she persisted in arguing, he finally shouted, "I am the chairman and I will hire whom I wish."

Although she knew already that as a part time teacher, she had no rights, she decided to pay a visit to the teachers' union leader. He was not very encouraging. "It happens all the time. We can't do anything. That's the whole idea behind part time temporary teachers - that they be only part time and used when needed." Debbie tried hard to save her job. She liked the school and had grown accustomed to the children and to the methods of teaching.

"I did a good job and received good student evaluations. So how can they fire me?" Debbie posed to the union man.

"You're not being fired, just not rehired. There's a difference," he countered. "Even if we contested, they would come up with some criticism - that you don't speak Hebrew fluently or that you live in Jerusalem and are thus too far from the school to be available to students. There's no end, really. They'll find something."

"I don't understand why he would want to do such a thing," Debbie's voice was penitent now even if not convinced.

"Probably wants to bring in his concubine. That's usually what it is, in cases like that. Hard to prove though."

Debbie was shocked at the flip way in which he sized up the situation and accepted it as though it were a very frequent occurrence about which nothing could be done. She wanted to stay in Israel longer but needed to work. She had counted on being able to continue at the school. Not knowing exactly what course of action to take, she decided to pay a visit to the district high school director of education.

Debbie soon discovered that to obtain an appointment with the director was no easy task. The secretary declared he was busy but that she should write a formal letter stating her "business." Debbie saw no alternative but to concede. She tried her best to explain her situation emphasizing the variety of subjects she could teach and including a *curriculum vitae.*

No reply. She phoned several times but was told the director was too busy to see her. She read between the lines; she was not important enough for the director or perhaps he and the new chairman might be friends.

One day Debbie decided to wait for him during lunchtime outside the building where his office was located. She had asked a student to point out who the director was. Then suddenly, the young student said excitedly, "That's him, with the three men, on the end talking." Debbie thanked the girl and approached the men. She had dressed to look her most elegant and beautiful. Now it would pay off.

"Mr. Salzman? Excuse me. May I speak to you," she said quickly.

The director, who had been engrossed in a lively conversation with the man on his right, looked up abruptly at what had interrupted his flow of words. The look of annoyed surprise softened into a smile as his eyes rested on Debbie.

"Yes," he said with a puzzled look.

"I'm Debbie Warshawsky, the girl who wrote you the letter about the job at Shemesh High School. I have tried many times to see you but the secretary insisted you were too busy," she recited her little speech as sweetly as she could and with a smile.

While she spoke, Salzman sized Debbie up without attempting to hid that fact in any way. He feasted his eyes on her voluptuous body, glanced a little too long at her breasts and then stared into her small heart shaped face. Debbie was too much in a dither to notice.

"So you're the one, ah ha. OK," he answering appraising once more, "Why don't you come by some afternoon after three and we can talk about it?" He paused for a minute, then added, "How about Tuesday at say 3:30 P.M.?" He spoke so efficiently that one would have thought he had rehearsed the speech. Debbie was elated.

On Tuesday, Debbie armed with another *curriculum vitae* and some of her publications, marched on the Director's office as though she were ready for battle. She arrived early, about 2:45 P.M.

The first skirmish was with the secretary who was still bustling about, trying to finish and get out as quickly as possible. When she saw Debbie, she let out a sigh of exasperation and said immediately before giving Debbie a chance to speak. "The Director is extremely busy right now and will be for some hours." She blurted out this information so convincingly that she would have believed it, had she not the appointment.

" But he told me to come at 3:30," Debbie protested confidently.

"What?" the secretary looked genuinely surprised. "I have nothing listed in my book."

"Well, he did," Debbie proclaimed emphatically. "Today *is* Tuesday, is it not?"

Just then, the door to the inner office opened and the director walked out. His eyes brightened when he saw Debbie.

"Dr. Salzman, this woman says she has an appointment with you." The secretary spoke in a shrill voice conveying the clear impression that she did not like being left out on matters and that she expected a denial on his part.

"Yes, yes, it's OK," he answered calmly, not in the least embarrassed. "You can do that in the morning," he motioned to the papers she had been sorting. "You don't have to wait. Why don't you go a few minutes early."

"Hmmmmph," was the secretary's reply and she made a move to leave.

"Come in, come in. Don't worry about her," Salzman bellowed after the secretary was well beyond hearing range. "What can I get you? A Kinley or would you prefer a Cola? But I'm afraid I have only the Diet version of these, he apologized again looking Debbie up and down. "But you certainly don't look like you need those."

Debbie was embarrassed by his stare but tried to maintain an impression of efficient composure. "Either is fine, whatever you have."

Yoav Salzman was a very tall thin man about 45 with dark hair and eyes and a dusky complexion. He slithered around the relatively small room with the stealthy slow movements of a panther, carefully stalking his prey. He went to get the soda from a small portable refrigerator and in a short while returned to give it to her, again letting his eyes linger just a little too long on her body.

"Sit down, please," he offered showing her a softly cushioned chair as though it were the only possible choice. He positioned himself in a swivel chair behind his desk but directly opposite her.

Debbie sat down in the chair he "suggested" finding herself sinking more deeply into the cushion than she had anticipated. She struggled to maintain an upright position but she kept sliding back into the pit of the chair.

Salzman smiled as he watched her struggle and lay back in his large swivel chair, turning it first to the left, then to the right before bringing it suddenly to the center. He was not unlike an army commander adjusting his position to focus directly on the best point from which to observe, disarm, and attack the enemy.

"Thank you for seeing me," Debbie stammered rapidly losing her composure in the awkward position into which she had by now sunk. "I wrote you the letter explaining why I thought I had received unfair treatment."

Salzman said nothing just making a fine adjustment with his chair. He had now achieved a perfect vantage point from which to probe his gaze up Debbie's legs beyond her short skirt which had all but disappeared into the chair.

"Did you have a chance to look at my *curriculum vitae*? Debbie asked politely.

He laughed and lay back still further in his swivel chair.

"No, should I have?" he said matter of factly.

At this point Debbie was caught off balance by his disdainful reply as well as by the sudden awareness that he was staring up her skirt. She struggled again to sit up at the same time pulling down her short skirt, alas, to no avail. Salzman knew his trade well. It was the perfect chair. It completely disarmed the victim.

"Well," she sputtered, "I wanted to emphasize the point that I would be qualified to teach also in other areas besides literature and grammar. For example, I also have experience in French and English as a foreign language and. . ."

He saw that Debbie would not relent so he interrupted with a quick turn of his chair. Debbie was so relieved that the stare had been removed that she stopped talking automatically. Salzman took advantage of the opportunity and said in a friendly matter of fact tone, "Look, I don't know what the problem between you and Shai is but he and I are good friends. We have been for years. I can't go against him. I just can't really."

Debbie started to protest that friendship should not make any difference. Again, he assumed an almost paternal air. "Bet Shemesh is a small place. It's not New York City. Everybody knows everybody else. I see Shai everyday. We have to keep peace."

He stopped for awhile as Debbie digested the horrible logic of a small town located in a small country. Then he brightened as though a light had just been turned on in his head in the form of a brilliant idea. "I have an idea. I'll arrange for you to have an appointment in the English as a Foreign Language department for the duration of Shai's chairmanship. Then when Radu comes back, you can go back to literature. I'll call Gila about it tomorrow; she's the chairperson there. Of course, it won't be exactly what you have now but it will only be for a short time. How does that sound to you?"

Debbie was surprised at the ease with which he solved the problem which had loomed so large to her. "Well, I suppose it's OK. I've taught ESL before," she smiled now as she spoke thinking that all was well Salzman was fingering her *curriculum vitae* now. "I see here that you live in Jerusalem. Pa'amalot Street. That's in the center, isn't it? Very nice."

"Yes, I like it very much," Debbie answered much more relaxed now.

"I come to Jerusalem every Tuesday to attend a philosophy seminar at the Bergenfeld Institute. I also do scholarly research, you know," he said mockingly obviously putting down Debbie's publications. "Anyway, Bergenfeld is not far from where you are. Perhaps I could come to visit you at this time."

He had said the last statement with such a serious face and with such a quiet, matter of fact tone, that it took a moment of silence before the full impact of its meaning descended on Debbie. The element of surprise is an Israeli forte and Salzman was a master of the art. "As a matter of fact, I'll be coming this Tuesday," he added breaking the silence.

"Oh," Debbie blurted out the truth which was the only thing that seemed to float into her numb mind. "This week I'm giving a poetry reading at Beit **Kaplan** in Tel Aviv, along with several other poets."

"Well then, some other Tuesday," he roared confident now that the bird had been captured.

Having made the statement about the poetry reading gave Debbie the momentum to answer again, and again it was the truth. "Well, I usually go folk dancing on Tuesday night to Weizmann Institute."

But Salzman was not put down. He laughed mischievously and started to get up from his throne of power. "Well, it's up to you. You decide." he finished non-chalantly.

Debbie mustered all her energy and quickly pushed herself up out of the imprisoning chair. Now it seemed as though she couldn't get out of that office quickly enough.

"Yeah, sure, goodbye," she mumbled almost without looking at him, took her bag and hurried out of the door. What a relief to be out in the fresh desert air! She felt like she had just escaped from some prison or had committed a terrible crime and was hoping to retreat unobserved. She sneaked away quickly.

Salzman was such a typical Israeli - non romantic, practical, logical, disdainful. His attitude toward women also seemed to be one shared by most traditional and macho types - that women were essentially mindless appendages to be used for sex and domestic purposes as needed. The stories of the independent, strong pioneer women, army officers and Golda Meirs were a distortion. They were strong only in their ability to be perfect slaves; the men were the real gods.

"No, I'm not going to put up with such a man," Debbie declared to herself remembering his slithering stealthy movements and his haughty air of superiority over her. She continued to go folk dancing on Tuesday nights and was neither reappointed in her own department nor newly appointed in the ESL department. The school year would soon come to an end and she would have to decide what to do.

How often friends had told her of the far greater social and professional opportunities in Tel Aviv compared to Jerusalem. "Maybe when the school year is over, I'll make the switch, try something new," she mused to herself and to others more and more as the spring wore on.

In the meantime, Debbie tried to see as much of Jerusalem and the events happening there as possible. Then one day in late May, as she was hurrying down Ben Yehuda Street, Cyril, the English doctor who was going with the South African artist called to her as he was approaching in the opposite direction. Debbie had mentioned a vague interest in moving to Tel Aviv one day earlier when she had met him on a bus to Hadassah Hospital.

"Hello, how are you?" he spoke quickly in automatic response to the speed at which Debbie had been walking. When she saw him, however, she stopped eagerly and completely since she liked him and thought him to be a very fine person. "Hey, are you still interested in moving to Tel Aviv?" he asked somewhat out of breath.

"I don't know, maybe," Debbie answered hesitatingly. "Why?"

"Well, Paula and I are getting married and I'm living in her flat now here in Jerusalem. I'll be leaving Tel Hashomer and accepting a position at Hadassah so I want to give up my flat in Tel Aviv. I thought maybe you might be interested in taking it. It's a really nice place in the center of the city." Cyril explained continuing to tell her about the apartment and its many virtues. He gave Debbie the owner's address and telephone number. The ball was now in Debbie's court!

CHAPTER 8
ODI ET AMO

There is nothing quite like summer on the beach in Tel Aviv. Even caricature posters of Tel Aviv beach tell only part of the story. For Israelis, the beach season extends from the end of March to mid November although if the weather permits, one may find beach lovers sitting on the sand even in January. Occasionally one may see Christmas tourists swimming! On Saturday morning from approximately 9 A.M. to 1 P.M., the sun is warm enough to encourage sun bathing also in the winter months.

But it is in the summer that Eros stalks the Israeli beaches. In June, July and August, the tourists descend on the hot coral sand as though fallen from some unseen paradise. Although the beach extends many miles, there is barely a space to steal especially on Fridays after 1 P.M. and on Saturdays. Tall flaxen haired girls from Scandinavia, ample nude apparitions from Germany and short dark curly haired husband hunting girls from the United States display their charms on the shores of the Mediterranean. (Unfortunately, the police come quite quickly to make the German girls cover up). Nevertheless, the scene is still somewhat reminiscent of a painting by Hieronymous Bosch.

To start the action, one needs to add the same number of young Israeli males. The outcome of this mixing may eventually be either positive or negative for one or both but definitely, it is guaranteed never to be dull or boring. The initial approach is an easy one; it is a free and very open environment. There are no taboos or restraints; it is not New York City. A typical scenario is as follows. A tourist girl will be sitting on the sand sunning herself or reading a book. A guy who has probably been spying her from a distant point, approaches and without a hint of shyness, begins a conversation often with the most obvious of "openers" such as "Ma Sha'a?" (What time is it?)

The tourist girl, especially if she is visiting Israel for the first time will fall for the bait completely and answer "I'm sorry, I don't understand Hebrew."The Israeli will then, pretending he didn't realize she was a tourist, respond with feigned surprise, "Oh, you don't speak Hebrew.Where are you from?" The tourist girl ,still unsuspecting, will say politely, the United States(or England, ect. as the case may be).

As he slants his way closer to her, the conversation will continue with such typical questions as, "Is this your first trip to Israel? How long are you staying? Where are you staying? Do you have family here. Are you alone?" The dialogue varies little. The authors are not the most creative people .

By this time, the guy has usually quite insidiously parked himself on the girl's blanket or towel. The girl may or may not welcome his interest but it will be difficult if not impossible to dissuade him now. He has basic but valuable information. From this point, anything could happen from just a friendly conversation to "drink coffee with me" (sex) to renewed contact eventually culminating in marriage (plus divorce?) and a New York address.

Some of these meetings may actually be accidental, that is, good looking guy spots pretty girl, presto, summer romance. However, in many cases, the meetings are planned, that is, an Israeli guy is looking for a tourist girl either for reasons of curiosity, something different, or with foresight towards emigrating to the United States. They will approach not only one girl but many in the hope of achieving their goal. There are some who "comb" the beaches approaching almost every unattached female in sight. It was written one summer in the Hebrew newspaper that police in Netanya (a popular summer resort) had to break up a fight among several Israelis about who had spotted the tourist first. The unsuspecting girl, being unaware of this phenomenon, may interpret the man's interest as being centered in her exclusively.

There is yet another difficulty foreign girls, especially Americans, face when they come to Israel which I will call "halo effect." They are now in the "Holy Land, the Promised Land, the land of Messiahs and Mystics, the land of their forefathers."

No longer are they "in exile" surrounded by a gentile enemy. Here at last they are at home; they are safe and can relax and let down their guards. Here at last are what their Jewish mothers always dreamed about - nice Jewish boys everywhere. A paradise for a nice Jewish girl searching for a husband? Right?

Wrong! Well, wait a minute. This is a relatively widespread myth and virtually every American girl is affected by it to a certain degree. So it deserves some discussion. It all lies in one's definition of a "nice Jewish boy." To be sure Israelis are nice Jewish boys, are they not? Yes, but they are not the same as their American counterparts. The problem arises when the American girl expects the Israeli male to behave and espouse the same ideas and values as the Jewish boys she knew in America. If she demands it, she is in for a shock. Israeli men are radically different from American Jewish men in dress, behavior, outlook, opinions, values and especially in the way they view and treat women. An American woman must learn to accept this difference if she is to have successful relationships in Israel This is often difficult since her conditioning and upbringing have been strongly oriented in another direction. These differences will appear again and again and often lead to conflicts.

And then, of course, there are those who are "not so nice." Israel, like any country, has its share of thieves, swindlers, money grubbers and the like. The new and naive American girl may look upon each street corner Romeo as the prophet Isaiah beckoning her to heed his words. If so, she is in trouble. It should also be mentioned that no American girl, regardless of age or level of education, is exempt from this naivete. Many an over 30 professional woman has had her heart broken (and sometimes her pocketbook) by being too trusting in the Holy Land. Just as the Holy Roman Empire was neither Holy nor Roman, so also the Holy Land or Promised Land is sometimes neither holy nor very promising.

It might be added that occasionally Israeli girls may be seen flirting with Anglo Saxon or European men but this is not as common and more often accidental. Basically, when it comes to marriage, an Israeli girl wants an Israeli guy. During the 1982 Lebanese war, many Norwegian soldiers served with the United Nations forces in Lebanon. When they came to Israel, especially to Netanya, on their days off, it was quite common for a certain few Israeli prostitutes to proposition these usually very young, very innocent boys for as much as $100 per night. Alas, some of these Nordic lads even had the misfortune of falling in love with these girls but we shall leave this tale for another time. For many years on Atarim Square in Tel Aviv, a major tourist complex, young towheads and dark kinky-haired Israeli girls could be seen "drinking coffee" together.

Needless to say, the beach is also filled with families, children, dogs and ordinary tourists not involved in the singles scene. Occasionally, there are also meetings between tourists, that is, for example, American girls with American or European men, but this does not occur too frequently since American rules of etiquette "Don't talk to strangers" and the negative connotations of a "pickup" are often operating preventing many potential opportunities. Quite possibly, the same factors responsible for so few people ever meeting in singles events in the USA are transposed to the Tel Aviv beach when these same people congregate there. To be sure, the action on Tel Aviv beach is definitely between the Israeli male and the Anglo Saxon, and to a lesser extent, European female.

To say that Debbie Warshawsky was a frequent visitor to this Mediterranean hothouse would be an understatement. Clad in her four year old American swimsuit (which she had bought on sale at the end of the season), a white pinafore over the suit and swinging her 1978 New York Film Festival tote bag, Debbie could often be seen walking on the beach strip down towards the area between the Sheraton and Yamit hotels, It was now 1988 and Debbie was at last a bonafide "Tel Avivi" having lived in the "big city" for several years.

During the summer months, she spent most of her free time either at this beach in Tel Aviv or in Netanya; sometimes she would even venture to the Sea of Galilee in Tiberias even though it would mean spending the night in a youth hostel. Sometimes she would go alone, other times with a girl friend or two.

She preferred to sit on the hot sand by herself and to drink in the magnificent clear blue sky and sparkling blue sea. The clarity and vividness of the scene always tantalized her. Gone was the film of pollution that always seemed to hover over New York horizons. The warm temperature of the water was also a welcome change after the perennially cold seawater of New York beaches. How wonderful it was to be able to run into the warm water with comfort and without that initial shock of ice cold water! Debbie loved to swim and would weave in and out of the heaving waves for hours.

After such tempestuous sessions with the sea, she enjoyed basking in the sun on her huge "Hello" beach towel. Or she would eat some of the fruits or sandwiches she had brought along in her New York Film Festival totebag. Unfortunately, her solitary idyl never lasted very long. Usually even before she had dried herself properly, the first "Ma sha'a" would come along. When she first arrived in Israel, she would naively talk with all of them. Yet when experience taught her that these types rarely became possibilities for good relationships or even just for friendships, she began to be less polite.

However, she soon realized that this was not a deterrent; in fact, very little could dissuade them once they made their approach. If she answered in a tactful way, "Well, I would like to rest for awhile" or "I would prefer to read my book now," they often reacted as though they had not even heard what she said. Later, she learned from an Israeli girl that the very fact that the girl would bother to give a polite answer would actually be an acknowledgement and encouragement for them to persist. As with the insistent shopkeepers in the market-place, one had to ignore them completely, not even glancing at them. Eventually for those who would not accept the hint (and there were many), one had to shout and become nasty. It has been said that some Israelis only understand this type of language and tone.

On one particular day, a young dark-haired Israeli about 22

accosted Debbie in the typical format - Ma Sha'a, Where are you from, etc. etc. Debbie answered that she had dropped from the moon. He raised his eyebrows in surprise and momentary bewilderment but quickly recovered and smiled. "Oh really, tell me, what is it like there?" Then Debbie said briskly, "I am very tired and don't want to talk now." When she lay down and covered her face with her beach hat, he disappeared.

Later when the sun had become unbearably hot, Debbie decided to move further down along the beach where there were large wooden umbrella shelters. Before long, this same beach Romeo reappeared and replayed the same tape. Debbie stared at him in disbelief. "You did me already," she accused.

He squinted, shielded the sun from his eyes and sizing up the situation said in an unembarrassed mocking tone, "Oh yes, so I did, sorry."

"How do you do it? Do you go from girl to girl all along the beach?" Debbie scolded, visibly upset now.

"No, of course not," he replied walking on. Then he turned around once more and smiled sarcastically, "Every other girl."

Such situations were common on all the beaches of Israel from Nahariya to Eilat. One time when Debbie was in Netanya, a popular beach resort between Haifa and Tel Aviv, a very short stocky man about 35 or 40 ran after her and started talking to her, much in the same manner. "I would like to speak with you." He seemed so desperate, somewhat different from the usual beach type that Debbie stopped to hear what he had to say.

In a very halting and limited English, he related his story,"I am from Kibbutz Dinosam in the Galilee, you know it, a big one. But I don't like anymore. The work is not good and all the time other people are deciding what you should do. I want to go out from it and go to the city. But I have problem. I have no place to stay while I look, you, know, for job, flat and so on and no money. Maybe I can, you know, uh, stay with you for awhile. Where do you live?" The words gushed out like a torrent, almost as if he had rehearsed them or repeated them many times before.

Even though Debbie had been in Israel quite some time at this point, she continued to be shocked anew everytime such a proposition was made. There seemed to be no end to the possibilities of requests. It broke her illusions of an idyllic kibbutz life. Myths die hard. This Izzy as he soon revealed his name to be, remained somewhat of a puzzle. Was he truly in earnest or was it just for sex or a guise to meet a tourist and go to the glorious "States"?

She had heard that there was a tendency for the younger people to leave the kibbutz life and seek greater opportunities in the big city. Kibbutzniks who divorced were also likely to break with the kibbutz; usually the husband would be the one to leave. Some kibbutzniks actually waited for the volunteers to come from foreign countries and eagerly sought out their company. For some, this proved to be a way out, an opportunity to go to a foreign country, be it the USA, England, Sweden or Australia. Of course, occasionally, the volunteer would remain to marry the Israeli and would eventually become a kibbutz member. In the case of Izzy, the decision was an easy one. Since he was perhaps only about 5 feet 2 inches tall, Debbie escaped by giving him some excuse of having a roommate.

Tel Aviv beach was dotted with hotels, cafes, restaurants, a marina with boats of all sizes, wind surfing centers and a large tourist mall called Atarim Square. The northern most part was primarily the tourist area; the section stretching towards Jaffa attracted more of the local and resident population. There in the hot summer evenings clots of people would gather to picnic or barbecue on the sand. Occasionally these huddles of Sephardic Israelis would be invaded by the appearance of the weekly meeting of the English speaking single parent group of the ACI (American Club of Israel) who would hold a barbecue on the sand. On Thursday evenings near the Dolphinarium, about 200 people mostly Argentinians and other South Americans who had settled in Israel, would dance up a sand storm to wild Latin American music. On certain other evenings, there would be "60's dancing" and Israeli folk dancing. Flickering here and there in the darkness on the water's edge, pensive fishermen could be seen. On the boardwalk, lovers promenaded. There was something for everybody on the shores of Tel Aviv beach.

Since Debbie was quite a pretty girl, she had quite naturally attracted many potential suitors of varying quality while sitting on the sun drenched sand. Then one day she noticed that not many men approached her anymore as they had a few years earlier. She assumed that the vast majority now knew what and who she was - a lower middle class girl who was living and working in Tel Aviv - not a rich American tourist. It was not exactly that she missed their attentions - for she considered most of them a nuisance - but it was strange that they should suddenly stop doing so.

"I guess maybe I look older now," she rationalized to herself. Time moved mutely in the sand. "Most of the girls on the beach are about 20, so of course, they will choose them instead of me. That's how it goes."

One day she was at the beach with an Israeli girl friend, Miri, and mentioned this observation to her. Miri thought deeply for awhile with a puzzled look of disbelief on her tanned face.

"Since when have you noticed this?" she asked Debbie who replied that she could not exactly pinpoint when it had started. She looked over Debbie intensely, gazed aside for a few moments and then rested her eyes on the bag in which Debbie had been carrying her beach things. It was a large blue plastic Shekem bag with lines of large Hebrew script running diagonally across it. (Shekem is a supermarket-department store chain usually reserved for soldiers and their immediate families and offering reduced prices). Debbie had purchased food in one of these for a month not realizing that it was not meant for the general public and hence had acquired several rather nice strong practical bags.

Miri's eyes seized on the bag. "How long have you been going around with that?" she quizzed Debbie pointing to the bag.

"Why?" her friend responded, "What's wrong with it?"

"Oh, that's a Shekem bag, don't you see, it means that you are an Israeli or at least that you are living and buying food here." Miri explained somewhat exasperated.

'Are you kidding?" Debbie cried. "You mean because of this

plastic bag they are ignoring me?"

"Sure," Miri was laughing now. "They want a tourist girl, not an Israeli or an immigrant."

Then Debbie recalled her large black "New York Film Festival" tote bag that she had taken to the beach in the past. One day, the thick strap had broken and Debbie did not have a needle strong enough to sew it, nor did she have any idea where to purchase one. It had seemed so much easier and quicker to take the convenient Shekem bag. The change had scared away most possible admirers since they assumed that she was a typical poor Israeli who could not even afford a tote bag and had to resort to using a shopping bag. It was all very clear and understandable now. Subtle clues reveal a lot.

The beach was conducive to easy conversation between people and Debbie often met other female tourists as well as the ubiquitous male tourist hunters. One day she chatted easily with a Swedish nurse who had been working in a United Nations military hospital in Lebanon. She had a few days off and was utilizing them to explore Tel Aviv. Karen described her life as an army nurse.

"Why do you come all the way to Lebanon to be a nurse?" Debbie asked her, "For adventure or are there not many job opportunities in Sweden?"

"Well," she answered slowly and matter of factly, "I'm 36 now and have been a widow for 3 years. My husband died of leukemia. I have a son, 14, who is staying with my parents. I would like very much to marry again."

"But is there any opportunity for this in the hospital?" Debbie queried, herself growing interested. "Are there so many men in the hospital and aren't the UN soldiers very young, usually in their early twenties?"

"Yes, that's true but there are also the officers who are older."

"And married probably," Debbie added mockingly.

Karen smiled seductively, "There are alone, far away from their wives and sick. So they are grateful for the attention and caring I give them. Right now, I know a Frenchman, an officer.

He is married but has already confessed he is unhappy with his wife and may not go back. So we shall see."

Debbie was amazed at her candor, cunning, and courage; she estimated that Karen would succeed. "Is it difficult to find a husband in Sweden?"

"Oh, yes," Karen declared strongly, "at this age, impossible."

At another time, Debbie met a Brazilian girl of 32, also a nurse. At first, like most girls, she insisted she had come to Israel "for a year" to get additional "nursing experience" in a different environment. With Debbie's prodding, the girl soon admitted that it would be nice if she would also meet a nice Jewish doctor in the learning process. She offered the excuse, "The Jewish population of Brazil, especially of my home town, is very small and I do not want to marry a goy." (non-Jew) She was working at Feldman Hospital in Haifa. Debbie wished her good luck.

And then there was the Dutch free lance journalist Debbie had met in a sherut on the way to Tel Aviv beach. She had come to Israel "to interview and write a book about Soviet immigrants." At first, she and Debbie discussed mainly the profession of writing but gradually the topic shifted to men. The difficult Israeli macho came under scrutiny and the Dutch woman related the saga of a "friend" of hers, also a journalist with an excellent job, who had come to Israel as a tourist and had met a tour guide on one of her excursions.

"He seemed so interested in her, and of course, she was wildly in love with him. It all happened so quickly. When the three week tour ended, she hated to leave but needed to return to her work in Holland. She went back but she became more and more unhappy. She just couldn't forget him. He had such a fascinating personality. Finally, she couldn't stand it any longer. She decided to give up her job and return to Israel."

Debbie groaned knowing already what the end of the story would be. He sounded like a typical Israeli tour guide: good looking, aggressive, friendly, charming, disarming. She saw the woman rushing back to Israel thinking she would immediately fall into the guide's eager waiting arms. But the memory of tour guides is not great and his arms were not there when she arrived.

"Can you imagine," the Dutch woman continued almost whispering now, "he barely looked at her. She hardly saw him at all." What the quiet unexciting Dutch woman did not realize or misinterpreted was that the tour guide's interest in her was not genuine but that of a clever tour guide eager to gain potential customers for his new tours or a guide's passing interest in his group members which could easily be transferred to a new group member.

The woman was devastated. She returned to Holland but failed to get her job or apartment back. She now works only as a free lance journalist unable to secure a new permanent job. Later, Debbie wondered if perhaps this "friend" might not have been the woman herself since she was also a free lancer.

While applying another coat of sun screen, the Dutch woman told Debbie about one of the Russians she had interviewed for her book, a man she apparently liked very much. She was bursting with enthusiasm and hope. Debbie hesitated to give her the warning about the Russians that her Rumanian girl friend had given her when she first came to Israel but felt she must to protect her from further hurt.

Debbie remembered being shocked when Marina had described the method by which some Russians plot to get to the United States. "The man looks for an American woman and courts her. Then he tells her he will divorce his wife and he will actually go through the divorce proceedings. But it is all just a show. He will then marry the American woman and go with her to the U.S. and wait the required time for citizenship. Once he has this precious possession, he will then divorce or ditch the American woman, return to Israel and remarry the patiently waiting Russian wife and bring her and their children to the US. They will then eventually also become American citizens and they will all live happily ever after," Debbie concluded sarcastically.

When Debbie had finished her tale of horror, she noticed that the Dutch woman's face had almost completely been drained of color. She had turned a deadly ashen gray and was sweating profusely. "Are you OK?" Debbie asked now worried. She surmised that her story had aroused her suspicion with regard to the true motivation of the man she had interviewed. "I think I'll lie down awhile," the women sighed and the topic was dropped. She was silent the rest of the afternoon.

One Saturday, Debbie was on her way to her favorite spot along the shore when the presence of two Israelis soldiers disturbed her vision. They were in full uniform each having a large machine gun drapped across his shoulder. "What are they doing here?" she thought at first. They seemed so out of place among the strollers, sun-bathers and swimmers. But then she remembered that they were probably guarding the beach with its many tourists.

The walked about one third block ahead of her and she, intrigued, followed them longer than was necessary. An old Arab man with his entire cleaning apparatus came trudging along rather slowly. His face was deeply wrinkled, several teeth were missing and his dry skin had a sallow color. His body was bent over revealing his age and the hard work he had done all his life. Upon seeing him, the soldiers immediately whisked him aside and demanded his identity card. Even from afar Debbie could see that this had not been done with any degree of politeness. She watched the bent old man crumble even more as he fumbled into his pockets finally producing the small card, the color of which alone would immediately identify him as coming either from the occupied territories or from within the Green Line. He looked away into the distance as the soldiers examined his card, trying perhaps to calm himself or to pretend that it really wasn't happening. With a commanding air, they then proceeded to ask him some questions. At this point, his face showed visible signs of anxiety as he tried to choke out a few words in reply. After a time, one of the soldiers quickly thrust the card back into the old man's hands and they went on. The old man took up his cleaning equipment and again resumed his meager scrap of life.

Debbie continued to walk after them, interested now in what they were doing. Soon she was the same scene re-enacted, this time with a pathetically thin young man about 23 as street cleaner. Again she was struck by the humble compliance of the Arab in the face of the soldiers' haughty commands. And yet what else could he have done? The soldiers themselves were mere boys, slight in stature, dark skinned Moroccan or Yemenite types - their duty to protect the beach. Yet the uniform and especially the guns invested them with the euphoria and confidence only power and control can give. This Saturday, Debbie arrived at her favorite spot late . She was more thoughtful than usual. Sunlight rained down with a vengeance that day, like a punishment, perhaps a precursor to hell. Now and then, large brown security planes swung low along the shore like a wrathful Old Testament Deity watching.

CHAPTER 9
TRIMALCHIO'S DINNER PARTY

To adjust to Tel Aviv was difficult since it was so different from Jerusalem, almost its direct opposite in every way. Debbie had now been living in "little New York" as they sometimes called Tel Aviv, for several years. She had been told over and over that there was so much more social life in Tel Aviv. There was, of course, a cafe life all year round. Especially in warmer months, cafe after cafe lined the sidewalks of Tel Aviv, most of them being found on the famous street known as Dizengoff. On Saturdays, from early morning to late at night, this street and the beach boardwalk were clogged with linked couples, some of which were occasionally pierced by a clinging toddler. Traffic was blocked off and the entire street became a river Styx of Tel Aviv family life.

The tables of the cafe would spread out insidiously deep onto the sidewalk leaving the passerby little space in which to walk. Almost always, the cafes were filled to capacity. People would sit for hours talking (usually quite loudly), laughing or just watching the people go by. It was a pleasant relaxed place to gather with family, friends or to meet new ones. And yet often only a thin layer of smiles and tanned skin would clothe a jungle of naked feelings.

Different cafes tended to attract different age groupings. There were some which catered to the young single crowd in their twenties. Here one could go with friends and very casually meet new prospects at a nearby table or hear news about a party that evening at someone's home. Usually a "Why don't you come by?" was quite common and freely offered. There were other cafes where a somewhat older crowd of 30's and 40's would congregate and still others were unofficially labeled for senior citizens. A very few would be professionally segregated, for example, so called "literary" or journalistic cafes where well known writers or celebrities from the media would be likely to appear. Young and not so young hopefuls hung around waiting to be noticed. Shades of snobbism could be felt. Often the popularity of various cafes would shift if the "in" crowd suddenly decided to select a new place in which to meet. Almost everyone had a favorite cafe where he occasionally or frequently liked to sit. There could be no doubt that the cafe was a major Tel Aviv institution.

Other opportunities to meet people were afforded by the boardwalk and its many lawn chairs along Tel Aviv beach. Or one could go to Netanya, a resort town about 20 minutes drive north of Tel Aviv. There, a large pedestrian mall, formerly Herzl Street, was dotted with tourist-type restaurants and shops. Kikar Atzmaut (Independence Square) had regular outdoor folk dancing, singing and concerts by the Netanya Orchestra featuring light classical music. Both tourists and permanent residents partook of these activities or simply promenaded up and down the street eyeing and evaluating each other. The weather was warm from April to November and was generally conducive to continual outdoor life. There was a beautiful beach similar to Tel Aviv but perhaps less crowded. During the summer months, Netanya was very popular with French tourists.

Occasionally during the summer months, there were "Big Events" in Tel Aviv's Hayarcon Park, one of the largest parks in Israel, an equivalent to an American state park. One year they featured opera tenor, Placido Domingo, violinist Pinchus Zuckerman and Zubin Mehta leading the Israeli Philharmonic Orchestra. Approximately 600,000 people streamed into Hayarcon Park that night to hear the free concert. The atmosphere was a congenial one and friendships were easily woven on the sprawling tender grass.

As far as other more organized social life was concerned, Debbie was introduced to it slowly. Or perhaps we should say, she discovered it gradually because no one introduced her to it. Quite the contrary! Debbie found the single people of Tel Aviv, especially the women, definitely unfriendly, even hostile.

This was quite a surprise for Debbie who had always expected that somehow Israelis should welcome her as a fellow Jew from

America and help to integrate her into her real "home" - Israel. Instead what she encountered was an extraordinary amount of hostile competition among a seemingly endless herd of single Israeli and immigrant women for the few available men. This phenomenon intensified as the age of the women increased, beginning with approximately age 28, worsening after 35 and becoming merciless after 40.

When Debbie left Jerusalem, her landlord who had been single gave her the name of a divorcee in Tel Aviv who was a close friend of his and was very much involved in the single life of Tel Aviv. The landlord felt that Mirra would help Debbie to make friends and tell her about the different singles groups, especially good private ones, she might join. Debbie eagerly called Mirra for this vital information.

The reception she received was not very encouraging. There were indeed some private groups but at first the all powerful Mirra drawled,"I don't know if the leader is accepting any more women. I will call to find out." Of course, the answer was negative. However, she had whetted Debbie's interest by telling her there were groups for all age brackets, even one for over 50 and over 60 which were quite active and had many members. Mirra cleverly softened her cruel stance by promising to try and find a time when Debbie might come as a guest; she would call her as soon as there was an opportunity.

In the meantime, she told Debbie of several singles dances which met weekly in various hotels in Tel Aviv. Here Mirra was most generous with details and enthusiasm; it should also be added, however, that these same details were readily available in all the weekly tourist bulletins. Debbie did not need Mirra's help for this. Naively, she hoped Mirra would be able to secure her an entry to the select groups.

For want of something better, Debbie decided to give the hotel singles dances a chance. One Thursday evening she and her Israeli friend, Shoshi, went to the Herzlia Hotel, a 4 star hotel in Tel Aviv. Like many hotels, the Herzlia allotted one evening a week to a singles disco or dance for those over 30. The entrance fee was modest and the requirements for entry none.

The discotheque was small but nice and quite crowded with people mostly in their late 20's and 30's. At first, Shoshi and Debbie danced together but Shoshi quickly struck up a conversation with someone dancing close by her. Debbie sat down at the table where they had been sitting, sipped her Cola and munched on the peanuts that had been placed on each table. Before long, a tall, thin young man about 34 or so with relatively long straight blond hair came over and asked Debbie to dance. He seemed nice and pleasant enough and Debbie danced with him several times. Finally, although it was quite late, he offered to take both Shoshi and Debbie home. He took Debbie's number and promised to call on Monday.

Monday afternoon, Shlomo did call. They had been speaking for about two minutes when he suddenly said, "I'll call you back in five minutes." and quickly hung up. Debbie was bewildered and waited but he did not call again. Later in the week, Shoshi called her and told her that a friend of hers had recognized Shlomo in the disco. "Tell your friend that Shlomo is married."

One of the disadvantages of the hotel's singles events is that there is a good likelihood that some of the participating guests may be married. Apparently, Shlomo was not at all unusual, as Debbie would still discover. The Israeli I.D. card states the marital status of the individual, so a married man is clearly labeled as such.. However, she learned that some Israeli men retained the old I.D. cards they possessed when single, so that they might utilize them for just such purposes of picking up girls in the future. One had to know all the tricks!

Debbie tried several of the other hotels and found them to be generally similar in format and atmosphere. They were well attended and most had an equal number of men and women. In some, the age groupings were somewhat older, perhaps from 30 to 50. It was obvious that a great change had occurred in singles events in Israel. They were much more accepted now in 1989 than they had been in 1981.

The dances themselves were comparable to similar events in

the United States. People came, eyed each other, sat down, walked around, danced with a few partners and left. Some met and left with a partner; others left alone with or without having exchanged their phone number with someone. One had to be careful not to get saddled with an "undesirable" too soon in the evening. Picking and pairing occurs fairly early. If one waits too long or wastes time, he may find all the desirable partners occupied. Hence, many girls refuse partners not to their liking and hold out for the one they want, preferring not to dance at all.

Complaints often heard from the men attending these and other events are that many of the women immediately question the dance partner, "And what do you do?" before they ask anything else. Some even continue to query the man if he has tenure *(kvi'ut)* in his job. (Many positions in Israel even in the business world carry tenure regulations. A person is hired for two or three years at the end of which he is either hired permanently or fired.) If the answer does not meet with the woman's standards, she will usually disappear quickly. Debbie once asked an Israeli girl why this was so and she answered very emphatically, "Well, no girl wants to get stuck with a man who can't support her. Life is hard here even if the man has a good job."

Initially, Debbie felt so anxious being on the sideline that she would dance with the first person who asked her even though she might have preferred another. However, she soon learned that so doing prevented her from making contact with the person she would have liked who was occupied with another girl by the time she had disentangled herself from the first one.

On the whole, most of the clientele who frequented these hotels were average people - blue collar workers; few were college graduates. Most of the men were probably seeking short temporary relationships some perhaps only overnight. It might be suspected that the women were perhaps more hopeful of something serious and long term. In general, it was thought that the hotel scene was not the best way for a girl desiring a meaningful relationship to meet anyone. Some even felt that only the married and the undesirable, that is, those who were not accepted into a private group, would go to the hotels.

Debbie tried each a few times and then gave up. Frustrated and disappointed, she decided to give Mirra another call.

Perhaps she had forgotten her promise to let Debbie know of private club events. She related her experience at the hotels stating that she had found the crowd uninteresting. "Well, she said all-knowingly with her heavy Israeli accent, "Nobody is going to the hotels."

"What, then why did you tell me to go there giving me all the specific days and places?" Debbie retorted barely controlling her anger.

"Well, I thought you just wanted to see, you know, what is going on. You are a tourist."

"I am *not* a tourist," Debbie screamed now giving her rage and frustration free rein. "I have been in Israel seven years and I want to go where Israelis go. It was awful. In these hotels, the guys are so aggressive. One time, the minute I walked in, a guy came up and wanted to dance. I didn't even have a chance to look around or find a place to sit down."

"Oh, you must be very attractive then," Mirra cooed jealously and then her voice became computer cold and matter of fact. "The groups are not accepting new members now, especially women. There are far too many women already and we want to keep a balance. I really have to go now. I have a date" With that, she hung up quickly leaving Debbie with a sinking feeling of having been betrayed by her own people and by her own sex.

Debbie wondered how she might be able to discover these groups on her own and get herself accepted without Mirra. They were all very private and did not actively seek new members. Israeli society in general is a very closed one where people often know each other from early childhood. It is difficult if not impossible for an outsider, especially a foreigner to get in. At first, Debbie asked Shoshi, her one girl friend in Tel Aviv, who promised to inquire about an "academic" group - that is, where one required a minimum of a B.A. degree for admission. The age grouping was late 20's, early 30's. Debbie had hopes of joining this group although she was already at the upper age limit.

For a long time, Shoshi was silent about the group although Debbie repeatedly hinted in this direction. Finally, she asked her directly and Shoshi in a very embarrassed tone told her that when she asked if she could bring Debbie, they stipulated that new women would be accepted only if they were under 30. The rationale was that if they were already over 30 when they became members, they would soon be too old for the group. Debbie was hurt by this and felt it almost to be a rejection of herself although rationally she knew better. She puzzled also over the age factor and wondered if this were truly the real reason or the fact she was an American. She knew that Israeli women viewed all foreign women, especially Americans, as potentially dangerous to their security in the sense that so many men wanted to emigrate and sought to do so by marrying American citizens. They were scared to death of losing the few available men they had.

Debbie was very disappointed in Tel Aviv. Physically, it was not a very attractive city with its endlessly repeating four story buildings. She had hoped for more social life and there was, only she was not part of it. The summer was hot and she wanted to have some fun. She was about to give up hope when she remembered the singles group she had once tried to join in Jerusalem where the organizer had also responded like Mirra. She also recalled what her friend Mike had told her about the organizer, that she had first crack at all the men and control over the women who joined. She also noticed ads in the *Jerusalem Post* calling for new members for a "Singles group now forming" and sometimes resolved to write and apply although she could never quite bring herself to do so. But now she thought to herself, "Hey, maybe I could start such a group. It would be nice to have people come to me for a change." The more she thought about it, the more excited and elated she became.

She carefully prepared the ad she would place in the *Jerusalem*

Post, the major English daily, and which would also appear in one of the major Hebrew dailies for 30 days. Using the correct words was of paramount importance. How could she attract good people, the kind she wanted? After much consideration and revision, she decided on the following: "Singles group now forming, women 30-45; men 35-50 for mutually shared activities. English and Hebrew speakers welcome. Tel Aviv, P.O. Box 2971, No. 3862."

Debbie was a bit hesitant to bring the ad to the advertising agency which took ads for the newspapers thinking it might provoke some giggles or wisecracks among the staff. Yet quite the contrary was true. For them, this type of ad was quite common. She noted that one of the clerks, a fake redhead about 40 looked interested. All she had to do now was to wait for the letters to pour in!

Debbie did not expect much of a reply to her ad and so continued to pursue other activities. Although she was still far from fluent, by this time her Hebrew had improved so much so that she decided to attend the Hebrew poetry readings that were held on the first Sunday of every month at the *Cafe Sifrut* (Literary Cafe). Several Israeli poets of varying fame read from their works, A small makeshift stage was provided in the corner of the cafe and the audience listened at large round and rectangular tables drinking their capuchinos and cafe au foches.

Debbie chose one of the tables that was still free. Everyone was in large groups talking loudly; she felt out of place alone. How different from the anonymous poetry readings in New York. She tried to appear relaxed and ordered cupuchino and apple strudel. At the next table sat five people engaged in friendly conversation, two women and three men men between the ages of 40 and 50. It was difficult to discern who was with whom. One of the men had glanced in her direction several times. He sat stiffly and erect in his chair, his eyes staring intensely at everything. Nothing would escape his scrutiny, Debbie included. He smoked constantly and held his cigarette in an awkward manner. After awhile, the look he cast Debbie grew darker and darker until finally, in a stern and disapproving tone, he thundered, "Why do you sit alone? Are you asocial?"

Debbie felt embarrassed and automatically accepting the correctness of his opinion, was about to offer an explanation when he motioned with a jerk of his head which in Israeli gesture language meant, "Come over and join us." She hesitated and then a long drawn out "Come on" reached her ears and as if mesmerized, she moved her chair over to his table.

"Why do you sit by yourself?" he asked again as she sat down and without waiting for a reply introduced himself and the others. "I am Yoram and this is Yakov and his wife Rina and Dror and his wife, Leah. Debbie helloed everyone around the table and smiled even though she felt out of place. The group did not seem to mind her joining them perhaps because she filled the place of the third partner. By this time the reading had started and the talking in the cafe abated.

Debbie sat facing the primitive stage. From this vantage point, she was able to observe the profile of Yoram quite easily. He was about 45, quite good looking, handsome even, in a very distinguished way. He held himself erect at all times and had a distant almost impenetrable aura about him like an ancient statue of Apollo or Caesar Augustus. His hair, which had once been black, was now partially gray yet still ample and wavy framing his classic face in a bouffant style. He was listening to the poets intently as though they were uttering profundities. Debbie's Hebrew was not yet sufficiently refined so that she could follow all the poets were saying. To grasp all the nuances, even most of them, would have been impossible even in English. Poetry readings were sometimes difficult in that respect especially if the poetry being read was of an intellectual and abstract variety. This particular reading was no exception to the rule.

Then an intermission was announced and the cafe resumed its former noise level. Yoram looked at Debbie sternly, "Well, did you enjoy it?" Again he asked in such a way as though he did not really expect an answer. "It was very good," she muttered demurely.

"Good? That's all you can say," he thundered again and then lapsed into a mini lecture of his own on the quality of the poetry that had been read. He spoke authoritatively as if he were an expert in the field himself. Debbie asked if he were also a poet and he laughed. "Well, yes, when I was a child, I wrote a few things but not now. Who has time for such things?"

Debbie resented his flippant know it all attitude but said nothing. He began to deluge her with the usual questions, all at once as if he were filling out a bureaucratic form. Where was she from, how long was she in Israel, did she have a family in Israel and so forth. She answered quickly like a robot trying hard to please, hesitating here and there only to decide if it was a "good" answer, that is, one he would like to hear. Apparently they were for he began to smile approvingly especially when he heard she had already lived in Israel for seven years.

The intermission ended and another poet began to read in a slow, monotone voice. This time Debbie understood little, the poet being obstruse and purposefully intellectual. Finally he finished and the cafe again resumed its dissonant harmony.

"Well, what do you think?" Yoram yawned this time waiting for her to answer although he again communicated with his attitude that whatever she had to say would not be of crucial importance.

"I'm afraid I didn't quite get all of it," Debbie answered honestly afraid he might quiz her and discover her lack of understanding himself.

"Why not?" he quipped with a puzzled frown.

"Well, first of all, I don't know Hebrew quite so well and. . ." Debbie tried to explain at which point he roared, "What, you are seven years in the country and you still don't know enough Hebrew to understand a simple reading like this. What is the matter with you?" Debbie, again accepting without question his right to criticize as well as his words as absolute truth, was about to stammer something in her behalf when he broke in like lightning. "The Russians, they are here less than a year and already they are talking." He spoke with a serious stern face and reprimanding air. "My God," he muttered shaking his head for effect.

"I do know it," she pleaded, "but not on a university level basis. You don't learn a language overnight. There's plenty of time. I'm not leaving." Now he smiled again just faintly for a few seconds, then reverted back to his earlier stance. Before they left the cafe, he had taken her phone number and said he would call her during the week.

As they started to leave Debbie utilized a short lull in their conversation to initiate a question of her own. "And what do you do, Yoram?" she asked demurely.

"I work at Tel Aviv Hospital," he answered curtly and with force, the way he seem to do everything.

"What do you do there?"

"I'm a doctor, what do you think, I am cleaning the floors?" he shot back with a defiant jerk of his head.

Debbie was immediately sorry that she asked that. "Of course, he was a doctor. It had been insulting," she chided herself and tried desperately to right her error. "Yes, of course, but I was curious to know in what specialty."

"A urologist, OK?" he hit back.

"Oh, that's very interesting," she added quietly but not very convincingly. The words tolled in her throat but they did not ring forth easily.

"Are you a *sabra*?" she continued trying to appear interested and pleasant.

"A *sabra*?" he repeated as though it were something wonderful to be. No, I'm not. I was born in Algeria. I come from the Sahara." He roared the last word defiantly and with a sense of awe. "It must be a fascinating place," Debbie offered shyly as if to compensate him for his loss. "My grandparents came from Poland, from Lodz," she explained. He grunted when she said "Poland" and looked away with an air of dismissal.

Just then a group from a nearby table passed by also on their way to leave. One of them walking last was a very fat woman about 35 or 40 . Yoram eyed her with a sharp clinical stab, then turned back to Debbie shaking his head in disgust, "What a disaster!

Suddenly he stood up imposingly and declared, "Let's go. I've had enough." He walked away from the table. Debbie, almost instinctively followed quickly but outside he went with his group waving his arm in an absentminded gesture of "Goodbye, see you around."

About two weeks after she had placed the ad, Debbie wanted to check with the agency whether or not there were any replies. Her curiosity could not longer be contained. She walked down Dizengoff Street toward the agency where she had placed the ad and from which she would receive the replies. She was deeply in thought about what she would do with the letters when suddenly she recognized the handsome man about 45 pushing a stroller with an active year old child toward her.

It had been about five years since she had last seen him but he had not changed at all. She tensed up not knowing whether to acknowledge him or not. She decided to wait for a cue from him. He noticed her looking at him and for a second there was a touch of recognition followed by a puzzled frown.

"Oh, what the heck," Debbie talked to herself. "I'll say hello. What can happen"? "Hi, remember me? How are you?" she called to him. It was at this point that she suddenly became aware of a petite dark young woman about 25 walking casually a few feet behind. Apparently, she had stopped to look into a shop window and hence was not directly next to him when Debbie had first noticed Kurt Nowozek. Now her dark eyes flashed questioningly at Debbie's intruding approach.

"Yes, yes, I remember, the American girl, many years ago," he answered with a wave of the hand and the same confidence and ease as when he had first breezed into Mrs. Levinsky's apartment. "I would like to introduce my wife, Rachel and this is our daughter, Nehamia, who is almost one," he continued quickly and proudly not so subtly conveying to Debbie that he was now a very married man.

"She's beautiful," Debbie cooed but Rachel made no sign of understanding.

"Rachel doesn't speak English very well. She has just come from Tangiers, Morocco three years ago," Kurt explained. "She knows French and is learning Hebrew." Debbie repeated her message in Hebrew and Rachel smiled. Debbie asked Kurt about his work and if they lived in Tel Aviv now but he soon began to fidget nervously about and mumbled something about having to meet some friends for coffee. Debbie knew the horrible truth that once a man was married, even small talk conversation was not longer a possibility so she bowed out gracefully with "It's been nice seeing you again." She looked at the trio once more and recalled his pompous speech about wanting a rich woman, house, expensive furniture, trips abroad, etc.

"Is she a millionnairess like you wanted?" Debbie laughed.

Kurt smiled shrugging his shoulders. "Quite the contrary," he said happily without a trace of regret. They said goodbyes and Debbie went on her way again marveling at the power of petite young dark Moroccan women. "Love does conquer" she thought to herself remembering his materialistic egotistical demands and how he obviously had willingly given them up for this woman. Such things did not happen to her.

Debbie continued to the advertising agency to pick up the responses to her ad wondering if there would be any. Much to her surprise, the clerk pulled out a huge batch of envelopes which had already been sorted and clipped together. Then she checked for additional replies which had newly arrived. All in all, there were at least 50 answers. "All those for me?" Debbie was stunned; she couldn't wait to get home and begin reading.

She was certain that 90% of the replies would be from women. Yet here again her fears were unfounded. Although there certainly were many more responses from females, the ratio was not as askew as she had expected. Eventually over the next few weeks, she collected 107 letters, cards, etc. - 60 were from females; 47 from males.

"Where to begin?" she thought. Among the men, there was a great variety in age, jobs, interests, background and educational level. From PhD to taxi driver, from 35 to 75 in age, from all backgrounds, sabras and foreign born, Ashkenazy and Sephardi - all had written asking to be in Debbie's group. Among the women, there was less variety. Most were, again somewhat surprisingly, professional women in very good positions, most were divorced, Israeli born and in their late 30's. So many people looking to meet. ..

Debbie was elated at the prospect of interviewing so many candidates for her "club." One air mail envelope from Sweden had caught her eye. "Even from abroad" she thought. This letter turned out to be from an Israeli doctor living in Sweden as part of an international health organization. He had seen the ad in the *Jerusalem Post* and conveniently planned to attend Debbie's group while he visited Israel to see his son and parents.

Like most ads, he sounded nice and sincere on paper. Debbie chose him the first to be interviewed since his time here would be limited. At the appointed hour he appeared. Debbie was immediately disappointed when she saw that he was shorter than she even though he had given his height as equal to hers. It seems to be a common policy that people placing ads often subtract years from their age and add several inches to their height.

Within seconds of their meeting, Debbie could immediately ascertain that this Swedish-Israeli health scientist was a brash egotistical and critical individual. He was 53 and had described himself as being handsome but was at best only average in looks perhaps even ugly to some. Instead of waiting to be asked questions, he immediately seized control of the situation by commenting, "One thing that worries me about your group is the age of the women. It could be a problem. They may be too old for me. "Why," Debbie asked puzzled, "They are all between 35 and 45."

"Well, yes," he hesitated and frowned obviously considering these to be too old. "So they are all younger than you," Debbie blurted out rather angrily now.

"Well, you see," he sighed softly trying to gain Debbie's sympathy. "I have only one son and he is with his mother. I would like to have another family with several children and for this I need a woman under 30 years old."

"Baloney," Debbie thought. "The old goat wants a young girl." She began to dislike this arrogant man more and more as the conversation continued. "And do you think that a girl of 30 will want to marry a man of 53? You would be old enough to be her father," Debbie argued.

"Well, I *am* a doctor," he said boastfully, leaning back in his chair, "Although I suppose a social celebrity or athletic hero could better command a younger woman."

"Well, perhaps my group is not for you," Debbie concluded, "Although I think the women are very attractive and interesting. At this point Debbie did not want him in the group even if he was a doctor. It was easy to see why he was divorced. He allowed Debbie to pay for her own coffee.

The next candidate was a decided improvement - a professor of Engineering at the Technical University. He was fairly tall, blond (although the hair was sparse and fading fast) quite good looking and pleasant, 49, divorced with one son. They met in a cafe and Debbie fired away questions as though the group actually existed and as though she were a professional organizer. The only problem with this engineer was that he was genuinely interested in the group and its activities - not in Debbie. Much to her dismay, he seemed barely to notice her except as a vehicle to other opportunities. Debbie liked him and hoped he would ask her for a date but he didn't. He asked her to inform him when the next party would be.

Another prospect simply did not show up for the appointed meeting. When Debbie phoned to inquire, he merely stated that he had changed his mind.

In the meantime, Debbie scanned other ads for possibilities. One in particular appealed to her intellectual bent. "Intellectual, 49, wishes to meet English speaking lady with whom to write book."

Writing a book with an intellectual would be a delight for Debbie and she visualized herself having deep philosophical discussions with a brilliant and handsome scholarly man and of course she, the poet, would do all the writing. She couldn't resist this fantasy and called the number he had listed. He spoke with a heavy Russian accent and sounded a bit "kooky" but she agreed to meet him in a cafe.

He was quite late but Debbie waited (as she always did) excitedly. She was not prepared for the shock that greeted her. Instead of a scholarly intellectual, Valentine was quite simply an unemployed weirdo with no place to live. He was staying "veet friends." It was immediately apparent that he was a "kooky" type, a new immigrant from Asiatic Russia. He claimed to have attended the *Moscow School of Dramatic Art* where he studied mime. Now he wanted to do "something else" but he didn't know what. His appearance, awkwardness and heavy Russian drawl created a ludicrous combination. He was at best a very strange fellow a kind of Mandrake the Magician type where you were never quite sure what he was up to.

Many questions later, Debbie finally mentioned the book he had spoken of in his ad. "What kind of book is it you want to write?" Debbie inquired as they drank coffee together. Valentine began to speak about collecting a group of philosophical essays he had written and making it a book. These "philosophical essays" were no more than Valentine's personal viewpoints toward certain situations and events, basically sounding like common sense and homemade remedies.

"Eet ees vat I dink about life, you know, verrry special." Since his English was severely limited, Debbie anticipated that the entire work would have to be rewritten. She thought that it was probably as crazy as he was. "The problem ees die Eeenglish" he admitted, "My Eeenglish ees poor and so I dought dat somevon like you. could help me.

"The ad mentioned 'writing a book together' Debbie reminded him, "But it seems that the book is already finished." "Vell, ve vould do die Eeenglish togedderk," he explained, "So eet ees still writing togedder, no?"

Debbie was peeved at having been misled. "Well, occasionally I do editorial work and translations for people and I would be happy to take a look at your manuscript. I usually work by the hour," she informed him firmly.

"Vell" he said, looking at her seductively, "I dought maybe, you know how eet ees, maybe vee vould fall in luv."

Debbie sighed thinking "O brother, he wants me to slave for nothing and probably take him in too and then to the

States,. . ." "Not so quickly," she said emphatically.

"Somedimes a gurl doesn't mind to help a fellow out a leetle, you know," he hinted again.

"Yes, I'm sure you will find someone," she said with a note of resignation taking her pocketbook and getting up. "I must go now, I wish you luck in Israel." She paid for her own coffee and left.

It was escape time again and Debbie found it necessary to take a short reprieve - a vacation from the seemingly bottomless stream of "characters." "How much crap can you take?" her girl friend would always say, "only in small doses." One always hoped that the next one would be different. But of course, he never was.

Debbie had seen an advertisement in the *Jerusalem Post* for a folk singing club sponsored by the British Immigrant Association for singles ages 30-45 called "The Coffee Club." Since she like folk music, she decided to give it a try. It met every other week in a community center. The "performers" were amateurs or semi-professionals (often aspiring professionals) from the audience who sang mostly American or English folk songs with an occasional Israeli or South American tune depending on the nationality of the performer. Led by an American immigrant about 40 years old, most of the audience which usually numbered between 100 and 150, were British or American.

Debbie was surprised at the high level quality of the singing and she was easily lulled by the melodic tunes. The group also seemed to be composed of nice people and the atmosphere was conducive to making friends although one could just as easily stay passive and aloof. It was held in the basement and as the crowd increased in number, people sat huddled closely together yet no one seemed to mind. At 9:30, there was a 20 minute intermission where people could talk and mingle and get refreshments.

The first few times, Debbie just sat quietly and listened. Then slowly she ventured to speak with a few people. Gradually, she began to know some men but although they were friendly, that was where it usually ended.. Once she struck up a conversation with a European man about 40 who walked her home, took her telephone number and seemed genuinely interested but never called. Another time, the situation was similar and although she saw the particular man several times thereafter on the main streets of Tel Aviv, she noticed he was always in the company of some young handsome boy.

Then one day rather unexpectedly, the phone rang quite late in the evening. "Shalom," the deep voice thundered in a way that indicated the receiver should immediately recognize it. And Debbie did immediately know it was Yoram. "Hello," Debbie greeted.

"What are you doing now?" he asked directly. She had barely finished replying when he ordered, "Let's have a coffee. I would like to speak to you.,"

Isn't it a little bit late? Debbie suggested.

"What," he snapped, "It's only 8:30."

"Well, I don't know," Debbie said hesitatingly.

"My God, she doesn't know. You are not getting married," he retorted.

"OK, Debbie agreed. Where shall we go?"

"Well, my house, it's very nice, you'll like it. All the women do." he boasted.

"I would prefer to go to a nice cafe around here," Debbie hinted weakly.

"Oh, they are all so crowded and noisy. We can talk better here," was the matter-of-fact reply. "Can you come?"

"I'm not sure I know the way. I have never been to Kiryat

Dworkin."

"Oh, you are so helpless. OK, I will come to get you."

After so many years in Israel, Debbie knew she could not possibly win. Most Israeli men simply did not take a woman out "on a date," that is, to dinner, a show, concert or dancing. Most expected a woman to give them a meal and later, "tender loving care." Many were even unwilling to spend money for a coffee in a cafe especially for anything more than a first date.

Yoram was right. The house was beautiful with a small lawn in the front and a large garden in the back. There were five rooms including a spacious living room. Attached to the house was a small office where he saw private patients and did treatments. There were paintings everywhere, most of which he quickly told her he had done himself.

He made black coffee as promised but that was all that was offered. It was supposed to be adequate for the entire evening. No excuse or apology was given. The generous hostess servings of the United States were not common in Israel especially in the home of a divorced man. Even the best servings were usually of the cheapest food possible.

They talked. Or rather he asked questions and Debbie gave answers. First he wanted to know how Debbie had gotten home from the poetry reading.

"I walked."

"What, you didn't bring your car?" he exclaimed, as if no one ever went anywhere without a car. "I would have taken you if you had told me you were on foot."

"Well, I don't have a car," Debbie laughed. "In fact, I don't even drive."

He sat up erect. "What, an American girl without a car and doesn't even know how to drive. I don't believe it!"

He always had a knack for making her feel small and inadequate. She suddenly felt ashamed for something she had never questioned before. She started to explain the difficulties of maintaining a car in New York City but as usual he responded to her comments as if he hadn't heard them.

"And why you don't know Hebrew?" I can't understand it," he shook his head.

By this time Debbie was becoming somewhat exasperated with what was supposed to be a"date" and should have been fun.

"Well, I think those are my concerns," Debbie replied sweetly, hoping he would change the topic.

But mercy was not forthcoming. "If you want to live here and be part of the life here, you must know the language like a native. And you have to be independent and get around, not always waiting for a bus." He preached at her in a harsh critical tone. Then she made the mistake of a lifetime, at least so it was with Yoram in the pulpit.

"I'm not sure yet how long I will stay in Israel. Maybe for good or maybe I'll go back to New York. I have an apartment there and my parents are there. They are still in good health but getting old and I am the only child. So, who knows."

This explanation would have elicited sympathy and understanding from most people but Yoram was furious, his face suddenly contorted with rage. He was beside himself.

"Excuses, excuses, you American Jews are all the same. Always some reason for not settling in Israel. Everything else always comes first. And then when they finally do come for a short period, what do they do? Write a book about Israel like they had been here all their lives. And they don't know nothing." He emphasized the word 'nothing'. "Why don't you go and volunteer in the hospital for handicapped children? Do something useful instead of writing some stupid poems. Oh my God!" he moaned as if in intense pain. "My mother had 12 children and she never wrote no silly poems," he added as if to sanctify his accusations.

For what seemed to be an eternity, Debbie was subjected to one of the longest tirades she had ever witnessed as Yoram gushed forth like a volcano about the question of all Jews living in Israel and the importance of their mission there. Wisely she thought it best not to interrupt him or argue. This was obviously a blind spot with him.

Debbie had not expected such an emotionally upsetting evening. She tried to change the subject by making a comment about his house being so beautiful and elegantly furnished. Surprisingly, it worked.

"I did most of it myself," he boasted and proceeded to point out various fixtures and conveniences he had added.

"It's so large. Don't you get lonely here by yourself?" Debbie tried to kid a bit hoping to change the tone of the conversation.

"Well, you know, I have not always been alone. Sometimes I have been living with someone for a time. But none of them has been suitable." He emphasized the word 'suitable' as though this would be a very difficult category for a woman to attain in his eyes. "Not so long ago, there was a girl living here from a kibbutz. She was very pretty but not educated. I can't be with someone who has nothing to say, nothing in the head, you know."

He laughed pitingly, "She cried so much when I told her to go. She loved me a lot. Even now she still calls me if she can please come to visit me."

"Does she?" Debbie asked cautiously somewhat sickened at the thought of this poor girl in love being thrown out so callously. He seemed not to care at all.

"Na," he frowned severely. "It's finished. I am not interested in her. She's a nice girl but not for me."

After awhile, as though he had completely forgotten his eruption, he frowned again and said, "Why do you always look so serious?"

"I didn't see any reason for laughing while you were arguing with me." Debbie answered tiredly. "You were very angry."

"Oh, come now, you have to understand these things. I'm a difficult man sometimes, I know. But you have no sense of humor at all."

Debbie sighed helplessly. "I guess not." She thought it easiest just to agree with him.

The reason for his change of mood soon became obvious. It was getting late and his mind had turned to the next conquest of the evening. "Come," he said simply as though that were all that was necessary. By this time Debbie had lost whatever attraction she might have felt for him. And yet for some strange reason of which she had only a vague awareness, she felt herself drawn to his commands.

She got into his big bed but instinctively stayed far on her side without even realizing how repelled even frightened she was of his power and yet attracted at the same time. The archaic desperation of her life clouded her judgment and prevented her from seeing Yoram for what he was.

"Well, are you going to stay there all night? It's OK with me. I will go to sleep."

Debbie smiled submissively and moved closer to him although she had difficulty relaxing. This only served to fire his impatience.

"My God, you are such an inadequate personality," he shook his head like a doctor who has just made a diagnosis of a hopeless case.

At least Yoram was consistent. He was just as commanding and cold in lovemaking as he had been in everything else. There was little tenderness and affection. The equation read that he was all wonderful and Debbie was woefully inadequate. The next morning after a meager breakfast of Turkish coffee and a slice of bread with jam, he took her to a central location in Kiryat Dworkin.

"There is the number 2 bus," he pointed to one of the many bus shelters, "It will take you to Tel Aviv. Can you find your way?" he laughed sarcastically shaking his head. "An American girl who can't drive, my God."

Debbie did not answer and got out of the car. He waved goodbye but the movement had more an air of dismissal about it than a farewell. As he drove away, she noticed a large "Pregnant is patriotic" sticker on his car bumper. These stickers had become popular after the Lebanese war when the prime minister called on the nation to replace those who had died. Some had adopted it as a general policy.

On the bus home, Debbie tried hard to forget the negative

aspects of the date and instead visualized herself pregnant and the beautiful wife of a respected medical specialist.

Her heart was like an empty stage ever anxiously waiting for a husband and children to make their entrances. She thought of her friends and relatives in New York talking enviously about her. "Oh, yes, Debbie Warshawsky, she went to Israel and married a doctor there. I hear she's expecting soon." How happy her parents would be! The fantasy was pleasant for awhile but Yoram's critical and harsh words cut through the illusion. "I don't know" Debbie thought. "It would be a big price to pay just to be married. Better to be an old maid in peace."

When the phone rang a few days later and her girl friend Sharon asked her if she wanted to go on a blind date, she answered an immediate "no." Debbie did not want to be with anyone else. Yoram had been quite enough.

But Sharon was persuasive and when Debbie heard that he was an American from New York who had been a hippie type in the 60's and had done many different things, she reconsidered and thought that at least he might serve as an interesting diversion.

"It will be good to talk about old times with another New Yorker and to be able to speak English fluently without first thinking about the level of the words and simplifying them for the Israeli listener." Debbie rationalized. She also chose to ignore Sharon's mention that he had one year earlier "become religious" and was currently "studying" at one of the yeshivas in the old city. She evaluated it as just another "experience" he was trying out. So she let Sharon give him her telephone number.

When Alan called from Jerusalem, Debbie was surprised at how long he wanted to talk and how many questions he posed. He especially emphasized whether or not she was divorced since as a Cohen[*], he would not be permitted to marry a divorcee. He inquired also about her Jewish and religious affiliations in New

---

[*] Persons with the name Cohen or Levi are thought to be descendants of the priestly caste and hence are subject to special laws.

York and Debbie listed her activities very carefully eager to make a good impression.

"Why don't we meet and talk some more. This is costing you a lot," Debbie suggested, "It's long distance, you know, and one half the cost of a call abroad."

"Well, I don't want to come all the way to Tel Aviv for somebody unsuitable," he replied quickly.

Debbie winced at hearing the word "unsuitable" again with the same stern intonation as when Yoram had used it. Finally, Alan thought Debbie worthy of meeting and so when she suggested "Peaches", a cafe near her apartment, he agreed to come.

Then suddenly he blurted out, "I have just one more question, I'm sorry I have to ask you because Sharon didn't know for sure."

"OK, what?"

"Well, have you ever been with a *goy*?"**

Debbie thought she must have heard wrong. "What did you say?" she cried.

"Look, I know it's not easy to talk about this especially over the phone, but I need to know because I can't go with somebody like that." Alan sounded nervous now.

"That's quite a question to ask over the telephone," Debbie moaned wanting to back out of the whole thing.

"Well, have you? Just say yes or no."

"No," Debbie shouted. "OK, she added, somewhat more softly.

"I'm really sorry. Things like that make it hard for me to find a partner. I'm 40 and by this age, most women have either been married or well, you know, have had experiences," he tried to explain in a rational way. But to Debbie's ears, it already sounded irrational.

"I'll see you at 8:30 at Peaches. Good night for now," Debbie answered not being able to continue the conversation and yet somehow not wanting to call it all off either.

Debbie was already waiting when Alan arrived at the cafe. There was no problem in identification since they had given each

---

** Goy - A derogatory name for a Gentile or non-Jew.

other good descriptions of themselves. At first they just exchanged small talk, how she had come to know Sharon, her life in New York, in Israel and so forth. He apologized for asking sensitive questions on the telephone "But I had to know, you understand." Debbie said "Yes." and quickly changed the subject.

Alan was quite tall, dark and good looking. At first, he seemed easy to talk to and they got along quite well. They were both from New York and knew common places. Again he asked many questions but Debbie did not seem to mind. He talked a little about himself. His was the typical story of a person who was struggling to find himself. He had "tried" many things from college to acupuncture but nothing seemed to be what he was searching for.

"Sharon tells me you were once a jazz musician. What did you play?" Debbie asked, genuinely interested

"Oh, that was just another 'lost period' of my life," He shook his head dismissing the matter as utterly absurd. "Listen, this place is too noisy. I can't stand it. Let's find a quieter place," he whispered suddenly leaning over closer to Debbie.

Debbie was quite surprised but agreed to walk with him, not knowing why he wanted a quieter place. They walked a while and Alan grew disgruntled with most of the places they saw which he viewed as "just as noisy." Finally he settled for a cafe-restaurant where at least there were fewer people.

As soon as they were seated, Alan, suddenly changed his whole tone and approach. Even his appearance was transformed. He grew solemn and intense as if what he was going to discuss was a matter of life and death. Before she could reorient herself, he was preaching to her, telling her about the "true way of life" he had found and how all other paths including hers were erroneous and would lead to disaster. He became increasingly fierce as he continued warning her as to what punishment would await those who did not obey the laws. To Debbie this sounded more like a Roman Catholic version of hellfire or something out of a James Joyce novel. Debbie realized that it would be useless to try and discuss anything with him. His commitment and belief were unshakable.

Debbie tried to be patient and listened for as long as she could tolerate it. Such intense absolutism and fundamentalism were alien and frightening to her. Finally, she made some excuse that it was late, she had to work early the next day, etc. etc. He accompanied her to the street where she lived but halted at the bus stop he needed. They said "goodbye" and for a moment he softened and became his former self again.

"A few years ago I would have kissed you, but now I can't," he confessed.

Debbie hoped that he might anyway just so he would appear more human again. During the "preaching" session, his countenance had taken on an unnatural other-worldly quality.

" I hope you will think about what I told you" he stiffened and maintained his distance.

"Sure," Debbie sighed and walked away.

She went home feeling sad. Alan was really a nice person but his mind was in chains and there seemed to be no escape in sight. She never expected to hear from him again, so she was surprised to hear his voice on the other end of the telephone a week later. After a few words of greeting, he dictated matter of factly as though he were reading a speech. "I just wanted to let you know that I have decided not to see you again. One problem is that you don't look Jewish so I would have a problem relating to you. You look so different from what I've been used to. And secondly you are not religious enough. You are not willing to accept the opportunity to learn God's law."

Debbie was shocked at the callousness of his words but she forced herself to be polite. "You needn't have called." she informed him in a serene soft tone. "I also understand that your kind of life is not for me but I wish you peace and happiness for the future. Goodbye now." She hung up quickly leaving him surprised and bewildered.

CHAPTER 10
THE GOLDEN ASS TURNS THE MILL ROUND AND ROUND AND . . .

In June, 1988, several cases of polio were reported in a small town in central Israel. Gradually cases were found elsewhere as well and the nation embarked on a widespread innoculation campaign. Complete vaccination was available for those who had never been and booster shots for those under 40 who had been vaccinated in the past. Debbie decided to get a booster dose. Many places, including schools were set up to dispense the vaccine.

One evening, Debbie went to get information at her local Magen David Adom (the Israeli Red Cross). It was already quite late and only a few patients were still waiting. When it was her turn, she spoke to one of the two doctors on duty. He was young, about her age, fair with a nice ample build and a pleasant round face. He explained everything very carefully to Debbie about the value of a booster shot. When she agreed, he gave her the injection.

Afterward, since there were no more patients waiting, he continued to talk to Debbie first about the polio outbreak and the innoculation campaign but then switched to more personal questions, as to where she lived, alone or with a family, her work, how long she would stay in Israel and so forth. Debbie enjoyed talking to this friendly and easy going doctor and he seemed to be genuinely interested in her also. They chatted energetically for some time when another patient entered. She thought she noticed a look of disappointment in his eyes. At this point, Debbie thanked him for the information, paid her fee and left.

She thought about him for a long time thereafter and walked by the Magen David Adom station more often than she needed to. She tried to think of some excuse to go in and see if he was there but couldn't come up with anything plausible. Then one night on her way home from the cinema, she walked by again and saw him parking one of the ambulances in the parking lot. When he noticed her, he called out loudly, "Hello, can I give you a lift, Miss Warshawsky?"

"Well, I only live two blocks away," she answered still recovering from the surprise of actually seeing him.

"So what," he smiled, "Come on, get in." He drove by her apartment to drop her off.

"So this is where you live. Very nice area." he continued.

"Yes, I like it very much, especially the park," Debbie agreed.

"Maybe I can come and visit you here sometime, that is, if you want." he asked in the same innocent tone with which he had asked the other questions.

"If you want to, sure, you're always welcome," Debbie said politely while at the same time subtly conveying to him with her eyes that she would like nothing better.

"How about tomorrow about five after I finish at the hospital and before I go to the clinic?" he shrugged hopefully.

"Tomorrow is fine with me. I am home by that time and it would be very nice to see you." she replied in a low quiet voice.

Debbie's comment was not mere flattery. She was eager to be with an attractive, interesting non-problematic man. It would be a welcome relief from all the undesirable and difficult singles. Ah yes, it sounded nearly perfect but there was one thorn on the stem. The doctor was married and had one small child. Yet by this time, even Debbie had learned the importance of snatching and savoring precious moments with special people when they presented themselves. She often regretted not doing so sooner.

Yuval arrived on time the next day. They had coffee, cake and interesting conversation. They were eager to know about each other. The transition to lovemaking was easy. He was a tender considerate lover, as relaxed in his manner now as he had been in the clinic.

Debbie had no problem in being aroused by his caring caresses and concern for her happiness. He had a strong stocky frame which made her feel feminine and secure. Of course, he could not stay very long but it is quality that counts, not quantity, Debbie told herself. She anxiously hoped that these pleasant interludes would continue. And they did. It was a marvelous antidote for the poison of the singles scene.

In the meantime, Debbie also sought the friendship of other women like herself. She had begun to value the importance of good women friends while waiting for Mr. Right to come along. One of her closest friends was a young woman named Yolanda from London, England who had been in Israel almost two years. She was 34 and like Debbie yearned to find a nice guy with whom to settle down. Confidential girl talk revealed that her encounters with men in Israel had been similar to Debbie's and that in general, she was disappointed with the single men she had met. Like many girls, she sought a solution to her problem by sharing a very good looking intelligent married man. She was a musician by profession and had many other cultural interests, therefore, she and Debbie had much in common.

Another good friend she had already known in Jerusalem was Israeli-born Zehava. After the breakup of a romance, she too decided to move to Tel Aviv. She was pretty, lively and thirty years old. She rarely lacked boy friends although she was beginning to discover that men of her own age or older already presented quite a few problems. The normal healthy guys of her youth had already been caught by more ripe and conniving types of women. She often dated younger men.

Zehava had read and devoured whole-heartedly the novels of Rona Jaffe which had been translated into Hebrew. As a result, she dreamed of going to the United States. Debbie tried her best to convince her that not every woman in the United States, in fact, quite few, lived dramatic and glamorous lives like the essentially upper class heroines of Jaffe's novels but Zehava's faith was unshakable. "Maybe you don't, Debbie" she had said solemnly, "but others do." Debbie decided that Zehava would have to find out the truth for herself.

One time Zehava helped Debbie read and translate the many

letters she received in response to her singles group ad. They were trying to categorize the answers in terms of "highly desirable", "OK" and "least desirable". It surprised Debbie how she differed from Zehava in grouping them. For example, Debbie was most impressed by a long detailed letter that provided much information and a good description of the person. She interpreted that approach as an indication the person was really interested in joining and that he was a serious, thorough, and reliable person. Zehava, on the other hand, wanted to put these letters in the "least desirable" category stating that "they must be very desperate to write all that and not have anything else to do. So they are probably not very good." She preferred the very short letters giving only a few details about themselves. "Those people, they are sure of themselves, they don't have to beg and convince and they are busy and active."

Debbie thought this to be very revelatory of the Israeli character which always strives to be strong and independent, at least in appearance and will go to great lengths to avoid appearing needy and desperate. They will shun someone who appears needy and dependent. This also explains the Israeli audiences in the cinemas who frequently laugh and begin to talk noisily whenever a scene from a foreign film shows a character being fearful, very sensitive, or very desperately in love. It seems they cannot tolerate or accept displays of the loss of emotional control.

Debbie tried to recall some of her old friends and was surprised at how many women she had met during her years in Israel. Some stayed, some left. Debbie's one time friend, Eti Rosenbaum, who had once given the party where everyone left when the food was gone, had moved to Haifa. At the age of 36, she was convinced that there was absolutely no chance to marry and so decided to have a child without being married. She had had a lover for a long time, a married man with three children, and he willingly fathered the child. Eti had a beautiful baby girl and the last time Debbie visited her, she seemed very happy and satisfied.

But Debbie also kept meeting new people. At one lecture on Middle Eastern politics, she met a widow from Peru, who was about 45, attractive and petite and had recently come to Israel. It soon became obvious that she did so in the hopes of finding another husband. She frequently asked Debbie of places to go and groups to join where one might meet someone. She went everywhere and tried everything but was disappointed. When she left one time to visit Peru, she did not return.

She met another English girl, Ann, who had been living in Israel for eleven years and had recently purchased her own flat. She was about 35, unmarried, and definitely looking.

Then there was Miriam, also from England who came to Israel at the age of 34, rekindled a relationship she had with an Israeli she had met in England and now at 38 was the married and happy mother of a little boy and twin baby girls.

And Marion from the United States, who at age 51 and single, had adopted a baby girl from Brazil. And Sharon, from England, who after having dated a macho type Israeli doctor for a year, became pregnant by choice at the age of 34. The fact that the father of her child has repeatedly and adamantly refused to marry her and has now retreated almost completely, does not bother her in the least. She is very happy with her infant daughter. Then there was pretty round faced Sarah, 31, who had recently come from Colombia, South America. She had studied in Geneva and was a simultaneous translator. She too could be seen frequently at familiar singles haunts.

As Debbie thought about each of these women, she realized each was very different but they all shared the same goal, to find a nice guy and get married. A few, like Miriam, had succeeded. Another good example was Gitel, originally born in Poland, who after the death of her husband had left England and come to Israel with her eldest daughter, then 33. She was about 56 years old, still quite attractive and very charming in personality. She had only been in Israel three months when she met Zev, a well-to-do widower her age, who also came from Poland. At first she was hesitant to accept his offer of marriage because it was so soon after her husband's death. Everyone advised her to take advantage of this miraculous opportunity and that many women would eagerly step into her place and perhaps would if she waited. An intelligent woman, Gitel realized the value of the jewel she had. Zev was a kind, considerate and cultured person. Gitel married him and has since led a very happy and interesting life. Her story seems to come more from a popular novel than from reality but it is true. The only regret she has is that it did not happen to one of her three single marriage-age children.

One day while waiting for a bus to Tel Aviv at the Central Bus Station, a petite girl came up to Debbie and asked, "You look very familiar. Didn't you used to dance at Columbia University?" Debbie vaguely remembered her but soon learned that Jody had come to Israel on a junior year abroad program at Tel Aviv University and stayed.

She had been studying for a master's degree in Nutrition at the university when she met a really nice guy from a kibbutz, also a student. They got married and decided to settle on a brand new kibbutz being formed in the Arava, an arid area near Eilat. "It was a pioneer settlement," she explained, "and there was a lot of hard work to be done, especially at the beginning. But now we have everything, it's quite comfortable and we are not that far from Eilat. You can visit us sometime." Jody seem to glow with health and happiness.

While Debbie was trying to recall some of the young women she had met in Israel, the memory of a very beautiful young petite girl named Beth came back to her. She had met her one day while having a routine checkup at the hospital. Beth was 31 but looked so much younger. She had come to Israel at the age of 17 to attend a three year nursing program at the Sharon Medical Center. Just like in a Hollywood film, she met a young doctor at the hospital, married him and eventually settled in a small town in the Negev desert. She worked as a nurse in the local clinic. The picture was perfect except for one detail. They were childless and Beth confided that she had been receiving fertility treatments at the hospital but so far, all were in vain. She sighed, "It's frustrating to work every day with young mothers and babies and not be able to have your own."

Through Ann, Debbie met still another girl from England, Paula who at 42 had been seeing an Israeli man in the process of obtaining a divorce. When he does, they will marry. However, she admits she is not in love with him, in fact, she finds him dull and boring. Yet since he is a nice and kind person, she is willing to make a compromise in order to be married and still have a child.

This was something Debbie could not bring herself to do although she also had this choice several times. She had met Craig from England through a mutual friend. He was divorced with two teenage children and had lived in Israel many years. He was pleasant, polite and seemed nice enough but somehow his personality came across as passive overly complacent, or just plain blah. In addition, he was very thin and a few inches shorter than Debbie. This would not have concerned her but whenever they walked together, he would always walk quite a distance away from her as though they did not belong together. Being with him was like being with a brother or close relative. When he decided to go to Australia to avoid military service, she did not miss him.

Most recently, she had met quite by accident a 36 year old widower with a five year old son. It was on the number five bus going down to the Central Bus Station. Debbie was sitting close to them. The man had reprimanded his son somewhat too harshly, Debbie thought, judging from the boy's sad and crestfallen face.

"He's really cute and so well behaved," Debbie commented as they got off the bus.

"Yes, you think so?" he asked puzzled. "Well, I suppose most of the time."

They continued to make small talk as they went to their new destinations. Debbie was on her way to Jerusalem; Menashe and his son, Shai, were on their way to Luna Park, an amusement park in Tel Aviv. Menashe was tall, fair and quite good looking but in a traditional and non-dramatic way. Debbie assumed he was married.

"Your wife didn't want to come?" Debbie queried checking on the existence of a mate.

"Well, my wife died two years ago," so it's just me and Shai. I go with him everywhere," he explained.

Debbie's ears perked up. "Oh, I'm sorry to hear that. It must be hard for you to care for a child and work at the same time."

"Yes, it is, but we manage, don't we?" he smiled at the child. Shai smiled too and nodded his head in agreement.

They were about to turn on the street for the bus to Luna Park when Debbie, searching for a way to keep contact, finally remembered her half forgotten, never materialized singles club. (When none of the men she had interviewed took an interest in her, she decided to drop the whole idea. The women she never met at all).

"I don't know if you would be interested," she began carefully, "but I have a group of people who are all single and we have parties and other activities once in awhile. They are all very nice. Perhaps if you are in the Tel Aviv area, you might want to join us sometime."

"Well, I don't know," he stammered visibly upset now, "but it's so soon. I know everybody is pushing me to get married. Just the other day, a shadrachan(matchmaker) called me up and wanted to match me with some women. I was angry with him and told him not to bother me again. I don't know how he got my number."

Debbie was surprised at the vehemence of his response. She had to think quickly to calm him. "Oh, I just meant to have some fun and participate in activities with people the same age and in the same situation as you. Most are single parents. There is no emphasis on pushing people together or matchmaking. No one is paired off; we function as a group. Why don't you think about it, take my number and if you want, you can call me to find out when the activities are. If not, it's OK too, nothing is lost."

He was somewhat relieved at this explanation and took Debbie's number. "It will probably be awhile till I call," he said sheepishly.

"Sure, whenever you want. Feel free," she smiled sweetly. "Well, I have to get to Jerusalem. Goodbye. Have a good time at

Luna Park."

"Thank you. Goodbye." Then they left. Debbie never expected to hear from him again.

She was surprised when he did call about two weeks later to ask if he and Shai might come to visit her in Tel Aviv and perhaps go to the beach. She heard notes of fear and hesitation in his voice but mixed with a certain eagerness.

They came a few days later, the little boy shyly carrying a gift. After they entered the living room, he extended his arms suddenly and held out what was a bottle of perfume.

"He wanted to give it to you," Menashe explained when Debbie looked surprised. She was happy at being treated like a queen especially after all the stingy men she had met recently. Yet her elation was somewhat dampened when she noticed both were wearing *kippas*.[*] She wondered if they had worn them on the bus also.

After some coffee and cake with polite conversation, they went to the beach which was only a few blocks from Debbie's house. They had a pleasant time. First Debbie went into the water with Shai who was somewhat afraid. She tried to encourage him and finally succeeded in prodding him deeper into the water. She thought of teaching him how to float but decided that would be pushing him too much. He was a nice little boy, always lively and cheerful. Debbie wondered how much his mother's death had affected him.

Then Menashe went into the sea with Shai. After they returned, they all took some photographs. Shai was delighted by Debbie's camera which he perceived to be a toy. After some practice, he was able to snap a picture of Menashe and Debbie.

After the beach, they decided to have dinner. The question was where. Debbie, being the "expert" on Tel Aviv, suggested a few places. She saw Menashe frown and hesitate and then it dawned on her suddenly that being religious, they must keep kosher and hence could eat only in kosher restaurants, of which there were

---

[*] kippa - worn on the head and indicating religious orthodoxy, that is, strict observance of religious laws.

few in Tel Aviv. Menashe shyly suggested a restaurant not far away which was strictly kosher. Debbie of course eagerly concurred in the decision.

They ordered dinner and settled into a conversation. Shai was eagerly devouring his French fries with huge amounts of ketchup, eating very little else. Menashe started to ask Debbie questions. At first, she thought they were rather harmless "make talk" type of inquiries but upon later reflection saw their significance.

"Do you plan to stay in Israel?" he asked quietly.

"I'm not sure yet, but probably," she answered honestly.

"Why did you move to Tel Aviv?" he asked with a very serious almost reprimanding look.

"Well, there were more job opportunities, the climate is better, and the social life more active," Debbie explained, becoming somewhat annoyed with always having to answer questions and justifying her actions.

"Oh, I thought maybe you didn't like Jerusalem. I wouldn't want to live anywhere else," he stated very emphatically.

"I lived in Jerusalem once, for several years, but I wanted a change. Did you ever live anywhere else?" Debbie asked more to make conversation than because she really cared to know.

"Well, some years ago, I moved to Hebron[*] and lived there for a year," he said non-chalantly.

At this point, Debbie was aroused from her boredom and a pain tore through her heart. "Oh no, a settler mentality" shot through her mind. Debbie was shocked that Menashe, who seemed so kind and caring a person in every other aspect, would do such a thing.

"Why did you do that?" she asked almost unbelieving.

"Why not? Jews have a right to settle wherever they want. The land is ours. We have to make that clear to the Arabs," he

---

[*] (Hebron is a city in the West Bank with an almost exclusively Arab population. For Jews to settle there meant provocation. They had to push their way in and it usually resulted in making trouble, creating hard feelings and even violence.)

declared strongly.

Debbie sighed. The answer to his comment would require an hour's speech, all to no avail, as previous experience with right-wingers had taught her. So she just said quietly, "That's not something I would ever consider."

After dinner, they walked about for awhile and then went to Debbie's apartment for a short period before they returned to Jerusalem. Debbie had had a pleasant time but she knew it was not promising.

The very next day, as if the encounter with Menashe had not been enough, Debbie was surprised by a telephone call from none other than Yoram. She had not heard from him since he had left her in the Holon bus station more than a year ago. It was typical of Israeli men that they expected the girl to welcome them with eager arms even though they had not phoned in ages. He spoke in a friendly manner as if he had just seen her yesterday. Not prepared for this surprise attack on Yoram's part, Debbie responded to him in the same manner. He said he was in Tel Aviv and wanted to come by to pick her up to go with him to have dinner and could she be ready in twenty minutes. Without thinking objectively, or perhaps not thinking at all, she spilled out the words, "OK, but make it a half hour."

"Oh you women always take so long for something so simple. OK, I will see how long it takes me," he sputtered impatiently.

Twenty minutes later, Debbie's doorbell rang. She was ready, having quickly thrown on a clean blouse and skirt. Debbie had foolishly expected that they would go to a restaurant for dinner but she should have known better. He was much too cheap for that and did not care enough for her to impress her.

They went to his house whereupon he took some meager portions of leftover chicken from the refrigerator and thrust them into Debbie's hands. "In the oven," he nodded his head to the small heater standing on the kitchen cabinet.

Debbie had never seen one like it before and proceeded to examine it before attempting to use it. Finally, she thought she knew how to work it and tried in vain to take out the tray. Either she didn't do it correctly or the tray was stuck. She fumbled with it for awhile when his booming voice broke in. "Oh, you are such an inadequate personality. You don't know how to do anything."

"Well, I've never used one like this before. I have an old one," she explained defensively. He took the chicken from her hands roughly and thrust it onto the oven tray with a jerk of his hand. "There's nothing to it."

Then the same scene was repeated with the heating of the bread leaving both of them exasperated. Finally, it was ready and he served Debbie a pitifully small chicken leg and a tomato. He took the remainder which was not much more.

They started to converse and Debbie momentarily forgot his treatment of her and chatted away amiably. He looked at her critically like a judge evaluating a murder suspect. "You talk so much, my God. Women should speak only with their eyes," he declared authoritatively.

"Who said that?" she laughed. "Some macho male?"

He covered his ears as though he were in excruciating pain from the loudness of her voice. "Shhhh!" he frowned, unwilling to listen to any more of what she was saying. Being shut up infuriated Debbie and she spoke even more loudly. He winced and covered his ears even more completely. Finally she gave up and was silent.

"That's more like it," he smiled sadistically.

Debbie wanted to explain herself again but soon realized that it was useless to talk with someone who wasn't willing to listen. He started to talk again as though nothing had happened but Debbie quietly ate the meager supper he had served.

"You see, you can be quiet, I knew it," he leered at her in triumph. He took her face and suddenly put it in between his cupped hands. "You have such a beautiful face, such a profile, but oh when you begin to speak, what a disaster!"

By this time, they had finished the meal if one could even call it that. There was still coffee to come so Debbie did not wipe the table deciding she would wait until they had completely finished. There were quite a few crumbs from the bread they had eaten but Debbie was not disturbed by them.

Suddenly like a bolt of lightning, he scowled and with a quick sweep of his hands, he wiped all the crumbs on the floor, yelling, "They're not going to move by themselves." Debbie, frightened by his outburst quickly got up, found a dishrag and cleaned the table.

"My God, you don't know anything," he fumed.

Making the coffee, normally a simple task proved to be an ordeal if one was preparing it for King Yoram. Debbie was anxiously concentrating on not making any mistake or doing anything he could find fault with. What she didn't realize was that he would search for something wrong. For her to pretend that all was well and to keep smiling just added to the burden.

He sighed a lot as if he were forcing himself to tolerate her stupidity or even just her presence. She tried not to notice and served the coffee careful not to spill any. She felt small and humiliated as though a heavy harness had descended upon her.

Finally, they finished and Debbie, of course, cleaned up without any help from Yoram. He left the kitchen immediately which gave Debbie a feeling of relief. At least she could tidy up in peace. When she finished, she went into the living room. She looked about for Yoram but he was not there. Then suddenly, she saw him standing under the bedroom door. He had heard her come into the living room.

"Come, I want you now in the bedroom," he ordered gruffly and demandingly. Then he disappeared into the room. Debbie couldn't believe it. After he had treated her so demeaningly all evening, now he wanted to make love. Or rather he wanted sex. Love was beyond his comprehension. She hesitated not knowing what to do. She couldn't bring herself to submit to him now and yet to leave meant going out into an unfamiliar neighborhood where there were no buses or taxis. She could be stranded and it was getting late.

"I'm waiting," he shouted threatingly.

Debbie took a deep breath, mustered up all her strength, quickly took her bag and tiptoed to the front door, praying it would be open. It was! She sneaked out quickly and as soon as she was clear of the house, began to run. She ran down his street and when she turned the corner, she stopped for a minute to select a house from which to call a taxi, looking first at the name of the street.

She chose a house that was well lit and rang the bell. Although she heard voices inside, they did not answer. She panicked. "Perhaps no house will answer, they are afraid and I will be here all night" raced through her mind. There was an industrial zone nearby and she knew enough not to venture near there. She would have to sit it out on the street. She walked over to the big picture window in the living room and saw people inside.

She knocked on the window and an elderly woman looked her way. Debbie smiled and held up her hand as if holding a telephone receiver. The old woman called a younger one who came from the kitchen. She immediately came to the window.

"Please, may I use your telephone to call for a taxi to Tel Aviv. I left my friend's house and I can't find a bus station," Debbie pleaded breathlessly. The young woman motioned for her to come to the door. Apparently she had not understood exactly what Debbie wanted. Debbie repeated only the key words, "Telephone, Taxi, Tel Aviv." The woman nodded and showed her the telephone. She called the information for the Holon Taxi Service and then ordered a taxi to come for her at the corner of Yoram's street and the street where she was now. They promised to come in ten minutes.

Debbie thanked the woman leaving five shekals under the phone and went back outside, Fifteen minutes later, a taxi appeared on the otherwise deserted block. Debbie waved her arm and he stopped. "Tel Aviv, Dizengoff ve Jabotinsky" she told the driver as she got in. "Kama ze?" (How much?) she continued trying not to show how desperate she was. "Twenty shekals," he answered. It was too much but it could have been worse. "Tov" (Good) she replied and sighed sinking back into the seat. It was a year till Debbie heard from Yoram again.

From one of the men she had interviewed for her "singles group", Debbie learned of the existence of the Tel Aviv ACI single parent group. She had dismissed the ACI from her mind, assuming that the Tel Aviv group would not be much different than the motley group she had met in Jerusalem. However, Dan informed her that the group was very lively and active and so large that they were split into two groups, one for over 40 years of age and one for under 40 with children under 14.

Debbie decided to give it a try and called the leader of the younger group to inquire about joining.

"Are you a single parent?" was the first question the leader, an American divorcee, threw at Debbie in a brisk and clip business like manner.

"Well, no, but I wanted . . . "Debbie replied hesitatingly.

"I'm sorry, the group is only for single parents," she broke in not allowing Debbie to finish her sentence.

"Well, I tried the young adults group, but I am too old for them. They are mostly in their early twenties. And the mid lifers who are supposed to be between 40 and 60 are actually closer to 60 and over. So I thought age wise I would fit into your group," Debbie tried to explain.

"No, you don't," she stated defiantly. "We are all single parents and we have much in common. Most of our activities are related to issues concerning single parents and the raising of children. I'm sorry."

"That's not really fair." Debbie said quietly.

"So, start your own group for singles over 30," the leader quipped. "I have to go now, one of my kids needs something. Goodbye." She hung up immediately.

Debbie felt so bad at having been so cruelly rejected by another American woman whom she felt should have understood and have welcomed her enthusiastically. It was at moments like this that Debbie felt like erasing herself from the entire scene. After two months had elapsed, so as not to make the connection obvious, she called the leader of the older group. After Debbie expressed her interest in joining, she too asked the crucial question, "Are you a single parent?"

"Yes," Debbie answered confidently. "I have a son, three years old."

"Are you divorced?"

"Yes, for one year."

They chatted a while longer and then the leader gave her the address of the member, at whose home the next meeting would be held. Meetings were usually held in different members homes except for the one meeting a month where both groups were combined, which due to its size met at the central headquarters in Tel Aviv.

Debbie did not like to lie but in Israel, sometimes one had to do certain things just to survive. One had to attack unfairness with unfairness. Later, she discovered quite a few singles without children in the group, especially men. None of the lectures dealt with children or with child rearing practices.

Debbie eagerly awaited the first meeting which was scheduled for the central headquarters with the two groups combined. Her eagerness and anticipation fizzled quickly when she saw the group in action. First of all, there were about twice the number of women to men. She wondered why it was always like this. Then she concluded that in general, men fear engulfment and involvement; women fear abandonment most. Is it any wonder then that women are seeking relationships at any cost and men wishing to avoid them. Hence they also avoid functions where meeting available women was a likely possibility. Yet 2:1 was not a bad ratio. She had known worse situations.

Debbie continued to attend the weekly meetings. Usually there was socializing from 8:30 to 9:30, then the program for the evening, usually a lecture by a visiting guest followed again by socializing. It sounds like a pleasant evening and it could have been but it was not. There was a jungle like atmosphere with a dangerous lion or tiger ready to jump at any time. The women were the lions and the tigers; the men the objects of prey.

Never before had Debbie encountered such desperate and aggressive females as in that group. Often as many as three women at one time would compete for the attention of one man. Each tried to outdo the other in charm, cunning and wittiness. The man would be passive basking in the attention of so many admirers fighting over him. For fight they did and not only during the brief socializing period.

Several times Debbie had been engaged in a serious conversation with a man. A woman, usually an Israeli (who were permitted to join) would barge into the conversation uninvited. Once she had been talking to a European man who was an amateur film maker. Debbie was interested in film and thought that he was interesting to be with. They were discussing Italian directors when suddenly a short fat, fiftyish Israeli woman came over and without waiting and without apology, not even an "excuse me," she blurted out loudly to him, "What did you think about tonight's lecture?" She totally ignored Debbie.

"Bertolucci is rapidly becoming one of Italy's top directors," the man declared to Debbie ignoring the intruder.

"I thought it was really great, didn't you?" the "bulldozer" cut in again, this time also moving her fat body closer physically. Both the filmaker and Debbie were obviously annoyed at her persistence and again ignored her comments. This time, he turned his body directly face to face with Debbie and away from the trespasser. He spread out his elbow in the hopes of completing his ostracism of her. Finally, she saw she would not succeed in gaining his attention and haughtily walked away. This scene was repeated again and again with only minor details changed.

The Israeli women soon became known as bulldozer #1,2,3, etc. Some of the men, including the one who had been interviewed by Debbie, stayed away from the meetings because they disliked women like this. He had said, "They are all so sad, lonely and desperate. I don't want to be near them. I want to be with happy people." Basically the men were afraid and justifiably so. Most, if not all, of the women wanted to marry again; many had several children and financial difficulties and were looking for support. A few of the Israelis admittedly sought a way to get to the United States; most just found life as a single difficult especially in family orientated Israel.

Some of the men actually made fun of the women's desperation. One time Debbie was in a car pool going to one of the meetings in a suburb of Tel Aviv. On the way, one of the men related how a woman had asked him to take her home. Then she invited him in for a cup of coffee. "I never got the coffee and that's all I really wanted," he roared with laughter.

"They're all like that," another man contributed and told his story which was quite similar. "I just go to hear the lecture. I keep away from them."

"You're very wise," a third one chimed in. "There are so many of them and so few of us. We have to protect ourselves. Ha Ha Some of them are pretty big. Ha Ha,"

Debbie squirmed when she heard what the few men there were in the group thought of the women. She reminded herself that she must never appear desperate.

The older group was somewhat too old for Debbie. Most of the people were in their fifties. To make matters worse, many of the older men had drifted over to the younger group in search of younger women. Although they technically did not belong there because they were over 40, they were eagerly welcomed by the younger women who wanted more men in the group to balance the severely uneven ratio of men to women. In the younger group, it was 3 to 4 women to every man. It is understandable that even a man in his sixties would be welcome. Needless to say, this "drift" did not make the older women very happy and at one point, the membership in the older group had dwindled to the point that they were in danger of extinction.

One evening, they called a meeting to discuss what they should or could do to remedy the situation. Someone suggested that each member bring one new person to the group. Another emphasized the importance of re-uniting with the younger group although attempts to do so failed in the past. The younger group wanted to remain independent. The leader related that she had received a call from the American Embassy where there were quite a few single parents who asked if they could join the group.

"But," she said with a frown, "I think we are all in agreement that we don't want to bring *goyim* into the group." There were nods of agreement among the eight people present. I told them that the group is just for people who have decided to settle here and they are just here for a fixed time."

Debbie was saddened to hear this harsh and what seemed to her unfair judgment of people who had not even been seen. Thinking that perhaps the leader, who was a woman, might not want any more women in the group, Debbie spoke to one of the men on the committee.

"I think maybe we should give the people from the Embassy a chance. At least, let them come once to look them over and then decide. They must be OK people if they work for the American Embassy, don't you think."

"Oh, come on," he answered as if her idea were absurd. "We want the group for ourselves. We don't want other people coming in." That was the end of that! Debbie fantasized about all the wonderful handsome men from the Embassy she could have met if only . . .

One week when the two groups met together, one of the women asked Debbie why she didn't attend the younger group. Debbie began to consider the possibility although she hesitated to approach the leader who had once been so rejecting. Now of course, she understood why; the last thing in the world they needed was another woman.

During the socializing, she came into contact with the leader and used the opportunity to ask her. She pretended that she hadn't known there were two groups.

"Haven't I spoken to you before?" she quizzed Debbie frowning as she analyzed her closely.

"I don't think so," Debbie answered as calmly as she could.

What is your name?"

"Gila."

"No, for sure not. I would remember such a nice name," Debbie lied.

"Yes, you think so?" Then she invited Debbie to come to one of the meetings. "See if you feel comfortable. Maybe you prefer the older group. Some do," she advised.

Debbie made a trip to Kfar Sava where most of the group lived.

It took more than an hour to reach the north Tel Aviv suburb and then she had to walk quite a distance down a dark deserted country street where the member lived. This was not so comfortable and she thought not to come there again.

The group was a nice one for the most part. Usually there were so many more women than men that the competitive aggressive spirit was not even aroused. When the two groups met together, there was more interaction in general. Individuals thought it was at least worthwhile to try to meet someone.

One time, there was a combined meeting in the center of the city, within walking distance of Debbie's apartment. The lecture would be given by a psychotherapist on the topic of feminist therapy. This theme attracted an almost completely female audience and three men. From the other side of the room, one of the men seemed fairly attractive and Debbie thought she might try to chat with him during the socializing part of the evening, provided that the 25 other women in the room did not have the same idea.

After the lecture, there was a question period and the man Debbie had noticed raised his hand and asked, "But what exactly is a feminist therapist?" The lecturer tried to explain briefly what she had already clearly stated in the lecture. Still he was not satisfied. "So how is this different from any other therapist?" he continued to press. He spoke slowly almost with a southern drawl combined with a midwestern twang.

The lecturer, growing more and more exasperated again tried to clarify the difference. He shook his head. "I don't get it. Why is this difference so important?" he said with a self satisfied grin, happy that he had made the lecturer upset and uncomfortable. Apparently the lecturer did not recognize the fact that he was merely heckling her and trying to put her down, not caring at all about the topic. She proceeded again to attempt to explain and justify her position.

"But you still haven't answered my question. What is a feminist therapist?" he drawled again.

At this point, one of the Israeli women called out, "Let's have some other questions. I'd like to know if you treat teenagers and if young people respond to this type of therapy?" At last, the focus turned away from him. He was obviously a woman hater and resented the lecturer for being a psychologist whereas he was a mere car salesman and a truly obnoxious and nasty person. Debbie spared herself the trouble of getting to know him.

She continued to attend the meetings even though she did not expect to meet anyone. Most of the members were American with a few British and South African and a few Israelis. It was a joy just to be able to speak English freely and without first having to lower the vocabulary and simplify the idea for Israeli ears. Most of the women were divorcees, a few were widows, all with children. Were it not for the competition and rivalry for the available men, some of them could even have made good friends.

Debbie did meet a few men while going to the group. The first was a handsome American from New York in his thirties, who had a PhD in archeology. As is the case with most men, he seemed nice and interesting in the beginning and keen on Debbie.

On Friday, they had agreed to meet at one of the late Friday afternoon restaurants featuring live singing and dancing. This was a custom popular with many Tel Avivians, especially singles. Debbie could not arrive until three o'clock but he said he would wait. It was to be their first real date.

When Debbie arrived, she looked for him before entering and saw him sitting at the bar talking to a girl. She motioned to him whether or not she should come in. For a long time, he did not make any move. She didn't know what to do and stood outside embarrassed. The girl collecting the fee pressed her to move so Debbie explained, "I'm supposed to meet a guy here but now he's at the bar with someone else, so I don't know whether or not to go in." He waved her to enter and she paid her entrance fee. Debbie went over to the bar and he directed his attention to her. After a drink, they started to dance. They danced for a long time and Debbie was beginning to tire. He tried to push her to make more vigorous moves.

"Hey, not so rough," Debbie pleaded trying to smile. "Listen, I don't feel so well, OK? I have cramps, just time of the month stuff, but still I would prefer to sit down for awhile."

He sighed as if disgusted and stopped dancing. They sat down and Debbie tried to be cheerful but his mood had clearly changed. Shortly thereafter, he wanted to leave. As he drove her home, he was sullen and silent.

"What's the matter? Are you angry because I didn't want to dance anymore? I just wanted to take a short break, that's all," Debbie tried to placate him.

"Oh, come on, you know what's what. Having your period, that's the oldest excuse in the book," she shouted at her with rage.

Debbie was bewildered at first then saw that the date was only a pretext to have sex. If that was not forthcoming, he did not want to be with her.

"Well, I could be angry too," Debbie exclaimed, "the way you let me stand outside the place. It was awkward and embarrassing. You could have come to the door to invite me in."

"I didn't come because I thought you wanted me to pay for you," he said matter of factly.

"It was only ten shekals. ($5) Do I look that needy? I thought you might want to be with that girl, so I hesitated. Oh, never mind," she said tiredly.

He stopped in front of her door. With barely giving her enough time to get out of the car, he slammed the door and drove off. Whenever she saw him again at the meetings, he pretended as though he didn't know her and always made a dive for a new young and pretty member.

There were all types of men in the group. There was a hard core of regulars; others came and went. One example of the latter was an Israeli named Yoav. She met him one Thursday when the group had assembled in Petah Tiqva, a suburb to the east of Tel Aviv. Debbie thought he was being kind when he offered her a ride home. There were no buses at that hour.

When they arrived at her apartment, he said very directly, "Let me come in for awhile."

"It's after 1 A.M. and I have to get up early tomorrow," Debbie excused herself.

"That's not so late. Come on, I took you all the way from Petah Tiqva," he argued. "That's a long way."

"I'm sorry," Debbie said firmly. "I didn't know it was a taxi. Perhaps some other time ok?"

Still angry, he took her telephone and said he would call. Several days later, he did call at about 10 P.M.

"Can I come over?" he asked immediately.

"Well, if you like, we could go to "Bananas" cafe for a coffee." Debbie suggested ignoring the intent behind his request.

"No, it's too late to go to a cafe," he stated emphatically.

"Well, then perhaps it's also too late for you to come over." Debbie argued logically, but it failed to penetrate him.

"If I came over, I meant to do more than talk," he stated somewhat dictatorially.

"I don't even know your full name or anything else about you. I like to know a person for awhile before getting so close," Debbie explained.

"Well, look, you have my telephone number, if you change your mind, you know where to find me," he said impatiently and without feeling. And just as suddenly, he hung up.

Debbie marveled at his ego and nerve considering that he was quite short in stature (much shorter than Debbie), barely average in looks and awkward and dull in personality. He said he was a business man, a word which serves an umbrella to cover many things, including "nothing." Soon thereafter, he stopped attending the meetings. She met him once more on the street and he tried the same tactic once more.

One of the first men in the group to ask for Debbie's number was an Israeli named Benjamin. He was also short and not particularly attractive but seemed to have such an affable, friendly personality that Debbie decided to give it to him. He was interesting to talk with and told Debbie that he wrote short stories in his spare time.

One day when Debbie had attended a meeting at Tel Aviv University, she met one of the women in the group there, one of the few French women. They talked for awhile, Justine saying that she was waiting for her date to go to a concert. They continued to converse until her date appeared - none other than Benjamin! Debbie was somewhat embarrassed but he did not seem to be.

One of the American women in her Ulpan, Denise, tried to encourage Debbie to come to the Book Discussion Club of the AACI. It sounded like something she would be interested in, so she agreed to come the following Tuesday. Denise had promised, "There are some really nice people there. I'm sure you can meet somebody. I did. I met a really nice fellow, an Israeli but his English is very good and he's interested in books. I have been out with him several times."

The group met every three weeks. A book, usually a best seller, was assigned and then the organizer of the group would lead the discussion at the next meeting. When Debbie arrived the first time, the discussion had already begun. One of the first people her eyes fell on was Benjamin so she slid quietly in the seat next to him.

"What are you doing here?" she whispered.

"Oh, this is an interesting group. They have read some good books and you have a chance to talk about it with other people," he answered amicably and with a gentle smile.

Denise had seen Debbie enter and was now casting anxious and furtive glances at her. As soon as the discussion was over, she zoomed to the place where Debbie and Benjamin were sitting.

"Oh, do you two know each other?" she said with a nervous laugh.

"Yes," Debbie and Benjamin said matter of factly. "I met him in the single parent group," Debbie continued, concerned about Denise's shocked face. Then suddenly she realized that Benjamin must be "the nice fellow" she had mentioned. She said she wanted to ask the leader about joining and so had an excuse to get away. By the time she returned, Benjamin had left.

"Is that the fellow you meant?" Debbie asked now.

"Yes," Denise said resignedly.

"He goes to the single parent group. Why don't you come to those meetings. It's a nice crowd even if you don't meet anyone," Debbie offered trying to be encouraging.

"Oh, I went a few times last year. It's not for me. Those women are very attractive and have nice figures. They are looking to get married again," Denise replied shaking her head. She was about 45, divorced, and quite overweight - not exactly the characteristics that would attract men in droves. Debbie did not tell her about Justine.

One evening after a meeting of the single parent group, Benjamin offered Justine, Debbie and two other Israeli women a ride back to Tel Aviv. As they were approaching Tel Aviv, Justine suggested, "Why don't we go and have a coffee at the Dan (Hotel). They have the most delicious cakes." All readily agreed.

Soon Debbie found herself sitting in the lobby of the Dan Hotel drinking a capucchino. However, as she looked around at her group, she felt depressed at being one of a harem of four with Sheik Benjamin basking in the center. He was obviously soaking up every bit of attention he was getting. Debbie wondered, "What am I doing here?"

Shortly thereafter, she discussed the scene with Justine. "I felt strange sitting there, four desperate women and one available man. It's pathetic." Debbie said sadly.

Justine laughed, "It's even worse than that, because he's not really available."

"What do you mean?" Debbie asked startled.

"Well, he says he's separated from his wife but he had been saying that for a long time. I heard that he's basically still married, living with her and all, but just not getting along. You can see why not." Justine laughed again. She did not take him seriously.

"I didn't think they would let married men into the group. It's supposed to be only single parents," Debbie asked disillusioned.

"Well, you know how desperate they are for men. It's better if there are more men there. If only a few come, it scares the rest away and soon none will come," Justine explained. "So let him come. What difference does it make? The "available" men in the group aren't really available either, If you know what I mean."

Debbie knew very well.

One evening, a new man appeared on the scene which made a grand total of three. At first, Debbie thought he was quite attractive, about 50, American, tall, with dark curly hair and still a lot of it. During the social hour, he seemed quiet and polite at first, but shortly after they started to speak, he began to fire a string of questions at her. He had her cornered in a part of the room and ignored her frequent hints that she would like to get some coffee which was in the next room. As usual, she allowed herself to be subjugated. She answered his questions docilely and never got to the coffee machine.

Perhaps it was her lack of firmness and sense of selfhood and her easy "nice" manner that made Debbie such a prey to men who were looking for women they could dominate easily and who would eagerly conform to their every whim and demand. Perhaps if she had said firmly, "Excuse me now, I'm dying of thirst. I'm going to grab some coffee. Want to join me?" and then making a strong move out of his stranglehold, whether he followed or not, would have communicated to this man, "This is not a woman you can push around" and quite possibly he would have disappeared in search of someone more pliable.

But alas! Debbie was pliable. When he offered to drive her

home, she accepted.

"I'm not going to offer to take you to a cafe, because I don't have six shekels ($3)," he said flatly. "And I don't believe in paying a fortune for a cup of coffee."

Debbie was somewhat taken aback by his arrogant statement. It was already quite late and she did not want to go to a cafe but still resented his commanding air.

"Are you going to invite me in?" he asked in a dare-you kind of way, as they approached her street.

"It's quite late, almost 12 and I must work early tomorrow. So I think not," she said as sweetly as possible.

"You don't know what you are missing," he argued sheepishly.

"Oh, I'm sure," she laughed, trying to keep things light.

"You may never have the opportunity again," he threatened in a jovial way but there was an undercurrent of stark seriousness in his gaze.

"A missed opportunity," she kidded.

"Someday, you may be sorry you missed all these great opportunities," he warned trying to appeal to her fear of loss.

"Perhaps," she sighed. "Here we are. Thanks so much for the ride. Will you be at the next meeting?"

"Who knows?" he shrugged his shoulders. She got out. He jus barely mumbled "good night" and drove off quickly.

Debbie did see him again but it was always when and where he wanted. He would never take her anywhere, not to a cafe, cinema, lecture or anywhere else. The places he would consent to go to were the various dance halls or hotel discos since he loved to dance. Yet even there, he insisted that she pay her own way. He exclaimed simply that he was penniless, his shrew-like Israeli ex-wife having taken his every penny. He did not have a steady job, just doing odd pieces of work as he found it. However, Debbie noted that when it came to lavishing expensive gifts and trips on his two spoiled teenage children, he would never tire of spilling out the shekals.

If Debbie complained about his never wanting to do what she

preferred, he just stated matter of factly, "Well, sweetheart that's my program. Take it or leave it."

For awhile, Debbie took it, even though it made her feel low and unworthy. She had lost all sense of self respect. In New York, she would never have accepted such a "program." But in Israel, she was lonely, he did speak English and there was not much other choice.

"I'm the best of the leftovers," he judged accurately, assessing his place on the singles market.

It was true! Often at the meetings of the single parent group, as many as three women would vie for his attention. It was pathetic to watch these desperate women trying to appear vivacious and so interested in the lecture of the evening or whatever else they had used as an excuse to talk with him. But yet, although many were attracted, few stayed with him for very long, perhaps because of his financial situation, perhaps because of his personality.

Debbie tolerate the status quo for longer than she should have always giving the excuse, "Well, it's better than nothing." But she was wrong. She finally decided to stop seeing him when he explained one day, "I'm looking for a *freyer*-ette,* a woman who will submit to my wishes 100%. She will always do what I want and not have any demands of her own."

Debbie argued, "Any healthy relationship involves a 50-50 give and take between the two parties, otherwise it is a sado-masochistic relationship."

"Well, sweetheart, that's what I want and I had it once until her 19 year old soldier son interfered. He threatened me and I didn't want to fight with him so I stayed away. She wants me back, I know but I don't want her now. She's gotten so fat. Her butt is twice the size it was."

Debbie decided she had had enough. There was no future with him and he would not change. He would crush her completely if she allowed it. She had worked hard to conquer her shyness and

---

* freyer - a Yiddish word, someone who can be taken advantage of easily, someone who is naive, gullible, easily deluded.

develop herself to be where she was today. She could not let someone like him destroy, perhaps in a short time, all that she had struggled for. It was only after she had been free of him for several months that she realized what a depressive effect he had exerted on her. What a heavy burden his presence and constant criticism had been! Better to be alone than to be in a destructive relationship!

The crooked seams of Debbie's life remained. As time went on, she continued to meet new men in the group, none of which was suitable. One was an elderly widower named Itzhak who liked Debbie very much. When he took her home once, he confided that he had been a widower for 32 years. He wanted to go out with Debbie and kept asking for her telephone number and she kept making excuses until he finally got the hint. He was about 70 and although he seemed like a kind and sincere person, Debbie felt he was much too old for her.

When Yehuda started coming to the meetings, Debbie thought he might be a possibility. An American teacher and counselor, he was tall, fair and quite pleasant looking. He was also attracted to Debbie and they went out a few times. Although he would only eat in kosher restaurants which severely limited their choice in Tel Aviv, at least he did take her somewhere. He was also quite interesting to talk with.

Debbie had been somewhat disturbed at hearing that he and his wife had divorced one year after she had twins and that he left the United States for Israel when they were five. Debbie wondered how anyone could leave twins being able to see them only once a year, sometimes less.

Once when they had come to her apartment after a date, he asked to see some of her writing. Like any poet, she eagerly picked her best poems, one which had been accepted by four journals (nothing short of a miracle, Debbie thought) and another which had been published by a Jewish journal. The first was a one page poem which portrayed women in different aspects of Israeli life showing the status of women in Israel.

He took the poem with a smile and began to read. As his eyes descended the page, the corners of his mouth also dropped until finally he was frowning and his face had taken on a scowl where the smile had been.

"Oh, this is awful," he said harshly.

"Why, what's the matter?" Debbie asked.

"How dare you criticize Israel like this," he thundered angrily.

"What do you mean "criticize Israel?" I am giving a description of the life of women here. It's a very realistic appraisal, exactly like it is with a note of humor," Debbie explained trying to defend herself.

"You're only a tourist here," he yelled. "What gives you the right to describe Israel?"

Debbie couldn't believe how fiercely he was reacting as though she had threatened him with a knife. "I've been living here for seven years. I think that's long enough to be able to judge a few things."

"You mean, you've been here for a year, seven times. You haven't actually "lived" here, become part of the country, "given" of yourself to the country."

Debbie did not want to argue and attempted to placate him by showing him what she thought was a positive poem. It was a true story about the boy friend of her friend, Eti. He had been in the Lebanese war and had seen his friends die while he escaped unharmed. When he returned home from the war, he was depressed and unable to study. Debbie had emphasized his "looking back" to see his unit go up in flames by making allusions to Lot's wife and the Orpheus legend. It is a disaster to look back.

She thought for sure that he could find nothing wrong with this very sympathetic and understanding portrayal of an Israeli soldier in battle. But she was wrong.

"This one is even worse," he snorted after he read it quickly and thrust it back into her hand with an air of dismissal.

"But it is a very sympathetic portrayal. There is nothing critical here," she argued.

His face grew dark and he frowned severely and with a scowl.

"You show the Israeli army in a bad light. You make him sound like some kind of nut case. Israeli soldiers are strong and brave. No matter what happens, they will be able to fight. They do not fall apart. So this is the kind of stuff you write. I'm shocked."

"Well, I'm sorry, you don't like it. Most people do," she retorted wondering what he would say to her more leftist poems.

He left her shortly thereafter, totally disillusioned, convinced that Debbie was some kind of ogre. She saw him again occasionally at the meetings of the single parent group but he kept his distance.

Often if the meeting was far away in one of the outlying suburbs, Debbie and others would get a ride from one of the older men in the group who lived in her neighborhood. On one such evening, Debbie got into the car and was surprised to find a strange passenger already there.

He was blond and very handsome and was coming to the group for the first time. He had seen the ACI advertisement in the *Jerusalem Post* and called the number given for details. Of course, being male, he was most cordially welcomed. He was born in South Africa but had lived in Haifa for many years. Now newly divorced, Debbie assumed at first he wanted to meet new people. She smiled at him, hoping to interest him and attract his attention before the meeting where she knew he would be stampeded by all the women.

"Where are you from?" he asked ostensibly to make polite conversation.

"From New York City," Debbie answered, "But I have lived here for seven years."

"Do you by chance know a place called Oyster Bay?" he asked non-chalantly.

"Oh, that's out on Long Island, in the suburbs," Debbie replied trying to be helpful.

"And where do you live?" he asked somewhat puzzled.

"In Manhattan, in the city itself," Debbie explained.

"How far is Oyster Bay from the center?"

"About 40 miles, about an hour by car."

"And what kind of place is it?" he probed.

"What do you mean?" Debbie asked not understanding what he was looking for.

"Well, what kind of people live there? Rich or poor? Are there houses or industry?" he continued more excitedly now and with a note of annoyance at having to explain what he meant.

"I don't really know it so well. It is mostly residential and I would say middle class or even upper middle class. But why are you so interested in this place?"

"I'll be going there in about three or four weeks and I just wanted to know something about the place," he explained pulling a map from his pocket. It was a map of Long Island. "I've been trying to find out how far it is from the city. I came tonight to see if anyone could give me information. Everyone in the group is American, right?"

"Yes, most." Debbie was disappointed now when she heard that he was leaving.

"Do you know someone there? Do you have a place to live? she asked simply.

"Yes," he said simply, "The only problem was to get a visa."

"How long will you stay?" He laughed as though that had been a ridiculous question.

"A long, long time," he declared simply.

"How long is your visa?" Debbie inquired.

"Six months only. But I may be getting married, so that doesn't worry me. Tell me, are the houses very big there? he continued obviously interested in how rich she was."

By this time, Debbie was tired of answering questions because she realized that she was just being used for information. The scene was clear now. She had heard that South Africans are eager to get out of South Africa, yet they don't want to come to Israel. They prefer Australia or New Zealand but it was getting increasingly difficult to get in. The United States was essentially closed to them. This man would enter the United States on his Israeli passport and he would be able to stay by marrying some poor slob of a woman.

Debbie thought back to the personal ad she had seen several times in the *Jerusalem Post* about a year earlier - "Attractive divorcee, 42 seeks sincere Israeli mate for life abroad." It had been an Oyster Bay address. Debbie wondered if he was going to her.

By this time, they arrived at the meeting place. Suddenly, the driver's girl friend who had been silently listening to the conversation, turned around and said to the man from Haifa, "Did you know, Debbie has her own apartment in Manhattan," she revealed the information proudly.

"That's nice," he responded with some degree of interest.

"She's considered quite a catch," the girl friend informed him with a wink. Debbie was embarrassed. They joined the meeting already in progress. She lost him as he started to mingle in the crowd. Later in the evening, he left with one of the women in the group but Debbie did not know her. He left for the United States three weeks later and has not been heard from since!

Although most of the women in the group were not interested in being friends, the competition for the men being too keen, Debbie did succeed in making one or two female friends. One of these was a very young and pretty divorcee named Susan who seemed less desperate than the rest. But like most divorced individuals, she was eager to tell her story.

And as most girls, she had come to Israel because she liked it but at the same time harboring secret hopes that she might lure one of those handsome sexy sabras under the *huppa* (wedding canopy), And she did!

Or rather she thought she did. Susan had met an Israeli on the beach, not long after arriving in Israel. He was charming, interesting and persistent. Never before had anyone wanted so much to marry her. She was quite literally swept off her feet. She adored him; he could do no wrong. They had a big wedding, mostly with his relatives and a blissful honeymoon trip to Europe financed with her money.

Things were OK for the first few months. Then he became

increasingly moody and irritable. Susan thought he was unhappy in the marriage and blamed herself. Perhaps she was not giving enough of herself, not loving enough. She suggested that they consult a marital therapist but he emphatically refused. They started to have bigger and longer fights about little seemingly unimportant things. He became critical of her appearance and behavior. Susan tried her best to please him but he became more nasty and sarcastic towards her, almost insulting although he always insisted he was doing it for her own benefit and to be helpful. By the time he was finished extricating himself, it was Susan who felt guilty.

Finally, things had worsened to the point that he began talking about a divorce. Susan couldn't believe it. She wondered what had happened to the charming curly haired easy going fellow she had met on the beach. She tried everything to save the marriage but he wanted a divorce. Since it had become impossible to live with him, she reluctantly agreed.

There was no pre-marital agreement. She had been so much in love and he had seemed so perfect that she thought there would never be any need for such a document. Although he had brought nothing to the union, he now insisted that half her property and money belonged to him. The case went to court and she, as a woman, was sure to lose.

Her lawyer was a clever man and saw the whole situation very clearly. He probed into the husband's background and talked with his present and former friends. Finally, there was a light. One of the friends, no doubt as unscrupulous as the husband himself, admitted that the husband had written him a letter in which he confided that he planned to seduce a rich American girl, marry her and then take all she had. He had boasted, "Things are going just as I planned. I've almost got her where I want her. And then I'll ditch her, take as much as I can from her and run. Then everything will be wonderful."

The lawyer wanted to see the letter but the friend hinted, "I didn't know it was so valuable. I don't know if I still have it."

"Perhaps for $5,000, you might look for it," the lawyer

suggested.

"I don't usually throw things away so I'm sure I still have it." It was not long thereafter that he "found" the incriminating letter and without a trace of guilt or betrayal, the friend gave it to the lawyer for the agreed upon price.

With the letter as evidence, it was clear that he had premeditated all the events and planned to cheat her and then to discard her. The court decided in her favor and he got nothing.

"I was lucky," Susan said with relief that was obvious even now. "I could have lost everything. So you see why I'm not so anxious to get involved again," Debbie then told her the story about the American woman who had sold her the toaster so many years ago.

CHAPTER 11
THE BARBARIANS ARE COMING OR THE EMPIRE IS FALLING

It was now the summer of 1993. The Israeli-Palestinian peace talks were progressing in Washington, the occupied territories were still closed and Russian could be heard everywhere. For Debbie, however, life continued as usual.

One day, she noted that it had been a long time since she had heard from one of her best friends, Yolanda. At first, she attributed the lack of communication to her friend's new job or to a period of intense musical inspiration. Debbie and Yolanda had much in common especially similar aspirations toward marriage and family life and similar negative experiences while striving toward this goal. Yolanda was 38 now and like Debbie heard the biological clock ticking loudly.

When Debbie finally gave her a call, she heard that Yolanda had a new boy friend and was seeing a lot of him. His name was Boris, he was 31 and a recent immigrant from Russia. In fact, he had only been in Israel for three months. Yolanda had met him in the *ulpan* (language school) where both were studying Hebrew. Yolanda had set great hopes for changing her single state into wedded bliss on the arrival of the mass Russian immigration to Israel. In fact, she frequented the government ministries dealing with immigrant affairs, donated food and clothing to the local absorption centers and enrolled in elementary Hebrew classes filled with the newcomers. Apparently her scouting had paid off.

Although Debbie also eagerly subscribed to various schemes to meet new people, she avoided the Russians. Her experiences with them had not been good ones, and she was very turned off by their crass almost obsessive materialism. Besides Debbie had already heard from several official sources that most of the immigrants came in family units and that the "singles" were almost always divorced women with children.

Yolanda began to think of Boris as a definite marriage prospect. She was surprised when he told her that he was going to Holland for a guided tour. "He's only been here three months and already he's going abroad on vacation. These Russians adopt a western life style very quickly," she declared somewhat proudly. She eagerly anticipated his return and in the meantime once again had time for Debbie.

Yolanda waited and waited. The tour should have ended by now but there was no sign of Boris. Perhaps something had happened to him, a terrorist attack or a criminal one, she thought. She was beside herself with worry. Finally one of his friends had pity on her and informed her that Boris had not planned to return to Israel. He had joined his wife and five year old son in Amsterdam. While he was waiting in Israel, they had left Russia for Holland and had made all the bureaucratic and other practical arrangements necessary for immigration, residency and work permits there. Yolanda was devastated. She had believed his every word. Yet when Debbie later tactfully suggested to Yolanda that she might write a short story about her experience, to warn others from falling into a similar fate, the latter was shocked and said she would not want people in general to know that such things were going on.

Besides the ACI, now and then Debbie and Yolanda tried several other activities with the same tireless hope of meeting new and interesting people. Actually, there was no end to the range of activities that were available in Tel Aviv.

In addition to the hotel groups which Debbie had already sampled, there were several other single groups usually organized by one person and sometimes meeting in different halls or private locations. Some would flourish for a while and then peter out. One such example was Leona's which often met Friday evenings in a private villa which she had rented for the evening. The entire first floor was the living room. About 200 people came predominately between ages 25 to 35. Debbie noted that in the younger groups, the number of men and woman were approximately equal whereas in the over 35 groups, there was a severe imbalance increasing with the age. The women painfully outnumbered the men with ratios too depressing to reveal.

One group where the balance was not overly askew met at the Amerika House, the twentieth floor of which served as a ballroom. The age range here was 45 to 70. Usually the music was a combination of disco and pop ballroom dances called "60's dancing" or "salon dancing" such as, the tango, passadoble, cha-cha, samba and rock and roll. There was a modest fee for entry varying between $7 and $9 per person.

There was another ballroom on the second floor on one of the main streets where they offered dancing almost every night, each day, however, catering to a somewhat different clientele. For example, one night was Sephardic night when the music and singer focused on Sephardic songs. Other evenings drew different age groupings. Many people usually came in pairs or groups and seemed to enjoy themselves. Debbie never met anyone at these places. She thought most of the men were too crude and aggressive and the women were rather flashy and made desperate attempts to appear younger. Gregory Roth types were conspicuously absent.

In recent years, various "60's dancing" groups had sprung up everywhere. Almost every community center had one "60's night" a week. They varied in age span. Tel Aviv University boasted two large and successful groups, one Saturday and the other Tuesday. The latter group was packed to overflowing. Israelis seemed to love especially rock and roll music and the tango. Debbie would often smile, even laugh at their enthusiasm for songs she considered old and dated.

Lectures and conferences were also a good place to meet interesting people although most of course were not exclusively for singles. There were always many lectures on middle eastern politics at the university which were usually composed of faculty members and students. Even those who were not, often had some relationship to academia, such as journalists and other media specialists. Debbie met quite a few interesting people this way, both men and women.

Almost always, the language used was English, especially if there were international guests present.

Lectures at the ZOA House (Zionist Federation of America) tended to attract an older right wing crowd (over 50). Debbie learned to avoid these since the views expressed by the audience were sometimes upsetting for her. For example, one night, the lecture had been on the Palestinian conflict and uprising. A middle aged, middle class American woman in the audience raised her hand during the question period and said in a very loud and angry voice, "Why don't they just send in the Air Force and blow Nablus off the map?" The lecturer of the evening replied, "And what do you think our image would be the next day in the media?" Debbie cringed. This group was not for her.

Debbie also attended archeology lectures even though this was not exactly her favorite subject. However, they were very popular especially the Tuesday morning series at the university. Each week a renowned archeologist would speak and present slides of his recent and important excavations. The auditorium was always full even though there was a fee. However, it was a predominately over 50's group. They also sponsored interesting outings to excavation sites that would normally be closed to the public.

Lectures on various aspects of religion had an appeal for many who were religiously inclined. Most of them were given from the point of view of a believer. Debbie had little interest in this yet many individuals attended such lectures or workshops even though they knew little about Judaism, often in the hope of establishing some roots or personal identity.

Lectures on health, business investments and psychological themes appealed to many and were always exceptionally well attended. The speakers were usually well known and respected in their disciplines. Since many single people attended such lectures, Debbie was convinced it was one of the best ways to meet a wide variety of people. Business investments attracted the largest numbers of men. Debbie tried to pretend even to herself that she was actually interested.

There was one group calling themselves the Single Academic Club which was exclusively for singles. Run by a thirtyish Israeli girl in her postage stamp apartment, it attracted mostly women. However, the lectures were usually interesting and the speaker a supposed expert in the field. After the lecture, which was always in Hebrew, there was a break for coffee, cookies and conversation, followed by a general discussion between the expert and the audience. The main problem was that the living room of the organizer was so small that the 35 people in attendance were sitting and standing in cramped and uncomfortable positions - often on top of one another. There was a $5 entrance fee. One time when Debbie ventured forth to the Academic Club, the topic was "If he says he will call, why doesn't he?" There were 32 women present between 25 and 35 and 3 men the same age.

Of course, one could always join the Tel Aviv Country Club for the appropriate fee. There they had many facilities including swimming pool, tennis courts, folk dancing, 60's dancing, all types of exercise equipment, classes of various kinds, such as yoga, aerobics and many other facilities. Alas, it was too expensive for Debbie and for many others as well. Her girl friend, Ann, had taken a subscription at the Hilton Hotel Sport Club in the hope of meeting visiting tourists but discovered that many arrived with wife and kiddies.

During her years in Tel Aviv, Debbie came gradually to learn that tours were a fairly effective way of meeting "quality people." The Society for the Preservation of Nature was one of the best groups. They offered tours to different parts of the country for one, two or three days, sometimes more. The advantage of SPN was that they searched the unbeaten pathways, places where the ordinary "tourist" trip didn't go. They usually had good attendance and interesting people. Debbie felt that here at least the misers were eliminated.

There was also an organized tour group for singles (late 20's, early 30's) plus many others organized by private individuals. It was a relaxed fun way to meet people plus seeing new things which is always refreshing in itself.

The ACI single parent group occasionally made outings where parents were permitted to bring their children. One time in January, Debbie joined the group for a trip to Mount Hermon in the north. She had never been there and thought this a good opportunity. As usual, there were many women and few men. One of the men was currently the boy friend of one of the long time members and during the bus ride to the Golan Heights, they were holding hands very romantically. Debbie thought it encouraging to watch this pair, neither of which was young. He had snow white hair and was at least 65; she was about 55.

Finally they reached the mountains. The view was magnificent and many people could be seen already on the slopes. The snow was fresh and immaculate. The group separated into different activities. One could rent skiis and equipment and go on the slopes, one could take skiing lessons, or take a ride up to the top on the cable cars, or go tobagonning or one might just take a walk in the refreshing snow and imbibe the beautiful scenery. Debbie and a divorcee from South Africa decided on the latter three. Later they visited the ski lodge and its gift shop and ate in the restaurant.

In the afternoon, while Debbie was watching the skiiers gliding down two of the major slopes, the man who had been holding hands with the group member on the bus came over to her. At first Debbie thought he was just being friendly to her because she was a new member and wanted to make her feel welcome. Yet it was not long before she realized that it was more than mere friendliness. She was shocked when he asked for her telephone number and if he might call her - all this within eye range of his "girl friend" who was speaking with some other members a short distance away.

Debbie was embarrassed and said, "Can't you see, Janet is looking this way."

"So what," he snorted, "I'm not tied to her."

"Well, I would really like to," Debbie lied tactfully, "but I couldn't do that to a friend. She's been very nice to me welcoming me into the group."

"Oh, don't be silly," he argued. "come on, give me your number. I want to get to know you better." By this time, he had pulled out a pen and notebook. Janet's eyes were glued on them.

"No, I'm sorry," she answered and began to walk away. He was angry and went off in a huff. Later, when they got back on the bus, he came over, ignored Debbie and started to chat with the South African woman sitting next to her, barely polite. When Debbie relayed her encounter with him, the South African woman commented, "Oh, he does that with all the women. He has boasted that he has had every woman in the group. I don't see how Janet puts up with it. I suppose she's glad to have him, given the shortage of men."

"The men certainly have their pick, don't they," Debbie concluded.

"Yeah, sad isn't it." she answered tiredly, sinking back into her seat.

Debbie noticed that one of the regular members, an American divorcee of 40 who was always quite vivacious was unusually quiet on this trip. When Debbie asked Doris if anything was wrong, she remarked, "Oh, I guess its just post visit blues or something."

Doris had recently returned to Israel after she and her only son had visited her parents in New York.

"It's just always such a hassle to get there. I have to get everything cleared with my ex first and that means lawyers and contracts to sign," she explained. "I hate it each time I have to go through it. Sometimes I wonder even if the trip is worth all the trouble."

"Why do you need your ex husband to make a trip? Are you not divorced? Debbie asked.

"Well, I need his permission to take my son out of Israel, even if just for a few weeks. And he won't sign it unless I put up my villa as guarantee."

"Guarantee for what?" Debbie probed.

"Well, if I don't bring the child back to Israel, the villa

automatically belongs to him. I have to put it all in writing each time." Doris sighed helplessly. "That's how it is. He knows I'll always come back. I would never give him the house, never. At this point, I still want to return, so it's OK," she added a bit more cheerfully when she saw Debbie's glum face.

"That's really awful. It must ruin any joy you would have from the trip." Debbie reasoned.

"Well, that's why I'm not exactly overjoyed at being back. And you know the problems being single here, of course," she added resignedly.

One of the men in the group, a newcomer from New York who had just published a book on engineering and was just "trying Israel out" had a more pleasant story to relate.

"Just for fun, I put a personals ad in the *Jerusalem Post* a few weeks ago," he said non-chalantly. "My God, I got so many replies I didn't know what to do with them. One of the women I met was a Russian, new in the country like me. She seemed nice but I guess I shouldn't have given her my telephone number because now I keep getting calls from Russian women I don't know. I suppose she is passing my number around."

He pretended to be so disturbed by this but could barely hide his glee. It was obvious he felt like a king making a difficult choice among so many willing slaves.

During her years in Tel Aviv, Debbie also discovered that there seemed to be no end to the number of self help and support groups which have sprung up. In addition to providing emotional support, it was also a good way of meeting people with problems similar to one's own.

Current phenomena or movements, such as, Rebirthing, EST, the Silva Mind Control Method, I-Am, Immortality and others have come to Israel and have been quite successful. Some sponsored weekend or week workshops in the Galilee or in the Negev in a vacation type setting which were especially popular even though they were also for the most part expensive.

Others were on-going support groups, such as, Alcoholics

Anonymous, Overeaters Anonymous, Infertility, Widows and Widowers and others. One interesting group which appeared within the last few years was called Anglo Saxon Women Married to Israelis. There were groups in almost every moderate sized community, usually in two age ranges, 20-35 and 35-55. The increasing popularity of these groups perhaps indicates that such relationships are problematic and that the people needed support, They would discuss common problems, such as, how to deal with his friends, in laws, language difficulties and areas of tension as well as sponsor activities. After much criticism as to why there was not an inverse group, that is, Anglo Saxon Men Married to Israeli Women, a small group was finally initiated. The truth was that there was really no need for such a group. These marriages seemed to work better. Eventually, other groups, such as, Dutch Women Married to Israelis, German Women Married to Israelis, etc. also came to life.

Debbie knew a girl who had gone to Alcoholics Anonymous in the hopes of meeting someone. She was not a drinker herself but calculated that such men were often abandoned by their wives and in need of help and support which she was only too willing to provide. Through AA, they would recover from alcohol and then hopefully become available males - for her. She finally stopped going when people kept asking her, "How long have you been dry?"

Debbie herself decided to try Overeaters Anonymous. She felt that perhaps being overweight might not be the most serious deficiency in a man, depending of course, on the amount. Since she was working in a town between Jerusalem and Tel Aviv on a translation job, she decided to try the group in that area.

The first shock that greeted her as she entered the apartment where the meeting was to be held was that the group was only women. Not one male to be seen. They were all considerably overweight and mostly in the older age group although there were a few her own age. Another surprise was that they were all married. Debbie's initial reaction was to wonder why they would have to come to a group like this if they were married.

They were all friendly and immediately started giving her a pile of pamphlets and other information, some of which was from AA. The leader explained that they based their principles on AA. They started the meeting with different members reading the 10 points of the program.

Debbie had to sit through it although it seemed very religious and unscientific to her. Instead of viewing their obesity as a physical and psychological imbalance, they approached and treated their problem as though it were beyond their control and they needed "a higher power" to help them. Then there was discussion with refreshments but Debbie did not participate. As the meeting was nearly over, a woman sitting close to Debbie said, although not in an accusing way, "I don't think you are really one of us." Debbie just smiled uncomfortably and was grateful when it was over. And yet it had been enlightening for Debbie to meet people with preoccupations completely different from hers.

Then there was Sunset Musicale which sounded so romantic in the advertisement - music, art, refreshments and good conversation - in the sunset of Friday afternoon. It was all to take place in an art gallery in Jaffa, the city immediately adjacent to Tel Aviv. Debbie decided to give a try.

The gallery itself was presenting several exhibitions of different Israeli artists. People were browsing then went upstairs to what was a living room type atmosphere. The crowd was predominantly older, (over 50) that had gathered around a large table of coffee and criossants. Debbie had come with a woman friend about 55. At one point, there was an elderly gentleman about 65 sitting by himself on a sofa. Her friend darted over and sat down beside him and initiated a conversation. However, moments later, his wife came from the refreshment table with two cups of tea and croissants in her hand. Debbie's friend got up quickly.

A performance by a woman guitarist who played a wide variety of songs, was the highlight of the afternoon. Then there was more mingling but Debbie left. It was Friday evening and there were no more buses running. The $7 taxi fare and the $8 entrance fee to the gallery had been expensive for what had been offered, sunset or not.

Debbie had never tried the marriage bureaus or any matchmaking services. She always felt very turned off when she saw these advertisements in the newspapers, perhaps because of her earlier experience with "Operation Marriage."

She had heard conflicting reports and comments about such agencies. Most were quite costly and one of the most expensive "Yentas" had recently been discredited entirely. One woman friend of Debbie's who had succumbed to the enticing promises of the matchmaker discovered that one of the men who had been sent to her had been the very same man sent to several other women as well. Apparently no attempt had been made at compatibility since all the women were very different. Debbie concluded that this was probably a logical and frequent occurrence, given the ratio of men and women who were "looking." And yet, her friend and neighbor, Hilary, happily related that one of the secretaries in her office, who had been married for one year, had met her husband in an agency. It was an encouraging story but Debbie remained unconverted. Perhaps someday...

Political activism was Debbie's primary interest since the start of the major Palestinian uprising on the West Bank and Gaza in 1987. She was still a member of *Peace Now* although she now took its activities more seriously. Through a visiting professor from New York that she had met in the ACI single parent group, she was also able to tag along with a left wing group of faculty at Tel Aviv University called "*Ad Kan.*" They had regular meetings between Jews and Arabs often with a lecture and sponsored occasional trips into the West Bank with the objective not only of promoting greater understanding but also to initiate plans for concrete action.

One Saturday, there was to be a joint meeting between the faculty of Tel Aviv University and Bir Zeit University, an Arab university which had been completely closed by the military authorities for two years. Therefore, the meeting took place in the Board of Trustees building. The discussion, led by the woman Dean of Humanities at Bir Zeit, was lively and engendered many good ideas. Debbie wondered how many would eventually be put into action since there was always a gap between eager proposals made during talks and the ultimate outcome.

After the meeting, Debbie spoke briefly with the chairman of one of the departments but the group from Tel Aviv University was ready to go so she was limited in her time to speak privately with anyone.

They drove with private cars back to the central street of Ramallah to wait for a sherut to Jerusalem. As they waited, Debbie looked about and saw several armed soldiers standing on the rooftops here and there watching the street with binoculars. Some shops were open on the street, the owners sitting outside ready to receive customers. Debbie felt strangely uneasy and wondered what it was like to live day by day with someone always watching your every move, especially if he was armed with a machine gun. She felt very sorry for them.

After they had been waiting awhile, a military jeep filled with soldiers drove by and stopping asked them what they were doing there. The Israelis in the group explained and they got into a discussion. Debbie remained silent and moved closer to the professor who had invited her. The commander of the soldiers talked for awhile with the organizer, a professor of social science. "I have everybody in my unit," he declared loudly, "from extreme left to extreme right but we never discuss politics. I absolutely forbid it. We couldn't do our work if we did."

The sherut came and they drove off. However, minutes later, shots were heard coming from the next streets. She felt certain that some teenagers had been killed or wounded as she read about every day in the newspaper. She wanted so much to go and see what happened but the taxi sped off to Jerusalem.

Most of the political activities Debbie participated in were organized by the Peace Now movement. They had demonstrations and made trips to the occupied territories. Debbie recalled the demonstration on Christmas Eve in front of the Municipality Building. The huge square was filled with people even though it was raining quite hard. Debbie stood, umbrella in hand, listening to the speeches. Another memorable demonstration was the one at the beginning of the *intifada* (uprising) when Allen Ginsberg spoke and read his famous poem, *Yahweh and Allah*. The crowd was so large that it was reminiscent of his readings in the sixties for Viet Nam and Bangladesh.

The most recent journey, demonstration, peace mission, whatever one might call it, was to the village of Nahalin, near Ramallah. Several villagers had indicated that they were willing to receive Israelis into their homes.

Nahalin had been the site of a massacre when about 3 A.M one morning, border police entered the village apparently to search for wanted suspects. There were accusations that the villagers had been taunted and incited. Eventually there were clashes between the villagers and the police with many casualties for the villagers. The Israeli authorities said that the matter would be investigated. Feelings of rage and hatred permeated the atmosphere.

The peace mission organized by *Peace Now* was designed to show the villagers that not all Israelis approved of the action taken by border police and to try to rectify strained relations between the villagers and the Israelis. A total of eight bus loads set out for the rocky terrain of Nahalin. About five kilometers from the village the buses were stopped by the military and ordered to turn back.

Some of the villagers had come to meet the buses. When they heard that they could not come in, they returned to the village to inform the others. It was then decided to hold the "meeting" in a nearby orange grove. The Peace Now group scattered throughout the grove sitting in small groups. Stones of all sizes lay everywhere. Representatives from the town came and a makeshift "stage" was erected. There were some speeches given by both sides and then some mixing between the Israelis and the villagers. Due to the limitation of language, this was often confined to hand grasps and other gestures of friendship and good will. One could deduce from the anguished looks and hearty grasps that these villagers wanted peace very much.

Debbie attempted to speak with some of the children who came from nearby villages out of curiosity. Few spoke English but one, wearing a Syracuse University T-shirt much too large for him, knew quite a lot of English because he had a relative in New York. They all seemed to be good and simple people and Debbie felt pity for their plight. That they were suffering was painfully obvious. They were surrounded and engulfed by a harsh terrain, the military, and a settlement within naked eye distance. They communicated both verbally and non-verbally that it was hostile to them. If only there could be more meetings like this one, and with everyone involved, perhaps peace would be possible. Debbie felt strongly that this was the only approach that would succeed in the long run.

On one occasion, a left wing group planned a trip to Gaza to speak with representatives of the workers and with the people who had been subjected to an unfair and unjust tax. Debbie joined the group partially because she was genuinely sympathetic to the workers but also partially because she wanted to see Gaza and going in a group made her feel more safe and anonymous. It would also be a topic of conversation for her since people often questioned her about the occupied territories when she visited the United States. She could then discourse freely on the woes of Gaza and make her ethical halo burn ever more brightly.

Most of the group went in private cars. Debbie and seven others were asked to go in the van brought by one of the members from a nearby kibbutz. Her girl friend, Hilary who lived in the next building to Debbie and had been an activist for some time, got in the front seat with the kibbutznik.

They went as far as the Gaza checkpoint where there was a delay of almost an hour while the organizers spoke (negotiated, argued, whatever) with succeedingly higher levels of the military to secure permission for all to enter Gaza. Debbie watched from the back of the van and wondered if they would be allowed to cross. She also observed the steady stream of Arab cars as they approached the checkpoint and were carefully inspected. Some were subjected to more security than others.

Finally they herded across and parked all the cars with the bright orange Israeli license plates. They were met by some of the Arab representatives who took a portion of the Israeli contingent in their cars with the bright blue license plates identifying them as coming from the occupied territories. The first letter of the license number also identified the city or town where they were from. The rest of the group, including Debbie were provided with large sherut type taxis.

The group then went to the headquarters of the Gaza Workers Union and spent several hours discussing the many problems these people faced in their daily work lives. An American lawyer and several Arab professionals were also present. In the afternoon, they visited the private home of one of the Gaza leaders for more general discussion.

Through her travels, Debbie saw that Gaza also had many different faces - the crowded city center and market place, fairly nice suburban neighborhoods, more modest simple areas, and finally the awesome poverty and gruesome conditions prevailing in the several large refugee camps. The contrasts were shocking as they passed by the Jebalya and Shati camps.

After once again changing cars at the checkpoint, the group left for their starting points continuing the lively discussions that had been begun at the meetings. Enthusiasm for proposed actions ran high. One by one, the passengers of the van got off until only Debbie was left in the back and Hilary in the front. Hilary called back to find out where Debbie wanted to be let off. She mentioned a main street near her house to make things easier for the driver. Soon after as Debbie was looking out of her window, she saw the driver park the van on her street and eagerly follow a smiling Hilary into her apartment building.

Although Debbie was involved in some serious activities, they were not sufficient to spare her the torment of meeting undesirable types of men. One day, not long after the Nahalin visit, her girl friend, Eti, called and asked her if she wanted to go on a blind date. She knew someone she had gone out with a few times but wasn't interested in, although he was a very nice person. Would Debbie be interested in meeting him? She could give him her number and he would call her.

Debbie was "burned out" with relationships but couldn't bring herself to say "no." "After all," she rationalized, "if a friend sends you somebody, he can't be all that bad, can he?" So she gave in and consented to meet him if he called.

One evening he did call and they spoke awhile on the telephone. At first, he seemed polite and asked her if she wanted to meet him.

"How about in an hour?" he whipped out the words immediately.

Debbie declined saying she was "going out with friends" this evening.

"How about tomorrow? Still busy? I think maybe you must work too hard," he said sarcastically.

"Tomorrow is better," she answered smiling. "Where shall we meet?"

"Well, I'll come by about 8 or so," he replied matter of factly. "What is your address?"

"I think I would prefer to meet for the first time in a cafe," she hinted. "Which ones do you especially like?"

"I don't like so much. We can decide after we meet." he argued cleverly.

"All right," Debbie yielded to avoid an argument. "But where shall we meet?"

"Well, if you don't want me to come to your place, I'll wait on the corner of Sokolov and Jabotinsky. I have a tan van, seats eight, you can't miss it."

The next day he waited in the assigned spot. Debbie climbed into the van. He was very dark, Sephardic looking with a round face. He looked her over quickly yet intensely. After the initial conversation, he talked about his life as a tour guide. In the meantime, he was driving aimlessly around the streets.

"Where shall we go?" Debbie inquired sweetly.

"Well, there's not much open on a Friday night," he tried to explain.

"Oh, but there are many cafes on Dizengoff that are open," Debbie argued.

He pretended not to hear and drove down Ben Yehuda Street which is for the most part closed. He stopped at a French croissant place.

"How about here?" he snarled, somewhat annoyed. "It looks closed," Debbie estimated although two people were sitting on the outside benches.

"No, it isn't. I'll ask," he stopped the car and went over to inquire. As Debbie had anticipated, the two teenagers had just sat down on the benches inadvertently.

"Yeah, it's closed," he came back feeling very self satisfied because he had put himself out. "I told you there's not much open tonight."

"Not here," Debbie repeated. "Everything is on Dizengoff. Let's go there."

Again, he ignored her suggestion and drove over to Ibn Givirol Street which was even more deserted than Ben Yehuda had been. "Look, everything is closed," he told her as though it were a reprimand. He pretended to be exhausting himself to find her a place when he knew all too well that on these streets, everything was quiet.

Then he drove back to where they had met. "Well, I think I'll be going back now. I have a lot to do tomorrow," he said in a computer like monotone. Debbie couldn't believe it. This was supposed to be a Friday night date. Then, instead of quietly getting out of the car and chalking it up to a bad experience, Debbie in her desperation to save the evening made a serious mistake.

"OK, let's go to my place and I'll fix some coffee," she heard herself saying. She didn't want to say it but felt compelled somehow to make something where there was nothing. She was again trying to make a very ugly frog into a handsome prince.

"OK, fine," he answered immediately finally having achieved what he wanted in the first place. He parked the car and they went to Debbie's flat.

He looked around appraisingly while Debbie made coffee and served him chocolate cake she had left. She herself drank orange juice. He quickly finished the coffee and cake as though he hadn't eaten in a long time. Then he asked, "Can I have some juice too?" Although surprised at his nerve to ask, Debbie served him a glass. He gulped down the juice in seconds and held out the glass, "Can I have another one?" Debbie was so shocked, she couldn't say anything yet gave him another glass. Finally satiated, he sank back into the sofa. Had Debbie a coffee table, he would have put his feet up.

Then they started to talk although Debbie was so put off by him that she had to feign any kind of interest. But of course, her best girl friend had sent him so she felt obligated to be pleasant. Finally the discussion turned to politics. He started to spit venom against the Arabs and the situation on the West Bank voicing extreme right wing arguments similar to Meir Kahane. "They have to get rid of them all. That's the only way there will ever be peace. Look at all the land they have in Saudi Arabia."

Debbie sighed, "That's too ridiculous even to discuss."

"Oh, are you one of those crazy American peaceniks. You people don't know anything," he laughed in the same condescending manner he had all evening.

"Like you said before, you have a lot to do tomorrow. So do I. Why don't we call it a night," Debbie suggested too weary even to be angry. She just wanted to be rid of him.

Fortunately, he left easily and quickly. Anyway, it hadn't cost him anything.

After he left Debbie wondered what she was doing with such an awful uneducated boorish person she would not have looked at in New York. How could her best friend have sent her such a person. No wonder she wasn't interested in him. When she told her what had happened, she too was surprised. He had taken her for a beer and salad and they had not discussed politics. Later she related the story to an Israeli girl friend and asked why so many men were like this. "Because the women do it, most of them," she explained, "They want to have a man and so they give them food and sex. They know that if they won't do it, another woman will. The men know this too, so why should he take you out when another girl will gladly invite him. That's how it is."

The new semester had begun which put a damper on Debbie's social activities. More leisurely days had allowed her the freedom to try many new activities and to attend many events. Now she only had time for a few.

One activity she continued was the discussion group she had joined. Actually there were several in Tel Aviv but most were Hebrew speaking. She had initially heard of an English speaking group from Oren Pitkin, an American from California that she had met at a lecture. Since the next meeting was to be held at Oren's home, he invited Debbie to attend. The group met every two weeks in one of the member's houses.

This particular week there were about 15 people present. Most were single although a few were married. They varied in age but most were between 45 and 65. The ratio of men to women was about equal. The one thing that all had in common was that they were all native speakers of English although they came from geographically distant places: the United States, Canada, England, South Africa and Australia. It may also be assumed that they shared an interest in current events and a desire to discuss relevant topics with others. However, as is often the case with singles, the main motivation may have been to meet people.

At the beginning of each meeting, a leader was chosen who would then direct the meeting although in an informal way. Each member was asked to suggest a topic for the evening's discussion. A few declined to do so but most chose themes of current interest. Then the group voted on each item, the one with the most votes becoming the theme for the evening's discussion.

The group sat in a ring formation and each person was then allowed five minutes in which to voice his opinion on the chosen topic. No one else was permitted to interrupt during this time. Occasionally the leader had to gently remind the speaker that his five minutes had come to an end. After each person had spoken (one could also pass), there was an intermission during which refreshments and light snacks were served. It was a congenial opportunity for the members to continue the discussion in a less formal way and of course, to get to know one another better. Then the leader would check with the group if they wanted "another round" which meant an additional five minutes for each person. Often the consensus of the group would be just to continue the informal conversation that had emerged during the break.

Although the age bracket of the group was somewhat too old for Debbie, she liked the people and continued to attend. It also felt good to be able to speak English fluently and at a high level without having first to simplify and eliminate words for an Israeli listener.

One evening after Debbie had been going to the group for a few months, two members of the group announced that they were going to get married. Jack was a 65 year old divorced engineer from Canada who had come to Israel one year earlier to work in one of the industrial plants. Rivka was a 54 year old English widow who had lived in Israel for eleven years. She worked as a hospital nurse. Everyone wished them well. They would have to get married in Cyprus since Jack was not Jewish. Marriages between Jews and non-Jews could not be performed in a religious ceremony, the only kind recognized as valid in Israel. However, secular marriages performed outside Israel were accepted as legal. The happy couple took off to live in Canada. But alas, we must be honest and tell the whole truth. Rivka returned to Israel after seven months alone. Rumors whisper that he hit her several times while drunk.

Although Debbie restricted her activities mostly to organizational activities, she did still occasionally have "encounters" as she did in her tourist days. But now she was wise and no longer a victim for every macho lurking in the shadows. One day, she was walking with her tray in the university dining room looking for a place to sit. Suddenly, a young guy about 32 walks brazenly up close to her and says, "I vant to spik to you." He was average height, blond and fairly good looking in a faded washed out sort of way.

Debbie was immediately put off by his aggressive behavior and quipped, "No kidding." He looked momentarily surprised but recovered quickly.

"I saw you enterrrr and I dought to myself, I must spik vit dat gurl," he tried again smiling in a charming way.

Debbie laughed at him because he was so obvious and continued walking. She sat down at a table already occupied by three people. But he was not to be put off so easily. There were no more available chairs so he quickly stole an empty one from another table and squeezed it in next to Debbie.

"Are you a toorist?" was of course his first question. Debbie decided to have some fun with him.

"No, I have been here for six years," Debbie answered defiantly and with an air that said she intended to stay.

"Oh, veddy nice," he said pretending to compliment but he was clearly disappointed.

"What do you study?" Debbie began her probe.

"Vel," he began pompously and full of enthusiasm, "I feenished die iniversitat and now I am die deerctor uf die bank. I haf vacation now."

"That's nice. What did you study when you were at the university?" Debbie continued to fish.

"Ancient History," he stated proudly with a toss of his head. "It vas so eenteresting."

"Oh, yes," Debbie exclaimed. I enjoyed it also. Did you like Lucretius? I never liked him. Too religious and conservative, old fashioned."

"Yes, you are right, of course," he agreed to Debbie's false statements.

"And remember Suetonius the historian. How modern and scientific were his theories at least when compared to Thucydides, who basically just wrote gossip. (But oh, what gossip!) Debbie continued with her erroneous comments.

"Yes, I remember," he said less enthusiastically now. He started to squirm becoming aware that Debbie was not just some silly girl but that she knew quite a lot. Recognizing that his total ignorance of ancient history would soon manifest itself, he tried to change the subject.

Debbie had finished her coffee and got up to go. "I vud like to call you. Where do you leef?"

"What will your wife and children say?" Debbie asked innocently.

He looked shocked, his fake charming and smiling manner disappearing entirely now.

"Why don't you spend your vacation with them? she accused, "instead of picking up girls at the university."

"My wife ees vurking so I can do vit my time vat I vant," he reacted fiercely.

"Well, I have to go now. Goodbye and have a nice vacation." Debbie remarked as she picked up her bag.

He got visibly angry and shouted, "I don't need you. I haf met already feefty gurls."

"Shalom," Debbie waved and walked away from him.

Many months later, Debbie once passed a bank on her way to the central bus station and happened to glance inside. She saw the ancient history scholar sitting and working in one of the teller windows. "Director of the bank, hah," Debbie gloated, now recognizing that he had garnished his mediocre life with the spice of many lies. "He is only a simple clerk. I should have guessed."

Occasionally, Debbie would meet interesting men that she would have liked to know better. Not all were like the tour guide. For example, one evening she had gone to the Cinematheque to see a German film that turned out to be very "epic, psychological, and poetic." For most of the audience, it was too slow moving. As it dragged on, more and more people left until by the end, only a handful of film diehards were left. When the lights went on, Debbie looked around the empty theater and saw a tall handsome man about 45 sitting in the row behind her. She considered starting a conversation with him and was wondering how to do it. On the went out, they walked in the same direction. Debbie smiled at him in a friendly way.

"You're one of the brave ones," he said also smiling, "staying to the very end."

"It *was* a little bit too long," she answered, "but interesting in many ways. German films usually make one think."

"Are you interested in film?" he inquired, now seemingly eager to become acquainted with her.

"Oh, yes, very. Are you also?"

After several more questions and answers, Debbie learned that this was Rafi Meisner, the Israeli film director who had made the well known controversial film, *Night Epoch*. He offered her a lift home and they chatted away eagerly as two people do when they discover similar interests. He mentioned that he was divorced and had one adult son. They exchanged telephone numbers and he promised he would call. He did call and they made a date for Monday evening. But early Monday morning he called and explained that he had received unexpected guests over the weekend. Since they were relatives, he could not leave them.

Debbie was disappointed and wondered if maybe he had just gotten cold feet. Eventually he did come but only once during the next week and in the morning. Debbie tried to call him quite often but there was never any answer. When she mentioned this to him one time when she again met him at the Cinematheque, he responded with, "Let me give you another number, where it will be easier to get me." He never called her again. She saw him now and then at film festivals and related events. He was always friendly up to a point but when she attempted to invite him for coffee or to go for a walk, he always declined excusing himself that he had to meet a friend or had an appointment to be somewhere else. In short, he behaved like a married man. Debbie assumed he already had a girl friend and perhaps even a wife, thus not wanting to get too deeply involved with her. Or perhaps he was just scared to get involved at all.

A similar scenario was shot at the Tiberias Film Festival when Debbie met Ben Isaakson from Israeli television. He was also tall, good looking, about 50 and he too exhibited much interest in Debbie at first even taking her back to Tel Aviv in her car. Like Rafi, Ben was divorced, having been married many years to a woman with multiple sclerosis, a progressive wasting disease. She was confined to a hospital permanently now where he still continues to visit her. Debbie thought he might be needy for human company. They also exchanged telephone numbers, etc. etc. However, when Debbie called him one Friday to invite him to dinner on Saturday, he spoke very curtly to her and hung up. Debbie assumed another woman was with him. She never heard from him. It was always that way. The good interesting men were immediately snatched up after their divorce and only the difficult problematic ones were available.

These men merely neglected to mention their girlfriends; their were others who "forgot" to reveal the existence of a wife. One day, Debbie was at Tel Aviv university and by accident walked passed the law school. She saw a large crowd gathering and tables set up as for a reception. Curiosity goaded her to her to investigate what was going on and she discovered there was to be a lecture given in honor of a retired dean of the school. As she was standing in the midst of the crowd debating whether or not she should attend the lecture, a tall blond man about 45 in military uniform decorated with numerous stripes casually started to talk with her.

They made small talk for awhile, then he persuaded her to attend the lecture. The dean had been a professor of his many years ago. She went and sat next to him. After the reception during which he spoke with several faculty members, he took Debbie to a restaurant. They got along very well and he too performed the ritual of taking her number and promising to call. He said he **was** divorced for 11 years and had one teenage son.. They had one more meeting where he just came to her apartment for an evening. Although Debbie would have preferred to go out, he seemed to balk at this idea and finally persuaded her that, "It would be so much quieter here and we can get to know each other better."

After that, Debbie did not hear from him. Then she decided to phone him only to discover that the number he had given her was always out of order. Debbie was disappointed when he didn't call her again and daringly decided to pay him a visit. After all, his telephone was out of order, perhaps he lost her number, perhaps something unforeseen had come up - these were among the rationalizations Debbie made for herself.

She went to Rishon Lezion, a town half way between Jerusalem and Tel Aviv and found the address he had given her. Yet there was no such name as Dan Eisenstein listed on the mailboxes or bells. She began to inquire of some of the neighbors, yet no one knew this name. She didn't know what was wrong. One neighbor after hearing Debbie's description of him suggested, "It might be Yossi Katz on the fourth floor but he is a sailor and not here much of the time." Debbie after spending hours looking for the name Dan Eisenstein in all three entrances, A, B, C,, finally gave up and went home dejected.

A few days later he called again explaining that his firm had sent him to Strasbourg, France on business. Debbie wondered if his calling at this time was related to her visit.

"Oh, did you visit the beautiful cathedral?" Debbie asked sweetly trying to ascertain the truth.

"Oh, yes of course," he answered.

"What did you think, of the astronomical clock," she continued to probe.

"I must have missed that; I didn't stay very long," he explained.

"Oh, come now," Debbie declared more aggressively. It is impossible to enter the cathedral without passing the huge astronomical clock. It is larger than an altar taking in the height of the cathedral. People make special tours of it."

"Well, how are you?" he said calmly, cleverly changing the subject.

"I called you several times and the telephone is always out of order" Debbie said with a tone of anger in her voice.

"Well, my roommate did not pay the bill and he is in Europe now and they shut it off, he replied matter of factly.

"Why don't you pay for him? How can you be without a telephone? She asked half swallowing his story.

"No, I won't pay his bills. Anyway he will be back soon and everything will be OK," he said again maneuvering his way out of a tight spot. He seemed to be very adept at that.

Debbie decided it would be better to question him in person so she agreed to his coming over to her apartment. Then she cornered him.

"I want to know who you are," she stated point blank.

He looked surprised. "What do you mean?"

"When I didn't hear from you for so long, I was concerned, worried even, so I came to visit you at the address you had given me. Only there was no one by the name of Dan Eisenstien there. I want to know what's going on," Debbie lashed out angrily, the frustration of the search still very much felt.

"OK, OK, don't get excited," he said calmly with a smile.

"What do you mean, don't get excited. I spent hours looking for your name, asking neighbors. I felt like a fool," she shouted.

"I didn't want you to call me or to come," he said quietly and simply as though it should have been clear to her.

"Why not? Are you married?" she retorted.

"Yes," he whispered.

"You told me you were divorced for 11 years, she flashed back with a hurt tone in her voice.

"I am."

"What? How can you be both?"

"I'm divorced from my first wife for 11 years," he stated leaving her to deduce the rest.

"But you married again," she understood now.

"Yes."

"Well, why didn't you just tell me instead of lying about it. Married men going out with others is not unusual here. But giving a false name, address and telephone number is just too much, "she fumed.

"I wanted to protect myself and my family," he declared simply as though he were the righteous one and Debbie the wicked homewrecker.

Debbie was fed up with him. How can you go out with someone and not even know his name! The whole fiasco catapulted her back to the saga of Eli Altoni and street #75 almost ten years earlier. "Dani Eisenstein continued to call once every few months wanting to see her. When he called again after a year elapsing to wish her a cheery "*Shana tova*" (Happy New Year), she hung up on him.

Again, this was not an isolated incident. A very nice man (they always seemed nice) that she once met at an exhibition in the municipality square had also lied telling her he was divorced giving her a false number. One time when she attempted to call him, the person who answered said there was no one there by that name. Israel seems to be full of married men on the prowl.

Another time when she tried the mid lifers group 40-60 of the ACI only to discover they were mostly 60+ she met a visiting American tourist. They started to converse and he expressed an interest in possibly settling in Israel in the future, only he was concerned about what kind of social life he would have as a widower. Helpful Debbie assured him that he would have an active and varied social life and invited him to a single parent group the following night in Holon. He was interested in going.

When they entered the living room of the hostess for the evening, Debbie remembered all eyes being riveted on the newcomer. When it was obvious that he was an American and a tourist to boot, one of the Israeli woman who admitted her desire to emigrate to the United Stated many times, zoomed over to Debbie and her guest.

She moved very close to him looking hypnotically into his eyes while she spoke, of course, totally ignoring Debbie. Several women vied for his attention throughout the evening but he did not express interest in any of them. Nevertheless, he was pleased with the group and soon concluded that indeed Israel is a paradise for a male. He could have his pick of many attractive women. His fears of a lonely existence were definitely laid to rest. For sure, they would fight over him!

Debbie went out with the tourist twice after the single parent meeting and enjoyed it very much. Unfortunately, his short vacation was coming to an end. Since she wished to continue the relationship with him, Debbie asked him for his New York address and telephone number so she might contact him when she returned to the United States.

"No, I am afraid that won't be possible," he explained.

Debbie was surprised. "Why not?"

"Well, you see, I'm still married. But I'm thinking of getting a divorce and then coming here. So far, I'm very impressed by what I have seen," he confided in her.

"What, you're married! You said you were a widower for eight years," she accused him loudly.

"I am a widower" he declared..

When Debbie looked bewildered he said softly, "but I remarried." One dare not be too trusting. Beware of the prowling tourist!

Yet not all men attempted to hide their marital status. Some are honest. Debbie once attended a three day anthropology symposium held at the Israel museum where she met Gadi Shapiro, a high level academic admininstrator. At first she was not particularly interested at him when he came over with, "Don't I know you from someplace?"

But after conversing with him for awhile, she realized that he was a very intelligent person even though he did not convey this impression. She met him again one day near the Hilton Hotel as he was heading for army reserve duty. They spoke briefly and then he asked her if she would go with him to a cafe sometime. Debbie agreed and he took her telephone number and address. About two weeks later, he called and they made a date for Monday at 2 P.M. with the intention of going into the center of the city to a cafe.

He arrived on time and Debbie invited him in. He made no move or mention to leave and Debbie wondered what had happened to the cafe idea. He sank back into Debbie's sofa as though he planned to stay forever. Debbie felt uncomfortable and impolite if she didn't offer him something; when she did, he responded eagerly, "Some coffee would be nice." Debbie made the coffee and served him some apricot cake she had left. He had often mentioned how fond he was of cakes. Still there was no mention of going to a cafe.

"Please help yourself," Debbie encouraged him pointing to the cake. He plunged in greedily.

"This is really good cake. What kind is it?" he inquired as he chomped away.

"Apricot," Debbie answered.

"Very good," he repeated as he savored the last few bites.

"I'm glad you like it. May I get you some more?" Debbie asked. He shook his head indicating "no."

"Well," he said putting the plate back on the table. "Now let's go to bed."

Debbie couldn't believe her ears, "What?" she cried.

"I said, 'Let us withdraw into the inner chamber' Is that better English?" he laughed.

"I don't think that is such a good idea," Debbie tried to be tactful. "I really don't know you very well yet. There is plenty of time."

He did not press the issue but he felt rejected. Two years later when they met again in New York, he remarked, "I think we have some accounts to settle don't we?" revealing that he had not forgotten. (They settled the accounts.)

In the meantime, love and romance had blossomed between her next door neighbor, Hilary and Asher, the kibbutznik, who had taken them to Gaza in his van one and a half years ago. The relationship had developed slowly. At first they just invited each other occasionally to their respective homes. At one point, Hilary even thought it was all over after her dog, having eaten garbage on the kibbutz, vomited on Asher's sofa. She did not hear from him for awhile.

However, they continued to meet at political activities; both had become involved in the Ramya Solidarity Movement, an attempt to save Ramya, the unofficial and unrecognized Bedouin village in the Galilee which had been slated for demolition by the government in order to make room for the expanding Karmiel settlements. After awhile, Hilary and Asher began to come to various left wing meetings, lectures, and panel discussions as a couple.

One day, Hilary ran into Debbie in the local supermarket and told her excitedly that she would be giving up her Tel Aviv apartment and moving to Asher's kibbutz located halfway between Tel Aviv and Netanya. He had requested and obtained a larger house on the kibbutz and she would be living with him there. They had already been spending weekends and other days off together so the move would just be an intensification and a cementing of a closeness that already existed.

Debbie was happy for the petite and pretty Hilary who was already 44 and had never been married. She was a gentle and good natured person, having made aliya 11 years earlier from Massachusetts. She had also lived in New York while a student at NYU. It was ironic that this should be happening to her since she had never even expressed much interest in meeting anyone. Asher, who was 46 and also a bachelor, had been born on the kibbutz and was an intelligent and dedicated peace activist who gave all his free time to this cause. They seemed to be very well suited to each other and everyone thought that they made an attractive couple. Debbie envisioned their story as a fascinating novel or Hollywood film.

In the late summer of 1993, Debbie read every day in the newspaper about the hunger strike and demonstration being made by the single parent immigrants from Russia. They complained of being ignored by the government and their plight truly seemed to be a severe one. Their number was estimated at 60,000 families. Debbie also learned that the vast majority of them were divorced women with children. The Israeli Garden of Eden for men was quickly growing into a jungle!

Debbie continued her ride on the carousel of love. One day, her girl friend, Rina, told her of the wonderful success she was having with the latest fad called *teleksher*. It was a new version of the traditional newspaper ad except that the prospective mates would call the telephone number listed in the ad, hear your message and then leave a message of their own.

Rina was excited. "So far I've received 300 phone call messages. Can you believe it?"

"Yes that's amazing," Debbie answered. "Have you met any of them yet?"

"I've met a few and they were all very nice. I was surprised," she remarked. "You can tell a lot by hearing their voices and by what they say. Then you can be more selective."

"Yes, I guess so. It sounds like a good idea," she agreed. She had already pointed herself in every direction. So why not? Love still hung on Debbie's walls and
>she
>>decided
>>>to
>>>>give
>>>>>it
>>>>>>a
>>>>>>>try.

Anne-Marie Brumm was born in New York City. She received a B.A. from Columbia University and a PhD from The University of Michigan where she also won two Avery Hopwood Awards for poetry. Having lived in Israel since 1980, she taught at Ben Gurion University in Beersheva and at the Hebrew University in Jerusalem. She is the author of two volumes of poetry, <u>Dance of Life</u> and <u>Sea, Sand, Stones and Strife: Poems of the Middle East</u>.

Her work has also appeared in many journals in the United States and abroad. She now lives in Tel Aviv working on a new novel entitled, <u>Mediterranean Notebooks</u>.